Everything
the
Heart Wants

Also by Savannah Page

Everything the Heart Wants

a novel

Savannah Page

LAKE UNION
PUBLISHING

Text copyright © 2017 by Savannah Page

Published by Lake Union Publishing, Seattle

www.apub.com

Amazon, the Amazon logo, and Lake Union Publishing are trademarks of Amazon.com, Inc., or its affiliates.

ISBN-13: 9781542046039
ISBN-10: 1542046033

Cover design by Michael Rehder

Printed in the United States of America

To every woman, wherever her path may lead, whatever her heart may choose, whomever she may love, however she may fly.

Home is the nicest word there is.

—*Laura Ingalls Wilder*

The real things haven't changed.
It is still best to be honest and truthful;
to make the most of what we have;
to be happy with simple pleasures;
and have courage when things go wrong.

—*Laura Ingalls Wilder*

One

We had a plan.

No one in the history of the world has ever said, "If you work hard enough and believe deeply enough, life will turn out *exactly* as you planned. You'll have *everything* you could ever want and then some." No one. Ever.

But still. We had a plan. And I expected that plan to go . . . according to plan.

I've never been especially fabulous at making decisions, nor particularly confident in the ones I do manage to make, but there are two things of which I am absolutely, positively, without a shadow of a doubt, 100 percent certain. And never in a million years did I imagine that these two ironclad decisions would be at odds with each other. That in what would be the great big novel of Halley Brennan's life, they were the choices that would make the novel both move forward *and* come to a screeching halt.

Adam Brennan and I had a plan, and it all started when we first met fifteen years ago during my sophomore year in college, when my good friend Nina invited me to spend Thanksgiving with her family. Nina's sophisticated, older, and very attractive brother Adam was there, home for the holidays while studying for his MBA. As soon as I laid eyes on the tall, dark-haired, brown-eyed sweetheart with the wide smile that creased his eyes, butterflies were set loose in my stomach. When I watched him set up the new TiVo for his father, and when I saw how he kissed his mother's cheek hello and goodbye—warm and appreciative gestures I'm sure all mothers wish for from their grown sons—serious crush mode set in.

Adam and I didn't have our first date until my senior year two years later, but you can be certain that if a plan wasn't already in the works for our future when we first laid eyes on each other fifteen Thanksgivings ago, there most definitely was one as soon as we broke apart from our first magical kiss on our first magical date.

Finding Adam was like finding a part of myself. It might sound corny or clichéd, but everything about finding Adam felt right. He turned out to be exactly what I'd been looking for, hoping for, planning for. He was *the One.*

During our first date, Adam and I reminisced about our backpacking trips to Europe—I'd recently returned from a summer abroad in London; he'd also studied abroad as an undergrad, in Edinburgh. On our overseas adventures we'd both kissed the Blarney Stone, taken the Berlin Underworlds air raid shelter tour, spent not one entire day but two in the Louvre, and opted to save a gondola ride in Venice for the next time we'd visit the romantic city, when we wouldn't be single.

I was an English lit major who had a subscription to the *Wall Street Journal* and an A in an elective introductory business class I'd taken to break up the Fitzgerald-Whitman-and-Shelley routine. Adam had studied business and marketing as an undergrad, and he devoured anything by John Irving and was unashamedly open about his love for the Little House books. "They make me feel like I'm coming home," he said.

I hadn't known I could love something coming out of someone's mouth as much as I loved that ridiculously endearing comment. That is, until Adam told me those three little words. When he told me he'd found his match, that I was his *One.*

2

I was the girl who loved sushi and couldn't handle hard liquor . . . often making really poor choices under the influence. He was the guy who knew how to *make* sushi and steered clear of anything harder than beer, wine, or champagne . . . because of an alcoholic uncle.

I was the girl who loved to jog and was intimidated by driving any and all LA freeways, despite having grown up in Pasadena. He was the guy who needed a jogging partner and had helped pay for college by couriering—he knew LA like the back of his hand and loved getting behind the wheel.

I was the girl who was interested in serious relationship material, wanted to call LA, or at least Southern California, my home, my Little House, forever, and had aspirations of traveling to Beijing, learning French, and writing a novel. He was the guy who had never been into dating around, had been born and raised in Glendale and had no plans to leave sunny SoCal, and aspired to a life filled with travel, delicious food, and an abundance of love . . . and he liked my novel-writing idea.

As if it were written in the stars, Adam and I were a perfect match. A perfect complement to each other, filling each other's gaps, each being positive when the other was negative, fitting each other like that proverbial glove.

As soon as I graduated from college, Adam and I moved in together, and our routines and lives melded together effortlessly. Our first place was a small one-bedroom first-floor apartment in a shabbier part of otherwise lovely Pasadena, complete with unreliable water pressure and a chronic ant problem. We shared Adam's barely-hanging-on Acura he'd had since before there was a *we*, and we were happy. Blissfully happy. He'd pour me a bowl of cereal while I battled with the showerhead; I'd stick to his travel coffee mug a Post-it with an *XO* or *You sexy thing* sentiment scrawled on it while he fought the classic start-the-car battle. It was a beautiful and uncomplicated and true love. In every way possible.

Upon completing his MBA, Adam landed a position at Disney, and after two years he finally began to see the benefits of his long hours and dedication. He was promoted to marketing department team manager. I couldn't have been more proud. We jetted off for a short but memorable weekend in Sonoma to celebrate.

"You make me feel like home," I told Adam on the night we returned after our brief getaway up north. We'd come home, left our luggage by the door, opened one of our souvenir bottles of Zinfandel, headed straight for our bedroom, and made love.

"I love you so much, Adam Brennan," I whispered against his lips, the sheet taut against our entwined legs. "So very much."

Adam had that charming sparkle in his dark eyes when he said, "*You* are my home, Miss Halley West." He kissed the top of my bare shoulder. "I love you. To the moon and back."

His fingers found their way to the base of my left shoulder blade, where he lightly traced my lone tattoo. My best friend, Marian Kroeber, and I had gotten them during spring break in Florida one year in college. While her rainbow tattoo, also on her left shoulder blade, was the result of an inebriated liking for something "colorful and cute" (not to mention it was on the first page of the parlor's portfolio), mine carried a bit of significance. It was a comet, and one with which I shared my name—Halley's Comet.

"Or, rather, to the edge of our solar system and back," Adam corrected, still tracing my tattoo. He kissed my shoulder once more. "My Halley."

Straight out of college, with Adam destined to flourish in his career, I'd found myself working a number of odd jobs, unable to land my desired position at a magazine or newspaper in need of an aspiring writer. Once I settled in as a receptionist for an advertising firm, around the time Adam was really moving and shaking at Disney, our future started to look brighter. Things were still meager some months, but that's nothing when you're twentysomething and in love and you've got your whole life ahead of you, promise on the horizon, and optimism packed in your pockets.

There was one thing my twenty-two-year-old self knew that Christmas season: I had a plan for my life, and Adam was unequivocally a part of it. So when he took me by surprise and got down on one knee in the middle of a Christmas tree lot, telling me that he wanted to spend the rest of his life with the woman who made him smile, who made him love, who made him feel at home, too . . . and who made him stamp, twist, turn, and fluff every. Single. Tree. In the lot, I knew not only that I'd met my match but that I had never been more confident and eager than I was in making this perfectly right decision.

Adam. He was my wonderful, confident decision.

I knew Adam was my *One* not only because of the way he securely held me against his firm, warm chest when the nights were chilly, or the way he let his kisses linger, his lips kissing at the kiss he'd left on my still-parted lips, or the way he looked at me from across a crowded room, as if he wanted to steal me away for an hour or an eternity, any measure of time to tell me how right we were for each other. I knew that Adam was my perfect match because when I imagined my future he was simply in it. He was my partner, my very best friend, my forever.

And for all the ways we complemented each other, made each other feel, and knew in our heart of hearts that we had been destined to find each other, there was one very important piece to the puzzle that could have been a game changer, a real deal breaker. Sure though I was about my love for Adam Brennan, I was also sure about my decision not to become a mother. Not then. Not ten years down the road. Not now. Not ever. I have never remembered a time when I pictured myself carrying a diaper bag, pushing a stroller, raising a mini me.

I didn't want to play mommy when other girls my age had baby dolls they pretended to nurse and sing to sleep. Sure, I had baby dolls. They were cute *toys* you could dress up, lay in a cradle, and read your storybooks to. And your friends always reached for their dolls during playtime, and you obviously didn't want to be left out, the weirdo who preferred her collection of Hot Wheels cars, much to her friends' chagrin. I did the proper little-girl thing and cared for my dolls. When I played house with my sister and our friends, I somehow found myself, by default, the single businesswoman without kids, or the married woman with a pet dog played by a little sister, or the woman who lived alone and spent her days brewing pretend tea and watering faux flowers.

It isn't that I dislike children. They're not my favorite of tiny creatures, but I don't run from a public playground in fear of their sticky hands and toothless smiles. When my younger sister, Charlotte, had her first, second, and third children, I was overwhelmed with a familial love for them I wouldn't trade for the world. I love being an aunt, and I adore her children (more when they're well behaved and not running amok, but I digress). But when I look at Charlotte's children, the ones I love more than any in the world, my heart does not long to have one of my own. My sister casually mentioned when her third, Leah, was born that she thought I'd get the baby bug. I was over thirty, at an age when the bug often came around, so I'd better beware.

Leah was a beautiful baby. Button nose, rosy cheeks, skin soft as could be and smelling like only a baby's can, and she always slept like a rock in my arms. No hassle, no fuss . . . and yet no itch, no bug. Charlotte's path was not—is not—for me. The millions of women who yearn for a swaddled bundle who's half them, half their partner aren't waving anything sparkly and shiny in the shop window that I long to have.

Do I lack that mothering gene, that maternal instinct? That hormone that "they" say is supposed to kick in, if not during your late twenties then certainly in your thirties? Where is that supposedly ticking clock that reminds you to get to procreating? That most Darwinian of urges, to participate in sexual selection so as to contribute to the rich tapestry that is the circle of life?

Steadfast in my decision not to wear that honorable badge of motherhood someday, I would responsibly mention this tidbit to every single guy I dated, just in case. Usually I did so on the first date if I thought there would be a second. It might seem forward and unorthodox, but better safe than sorry. Procreation is nothing to take lightly. I didn't want to risk falling in love with a man who could not accept my lacking the momma gene. I didn't want to love hard and lose big. Better to know straightaway. If I were to someday meet a man, fall in love, and choose to spend the rest of my life with him, I wanted it to be filled with freedom, adventure, and the ability to live tethered only to each other. There would be no room for three or four or more in our coupled-ness. I wanted a life free of children, and he would need to want the same.

So it was on our very first date, at a coffeehouse near my college campus, that I posed the ultimate potential game changer to Adam.

"I don't know about you," I told him, "but I think this date's going really well. And, at the risk of sounding cheesy, I really like you."

Adam chuckled and said, "And *I* really like *you*, Halley."

"You're probably going to think I'm wacky to say this on a first date, but I have to put this out there. Right away."

"Okay."

Adam's calm and confidence were infectious. This was never an easy thing to discuss, especially on a first date, despite the number of times I'd done it. But Adam's mere presence and those soft, inviting eyes of his made it easier.

Adam has *it*, and that made posing the game changer all the more consequential. Because *it*, as my friend Marian and I defined *it* back in college, is not just a man's ability to call up butterflies in your stomach because he knows just what to say to make you feel *just* what you want to feel . . . and because he has a head of hair you can picture tangling your fingers in during the best sex of your life. It's his effortless yet genuine charm and his honest smile. It's the way he leans forward in his seat and actually listens to what you're saying and the way he laughs when you say something you thought only you would find funny. It's the cup of coffee he buys for the homeless man outside the coffeehouse, the appreciation for the folksiest of tunes playing in the speakers overhead that he shows by tapping a beat on his thigh. It's the *it*-ness he oozes because he is your *One*. He is the man your parents always hoped you'd bring home *and* the man you always hoped you'd find—the find of a lifetime.

Adam's *it* factor (and those eyes—*god*, those eyes!) therefore made bringing up this game changer easier, but also terrifyingly risky. What if he *wanted* children?

"This is something really important to me," I said. "I think it's fair you know right away, before we take things further." I swallowed hard, then came right out with it. "I don't want to have children."

Adam didn't say anything, and neither did his facial expression, so I said, "If that's a deal breaker, I understand."

At last he sighed in relief as he said, "I thought you were going to say you were terminally ill or something."

"Oh no."

"Good. Because I'm really enjoying our date. And I'd like to ask you on another." He quickly backpedaled, adding, "Of course, if you were sick I'd still want to take you on another date. I wouldn't be entirely fond of the whole limited-time thing, but . . ."

"Right," I said with a smile I couldn't have hidden if I'd tried. Yet I had to hear an actual answer. "So . . . my not wanting to become a mother—*ever*—doesn't bother you? You don't want to have kids, either?"

"Can I ask why?" Adam asked, plunking both elbows onto the table. His thick eyebrows rose slightly, and one corner of his lips turned up with intrigue.

I gave him the usual laundry list of reasons I gave any guy who asked: no maternal urge; have never seen myself as the mothering type; don't want to be pregnant; don't want to be responsible for the creation and development of another human being; like my freedom; oh, and, I suppose, yes, some kids seem to turn out to be terrible monsters, as do some mothers. My own mother comes to mind. Not that I'd allow someone else's children or my mother to dictate my procreational future. Still, it was something to take into consideration, however lightly. At the very least, it was another bullet point to add to the list.

"Wow," Adam said when I had exhausted my reasons. "You've got this figured out."

"There's an expectation placed on women to become mothers. And I think most guys would be surprised to know where I stand, and . . . I don't want to waste anyone's time."

"I get that."

"It's a choice for some couples but not all. It isn't what I want."

He nodded.

"Are you okay with that?" I asked.

"I've never actually given it much thought, never stopped to imagine a life with or without kids." He shrugged. "I'm okay if you are."

"You're okay with *not* having kids? It's an important decision."

I could feel a blush coming on. Talk of the far future on date one, even with Adam, was not exactly comfortable. But if Adam and I were going to pursue a relationship, honesty was of the utmost importance. Especially about something this consequential.

I swallowed and continued. "I know I'm still young," I said, "and people say maybe I'll want one in the future. Who knows what could happen. But I have to be honest with you: I don't want children. Is that a game changer for you? A deal breaker?"

Adam cupped his large hand over mine and said, "If you're trying to scare me off, Halley, you're doing a terrible job. There's no game changer here." He squeezed my hand, then sat back and took a sip of his coffee.

"Seriously. Picture it."

"Picture it?"

I tapped a finger on the table and leaned forward in my seat. "Picture your future. Kids . . . no kids . . . What do you see?"

He raised his brows inquisitively, sexily, and said, "You."

It. It was there, without question.

"So, seriously," he said, "what are you doing tomorrow night?"

I sighed in relief.

No game changer here.

I am thirty-four years old now, and I am as resolute tonight as I was that afternoon at the coffeehouse that motherhood is not written in the stars of my universe. And Adam was on board with that. We agreed on what mattered most to us and could take it to the bank. We've been happily married for eleven years, and the topic of children is reserved for referring to Charlotte's growing brood, Nina and her husband Griffin's heartbreaking difficulty trying to conceive, and the talent of the cast of *Stranger Things*. Our thirties are turning out to be as hopeful and as lovely as imagined, filled with that freedom, adventure, and ability to live tethered only to each other. Everything was going just fine, until the game changed. Until everything was turned on its head.

I lean back in the swivel chair and gently shove away from the desk, spinning counterclockwise for a beat before the armrest hitting the desk's edge halts my brief ride. I tuck one leg to my chest and sigh, replaying the conversation Adam and I just had on the car ride home. It wasn't supposed to end up like this.

Adam and I have been through valleys before. There was the scary four-car pileup on the 10 I got myself into and broke my arm in. There was the economic recession that affected Adam's department and salary and nearly cost him his position. There was the emotional roller coaster ride that was Nina's trying to have a child for a decade. There was the loss of elderly loved ones, the hikes in rent, and the workplace tension that could wedge its way through the front door, resulting in snippy comments and unnecessary home-life tension. It was a marriage that was rife with all the love, frustration, and ups and downs you sign up for when you say, "I do."

But we'd always come out on the other side. We had our plan. We had each other.

This, though? This changes everything, and for the life of me I can't see how we will crawl out from under this one.

Letting out a soft, low groan, I tilt my head back and let my eyes fall to my bookshelf. I scan the titles: *On Writing. The Art of Fiction. Story Genius. The Elements of Style. The Baby Name Wizard.* All tools of the creative-writing trade. The last book, originally bought to assist me in creating character names in my fiction, has taken on a new meaning. My eyes bore into its vibrant orange-and-green spine, and nausea washes over me like a tidal wave. I fold my hands over my stomach and squeeze my eyes shut in disbelief.

A *complete* game changer.

Two

As soon as we arrived home for the evening, I headed straight for the home office and finished the day's work at last, later than usual. Afterward I locked myself in the bathroom with a good book and a steaming bath—a respite that was never more needed than tonight. Now my nerves have settled some, but the nauseated feeling that came over me earlier still lingers.

When my eyes fall to Adam as I enter the living room, the nausea swells once again.

"Sent your e-mail?" Adam asks me.

I finish tying the drawstring of my pink flannel pajama bottoms and nod.

In our rush to make it over to Westwood for dinner at Nina and Griffin's, I hadn't had enough time to send my editor the final notes on my article for next month's issue of *Copper*, the women's magazine for which I write.

"Rest assured, the women of Los Angeles will now know that rhubarb's the new kale," I answer with mock enthusiasm.

"Phew." Adam, lying across the length of the sofa, cell phone in one hand, drops his free hand to his stomach and says with a smile, "Good thing. I was about to make myself a *celery* smoothie."

"Just wait. Celery will be the new rhubarb before the end of the year."

I grab the remote from the coffee table and sit in the chair opposite Adam, relieved that the hostile conversation on our ride home has been left in the car. The remaining nausea will just have to subside with time, I suppose.

"You know," Adam says as I flip on the television, "you could float your résumé around."

"I love writing," I say in defense of my position at *Copper*.

"I meant to some other magazines," he clarifies. "Ones you could feel invested in. Where you could write what you really want to write."

"It's taken me a long time to get to where I am," I point out, slightly agitated.

"I know. But you and I both know the articles you're usually assigned aren't exactly . . . your passion."

"I know, Adam. I just have to pay my dues," I say with a cavalier shrug.

After years of working one random job after another, the goal being to make rent and pull some weight around here, I finally found actual writing work three years ago at a local women's magazine. I'd done some stints for other magazines and a small local newspaper, but none of them had required penning my name to anything more than tax forms and paychecks. When *Copper*, whose circulation was small but growing, offered to take me on as a junior contributor, I jumped at the opportunity. Three years in, I still enjoy the work, and I put my best foot forward. But Adam's right that I'm disappointed with my current standing at the magazine. Though I'm contributing to a number of articles each issue, I don't feel the passion that, pretentious as it may seem, I think a writer should feel about her work. I want that passion, that inspiration and unadulterated dedication to what my heart desires to create and share. I want to write about topics that matter to me, that move me, that move my readers.

Look at Adam. He's worked around the clock to get to where he is today, and while he's smart as a whip, he wouldn't have made it if not for his passion. He saw promise in a start-up that makes software to teach children how to bring their drawings to life with animation. With a vision and his passion, he took a pay cut to leave Disney and fill the start-up's marketing director position. Its success is now cosmic. He loves what he does, and every single day he is a reminder that if I put in my time and keep sticking to what I'm passionate about—my writing—I'll have my own cosmic success someday.

"I did get to write that piece about women making significantly less than men in the workplace," I mention to Adam, upbeat. "I really enjoyed that."

"I know you did. It was a great article." He smiles. "I just want you happy, Halley."

"I am."

If writing about kale, ballet flats, and how to most effectively spring clean gets me the occasional topic I want to sink my teeth into, like the diversity of what happiness is to different women, or how to overcome self-doubt, or what a work-and-home life balance means in a world that's on a constant fast track, where everyone's jockeying to be the most liked on social media and striving to have the biggest to-do list, then I can pay my dues. To write about the things I want to read, the things that move me, the things that matter to me, I can start with the fluff. And then, hey, maybe I'll take my own advice, get over self-doubt, find the time and courage, and take my years of experience in the magazine world and finally pen that novel. It's an idea.

"TV show or start a movie?" I ask, scanning through the never-ending list of Netflix options.

Adam doesn't respond. He's typing on his cell phone. I repeat the question.

"Doesn't matter." His eyes stay on his phone.

"We don't have to watch anything," I say.

He moves in his seat some, one arm now crooked behind his head. "Sorry, it's Nina."

"Say thank you again for dinner."

"She says we should've taken the leftovers."

"She's the expectant momma. She can use them more than we can."

A smile spreads across Adam's lips, and his fingers type a response.

Nina and Griffin had had tonight's dinner planned for weeks. There was something special that they had wanted to share with Adam and me, and we were not to be late. Nina was preparing coq au vin and it was, in her words, "a terribly difficult dish to prepare." It deserved all the promptness its consumers could extend.

Nina is a whiz in the kitchen, the perfect housewife who is also the perfect working woman, an editor at a midsize publishing house. What can't Nina do well? (Months ago Nina would have argued 'make a baby'—what most women should be able to do—but after ten years of trying, she has, at long last, managed to pull that one off, too.)

In college Nina and I ran track together and became very good friends. She is two years my senior. During those final years, I sorely missed having her just a few campus apartment doors over, but we kept in touch. (Dating her older brother kind of aided in that.) We jogged, shopped, and grabbed a coffee together whenever we could, and I've always considered her my sister. Not just because she is now, in fact, my sister-in-law, but also because I get along with her just as I do with my actual sister, Charlotte. Nina's easy to be around, and she's one of the kindest, most positive, and most genuine people I know. She's a lot like her big brother. I love her to death. And, yes, as someone who can't do more than whip up pancakes and scrambled eggs, I'm more than punctual when she's wearing the chef's hat.

"So what's this special news?" I asked a glowing Nina during dinner earlier tonight. She carried off the pregnant look like a model.

Griffin held out the bottle of wine, offering a refill, and I obliged, saying, "It's not twins, is it?" I tried to read Griffin's expression, but I got nothing more than an indecipherable smile.

"Twins?" Adam said, voice rich with intrigue. "Oh, Nina, is that it?"

"No, no, no." Nina immediately quashed the suspense. "Baby Rylan is solo."

"Well, is everything fine?" I asked.

Nina briefly glanced at Griffin, then looked to Adam and replied, "Yes. Everything's fine."

Adam reached for my hand under the table and gave it a squeeze. He was wearing a genial expression.

"Nina and I," Griffin began, "would like to . . ." He looked to his wife, who sat straight yet comfortable in her seat. Her dark-brown hair, which had been cut into a severe bob for as long as I'd known her, now hung in glossy waves, touching her shoulders. Grown out, it is what Nina refers to as her "mom hair," whatever that's supposed to mean.

Nina set her glass of ice water down. "We'd like to ask you two to be Rylan's godparents," she announced. Immediately, looking straight at me, Nina added, "It doesn't mean you'd be his legal guardians in the event Griffin and I . . ." Her face twisted into a grim expression. "We know you guys don't want children. Griffin's brother and his wife agreed to guardianship. You guys being Rylan's godparents would be more symbolic. To see him through whatever spiritual journey he takes, to be his mentors—"

"To be the ones who give him random gifts and take him to Disneyland just because," Griffin added with a chuckle.

"I know it might seem early to ask, seeing how he's still a bun in the oven, but—" Nina said, and Griffin excitedly cut in.

"We figure we've been waiting ten years, so what's a few months early?" he finished. Nina and Griffin shared an enamored look, clearly elated they were finally where they'd always wanted to be.

"Oh, Nina, of course. Griffin"—I dabbed at my mouth with the cloth napkin—"we're honored."

I was surprised not to see Adam's face express the joy I was sure we both felt at being granted such roles in our nephew's life. It was just . . . blank.

"And of course you'll be a part of the baptism," Nina added, rubbing both hands across her small bump, a habit most pregnant women seem to adopt, unaware, but one that I'm sure Nina does more than most. This was her now, the moment she'd been waiting for so long, and I was undoubtedly happy for her, and to be a part of it. But why, for goodness' sake, wasn't Adam showing the same sense of joy?

"Absolutely," I said enthusiastically. I patted Adam's leg.

"Absolutely," Adam repeated, although his tone lacked an appropriate level of enthusiasm. "Anything we can do for Rylan, we're here for you guys."

As Adam and I sat in the predictable evening freeway traffic on our way home after dinner, Adam, in a low, somewhat chilling tone, said, "If being Rylan's godparents meant we'd have to become his legal guardians in the event of a tragedy, what would you do?"

"What?" I said to his unexpected question.

He turned the radio down so low I could no longer hear the heated discussion about the arctic shelf on NPR. Adam repeated the question, tone just as cold.

"I don't know," I spluttered. "What's the point of the question when that's not something we're dealing with? I'm elated to be Rylan's godmother. I'll spoil that kid with love and toys and Disneyland trips"—I laughed—"and he'll have a life rich with love. And if something awful were to happen to Nina and Griffin, I think Griffin's brother and his wife would fill the role as parents perfectly. There's no need for hypotheticals."

"Halley, I know you don't want a baby."

My ears perked up. *Where* was this coming from?

Adam kept his eyes on the road, though we were in bumper-to-bumper, completely halted traffic, the searing red of brake lights filling the car.

"So you don't even want motherhood if it meant, I don't know, taking in a family member? Even if he wasn't a baby, but six? Or a teenager?"

"Where are you going with this, Adam?"

"I'm asking, under all circumstances, you do *not* want to have a child?"

He finally looked at me, and his eyes, even amid an irritating red glow, were crystal clear. I could see the chocolate of his irises, the black of his pupils, the bizarre longing that filled his eyes and entire face.

"Adam." I shook my head in disbelief. "I would do what needed to be done in the best interest of my nieces and nephews, absolutely. If that meant becoming their legal guardian, we'd figure something out." I shook my head some more, trying to dislodge the discussion from my brain, our mouths, the car. "I don't know what would happen," I continued, "and I really don't see why we need to discuss it. We are *not* Rylan's guardians. We are *not* Alice, George, or Leah's guardians. Charlotte's gotten that all taken care of and—and—and I don't see what good can come of having this kind of inane, hypothetical, pointless conversation!"

The car was silent for at least a minute before I said, "Why are we having this discussion?"

From his profile and the pressure building in the car, I could tell my husband was conflicted. He was holding back. His grip on the wheel was tight, his jaw locking and unlocking. This was a side of Adam I had never seen. Even when his colleagues at work had disagreements and he'd let off steam when he came home, he kept his cool, as if he had everything under control.

"Adam? Isn't being an uncle and a godfather, even without custody rights, enough?"

Eyes focused straight ahead, Adam simply replied, "No."

The red lights suddenly felt brighter, my cheeks suddenly felt ablaze, my stomach suddenly felt too full to hold the coq au vin.

"What are you saying, exactly?" I managed to mutter.

Adam slowly drew his gaze my way. "I'm saying that I think I want to have a child after all, Halley."

We were nearly home, exiting the freeway and making the left onto the street that would eventually drop into our neighborhood, when I spoke the first word since Adam delivered the bomb of the evening.

"How long have you felt this way?"

"Awhile."

"Awhile?"

He sighed, then said, "Don't you think it's beautiful, what Nina and Griffin are experiencing?"

"So your sister's having a baby and you want one, too?"

I bit the inside of my cheek and looked out my window. I tried to focus on the cars parked along the sides of the street, the dark palm tree silhouettes high in the night sky. Anything to keep from growing angrier at the turn of events in what should have been a lovely evening.

"They're not like puppies, Adam." I couldn't suppress the rage that was boiling inside me. How could Adam bring up something that was settled years ago? From the get-go. On our first date!

"I know that, Halley." He stopped at a stop sign, and instead of reaccelerating after a couple of seconds, he remained behind the thick white line.

"I didn't think I wanted that for my life," he said. "But seeing how happy Nina and Griffin are . . . how amazing the concept of having something that's part you, part me, together is . . ."

"I think it's really great that they're finally pregnant, Adam," I said. He began accelerating, crossing over the white line in the blink of an eye. "I really do. It's fantastic."

Nina and Griffin had been through the wringer trying to conceive—ovulation kits, ultrasounds, sperm motility and egg tests, fallopian tube exams, IVF. After two years of failing to conceive by simply trying and two additional years doing all sorts of tests, Nina treated herself to her first round of IVF on her thirtieth birthday. Lucky for Nina and Griffin, both have successful and prestigious careers—Nina as an editor and Griffin as a corporate attorney and partner at an esteemed law firm—and they were able and willing to spare no expense for their dream of having a child. When the IVF didn't take the first time, they tried a second, and then a third, and a fourth. Surrogacy and adoption weren't at the top of their list (at least quite yet), as Nina had a deep desire to carry a child. Then, like a miracle, during the fifth round of IVF, Nina got pregnant. Tragically, she never made it to her second trimester, experiencing a miscarriage.

At that point the doctors said it didn't look as if conception would be an option, and Nina and Griffin decided to stop trying. It was too painful to try and fail, time and again. But they never lost hope. Nina turned all her attention to her career, and Griffin to his, and they started to gather information about adoption. No heavy homework, only light doses of information. Slivers of hope. Then, after three years of not trying and always hoping, Nina became pregnant. No IVF, no special exams or fertility treatments. The good old-fashioned way had done the trick, finally. It was, as Nina and Griffin often say, a miracle. I'm not one to believe in miracles, but Nina's pregnancy made me a believer in at least one.

"I understand why you're caught up in the emotion and excitement of Rylan. Especially given the miraculous circumstances," I said to Adam in an understanding and collected tone, despite the frustration bubbling within. "But in the end, Adam, we made a promise to each other. We have a plan—no kids."

Adam didn't respond, so I looked out my window and continued. "Our lives are not Nina's and Griffin's. They're not Charlotte's and Marco's. They aren't anyone else's but our own, and our lives do not include a future of requesting a high chair or crayons with a children's menu at our dinner reservations." I looked to my husband.

"Halley." Adam paused for a lengthy exhalation. "Look, all I'm saying is that I think this is something I want after all."

"*All* you're saying?"

Adam's eyes moved from the road to me. "And *yes*, I *know* we planned on being the couple who never had kids."

"That's right we did!"

"And we've always been honest with each other."

"Yes, we have."

"Well, this is honestly how I feel." He turned onto our quiet street and proceeded to roll up to the closed gate of our condominium community.

"How long have you felt this way, Adam?"

He hesitated before answering. "Err . . . since . . . we found out Nina was pregnant."

"*Three months?*"

"Well . . . I've actually been thinking about it . . . for a while."

"What exactly is *a while?*"

Wearing a blank expression, he replied, "I guess the past year I've been . . . thinking about it."

I swallowed in astonishment. "The past *year?*"

"What with Nina and Griffin trying all this time, children always being a topic of discussion. Us getting older. It was only *thinking*, Halley. Hardly a crime," he said dismissively.

"But for three months you've . . . what? Been *decided*? Y-y-you want us to be Nina and Griffin? You want what they have? You want . . . a *baby*?"

He said nothing. He only looked at me, that same chilling blank expression on his face.

"Omigod," I muttered. "What is happening?"

When Adam propped baby Rylan's first sonogram image on our entry table with the rest of the collection of photographs, I thought he was a proud uncle. When he insisted to Nina on introducing Rylan to the world's greatest artists, and to teaching him about shading and composition, I thought he was a sweet big brother. I never imagined he wanted those things for himself . . . as a *father*.

"How could you keep something so *huge* from me?" I said, choking on my words.

Adam's voice was steady, his words forthright. "I wanted to be sure of my feelings before I sprang what is obviously horrifying news on you."

I gripped the sides of my head in sheer disbelief. "What are you saying, Adam? That you want to keep *thinking* about a baby or—"

"I'm not saying I want you to commit right now to us having a child."

A car pulled up behind us, ready to pass through the gate that Adam had yet to open with the punching in of the key code.

"I'm just saying that this is something I want, and I want you to be open to considering it, Halley."

My heart raced; my mind churned a thousand jumbled thoughts at once. How could this be happening? How could we go from being a joyous aunt and uncle to this, in the course of one brief evening? Or, evidently, over the course of three silent months? A *year*?

"I'm sorry," he said after a long, hot silence. "This isn't easy to say."

"This isn't easy to hear!" I squeezed my eyes shut. I could feel my chest tighten. I rolled my window down in desperate need of some air, some space. I had to calm down. "It was always supposed to be Halley and Adam against the world," I wheezed. "Not Halley, Adam, and Baby."

"I know." Adam rubbed my thigh in that comforting way of his. However, no amount of comforting could be achieved in that car at that moment. I still couldn't believe what I'd heard.

"Dammit. We talked about this." I squeezed my eyes shut again. Could I turn back the hands of time? Pretend this car ride never existed? Have been *more* clear about not wanting a child when we met?

"I know we did," he said.

"On our first date!"

"I know. But things . . . can change. People can change."

"Unbelievable."

"Look," Adam said, voice still calm, "I didn't want to just come right out and lay it heavy on you and say *I want a child*. But . . . this is how I feel, Halley. I've given it a lot of thought." His face looked pained—brow knit, upper lip slightly curled.

The car behind us honked, and Adam reluctantly rolled down the window and punched in the gate's code.

"How about you think about it? Give it some consideration?" he said. "And we can talk about it when you're ready?"

"There's nothing to consider. I'll never be ready."

"Halley."

"This isn't fair, Adam." I bit back the tears I could feel forming. "It isn't fair to throw this kind of a thing at me, knowing how strongly I feel. We both agreed we didn't want this."

"I know." He pulled into our driveway, parking alongside my car. "But it isn't fair to either of us to not be honest with you."

I held my head high and opened my door.

"Fair enough." I didn't know what else to say. I didn't want to have to say anything. I had to get out of the car. I wanted to walk inside our home and return to the way things had been. "I have to send that e-mail for work," I said dismissively.

"Hey, Halley," Adam called as I slid out of my seat. "I think you should add in your e-mail your proposal for that recurrent feature about strong females in literature." He gave me that warm, encouraging smile I'd climb the highest of mountains for. "It's a really good idea. And one you're passionate about."

I nodded, affected a weak, tight-lipped smile, then made my way up the walkway to our home.

When Adam and I stood at the altar, we did so with a mutual understanding of what family meant to the soon-to-be Mr. and Mrs. Brennan. I'd even asked him about not having kids once while we were engaged, wanting to be certain I was not going to deprive him of something he might want someday. His answer was what I'd hoped it'd be—"No children, no problem"—and one I expected never to change. How could it now? Besides, isn't it usually the woman who gets the baby itch? How could this be happening? And, more important, what the hell were we supposed to do about this revelation?

Sitting down at my computer to send my e-mail, then taking the bath and reading the book afterward, helped bring the tension down, but it is still there. It lingers overhead like a San Francisco fog.

I mindlessly flip through one Netflix show after another, nauseated and unable to make a selection. I'm mentally preparing myself to hear another remark from Adam, as he exchanges texts with Nina, about the wonders of having a child. I'm also hoping that this is something the two of us can put to rest with a good night of sleep, and that we can wake up to business as usual, where Adam will pour me my bowl of muesli and I will stick a love note on his coffee cup. We'll come home after work and exchange our highlights and low points. Before bed I'll grab a book to read, he'll sketch or flip through a magazine, and maybe we'll make love, *without* the intention of procreating. The way we always had and were always supposed to.

Adam laughs to himself as he types on his cell phone, so I ask what Nina's said.

"She's just wondering if Mom still has this ridiculous lederhosen outfit I wore when I was a kid."

I know the outfit. I remember the photo. It's adorable, Adam with his unruly mop of brown hair and those chubby pink cheeks. He's sporting an outfit that was intended to be a Halloween costume but was actually a childhood favorite he'd begged his mother to allow him to wear to day care, day after day.

"Oh, she'd never get rid of that," I say as Adam types a response. "In fact, don't we have that in a box somewhere?"

"I think so."

"What? Does Nina want it for Rylan?" I'm giddy at the idea of seeing my future nephew in it. "You should give it to her. I'm sure your mother would love to see photos of that."

Adam doesn't respond.

I'm about to ask if he wants to settle on an episode of *Friends* when he says, "You'll think about it, won't you, Halley?"

"Honey, it's your outfit to give or keep. It's not up to me. I do think Nina would lo—"

"Not the lederhosen. The baby." He rolls to his side and looks at me. "Can you at least *consider* having a baby?"

"No." It isn't a harsh no. It isn't stilted, nor is it bratty. It's honest. Like his asking me, my answer is genuine.

He sighs heavily and says, "Please, just consider it, Hals."

"I did. A long time ago." I turn off the television and stand, ready for bed. "Come on. Let's sleep." I hold my hand out to him, hoping he'll keep that beautiful mouth of his shut and just let us go to bed, put to rest this nonsense about upending our lives over something neither of us really wants. Go to bed the happily married couple without children we want to be now and forever.

With the duvet pulled over our bodies and my bedside lamp already turned out, I give Adam a long and passionate kiss. It's a kiss that doesn't necessarily invite something more but that lets him know that I love him, only him, and want to keep us. I don't want to argue, to go to bed angry.

His kiss is not as intense, but it's still heartfelt. It tells me what I need to hear, what I want to feel. That he's mine and I'm his. He wants to keep us, too.

He rolls to his side of the bed and turns out his bedside lamp.

"Good night, Halley."

"Good night, Adam."

But it's the lack of the habitual *I love you* before we go to bed that tells me I, alone, just might not be enough for my husband.

Three

A whole week passes, and much to my surprise the B word is not brought up. Not even the morning after our disagreement, when I figured chances were high Adam would at least ask if I'd slept on things. Nothing. That's exactly how I'd hoped things would go down. However, the resulting week has been anything but what I hoped for. Adam seems to be distancing himself from me, or at the very least letting his reserved side shine brighter than usual. He's brooding. Things seem different between us—there's a lot of quiet space.

For instance, Griffin's law firm happened to have some extra tickets to the sold-out ballet I'd wanted to see, and when they arrived in our mailbox one afternoon, Adam stuck them under a magnet on the fridge without mentioning their arrival. I happily discovered them while preparing dinner and asked him if he had the date marked on his calendar—it's a Friday-evening performance, and he'll need to leave work early to beat the traffic. His answer was a simple, "I'll have to check."

"We've been wanting to go to this for a while," I said.

"We just now got the tickets."

I tried to ignore his unusually direct tone.

"Well, let me know," I said.

"I will."

It wasn't just the incident with the tickets, but with the way conversation was flowing between us in general. Like a foreign language. Adam has a strong introverted side. Though he's confident and a born leader, he tends to be soft spoken, a nurturer by nature. With me he's fun, carefree, gentle, an open book. His keeping discussions succinct at the dinner table—emotionless and strictly about work—is out of the ordinary, and the shortness of his responses is unsettling. A small part of me—a very small part—wants to bring up the B word simply to move on from it, so we can carry on with the way our lives are supposed to be. Get beyond this. If he won't talk about it, then I will, because we need to find our way back to normal.

The thing is, I know negligence can lead to festering, and festering is childish and dangerous. It can be the prologue to a disaster in a marriage. Because just as much pain and damage, if not more, can come from the things you don't say as from the things you do. And the longer Adam and I neglect to deal with this enormous grey cloud, the greater I fear our problem will become. I have to find the right way to broach the topic of parenthood. A way that allows us to move past this quiet space that's become so loud I can't hear myself think anymore.

Unsure of where or when to begin, I consider rallying my sister, Charlotte, to my side. If anyone knows about the struggles of married life it's her. She and her husband, Marco, tied the knot straight out of college, eleven years ago. Like Adam and me, she's seen the marital peaks and valleys, though she's seen more valleys than we have, and more than I think she ever imagined. Her first and third children were not accidents but what she lovingly refers to as "earlier-than-expected blessings." Charlotte's still finding herself—aren't we all?—and she's a real-life testament to what it means to work at a marriage.

Marco works for a reputable PR firm, and Charlotte's a stay-at-home mom. They have a lovely two-story home, complete with the white picket fence and red front door, in a safe, family-friendly neighborhood in Burbank. They're active in their kids' lives and take at least one big family vacation each year. They don't yet have the dog to complete the picture-perfect family, but six-year-old George has made out his Christmas list months in advance, and there's only one thing on it.

At first glance, the Millers *are* that picture-perfect family. Inside, though, Charlotte struggles with keeping up and being happy. Marco struggles with keeping it together and being present. As Charlotte says, they have their challenges, and every day they have to work at them. At the end of the day, she loves her husband and children, and she knows Marco loves her and the children, too. At the end of the day, you remember to count your blessings and not your frustrations.

However, though Charlotte no doubt has loads of marital advice and experience to offer, and is always a supportive ear and an encouraging voice, my baby trouble with Adam isn't something I want to burden her with right now. She has enough going on with three young children. The last thing she needs is her big sister saying that she's faced with a hypothetical child changing her life, that a stress is being put on her marriage. Charlotte will be torn between telling me to stay true to who I am and what I want, and telling me to do whatever it takes to keep my marriage strong. She's Adam's biggest fan, and as a mother herself, even knowing how strongly I feel about the matter, I can easily picture her telling me to just consider what Adam's asking. I could imagine her saying, "It isn't like he's asking you to travel to Mars or something, Hals. It's a baby. Millions of women have them. All over the world. Every day."

Talking to Nina is out of the question. It isn't that Nina would instantly side with her brother. It's that she's been riding the Baby Express for years, and I know, especially given her hormone swings lately, she'd say it'd be fantastic to be pregnant at the same time. How could I not want what she's experiencing right now? Though she knows my staunch views on motherhood, there's still a chance she'll tell me to buck up and get knocked up, and that's a chance I'm not willing to take. And I couldn't prattle on about how much I don't want a baby, when she so clearly would travel to Mars for one.

I decide to call up Marian Kroeber, one of my dearest friends from college. She isn't my last choice, just my most sensible. Exactly the woman I need in my corner right now.

Marian is outgoing, honest, sympathetic to a fault, fun loving, and likes a strong cup of coffee. Sometimes a strong shot of whiskey. She may not have the greatest track record with men, and on occasion lets her bitterness about love color her opinion of them, but she's never dishonest or mean spirited with her advice. She always does me a solid, even when I don't necessarily deserve it; she always has counsel, even when I may not necessarily want to hear it. She's the kind of best friend every woman should have. I count my lucky stars I have her, especially at a time like now.

Taking lunch in the office at my desk today, I balance research on the long-term effects of Kegels practice for my next *Copper* article with a call to my main girl Marian.

"Halley! How's life at the top of the women's magazine world?" Marian's voice bubbles through the phone.

"Glamorous as ever," I say with a laugh.

"Uh-oh." Her voice turns down and thickens with concern in half a beat. "Troubs at work?"

"Troubs at home." I sigh, then get right to it. Refraining from a dramatic buildup makes my problem less grave and less real, as does referring to it as *troubs*. "Adam thinks he wants a baby after all." As soon as I say the words, though, I know that my problem is more than a troub. It is every bit real and grave.

"What?" Marian practically shouts into the phone.

"I know."

As soon as Marian processes that what I'm telling her is not a terribly delayed April Fool's joke, she sympathetically listens as I give her the details, inserting *mmmhmm*s and *aha*s in her characteristic multi-tasking way. She's on the road, making her afternoon rounds as a pharmaceutical sales rep. When I tell her that Adam's acting distant, almost distracted, "like something's really bothering him," she interrupts with a throaty laugh and says, "Yeah! It's called you being preggers with his progeny."

"I know," I say, deflated. "But when something's bothering Adam, he tells me, and we work on it."

"Like when you decided to paint your living room eggplant and he hated it?"

"Like that. Just . . . not." I draw a circle with my highlighter around the graph at the bottom of the second page of research on my desk. "Bigger. This is a baby, not a bucket of paint, Marian."

"Po-tay-toe, po-tah-toe, you know what I mean. He's honest when there's a problem, and you are, too."

"Exactly. And he was open telling me he wanted a child, like I'm open in telling him I don't."

"The ideal couple. God, you guys make me sick," Marian says in her teasing way.

"He's obviously bothered about this baby talk, but he just broods about it."

"You know I love you and always have your back?"

"I do."

"His brooding and your trying to ignore things are one and the same. There's a problem in the Brennan home, and it needs fixin'."

"I just want this heaviness to go away, Marian."

"I know you do, hon."

"I'm so angry at him for doing this to us. So angry!"

"You have every right to be."

"God, I don't know where to go from here."

"The way I see it, you can sweep it under the rug, try to forget it happened, and hope he does, too."

"Yes, but how mature is that?"

"Eh. Works for a lot of couples."

"Not for us." Adam and I are bigger than that. Our openness is one of the things that's made our marriage so strong. "Besides, that hasn't exactly been working out so well."

"So that leaves the other option. Dust off your balls and come out and talk about it, Hals," Marian says, perky.

"I have only one thing to say to him about it." I heave a sigh and drop my highlighter into the pencil cup on my desk. "And if he hasn't changed his mind, then what? I guess we can just keep waiting and see-ing and trying to work things out—him hoping I'll give in, me hoping he'll give up. Then we're right back here, where we started. And god knows what kind of a wedge of tension will be between us by then."

"Let's not get ahead of ourselves," Marian soothes. "Maybe he's going through a phase." Her tone is hopeful.

"I can't believe this is even a thing," I mutter, dropping my elbows to my desk.

"*I'm* surprised this is a thing. I thought you guys had this topic wrapped. Like, years ago?"

"We did. On our first date."

"Men." She makes a *tsk*ing sound. "Always complicating shit."

"I love Adam," I say, growing despondent as we talk about my marital troubles. *Me? Adam? Marital . . . troubles?* I cannot believe the words—the reality.

"I know you do. We all love Adam. Who doesn't *love* Adam? And that tushy of his," she trills.

I chuckle at the memory. Adam will never live down Marian's tushy comment. Marian ran track in college with Nina and me, and during one of our meets, when Adam and I were just starting to date, he came out to watch a relay. Marian, exhausted from the run and dripping with sweat, must have hit the wall, because she had mistaken Adam for a guy she'd been seeing from the law school, who, like Adam, tended to wear dress slacks and shirts to even the most relaxed events, like a track meet. Before I got a chance to introduce Marian to Adam, she grabbed his ass and called it a *tushy*, and said something off color about her reward for running her hardest. When Adam turned around, Marian could have eaten her words, but she just came right out with, "My apologies. Not for the fine tushy remark, but for grabbing what is Halley's and not mine." For a good year, every time Marian saw Adam she'd whistle and say, "Fine tushy you got, Adam."

I appreciate the happy memory and say, "Maybe he will forget about it and move on."

"The tushy comment? Never."

"Marian," I groan, and she laughs. "And maybe this grey cloud over us is about something else entirely."

"Maybe." Her tone suggests otherwise. I know as well as Marian that that isn't the case, though it feels good to have a small ray of hope.

"It isn't fair. You know?" I say.

"I know. Life and love ain't fair."

"Maybe you're right, and it is just a phase." I try to convince myself, clinging to any ounce of hope I can find. "I bet once Nina has the baby, he'll see what hard work it is and forget all about it. He just doesn't realize that part of it."

"Or he'll see how adorable it is and want one even more."

"Oh, Marian. Always devil's advocate."

"Halley, give it time. Don't expect the worst, but don't plan for the best."

"Marian Kroeber's words to live by."

"If you want my honest advice—" Before she can finish, the line clicks, and she says, "Sorry, incoming call I need to take. Just a sec." Such is the life of a successful and busy pharmaceutical sales rep.

Straight out of college, Marian decided to give the pharma industry a shot. When she heard there could be a lot of money and perks in it, particularly for women, she put aside any feminist qualms and embraced the industry with open arms. As she once put it, if she could put her brains and natural saleswoman abilities to good use *and* let those long, trim legs of hers help her out, why not?

The truth of the matter is, Marian's a workaholic, and her position as one of the leading sales reps in her company suits her well. She's single; has no interest or time for a pet; loves to travel and meet new people; enjoys cocktail parties as much as any thirty, flirty, and unattached woman; and lives by the motto, "My thirties won't break me; I'll break them." She's doing a smashing job. She may lament her lackluster relationship situation from time to time, but honestly, where would she find the time for a boyfriend?

"Sorry," Marian says, coming back on the line. "Never a quiet moment here. Look, my honest advice is that it's either going to get fixed by Adam changing his mind—it's just a phase—or by the two of you seriously talking it out and figuring where the hell to go from here. There's no easy answer, babe. At least not right now."

"I know. I'm hoping for the former."

"I am, too. But you guys have always been open and honest. *Talk* about it."

"I can't remember the last time we had sex," I say at random. All the research about Kegels and procreation remind me of the unfortunate reality in my bedroom.

"Dry spells happen," Marian says.

I lean back in my chair. "Hey, do you do Kegels, by chance?" I ask.

Marian laughs loudly. "Is that a proposition?"

"I'm working on an article."

"Aha. I sure do. Why?"

"Well then, you may be happy to know you fall into the sixty-seven percent of American women who do."

"That's a real statistic?" she says in disbelief.

"Apparently." I shuffle my stack of papers into one neat pile. "Although we probably have an entire department solely dedicated to making up fluff reports like this."

"Got to sell the mags."

"Exactly."

"Well, speaking of selling, I've got to run, girl."

"Me, too." I've got ten minutes before my first afternoon meeting and need to finish my prep.

"Keep the lines of communication open," she adds before hanging up. "Don't let words go unsaid, feelings unshared." I know this advice is particularly hard for her to impart.

"I love you, Marian," I say, appreciating another one of our heart-to-hearts. "Talk later?"

"Always."

In an effort to blow away that grey cloud, and maybe even spice up our sex life, I start with tacos. I know, I didn't think this through very well, but Tito's Tacos are by far the best tacos in the world. And they're *our* tacos. Good always comes of a night with Adam and me sharing a bag of Tito's Tacos. Maybe the comfort food will loosen Adam up, remind him that the two of us are really good together, that we have something special. That we don't need anything or anyone more.

I don't know where to begin with the elephant in the room, and I kind of resent having to be the one to do so. Because after all, I'm not the one who wants to renege on a promise we made to each other when we got married. I don't feel any different about our future. Of course, if I leave it all up to Adam, god knows how long this awkward distance and silence will carry on between us. Is he *honestly* waiting for me to change my mind?

So I have to step up to the plate. Somehow.

I figure I can start with tacos, and then we can talk about more than work. Maybe we'll have sex. And somewhere in all of that, maybe I will find the courage to ask Adam if he's still feeling as if the two of us are not enough. But what if he says he is? What then? And that possibility is why I can't "dust off my balls" and bring up the B word on my own straightaway. Why I can't think past the tacos, talk, and sex. This is why I need Adam. I need him to tell me that the distance and silence are all because of some stupid whim he didn't really think through. That he's sorry we even got to this weird point. That all he wants is me, that I'm enough, that he's sorry for thinking of breaking the rules. That we can go back to being just the way we were.

Unable to stand the building tension and suspense about what will come of Tito's Tacos night, I break open my ice-cold bottle of Corona before Adam's home. The room's filled with the spicy scent of the dinner still in the bag—cilantro, onion, and grease. It, like the memory of Marian and Adam's first encounter at the track, makes me happy. I'm reminded of simpler times, back when Adam and I were just settling into newlywed life and we initiated Taco Tuesday. Back when cheap tacos were considered a splurge, reality TV was still relatively entertaining, and babies were never on the brain.

"Hey," Adam says, startling me as he walks through the front door. "Smells good. Tito's?"

I can't help but beam as I watch him set his leather messenger bag on the sofa and walk toward me in the dining room. He undoes the top button of his pale-blue dress shirt. It's one of my favorites for the way it fits as if it had been tailored just for him, and for the way the color complements his naturally golden-tanned skin and dark-brown hair. His eyebrows, a slight shade darker than his hair, rise expectantly once he eyes the bag of greasy comfort food. Even after ten-plus years of marriage, Adam can still make me light up by simply entering a room. Even a room that has a big grey cloud hanging overhead. I love this man with every fiber of my being. I'm suddenly hit with a deep longing for our old Taco Tuesdays, not tacos to try to solve a marital problem.

I love Adam. He's still my home.

So why in god's name am I nursing a beer because I'm afraid of dinner conversation with him? Because I'm nervous about what he may tell me, if he's honest and open? Because I'm terrified of discovering what the truth might be?

"You *did* get Tito's," Adam confirms. He looks up at me, wearing a small, crooked smile. "It isn't even Tuesday."

We've long since turned Taco Tuesday into Tacos When We Feel Like Them, but his comment still warms my heart. Simpler times.

"Want to watch some TV?" Adam asks, a plate of tacos now in one hand, bowl of tortilla chips in another. He moves toward the living room.

I resume my seat at the dining table after fetching a spoon to serve the salsa. "Maybe later."

"Okay." He spins on his heels and joins me at the table. He pops open his beer and tips his bottle to mine in a mock clink.

"Actually." I wince, wishing the Corona would do a better job of calming my nerves. "Maybe no TV for the night. Maybe we can play cards or go for an evening walk or something?" Anything.

Adam makes a puzzled face. "Okay."

He's licking his fingers after one finished taco while I haven't done more than take a single bite. I was dying to sink my teeth into dinner before Adam came home, but now that he's here, all I can think about is where to begin. Why this is so difficult, so awkward. How to say the words I don't want to have spoken.

What little gumption I can find surges forth as I say, "Adam, honey, are you okay?"

He sounds an *mmmhmm* as he takes a large bite.

"Work good?" I've already resorted to the idle small talk I've despised this past week—the only kind we've managed to have.

"Work's great. And you?" Before I can answer, he asks, "What's going on with that feature proposal? You pitched it to your boss, didn't you?"

"I did."

"And?"

I'm not particularly interested in talking shop, but I did pitch the idea to my boss, Chantelle, and I do have some news regarding it. News I would normally be ecstatic to share with Adam, but that isn't what I want to talk about tonight.

Nevertheless, since it is something I'm happy about and know Adam will be, too, I tell him, "Chantelle loves it. She loves it so much she wants me to put together a sample piece, and she'll toss the idea around with the editors to see what they think."

"Congratulations, Halley." Adam brushes the salt from his hands and claps them together in praise. "That's my girl. I'm so proud of you."

"It isn't a feature yet, but hopefully." His pride and joy are infectious. My shoulders rise as I think how encouraging the news I received this morning is.

"Which strong female in literature are you thinking of pitching?"

I shrug, picking at the shredded lettuce on my taco. "Anne, I'm thinking. Of Green Gables." I think of when we were first dating and staying up until the wee hours of the morning talking about everything from high school experiences and current events to film, music, and literature. Favorite bands, least favorite movies, and all-time forever-favorite books. "Or Laura," I say, "from Little House."

"I like it. That's the reason for the tacos, huh?" he says with a devilish grin.

I give a deflated look at the barely touched meal on my plate, lettuce now littered about like sad confetti. I suppose Anne or Laura could have been the reason for the tacos. In fact, I wish they were. And with that open window, I say, "Adam, are we . . . all right?"

"What do you mean?"

"I feel like we haven't really been . . . close. This past week. Since"—I choose my words carefully, not wanting to nose-dive into baby talk—"the night we went to Nina and Griffin's."

Adam nods slowly, almost meticulously. I wish he'd say something. Anything. His eyes are transfixed on what looks to be my plate.

"I feel like we haven't really connected," I blurt. "We seem a little distant."

Adam looks straight into my eyes. "Halley, I love you."

"I love you, too."

He reaches his hand, palm open, across the table. I slip mine into it and smile weakly.

"We're going through a little rough patch, that's all." His thumb strokes my hand in an almost reassuring way. Almost. "We'll figure it out," he says. Again, in an almost reassuring way.

I nod vigorously, feeling the needling sensation of tears prick the backs of my eyes, the depths of my throat. I am not going to cry. I am not going to cry. There's nothing to cry about. A "rough patch" is what this is. A disagreement we have to work through. That's all. I try not to think about how this is a rough patch only because *he* decided to make it one. Everything was just fine before he changed his freakin' mind! But in any event, we love each other. As Adam said, we'll figure it out.

"I'm happy with you," I say, successfully able to suppress the tears, my voice strong. "I need only you." He smiles weakly at my comment. "I love you so much, Adam."

"And I'm happy with you, Hals. Come here." He lets go of my hand and waves me over.

Seated in his lap, I drape both arms around his neck. He kisses the tip of my nose. "You still hungry?" he asks.

I look over my shoulder at the mess of a dining table. I pluck a chip from the bowl and offer it to him. He shakes his head, and I eat it. "Stuffed," I answer.

"Me, too. Want dessert?"

I wrinkle my nose. "I didn't pick anything up. Unless you want to go get some frozen yogurt?"

The corners of Adam's mouth pull up, and he looks off to the side. "That's one option . . ." He nods toward the bedroom. "Or we could go to bed early?"

I all but leap from his lap, grabbing his hand and loving the way it engulfs mine. My hands always get lost in his.

"Forget the frozen yogurt," I say hurriedly, leading the way to our bedroom, Adam laughing as he follows.

With one arm wrapped around me, Adam holds me against his bare chest. He brushes the auburn strands of my hair from my shoulder. They tickle as they fall across my back.

My eyes move to the fine contours of his stomach. I can feel and hear his heart beat strong and steady against my cheek. His chest rises and falls with each breath he takes. His fingers brush through my hair, and I close my eyes.

"I don't want to be anywhere else," I whisper. "With anyone else."

"We're perfect together, aren't we?" Adam says.

I smile to myself at his not-so-subtle hint about our perfection not just as a couple but also as sexual partners. Even when we'd first become intimate, we fit together as if we'd had years of practice. Adam once said when we were first dating that he couldn't believe how perfect we were together—how we moved together just right; made each other feel better than seemed physically possible; effortlessly fell into place the way every couple aspires to.

I told him I bet he said that to all the girls, to which he replied, "Just the one." It was the perfect line, not because it was true and simple and romantic but because it was the kind of line a writer looks for when she's working on that flawless meet cute for the couple that ends up happily ever after. I liked the way it came out of Adam's mouth, and I like that today, all these years later, and despite the awkward space of the past week, it is still true. We *are* perfect together.

"Impossibly so," I say.

Adam pulls me tighter against his body, and I slide on top of him. Our lips touch—electric chills fly up and down my arms and spine— and I taste the salt still on his lips from dinner, the salt of his sweat, the salt of my sweat mixed with his. His tongue dances with mine in as perfect a dance as the one we just did together in the sheets. It's hungry, unselfish, and careful, all at the same time.

When I emerge from the bathroom, towel drying my hair after a long, steamy shower, Adam's at his sink, brushing his teeth. His hair's still wet from his shower, at its darkest and slicked back. A thick strand hangs near his right ear, and he swats it back as he leans to spit into the sink. I can't help but smile as I stare at my husband. This is enough for me, all I want. Exactly what I want.

Overcome with exhaustion, I follow Adam into our bedroom, deciding to forego blow-drying my hair and opting to deal with the mess in the morning. Snuggling in Adam's arms is what I want to be doing right now.

Adam turns on both bedside lamps before slipping under the covers. He punches down his pillow exactly three times, then takes a long drink of water from the glass that's always on his nightstand. He clears his throat and takes another drink before crashing his head onto his pillow, but not without his routine deep groan. It's the same thing every night. I find it charming. Every couple's got its nighttime rituals. Adam's got his fluff-sip-and-groan deal, and I've got my application of hand lotion, the tightening of the hospital corners on my side of the bed, and, of course, the pill regimen.

I shake out one multivitamin followed by extra doses of vitamins C and E, and then move to puncture the blister pack for one of my birth control pills.

"Have you thought about stopping taking those?" Adam says.

I close my hand over my routine pills and glance at Adam. I say nothing. I know to what he's referring, but I answer, "I take extra vitamin C and E for my skin and immune system. Maybe they're nothing more than placebos, I don't know."

I'm about to take a drink of water when Adam says, "Your birth control, I meant."

Perhaps this is what I deserve, since I've done a bang-up job of talking through our dilemma tonight.

I turn and look at him head-on. "I've been taking these since I was nineteen, Adam. No, I haven't thought about stopping them." I hold up my fist of pills. "Why would I?"

He props his head up on an arm and shrugs. "I thought you'd . . . consider."

"Consider getting off the pill?"

"Yeah."

"I never said I'd consider getting off the pill."

"You said you'd consider getting pregnant."

"No." Indignant, I hold up one finger. "No, I never said that."

I did *not* say I would consider getting pregnant. Or going off the pill. Or anything that involved changing my mind about our mutual decision on a childless life.

"Halley, have you given this any more thought since we first talked about having a baby?"

"First off, please don't say, 'talked about having a baby.'"

He tosses up his hands in response.

"Second, it's all I can think about." Adam's face lights up as I say this, but before he can speak, I add, "Ever since you dropped that bomb on me, all I can think about is what we're supposed to do about this *massive* disagreement. We both suddenly—apparently—want different things out of life. And those two things, Adam, do *not* go hand in hand. They're like water and oil. So have I given it any more thought? How can I not? You're asking me to consider having something I don't want, and I'm waiting for you to consider not having something you apparently do."

I was talking in circles. Thinking in circles. This was going nowhere.

I clap my hand without the pills to my clammy forehead.

"Halley, I don't mean to upset you." He sits upright in bed, his arms helplessly by his sides. "I just want to talk."

"Good. Yes, I want to talk, too."

"What if you just got off the pill and we can see what happens?"

Is he mad? He's truly lost his mind! With that idiotic suggestion, I wash down my handful of pills.

"Halley," he grumbles.

"'We can see what happens'? *See* what happens? You *know* what will happen."

"It took Nina and Griffin a very long time."

"So you're saying you're okay with potentially trying for *ten* years to 'see what happens'?"

"It wouldn't take us that long," he says, with no medical evidence to back his claim. In his defense I don't, as far as I'm aware, have an oddly shaped uterus like Nina's, which makes it nearly impossible for her to conceive. But still! The nerve.

"You're a doctor now?" I snap.

"It most likely wouldn't take us that long."

"Oh joy! Waiting on pins and needles every month to see if my period comes. That's just how I want to spend every twenty-eight days. And *not* for the same reason you're waiting!" I take another drink of water, then slam the dresser drawer closed with a swing of my hip. "No, Adam. I'm not going to live like that."

"Okay, here's an idea," he says, suddenly eager, eyes bright. "Our Thanksgiving trip to Maui."

"Yes?" I'm curious where he's going with this. Nearly every big holiday Adam and I take advantage of the time off from work and set out on a romantic vacation. In three months we're headed to an all-inclusive Hawaiian beach resort. The mere thought of it as we argue about babies makes me want to grab my boarding pass and bikini and jet off right now. Come to think of it, maybe that is just what Adam and I need . . .

"Let's go," he says, "and have a completely indulgent vacation. I'm talking every massage and kayak adventure, all the yoga on the beach and obnoxious cocktails we can imagine. The works. We don't do our usual all out, we go *all* out." Music to my ears. "And it'll be our babymoon." Needles in my ears.

"Our *what?*" I say, beside myself.

"Well, our prebabymoon, if you will. It's where—"

"I know what they are. What I don't get is why *we*"—I motion between us—"would be having one."

"Halley. Come on."

I'm sick to my stomach. "A prebabymoon? One last hurrah before we turn our lives upside down? Can't you see this is part of why I *don't* want a baby? I don't want to have to 'live it up' before we make a life change."

"Halley."

"No."

Cheeks turning red, Adam throws up his hands again and says, "Fine. Forget about it."

"Forget about the babymoon . . . or the trip itself?" My mouth slowly begins to fall in disbelief.

He doesn't respond, so I repeat, this time louder and angrier, "The Thanksgiving trip *itself*, Adam?"

He runs his hands through his wet hair and ignores my question. "Okay." His voice is steady. "Just hear me out, Hals. Are you afraid of what having a child could do to your career? That you'd have to take maternity leave?"

"Yes, for one."

Granted, my career isn't all that impressive, and most days I'm not exactly pleased, much less enthusiastic, to be writing about "Miniskirts: Are They Really Inappropriate after Thirty?" But working at *Copper* is a position in the writing field, something I've always had my heart set on. I'd be daft to do anything to jeopardize my career, and having a baby would do just that. Look at what happened to Charlotte when she became pregnant with Alice. She let go of her dream of becoming a lawyer. Eleven years later she still regrets her decision, though she loves her daughter to death and would have her all over again. (Though perhaps a bit later.)

"Okay. I've got that covered." Adam's eyes light up, hopeful. "I can work from home, be a stay-at-home dad."

"Round-the-clock dad? Getting up several times in the middle of the night for feedings? Constant doctor appointments?" I run on, ticking items off with my fingers.

"We'll bottle-feed, and I'll get up. I'll do the appointments."

"Finding a day care if you can't manage working from home? Nina's already on a waiting list," I say, incredulous. "And a long one, at that."

"We'd get a nanny."

"And win the lotto?"

"We'd manage," he insists.

"I don't want to manage. I want to live, Adam."

"Halley."

I continue ticking items off one by one with my fingers. "Potty training, PTA meetings, recitals, teen angst, college tuition—"

"First words, first steps, first *I love you*s," Adam counters in an aggravatingly cheerful tone.

"Moving to the burbs when the kid gets older, so we can move to a neighborhood in a 'good school district.'" I use irritating air quotes.

"What's wrong with that?"

"First, I'm not a burbs girl." I begin pacing. "Second, the thought of having to plan our living arrangements—our mortgage—around a child's elementary education is . . . well, it was hard enough to find a place we both love that's close to both our offices and not a gajillion dollars!"

"Halley."

"No, that's not even the half of it. I don't want to shop for ever-growing feet, and I don't want to go to soccer games every single weekend or plan our vacations around a child's school schedule. I don't want to fret over babysitters so we can have a simple night out at the movies or dinner. Dinner without high chairs. Movies that aren't animated, or the early matinees where breastfeeding moms and crying babies are welcome. And breastfeeding!" I stop my pacing.

"I already said we'd bottle-feed," he cuts in, yet again suggesting something that is neither here nor there. There will be no bottle-feeding because there will be no baby.

"No, Adam." I shake my head, my arms crossed over my stomach. "No toys all over the rug and sippy cups in the dishwasher—"

He meets me head-on and says, "Yes to packed Christmas stockings, Bring Your Child to Work Day—"

"No to helping with multiplication tables. I can barely do them myself anymore."

"See, an opportunity to learn!" He's grinning.

"Oh god." I clap a hand to my head.

"Yes to handmade art, macaroni necklaces, finger paintings we put on the refrigerator—"

"No to the birds-and-the-bees talk, dealing with other kids' parents at school and birthday parties, and the entire responsibility and role of parenting!" I exhale loudly, waiting for Adam to add to his list of reasons why we should become parents.

But he doesn't respond. Rather, he sits there, the sheet bunched around his waist, shoulders slumped slightly forward. He's wearing an expression that says both that I haven't changed his mind and *Are you finished yet?*

I'm not, so I say, "I don't want to be pregnant." This should cap the opened bottle.

"It's only nine months," he counters. "Time will fly by."

"Omigod." I toss up my hands, incredulous, nostrils flaring. "Easy for you to say!"

"We'd be great parents."

"You don't know that." I charge to my side of the bed and begin tugging at the corners of the sheet.

"Are you worried about motherhood because of your mother?"

I let go of the sheet and stand tall. I close my eyes and press my fingers to my aching temples.

Adam knows as well as I do that my mother did a piss-poor job of wearing the mommy pants. I was an accident—that's right, *accident*, not "earlier-than-expected blessing"—and so was Charlotte. If it weren't for our loving and dedicated father, god knows what street corner I'd be working in Hollywood or what back alley Charlotte would be lying in. When I was growing up, my mother, Monica, was notoriously flighty, forgetting to serve Charlotte and me breakfast half the time and choosing parties with friends over helping with homework. To call Monica a part-time mother would be giving her far too much credit.

I was in fifth grade when she and Dad called it quits, and she went from flighty to practically nonexistent. That might have been a blessing, but she became that embarrassing older woman thinking she's half her age and forgetting about the ex-husband and two young daughters she left behind in her serial dating, multiple moves, and constant career changes. Instability was her middle name. She dated up and down the roster of pathetic divorcés, even a fair share of married men. Despite it all, my father never uttered a foul word about her or her hazardous behavior. He simply learned to juggle the roles of father *and* mother, and I think he loved us even more fiercely because of it.

During my college years, my mother decided she wanted to try to become friends with Charlotte and me. Said she might not have excelled at being our mother, but could we give friendship a shot? Needless to say, her penchant for living life on the edge and forgetting that once a mother, always a mother, regardless of any friendship you may try to cultivate with your daughters years later, have brought us to today, when my mother and I are not on the best of terms. After thirty-four years we've reached lukewarm waters. We don't overly engage, we try to keep it civil at family birthday parties and events, and on very rare occasion we will have an easy two-minute phone call (usually out of the necessity to coordinate said family events).

However, I do not read my mother's shortcomings like some kind of tea leaves for my future. I'll never know if her feeble mothering attempts truly influenced my choice not to have children (how can I?), but what I do know is that I've made up my mind, Mrs. Brady or Monica Lenz as my mothering role model.

I open my eyes and remove my fingers from my temples, the pulsing beginning to lessen, though only slightly. "No," I tell Adam simply. I point out that I have my sister, Charlotte, as a prime example of motherhood done well. Sure, she's exhausted, and the start of her little family began sooner than she'd anticipated, but she's a wonderful mom. If she, also a daughter of my mother, could do it, of course I could.

"Then why won't you at least *consider* having one?" Adam pleads.

"I *have* considered it, Adam. Every woman does. I even reconsidered it when Nina got pregnant the first time, before she miscarried. And when Charlotte was pregnant with her three, I thought about it. I imagined myself in their shoes and thought, *Does this look like something I want after all?*"

"And?"

I groan. "And nothing's changed. I know what I want and what I don't, Adam. I want you. And I don't want a baby."

"Look, I'm not asking to have one in the next nine months."

I gesture to the dresser where I keep my pills. "It sure sounds like it, me stopping my birth control and turning our trip to Maui into a last hurrah."

"Can you be open to the idea? Or how about adoption?" He suddenly looks eager, renewed, hopeful. "If being pregnant is the problem, what about that?"

"Adam, the being-pregnant part is an infinitesimal part. And even when you take the crazy that comes with raising a child and all the responsibilities . . . when you take all that tough stuff and set it aside, I still know, deep down, that I don't want to be a mother. Even though I'll be missing out on all the joy that parenthood does bring, it's not for me. It's just . . . who I am. Plain and simple." Adam now looks defeated, no longer hopeful. I sit on the edge of my side of the bed and ask him, "You know why I don't want a child. Why do you want one?"

After a short silence, he presses a fist to his heart and says, looking straight into my eyes, "I feel it in my soul, Halley. In my heart. I can't explain it."

"You can't explain it. That's great." I can't hide my sarcasm. "You want to upend our lives because of something you can't explain?"

"I guess since Nina got pregnant I've really started looking at kids differently, thinking about babies," he says. "This isn't something I've *ever* done, really think about having children. Ever." His fist drops to the scrunched blankets across his lap. "Maybe that's the problem," he says with an ironic sniff. "You did all your thinking a long time ago. I'm thirty-eight, getting older, and looking at life through a clearer lens that comes with age . . . I don't know. That's why I haven't been myself lately. I don't want to be angry with you, Halley, but every time you say you don't want something that's become so important to me, I deal with it by shutting down. It's not fair. But I do know that I have to be completely up-front with you."

"I appreciate that."

"What I mean to say is . . . god, this is hard." He pauses. "I'd love it if you would consider having a child."

"I know that."

"But if that's all you did . . . Consider? And we never actually *had* one . . ."

"Yes?"

He closes his eyes and sighs.

I clap a hand to my heart. "What are you saying, Adam?"

"I really want a child, that's what I'm saying." He exhales a very long and heavy breath. "I know this wasn't how things were supposed to be, Halley. I'm sorry." He gives me a sideways sympathetic smile. I don't like it. It's as if he feels sorry for me. As if I'm to be pitied for standing by my convictions.

"I feel sorry for *us*." As soon as I say the words, I feel the stinging sensation behind my eyes that warns me the dam of tears is about to break.

Adam and I—my husband and I—are at an impasse. The dam is about to burst, the grey cloud is hanging low and heavy, that fat elephant is pressing against the walls of our bedroom. Every horrible cliché is rearing its ugly head, and all either of us can do is stare at the other, speechless.

Scrambling, I finally blurt out, "What should we do?"

"I don't know."

Wrong answer. Adam *always* has an answer, and a good one. A real and workable one. He's the problem solver, the one who steps up if I step down. The positive to the negative. The perfect match. *My* perfect match.

I grip my heart, as if that'll somehow help the sudden burning sensation that's seized it.

"Things clearly aren't working the way they are now," he says, only adding to the fire. This is not what he's supposed to say. He's supposed to cry with me and hold me and tell me that we'll figure it out. Because we can. Because that's what soul mates do!

Desperate, I suggest, "Let's go take that Thanksgiving trip now! And go all out. Pamper ourselves, remind ourselves that together we can overcome anything." I press my hands to my heart. "That we can be happy, just the two of us."

Adam only looks at me with two slightly raised brows.

"I'll ask Chantelle for the time off," I add. "What do you say? We need this, Adam."

"Halley, no."

"No?"

He sighs. "I . . . I can't think about vacationing right now."

"What?"

"We've got bigger problems than vacations, Halley."

Not thinking, and being spiteful, I say, "Fine, whatever. Let's just cancel the vacation." A painful stinging knot settles in the back of my throat.

"Fine," he says.

His response is not what I expect. "Great! So you want to bail on our life plans *and* our Thanksgiving plans? What's next? You want to bail on our marriage, too?"

As soon as I say it, and as soon as I register that Adam is not saying anything, I regret my rant, my insinuation, the whole damn evening.

"Omigod," I breathe, cupping a hand to my mouth. "Do you want a di-di-di . . ." I can't bring myself to say the word.

"Christ, Halley." Adam gruffly crosses his arms over his chest. "No! Of course I don't!"

Relief ushers the knot out of my throat and suppresses the tears, but the simple fact that the idea of our marriage failing presented itself, even if it was wholly my doing, leaves behind a small stain of disturbing doubt.

"Then what?" I mutter, helpless. "What do we do?"

"Maybe . . . ," he begins, sounding equally helpless. "Maybe we should see a therapist?"

"A therapist?"

I don't know why, but I'm skeptical. But I'm also desperate. And so is Adam. We have to try more than Tito's Tacos and a horribly heated, unproductive argument before bed to solve our marital problem. Therapy it is.

"Deal," I say, snidely thinking, *You do remember the concept of a deal, right, Adam?* Instead I decide to put to rest for the night, and hopefully for good, my anger and resentment toward my husband and this ridiculous dilemma. "I'll call around for an appointment first thing in the morning."

Four

"You're just upset because you didn't hear what you wanted to hear," Adam says brusquely as he shuts our mailbox with more force than necessary.

"And you're telling me *you* heard what you wanted to hear?" Arms akimbo, I stand in front of him, impeding his path to our condo.

"Of course I didn't."

As agreed, we met with a therapist. Her twenty-plus years of marital counseling and one available hour at the end of today meant she was qualified to help Adam and me climb out of our mess. Unfortunately, halfway through the session it became clear that her advice was hardly worth considering.

"Good," I say, turning on my heel. "Because suggesting we should probably consider a separation is nonsense."

Adam and I stalk to our front door.

"Let our heads get clear by being away from one another," Adam mocks the therapist. "Take time, space, reassess. It's ridiculous."

"That's the easy route," I say. "Walking away. We're not . . . going to fail."

"I agree. I'm not a fan of what she had to say, either. But Halley." Adam pushes open our front door, the mail tucked under one arm. "What do you suggest we do?"

"See another therapist." Isn't it obvious? This one clearly didn't work for us, so onward we search. And again and again, until we've exhausted our options.

"All right," he says in a confident way. "I was thinking the same thing."

I follow him inside and charge to the kitchen, where my laptop and a notepad and pen are leftover from the therapist search. "One of the doctors I called didn't have an opening until next weekend," I say. "I'll call him back and book him?"

"Sounds like a plan."

"And I'll call a few more and book a third." I force a weak smile. "Just in case."

"I was thinking the same thing."

And so it went. Therapist Two didn't suggest a trial separation so much as he suggested that I needed to play on Adam's team, so to speak. I needed to find it in my heart to respect Adam's sudden wishes for a child, and if that meant considering and perhaps having a child to, and I quote, "save our marriage," I should make such sacrifices. Because, and I quote again, "Isn't that what true love is about?" I wanted to stand up and shout, "Isn't true love *not* about coercion? *Not* about promising one thing and doing another?" It came as no surprise that Adam didn't think Therapist Two was as terribly misguided as I did.

Needless to say, Adam and I have become more agitated with one another these past few weeks. Our home is quickly deteriorating into one of those households you see on reality shows where parents cry out for help reining in their unruly children—except that in our case there are no children. Left and right we're sharing pointed glances, snapping retorts, and practicing the golden rule of "If you can't say anything nice, then don't say anything at all." Which can be just as venomous as actually saying something when in your everyday life you usually communicate, laugh, and exchange warm glances. Silence has never felt so cold.

Therapist Three turned out not to be any different from Therapist Two in that a side was clearly taken. She wasn't as bold and insulting as Therapist Two in suggesting that one party align with the other, but when she looked directly to Adam and said, "Having a baby is something very different for a woman than for a man. I don't think you understand what you're asking of your wife," I was fairly sure this therapist would be meeting the same fate as her predecessors. The takeaway from all three was clear: one of us had to change our mind, or . . .

I couldn't think about *or.*

The entire drive home Adam ranted and raved about how sexist Therapist Three was, how backward it was to look at children through such a narrow scope, and on and on it went. If I put the kibosh on Therapist Two, then Adam could do the same for Three.

With three failed counseling sessions and three argumentative weeks down, Adam and I are no closer to a resolution. We find ourselves at the same damn impasse, under the same heavy grey cloud. It's amazing and depressing how thirteen years of a cultivated love can deteriorate so severely in such a short time.

"We're getting nowhere," I grouse the night of our session with Therapist Three. I take my regimen of pills without a second thought, then begin to tighten my side of the bedsheet. "I don't want to fight anymore, Adam. I'm so *tired* of fighting."

Adam, already in bed, looks up from his magazine. He's wearing that familiar blank expression I've grown accustomed to since the B word became a thing.

"I don't want to fight anymore, either, Halley." His voice is calm, crisp.

"What do we do?" I'm about to suggest trying yet another therapist, even though I feel utterly hopeless at this point. When one side is taken, the affronted party is incensed, and when one suggests we separate—

"Maybe she's right," Adam says.

The therapist today is right? Adam agrees that asking me to have a baby—to seriously consider one—isn't fair?

"The first therapist," he continues. "Maybe she's right."

My heart begins to burn. Adam closes his magazine and rests folded hands on it.

"Right about what?" I ask.

"I think we need to step back."

Immediately outraged by the finality in his tone, the doomsday-ness of his words, I stammer, "So—so you want a . . ."

"I think a separation would be good for us. To step back and figure things out."

The burning in my heart disappears, just like that. Now I feel . . . nothing. Emptiness. Hollowness. It's a dark cave in my chest where, against the odds, I can hear a thudding *thump-thump-BEAT* that rings through my body, my ears. I'm alive, yet I feel as if I'm in free fall.

"Or see another therapist!" I blurt.

Adam shakes his head, his eyes trained on his magazine. "I don't think counseling is helping, Hals. In fact"—he looks to me—"I think it's making things worse. We're always fighting. Everything is so *tense*. Maybe the first therapist was right, and we need to figure this out . . . with some space between us."

"But we're working on a *marriage*, Adam. A *union*. We're supposed to figure things out *together*."

"And the status quo isn't working."

I clap my hands to my head and collapse on the edge of the bed. I can't believe my ears.

"We both know we're not our best selves right now, Halley." His words come out shaky, rattled by the striking turn in the conversation, in our lives. "We owe it to our relationship to try something different and see if it works. We're not . . . good around each other right now." The words pain him to say as much as they pain me to hear. His eyes are squinted, the corners wrinkled, his bottom lip tucked in an uncertain bite.

He scoots closer to me and rests a hand on my lower back. "I think we're better working through some stuff . . . away from each other. Fewer fights like this . . ."

"Are you seeing someone else?" I don't know why my mind goes here. I suppose it's the standard conclusion women in romantic books and films come to when their husbands suggest a separation. And doesn't every woman know that a separation means only one thing: that you're merely gearing up for that inevitable divorce? There is no getting back together once you step back. You get used to being apart and realize being separated is exactly what you needed, and you like it, and you don't want to go back to the way things were because things are suddenly so much better apart!

I can feel the awful, familiar tightness in my chest reappear—a burning filling the hollow space. My stomach gurgles; my heart beats even harder, faster.

"I am absolutely not seeing someone else," Adam says, and I believe him. I have no reason not to. If there's one thing I know Adam is not, it is unfaithful. Seeing how he's going back on his promise of a childless union, I find some room for disbelief, but if I'm truly honest, Adam's as straight as an arrow. I'd be willing to bet that he'd stay in a childless and perhaps even miserable marriage with me before he'd cheat.

And as soon as this thought crosses my mind, I have one of those bizarre feelings where you're seeing something clearly for the first time, and you're simultaneously elated and terrified. If Adam's life will be unhappy and unfulfilled because of me, and if my life will be filled with resentment and contention because of him, then maybe Adam's right. We aren't our best selves right now. We're not good around each other right now. Maybe, given the situation, we do need to step back, take time, assess, and try to work out our together, apart.

The severity of our situation, the harsh reality that lies within my discovery, hits like a ton of bricks. There's only one thing I can say. "A separation?"

"Yes."

"For how long?"

"I . . . don't know."

"And . . . then what?"

"That's what we'll figure out."

Adam is calm and collected as he discusses the bleak and vague future being laid before us, but I can see in his eyes and the way his shoulders uncharacteristically sag downward that he's anything but collected. Adam's reeling inside, like me. This isn't what either of us wants, yet it's what we both need.

At last he says something that brings me hope. "If we're going to keep our relationship strong and honest, I think we should give this a try, Hals. We should try whatever we can."

"We should." I slip into place in my side of the bed, slowly trying to register what on earth is happening.

"I love you, Halley." Adam unexpectedly takes my head in both his hands and plants a firm kiss on my forehead. "To the edge of our solar system and back."

That does it. The tears come. I hold them in long enough to say, "I love you, too, Adam. To the edge and back."

They are the heaviest *I love you*s we've ever said. The heaviest I think I'll ever say in my life.

With nothing and everything more to say, we turn out our lights, lie down on our own sides of the bed, and fight for the restful sleep that never comes.

It is the next morning, in that first second of being awake, when you register you're no longer asleep, that I become conscious that it is a new day, and I feel good. It is in the following second, when I remember the events of the night before, that I register they were not a nightmare, and I feel incredibly sad.

Unsure how to carry on given the newly made decision, I skip breakfast. I forfeit the most important meal of the day for two reasons: I have zero appetite, and if I don't eat, I can avoid having to see Adam. As soon as I wake, Adam is already in the shower, so I slip on my running gear, double-knot my neon-pink laces, the condo key tied to one, and hit the pavement.

By the time I return home, Adam is already gone. So, following in his footsteps, I get ready for the office. I suppress the urge to bawl my eyes out in the shower and call up my best girlfriends to lament the scary state of my marriage, and I go to the office. I have never been more grateful for a day packed with back-to-back meetings. I have no choice but to keep my personal life at home and plow through the workday. I stay an hour later than usual, both because I want to avoid facing Adam for the first time since talk of separation, and because it feels really good to bury myself in my writing. Even if my current article is titled "To Conceal and Contour."

It isn't the easiest day at the office, though. Many times, I have the urge to pick up my cell phone and call Marian and spill the beans, or shoot Adam a text. Something along the lines of, **Hope you're having a good day**, or **See you tonight. XO**. Something kind of neutral and loving. Something that says I'm thinking about him. I know that as soon as I do that, though, I'll spend the remainder of the afternoon anxiously checking and rechecking my text messages, hoping for a response. Hoping for a text that reads something like, **Let's forget about this separation nonsense**, or **You're all I'll ever need, Halley. Come home**.

I have one urge that I do give in to today—to downright cry, alone. I take my tears to the women's bathroom, and seeing how it is the first real, tissue-needing cry since Adam and I started on this rocky path, I let the tears come, unrestrained. They aren't tears of anger so much as they are tears of sadness and hopelessness. Tears of shock that come as unexpectedly as the reason behind them. I know they are the first of many, yet I feel somehow better afterward. My eyes look as if they've taken a beating, but it feels good—if that can be an appropriate word in this case—to acknowledge my pain.

Utterly spent, I come home to an empty condo. I usually beat Adam home from work, but I stayed later today. Perhaps he has the same game plan. I don't allow myself to ponder where he is or why he isn't home yet. Instead, I sit in front of my computer and continue the work I halted at the office. It's during my *Anne of Green Gables* research for my *Copper* passion project (I can't work with Laura right now) that I fall asleep at my desk. It's half past nine when I wake to hear Adam turn on the shower and whistle that no-name tune he whistles every single night.

I notice his running clothes and Nikes in the bedroom, piled by the bathroom door, which is slightly ajar. A pang of sorrow hits as I think of how Adam and I used to jog together. Not all the time, but only in the alternate universe of what is our new *now* am I a morning jogger and he an evening one.

I crawl into bed without so much as taking off my makeup or brushing my teeth—activities that would undoubtedly force me to interact with Adam, or at the very least come into contact with him. The prospect of what we wouldn't be able to say to each other is too much to bear. I pull the duvet halfway over my head and shut my eyes. Before Adam can step from the shower and conclude his habitual tune, I fall into some much-needed sleep.

On night two Adam gets home, again, later than I do. This time, however, he joins me in the living room for the remainder of the *Friends* episode I'm watching. We finally share words, though they are brief and only about work.

"Work going well?" Adam asks.

"Yeah," I reply. "You?"

"Busy. But good." He looks at the TV screen, lets out a single beat of laughter, and says, "Ah, this is a good episode."

Then we sit next to each other and don't say another word until lights out.

"I love you, Hals." On one crooked arm Adam leans over onto my side of the bed, and we kiss.

"I love you, Adam."

They aren't heavy *I love yous*, but their lightness isn't exactly something to boast about, either. They are habitual in a world that is becoming anything but familiar.

We do versions of this for three days, never once mentioning our supposedly impending separation. Perhaps both of us would rather forget it was ever mentioned? Maybe delay and denial feel less painful than the cold, hard truth.

It is on morning four when I receive an early-morning text, right as I'm about to take another atypical solo morning jog. It's from Nina. She says she'll swing by after work with the tube of lipstick I left on her guest bathroom sink when Adam and I visited for dinner. It isn't as if I don't have other lipsticks tiding me over, though that particular MAC shade of pink is my favorite. One I've worn since college. I could get it from her whenever we see each other next.

Don't make the drive for that, hon. But thx! I text.

Nina texts back, I miss you and I want to visit.

I consider asking Adam if he knows anything about Nina's plans, and then I start to imagine what he must have said to her about our plight. Did he run to his little sister and tell her I was cruel and selfish, refusing to give him something *she* values so highly? Are we already at that immature stage in a separation of designating whose friends are whose, what relationships have to change, sides forced to be taken? I can't picture any of it. This is Adam and me. Nina and me. Things surely could not deteriorate to this.

So I do the least anxiety-causing thing I can think of, and the most realistic. I view Nina's invitation as a hand held out to a friend, a sister-in-law who has always been more sister than in-law. I miss her, anyhow, and even though I don't like the idea that Adam has talked to someone else about our marriage troubles, thereby making them that more real (I know, calling the kettle black), I am relieved Nina already knows. Because the sooner you start talking, the sooner you get to fixing. At least that's what I hope for.

"You are too sweet, Nina," I say when Nina shows up at my front door after work. She has a bottle of red wine in one manicured hand and a tube of my favorite lipstick in the other.

"If I were sweet"—she looks to my lipstick—"I would've brought this by sooner."

I take the wine and lipstick. "You're ridiculous." I fetch a wineglass for me and, from the fridge, a bottle of sparkling water for Nina. We move to the living room.

"Got to say, as always, you look great, Nina." Her face has become more round and soft, a lovely effect of pregnancy that she wears flawlessly. Her lips are lightly colored with her signature mauve lipstick, probably still the YSL color she's worn since college. She's wearing the most darling skirt, a Ted Baker judging by the large-print flowers, with a fitted black tee. If Adam saw her right now, I could picture him telling me, *See, pregnancy isn't awful. Nina looks great, and you'd look so beautiful pregnant, Halley.*

"So, how are you feeling?" I ask, tucking a leg under my seat.

"Fantastic," Nina says. "With that awful first trimester morning sickness at all hours of the day long gone, I feel like a million bucks."

When Nina first began experiencing morning sickness morning, noon, and night, I remember commenting to Adam how misguided the term was. He'd said something about how Nina probably just got the short end of the stick, that the term probably existed because most women do experience sickness only in the morning. I laughed and made a curt remark about how that's one of many ways pregnancy and motherhood blindside a woman. No, thank you.

I blink away the unpleasant memory of Adam and say, "Well, it shows. I'm glad to hear you're not feeling so sick anymore."

Nina places a throw pillow behind her back for added support. "I may not be throwing up anymore, but now my feet are already starting to swell. These are some of the last shoes I can tolerate that aren't comfy sneakers or slippers." She laughs to herself.

"You could do worse," I say of her fashionable black patent leather ballet flats.

"Did you know Rylan's about the size of a cauliflower now?"

Nina pulls her cell phone from her large designer handbag. While I consider the peculiarity of how produce is commonly used to describe a baby's growth, Nina opens an app on her phone. The app tracks the growth of the baby, alerts you to interesting facts about the baby and your pregnant body, and tells you what to expect week after week.

"That's amazing," I say, impressed at how something so large, relatively speaking, is growing and thriving inside little Nina. It is called the miracle of life for a reason, and I'm happy Nina is getting to experience every bit of it.

Nina kicks off her shoes and props her feet on the ottoman. She takes a drink of water. "So, Halley. How are *you* doing, doll?"

It's uncanny how direct yet polite Nina is, like her brother. It's equal parts cut-to-the-chase, and kindness and courtesy. It's evident Nina and Adam's parents raised them to be kind and understanding children, composed and empathetic adults. Adam would make a spectacular father. I have never doubted that.

"I've been better," I say.

"I'm sorry." She rubs my arm.

"I love that you're here, Nina. But did Adam, by chance . . . ask you to come over?"

The idea then strikes me: Is Adam trying to find an easy way to initiate the separation? Is he so scared to come to me directly and ask me to leave our home that he employs his sister?

Now I'm just being foolish and paranoid.

Nina shakes her head. "Adam and I've talked about what's going on," she says. "A little bit, not much detail. I'm here on my own, for my friend who's obviously going through a difficult time."

"Thanks, Nina."

"I know if Griffin and I were going through something like this, I'd want you around." She then quickly adds, with a worried look on her face, "It's all right that I'm here, right?"

I laugh. "You never have to ask, Nina."

I catch her up on all the details that Adam's left out—which, to my relief, is quite a lot—and I'm careful with how I phrase things. Adam is not the enemy or the victim, and neither am I. We are a married couple at a low point and we're trying to figure things out. After I tell Nina that we're as distant as we've ever been, I ask, "Um, Nina? Do you know if . . . if Adam expects me to leave our home for our . . . separation?" I ball both of my fists, anxious about her response. "Is *that* why he hasn't brought up the separation idea again?"

"To not be with you is the last thing Adam wants," she says. "He's as torn up over this as you are."

"He suggested it," I say quickly.

Nina only nods.

Just as quickly, I add, "I suppose it's not a bad idea, the separation. Actually, I don't think I can quantify it—good, bad. I mean, who knows how to deal with something like this when you've never had to? When you've never thought you would *ever* have to?"

Nina keeps nodding, her mere presence comforting.

I don't want to make Nina feel as if she needs to take sides, so I say, "Adam's probably right that we should give each other some space. The way things are now, I don't see how we're going to reach a conclusion, at least not without building up the tension till someone bursts." It's a logical line of thought, but it's far from easy to swallow. In theory it seems sound, at least worth a try. In practice I'd rather go to bed for a month and sleep away the problems.

"He's looking for an apartment," Nina says with as much forced positivity as she can muster, given the situation at hand.

It's as if a knife slices through me. My husband is already looking for another place to live. With every step toward separation, I'm getting closer to being without Adam. It's the theory versus the practice. Denial is dead, and reality sets in.

I'm crushed.

I bite my bottom lip. "He . . . is?"

Nina looks heartbroken, as if she wishes she were recounting only the scoop on this afternoon's episode of her favorite soap and not the reality that is her brother's and best friend's lives.

"But it isn't looking promising yet." She squeezes my knee. "Everything's without vacancy or too expensive or too far from his office."

"No," I say, scrunching my brow and getting a hold of my thoughts. "I'll move out." I finish my wine.

"He doesn't want to make this harder on you," she says, now undoubtedly assuming the role of intermediary. Separation never felt so imminent.

"No, my staying here with all these memories"—I cast about the room—"will certainly be harder. I couldn't do it."

Nina rubs my arm again, and I say, "I'll stay with Marian."

I haven't asked Marian yet. In fact, I haven't even breathed a word about the separation to her. I figured once Adam and I made a real move toward it, then I would. Doing so now would just make things more . . . real. Although I'm starting to feel that this talk with Nina is move enough. Things *are* real. This is not a bad dream from which I'll wake, nor something a Snow White kind of sleep will make dissolve. This is what has become of my life, as unexpected and as unplanned as it may be. It's time to face the music. I am separating from my husband.

"Old roommates reunite," Nina says with a cheery smile. I adore how positive she's trying to be through all of this.

I sniff a laugh. "Not exactly under the dream circumstances, but yeah." I roll my empty wineglass between my hands. I'm temporarily mesmerized by the way the rich red drop of impossible-to-reach drink rolls around like a bead of uncatchable, unstoppable mercury.

"I'm sad, Nina. Heartbroken and sad."

"I know you are."

"And Adam can't do anything about my sadness." I draw my gaze from the mercurial bead to Nina's chocolate eyes. Her uncanny polite directness isn't the only thing she shares with Adam. I swallow hard. I miss Adam and the way things were.

"That's why I'm here," Nina says, encouraging. "That's why you have a friend, a sister, to help with that." She pulls me into a hug.

"Hey." I decide to turn the conversation. "I think Adam's going to be busy with work during that ballet. You want a girls' night?"

"He doesn't want to go, does he?" she says.

Adam is no Philistine, and ordinarily he'd have no qualms about accompanying me to a ballet or symphony, the kind of date I'm more prone to choose. However, it isn't a matter of whether or not Adam wants to go. I'm deciding that, given our separation, this is something I'm going to try without him. The big deal isn't going without him or having a girls' night, it's my deciding to try to realize the reality of our separation—move beyond theory and get to practice. There will be many things Adam and I will temporarily no longer share, and a ballet seems like one of the easiest to start with.

Adam arrives at the tail end of Nina's visit.

"Stay for dinner, Nina," Adam offers. "We can all go out somewhere, maybe meet Griffin someplace?"

"Thanks," Nina says, "but I've got dinner in the Crock-Pot, and I'm feeling too tired to be anywhere but home, dressed in my pajamas." She glances at her swollen feet.

"Thanks for coming over," I tell her.

We hug goodbye, and Adam gives his sister a kiss on the cheek as she's out the door. Before Nina turns away, she darts her eyes from the back of Adam's head to me, and gives a thin smile. A *Keep your chin up, girl* smile mixed with *I'm so, so sorry.*

Once Nina leaves, the place becomes considerably quieter.

"Um, takeout for dinner?" I say, keeping it brief.

"Sounds fine." Adam pulls out his cell phone to place the order.

"I'll take my usual, with the yellow curry."

"Are you sure about Thai again? We had it the other night."

"Then pizza," I say, lackluster. "I don't care."

"I'll order Thai." He says this as if it takes all his energy.

This is our new normal. This is the Brennan household. Terse, tight, and terrible.

When I tell Adam my plans to enjoy the ballet with Nina, so he doesn't have to deal with making it work with his schedule, I catch a small flash of sadness streak across his face. It's as if he recognizes, as do I, that this is really happening. That there is going to be a separation, and that it will hurt. It already does, and we haven't even reached for the first piece of luggage. There isn't even three feet of distance between us on the sofa as we eat dinner in silence, but it may as well be the ocean.

Five

The following evening, as Adam sits in bed with his computer aglow on his lap, a small sheaf of papers at his side atop the duvet, I announce that we are one step closer to our trial separation.

"What do you mean?" he asks, looking up from his laptop.

"I mean that I'm moving out."

"No, Halley. You stay here. A separation was my suggestion. I'll move out."

I apply my hand lotion and shake my head. "No," I say, eyeing my sparkly princess-cut wedding ring. I'm careful not to press lotion into it. I've always refused to take it off, even when applying lotion, because I nearly lost it once by doing so. Ever since, Adam made me promise to keep it on, no matter what. If that meant excessive ring cleanings, so be it. As I look at my wedding ring, as we discuss who will live where during our separation, I can't help but wonder if Adam would mind now if I took it off.

I sigh. "No," I say again. "It's *our* problem, and I don't want—" I stop myself. "I can't live here. Not without you."

"I've been . . . looking for an apartment, Halley," he says with hesitation. His forehead knits and his eyes narrow.

"I heard." My voice is steady. I rub the excess hand lotion onto my forearms and elbows.

He closes his laptop and sets it aside. "I'll leave as soon as one becomes available. Besides, moving's a hassle, and I don't want you to have to do tha—"

"It's done. I'll be out by next week."

"You found a place?" he asks, surprised. "So . . . *fast!*"

I take my routine pills. "I'm rooming with Marian."

I asked Marian earlier this afternoon if she could use a room-mate for a while. After a lengthy call about everything from how Adam and I came to this conclusion to if I was still all right with bar soap—she wanted to make sure I felt right at home in my . . . new home—it was settled. Old roomies were, as Nina said, going to be reunited.

"Ah." He purses his lips in surprise. "All right then."

I slip into bed. "Good night, Adam." I try not to sound resentful. But I am. I resent Adam's choice to change our future. If I'm not careful, I'm going to resent him, and that, ironically, is the very thing that would terrify me about having a child. If I start resenting him now, I might as well buck up, have the kid, and go on with my inescapable resentment. That's the worst thing I could do, I know, and a child would never deserve to bear the brunt of such resentment. (God knows Charlotte and I can attest to the hurt a child feels when it knows it's unwanted.) How selfish it would be to have a child to keep Adam, how selfish to do that to an innocent person. If only Adam could understand this. If only he could see my side of things.

Perhaps, though, he's not supposed to. Perhaps—and I hate think-ing this—this separation is the catalyst for his moving on without me, and me without him. After all, isn't that what happens when a couple separates? Who am I to have faith that what Adam and I have can some-how let us transcend what so many separated couples cannot? Just the same, a separation to save our marriage is worth a try. Because if you don't have hope, what the hell have you got?

"Is that it?" Marian says in disbelief. She cranes her head out her front door and looks left and right.

"I wish I traveled this light," I say, my purse slung over one shoulder, a tote bag over the other, and a large duffel at my feet. "The rest is in the car."

Marian helps carry the rest of my belongings up the stairs to her town house, located on the second and third floors of her building, a ten-minute drive from my condo. To my delight, and certainly to Marian's, who's got a very sleek, sophisticated, and minimalist approach to interior design, I don't have much stuff. Her luxury midcentury-style town house is quite spacious, in any event. Complete with a guest room with its own en suite full bath, Marian's place will be more than sufficient while Adam and I spend a while—whatever *a while* is supposed to be—apart.

Once the last of my luggage is brought up and added to the heap in the center of what is now my new bedroom floor, I walk out onto the enormous balcony. It wraps around, like an L, with access from the kitchen, which is straight from an upscale magazine with its very clean lines, glossy white cupboards and drawers, and smoky-grey granite countertops. The balcony extends around the living room, whose walls are mostly floor-to-ceiling windows and doors, and ends at a large sliding glass door that opens into Marian's master suite.

I grip the top of the glass balcony and close my eyes, letting the rays of the golden early-evening sun warm my arms and face. I briefly considered going to college up north—San Francisco, Portland, or Seattle, for a change of pace—but I couldn't imagine giving up the near-constant shine of the Los Angeles sun, her expansive blue skies, her endless palm trees that wave hello.

"It's not a beach view, but it works," Marian says from the living room. She joins me on the balcony and drops onto one of her two chaises, slipping on her oversize designer sunglasses.

The view may not be of the beach, but the residential street below is lined with palm trees, and along the other side of the balcony is a view of the lush town house community's garden and courtyard, set against the backdrop of the striking San Gabriel Mountains. Street noise is minimal. You don't come face-to-face with your neighbors on the balcony, as Adam and I do if we're out on our small one off our kitchen. The sun bathes this balcony in light, spilling on into the large living room. It's absolute perfection. Adam and I have a beautiful and nicely sized condo (as well as a nicely sized mortgage), but it pales in comparison to Marian's swanky digs.

"I can get used to this," I say.

"Get used to it. You're here for as long as you like, Halley. However long you need."

However scenic the view is, however luxurious the town house, and however fantastic the company, I hope Adam and I won't need very long. It hasn't been more than five minutes since I've settled into my new place, and I'm already missing my husband. Who am I kidding? I've been missing him for weeks. But with Marian's spare key—my key—snug in the back pocket of my jeans, the missing him hits harder than ever.

I'm grateful for Marian's step-up-to-the-plate attitude tonight when she insists we go for a run. I can't remember the last time we ran together—could it really have been back in college? I love the route she leads us on. We find a lengthy stretch of sidewalk uninterrupted by stoplights or crowds waiting to cross the street—no small feat in the heart of Pasadena—and cross through Central Park before concluding with a few trips up and down the stairs of a pavilion that's quieted in its after hours. It's in the tranquil town house courtyard, where we take the opportunity to stretch and hydrate, that Marian gets to the heart of the matter.

"So," she exhales, "you're on some kind of a timeline thing?"

"Huh?" I ask, stretching my hamstrings with the assistance of a bench.

"You and Adam. Do you have a certain date for when you're supposed to figure this all out?"

She adjusts the lower rim of her teal sports bra. Marian never ran in more than a sports bra up top back in college and, like her flat, toned abs, some things don't change.

"Not exactly," I say. I use the hem of my tank top to pat away the sweat around my eyes.

"Well, I think you should." She, too, begins to stretch her hamstrings.

"Sick of me already?" I tease.

"You need a plan."

"You're saying magical words to me, Marian."

You'd think someone who strives to have her act together and be prepared would have nailed this one. It's been a messy few weeks, with days going by that I can't even string two sentences together with Adam, much less sit down at the table with a red pen and a calendar.

"There has to be some goal, something you guys have to achieve from this separation," Marian says soberly. "Right? Or why the hell else are you doing it?"

"A big reason is that it's toxic when we're together. We need our space."

"I get that. And then what?"

It shouldn't surprise me that I've surrounded myself with direct friends and family. They clearly make up my deficit. I vacillate some as I tell Marian I'm not exactly sure . . . time will tell . . . yada yada. All fluff, no substance.

"We haven't really talked about it," I say.

"Okay." Marian waves her hands, halting the aimless conversation. "How's this? Your goal in this separation, however long it lasts, is to focus on *you*. Do you. Do what makes you happy."

"Adam—"

"And don't say Adam makes you happy." She wrinkles her nose. "Because honestly, honey, he doesn't right now."

I nod at the harsh reality of her words, and she continues, now stretching her quads.

"I'm not saying you should try to forget about Adam," she says. "That's not going to help. But I don't want you to mope or dwell on him and the problem. Constructive thinking is one thing, a river of self-pity and tears another entirely."

"Right." I give one strong, affirmative nod. God, what would I do without Marian?

"You find yourself," she urges. "He, hopefully, finds himself. And I think you guys should still talk, maybe even see each other now and then? Don't completely ignore each other."

"Just give each other space."

"Yes."

"I like that," I say, even though I can't picture how we get from here to there.

"Aaaand," she trills, "maybe, when you feel a little more clear-headed, like you've been doing you, have your space, and babies and marital dramas are not all that's on your brain, see Adam. Maybe even have a date. Or at least a hookup."

I burst out laughing. "If sex couldn't fix things before, I don't think it will now."

"All I'm saying is you're still married. Don't shut each other out. Because then you might as well just call for a divorce now."

The power of this unspeakable word hits like stone, and Marian recognizes its weight immediately.

"I'm sorry, Hals." She's quick to apologize. "That came out wrong."

"I know what you mean." I wince, then say, "Don't shut each other out but give each other space. Get clear heads again."

"Precisely. But first, set a date. An actual date, a week, a weekend in some month, *something* when you two talk about where to go *after* the separation. Plans are good." She plants a hand on her hip. "I know they don't always pan out, but they're good to have."

"Yeah," I say with a small smile. "Speaking of plans, Adam and I are supposed to go to Maui for Thanksgiving."

"Omigod, that's right! And?"

I shake my head. "Again, it's something we haven't really talked about."

"Well then, there's another thing you need a plan for. One"—she holds up an index finger—"a timeline, a date. And two"—she holds up a second finger—"vacay plans. And then, before you know it, you and Adam will be all made up, and you'll be basking in the sun on the white-sand Hawaiian beaches, getting tanked, tanned, and screwed." She winks. "The good kind."

"Oh, Marian," I say with a needed laugh. I grasp for some more levity. "Maybe you're right. Maybe we'll have a Miranda-and-Steve moment on the Brooklyn Bridge?"

"Omigod, totally romantic!" Marian presses her palms to her heart and swoons. "A Brooklyn Bridge kind of makeup, and *then* off to Maui!" She flies a hand through the air before returning it to her heart.

As much as Marian embraces the single life, she's a hopeless romantic. She'd never admit as much, but you'd have to be blind not to see what a fan she is of big romantic gestures. Every rom-com, every chick flick and chick lit book, every grand proposal and sappy reunited-lovers story on the *Today Show* gets her heart all aflutter. She says she isn't holding her breath for her own fairy-tale romance, but I know she's got her fingers crossed behind her back.

"It's a fun thought, but let's not get ahead of ourselves," I say, leading the way out of the park and toward her—*our*—home. "We don't even have a cool place like the Brooklyn Bridge to meet."

"What are you talking about? The bridge over the Long Beach Freeway on Colorado Boulevard," Marian jests.

"Oh god, how *totally* romantic," I joke back. "And while we're at it we can stop by Starbucks for a celebratory Frappuccino."

Marian laughs. "Hey, it could happen."

I shrug. "Could happen for you, too." I can't help myself.

"Ha! I'm a love-'em-and-leave-'em kind of girl."

I look over at her when she says this, and there's a look of compunction on her face. It's quickly washed away when she says, "Sun's setting. It's officially evening."

Immediately I'm prepared for Marian to suggest we call for a ride and hit up one of LA's hottest clubs or change into our sluttiest clothes and hop some nearby bars. She surprises me when she suggests we stop by Vroman's Bookstore and grab all the celebrity gossip and beauty magazines we can find.

"Not to support your competition," she adds. "Competitor research, we can call it."

"Or just the medicine a girl could use right about now," I say.

"To Vroman's it is!" Marian says, excitedly bounding up the stairs to our town house. "God, we're going to be great together, Halley. Not that I ever doubted it." She pauses for a moment, key turned halfway in the doorknob. She looks over her shoulder at me and says with a bright white smile, "I know it isn't the best of situations for you for why you're here, but it's really good for me."

"Everything okay?"

She finishes unlocking the door. "Of course! I'm fabulous and on top of the world, Halley! I'm just really happy to have a roommate. To have you as a roomie again. It's really nice. Really nice."

That it is.

Six

The unusual and light summer rain that surprised Pasadena this early evening lets up. The sun is shining its farewell rays for the day, and the pavement and sidewalks are glistening. The scent of wet concrete wafts all around. When I look up into the sky, I can make out a fraction of a faint rainbow peeking from behind the mountains, the buildings, the dispersing clouds.

At long last I decide to give my sister, Charlotte, a ring. Not just a call like the ones we usually have where we catch each other up on the little things in record time so she can get back to fighting the fires little ones like to start. Rather a lengthier (and no doubt weightier) call, wherein I confess the marital drama that I've been worried she'd be hypersensitive about, and wouldn't want to believe or process.

I pull up Charlotte's number on my phone during my walk home from work. Living with Marian means being able to walk to and from my office. It's a slow-paced fifteen minutes, and something I figure I'll be able to do for only a limited time, from my new residence. It is also a small way to *do me*, as Marian suggested. A lot like my jogs, these walks are a way to seize the peace, gain clarity, and think through my predicament.

When Charlotte answers, I am not surprised to hear her kiddie circus shrieking in the background. At ten, six, and two, Alice, George, and Leah make up a full choir in the Miller house. There is never, and I mean never, a moment of silence when Charlotte and I talk on the phone. Rarely there may be thirty-second interludes of uninterrupted conversation, all while one child snatches a toy from another's hands. Then as soon as the toy robbery is complete, there's the predictable chorus of crying, whining, and protesting, followed by Charlotte's combined efforts to scold, soothe, and make right. Jockeying for Charlotte's attention is a game at which I declared myself a loser a long time ago.

Adam asked me once if my not wanting children had anything to do with the inability to hold an honest, uninterrupted, one-on-one telephone conversation with Charlotte. Like my mother's inability to snag a Mother of the Year award, perhaps on some level this reinforced my childless choice.

I'm rational enough, though, to acknowledge that life largely is what you make of it, and the choices you make are symptomatic of who you are, your beliefs, your personality. I am not Charlotte and she is not I; therefore it follows that my personal portrait of motherhood could be something else entirely. It would be unfair to have decided kids aren't for me based on the difficulties I watch my sister go through.

So in a straightforward answer, no, my choice of a childless life is largely independent of what I witness with Charlotte, just as it is largely independent of the way my mother chose to raise—er, *not* raise her daughters. Though Charlotte and I may share our father's slight overbite, a love of frozen chocolate bananas, and an appreciation for Bette Davis films, we are quite different, and therefore would most likely be very different mothers with very different households.

I was the daughter who, when asked what she wanted to be when she grew up, answered at various stages in life *dancer, writer, doctor, artist*. Charlotte's answers included *teacher, singer, lawyer, chocolate maker*. Both very typical answers from kids who would eventually discover that a degree in the liberal arts guaranteed a teacher's position as much as it guaranteed a spot on the Rockettes' lineup (especially in a wayward economy). It was during college that my childhood idea of *writer* began to take hold as I pursued my degree in English literature (still as much a guarantee of landing a writing job as of landing that teaching position). It was also during college that Charlotte's childhood idea of *lawyer* began to take hold. It was Charlotte's plans to become a mother someday, however, that also took hold and changed everything.

Charlotte and I were always encouraged by our father to follow our dreams, whatever they might be. Chocolate maker included. (Even though he could never hide his hopes of our following in his footsteps and pursing the sciences.) As determined and hardworking women, we were told we could become a writer and a lawyer, and that's exactly what we set out to do.

Charlotte also studied English literature, but she had the desire to attend law school afterward, and, in her words, see if she was any good at fighting for the little guy in the legal world. She and Marco, her college sweetheart since freshman year, married a few weeks after graduation, and come the fall semester, Charlotte was geared to begin her legal studies. Weeks before the semester started, though, Charlotte found the second part of her life aspirations met. She was pregnant. It was a blessing that came a few years too early in their marriage (their words, not mine), and one that changed the course of Charlotte's career and life. She's never outright said that she regrets having a baby much earlier than she and Marco planned, but she has said that she regrets never having gone to law school. I don't know if saying one automatically means implying the other. The correlation is blindingly apparent, if you ask me.

I say all of this not to point out that Charlotte chose to be a mother and not follow her career path, and that I chose not to be a mother and have therefore followed my career path. I am writing, but I'd hardly call what I'm doing my passion. I say all of this to point out that Charlotte knew what she wanted; she had a goal. She's a brave woman who does what needs to be done and will find the joy in it, even during the roughest of days, the most interrupted of phone calls. Charlotte's also the woman who, exactly because she chose motherhood (or, rather, because motherhood chose her), has had to make concessions. She's had to put part of her dream aside. I suppose there's beauty in that because she always wanted to become a mother. Like Nina, she's always seen herself as a mother as much as, if not more than, she's seen herself as a career woman.

Yet no matter how you slice it, motherhood has made Charlotte's path trickier. It changed everything. Because once Alice was here, the question became, what about baby number two? Because she and Marco didn't want a giant age gap between the children, even if number one had come earlier than planned. And then, since they had always planned on having three children, they didn't want to put off their youngest for too long, either. They considered it, but then, as Charlotte says, after a night of too much chardonnay and not enough precaution, baby number three came along.

There would always be the opportunity to go back to law school and become a lawyer, Charlotte said. Once the kids were grown and more independent, she could finally turn the focus more toward herself. But a woman's eggs have an expiration date, and the months between one birth and the next begin to stretch and stretch. That window stays open for only so long. So she chose to follow the path she hadn't quite seen herself on at this point in her life. And she made the most of it. And then the years rolled by, and she started to ask if she was happy, if this was what she should be doing after all, if this was even what she wanted to be doing.

And that is where Charlotte finds herself. With three children and a husband on the front burner, her career on the back, struggling to keep going strong. I'd be remiss if I said I don't hear the desperate cry for sleep in Charlotte's voice, or notice the way she pauses at a clothing advertisement covered in blazers and pantsuits, or catch the empty gaze as she looks out at her living room strewn with toys and mutters under her breath the double entendre, "What a mess."

So I suppose, upon further examination, on some level Charlotte's choice to become a mother does further cement me in mine to refrain. It's on a grander level, though, that Charlotte's path may very well be no different from my own. From the one I'm on with Adam. Neither Charlotte nor I was naïve enough to think that come thirty we'd have it all and want for nothing. But we both certainly thought that by thirty-four and nearly thirty-three we'd be on the path to what we wanted, that we'd have things mostly figured out. Things could always be worse, of course, but you can't blame a woman for looking at her life—three kids before thirty . . . a pipe dream of a law degree . . . a marital separation . . . a sense of losing control, or realizing you never had it to begin with—and wondering *how* it came to this? How did we let ourselves lose sight of who we are and what we want out of life?

It is for all these reasons that I have delayed so long in sharing with Charlotte that I, too, am scratching my head and saying, *What the hell happened?* It can be a dangerous precipice, looking at your life and questioning if what you've done is what you should've done, and one I know Charlotte teeters on the edge of constantly. It's why I choose to be very careful with how I bring up my quandary. Charlotte's stretched thin and I don't want to burden her. But I have to talk to my sister, because, as these things usually go, she needs me as much as I need her. Interrupted though our calls may be, I know she always values our conversations—her chance to escape the crazy.

"Oh, Halley, it's so good you called now," Charlotte says. A rustling sound comes over the line, then she exhales and says, "Okay. Peace at last."

"This an okay time to talk?"

"It's never and always an okay time to talk," she says. "You know I'm always in need of some adult time. It's hard to find, because the kids are constantly hanging off me like monkeys. But now's actually a great time. I'm in the closet!" She squeals like one of her children.

"The closet?" I say with a chuckle of disbelief.

"I know. Totally a confession from a *Dr. Phil* mommy panel, but I'll take the quiet where I can get it. I tried it before, the closet. But it was just so darn crammed I couldn't even close the door, much less fit inside it. But now"—she imitates a cartoon villain's laugh—"now it's all cleaned and Mommy's got herself her own secret cave."

"Charlotte, you're the best." Though I don't want to rob her of the peace in her newfound hiding spot, I can't help but ask, "Where are the kids?"

She loudly exhales again. "Alice is at the dining table doing homework. George and Leah are glued to the TV with a movie."

"Gotcha."

"When I emerge, it'll be a small wonder if everyone's where I left them, but that's for me to deal with in twenty. Right now it's you, me, and"—she makes a groaning noise—"a pair of shoes I swear I gave to Goodwill. Huh. They're actually really cute, and I'm kind of glad I didn't give them away." She sighs. "Who am I kidding? On what occasion would I need a pair of sparkly high heels?"

"I heard those mommy-and-me playdates can be quite the black-tie events," I tease. "Shoes and kids aside, everything good?"

"Same-o. Marco's busy as ever at work. It's good, though. He needs the promotion, because the kids aren't getting any cheaper. Oh, and Alice, by the way, is very excited to see her aunt Halley and uncle Adam at her science fair."

Caught up in the drama of my own life, I'd completely forgotten about my niece's upcoming science fair. It's been on the calendar for weeks. I'm grateful for the reminder, and also peeved that I let myself get lost in me-me-me.

"Alice is so cute," Charlotte says of her firstborn. "She's made everyone name badges, and they're on different planet and moon cutouts. Completely adorable. She's such a smart kid."

"Dad'll be proud." Our father, the astronomer, is delighted that his granddaughter has taken an interest in the sciences. He has not an ounce of hope for his liberal arts daughters.

"Don't you know it," Charlotte says. "Alice's science teacher told me he's really impressed with her, and that her project has a very good chance of ribboning. Lunch afterward just may be more celebratory than we think. I hope she wins."

Even if Alice doesn't ribbon, she has two phenomenal parents who have instilled in her the concept of gracious losing. If someone at the age of ten can identify nearly all the elements on the periodic table, I don't doubt she has the maturity and smarts to keep her head high if she doesn't win.

"I wouldn't miss her fair or what just *has* to be a celebratory lunch for the world," I assure Charlotte.

"And Adam?"

I bite the inside of my cheek and notice that my walking pace immediately slows at the mere mention of my husband's name.

There's no easy way to say this, so I just come right out and tell it to Charlotte straight.

"Adam and I are separated."

I can't tell if the sickly iron taste in my mouth is from biting my cheek too hard or from the foul taste of the words themselves.

"What?" Charlotte breathes out in complete shock. "Omigod, Halley! What happened?"

I waste no time in assuring my sister that Adam and I are trying to work things out, that by no means are we googling divorce attorneys. As soon as I say this, I can't help but wonder if that really is true in Adam's case. I certainly don't want a divorce. I can't imagine Adam's already thinking of such possibilities, given how we found our ways to our separation. Neither of us ran for the door, neither of us wanted to talk about that elephant in the room, and neither of us really has any clue what we're doing now that we've technically separated. I'm sure jumping to conclusions like divorce would only further complicate things at this point.

"So . . . what happened? Why are you . . . separated?" Charlotte says the word *separated* in a way that suggests she, too, has a nasty iron taste in her mouth.

I catch Charlotte up on everything. It's a godsend that this is one of the rare phone conversations we are able to have uninterrupted. Even though the topic of conversation is surely not what Charlotte could have seen coming, from the way she listens intently and says, "Oh, Halley," with deep, groaning sincerity, and from the way *I'm so sorry*s slip out between anecdotes, it is evident she's pleased to be in the loop, to lend a hand where she can in this adult matter. To, thank god, have a moment of peace to take in something neither of us saw coming . . . and neither of us has a clue how to deal with.

"Why did you wait so long to tell me, Halley?" Charlotte chides once I finish recapping.

"You don't need more stress," I say.

"I appreciate that." Before I can say something next, she adds, "You think I'd tell you to stop the stupid fight and just give in to Adam and consider a baby, huh?"

"Honestly?"

"That is the best policy, isn't it?"

"Honestly, I didn't want to drone on to you about my problems with motherhood when—"

"When it's eating me alive?" she cuts in.

"Mmmhmm."

"Hals, life isn't exactly what I thought it'd be at this stage. I'll give you that. And yours clearly isn't, either."

I sniff in response.

"There's bonding in that," she says. "Understanding."

"Thank you, Charlotte. I suppose part of it is that by constantly talking about it, it's that much more real."

"I feel you." After a short pause she asks, "You want my advice?"

"Please."

"Don't."

I wrinkle my brow. "What *don't*?"

"Don't do it." Charlotte's voice is strong. Not a single hint of hesitation lingers behind her blunt words.

"I don't want a . . . divorce," I say, wincing at the thought.

"No, don't have a baby. For Adam. For your marriage. For any reason other than if it's what you really and truly want, in your heart."

I don't say anything, because Charlotte's advice is the last I ever expected to hear from her. From Marian, yes. Nina, perhaps. But Charlotte?

"Don't get me wrong," Charlotte adds. "I love my children. With every bone in my body. And motherhood is a beautiful thing and it's completely worth it. *But* if there's one thing I know for sure, it's that having a baby when you're not ready . . . complicates things. And having a baby in order to save a marriage is the *worst* reason in the world. It's completely selfish, and it's not a guarantee it'll work."

"Charlotte." I swallow the sudden lump in my throat and stop at a bench along the sidewalk. "Is everything all right?"

"Everything is what it is, Halley."

"That's a crap answer. Charlotte, what's going on?"

"Look, Marco will be home any minute, and I haven't even started dinner yet. God knows what the kids have destroyed by now."

"How are you doing? Really. I've been going on about me and—"

"Ha! Hon, you're the one with huge news."

"How are *you*?"

Charlotte's an expert at putting herself second, or fifth.

"Things have been better," she says nonchalantly. "But what you're going through is *big*, Halley. And that's what we need to be talking about. You and Adam are *separated*."

"We've already covered that news," I mutter. "Charlotte, please tell me if you need anything. Help, advice, a girls' night out." I say this last part with a light laugh, and Charlotte, too, laughs some. "Don't pull a me and keep things inside because you're worried I can't handle it," I tell her.

"I won't," she assures me. "All I'm saying is if you want my honest opinion and you value it, do *not* have a child for the wrong reasons. I know you, Halley, and you've never wanted to be a mother. I know you love Adam fiercely, but there's a limit to how far one can go for someone . . . for something they want in life."

Her words stick, and long after we've disconnected, I can't shake them. She's right that having a child for the wrong reasons is selfish, even damaging. And there's no guarantee that by having one you'll fix your problems. In some cases you'll just create new ones. I'm encouraged to hear from Charlotte what I obviously wanted to hear, advice that I can digest and that jibes with my own opinion. What I can't let go of and swallow, however, is that these words of wisdom come from *Charlotte*. Does she say them because she wishes she could turn back the hands of time? Does she actually . . . *regret* her choices? Did she have her children for the wrong reasons? Has she reached that limit she mentioned, where you've gone as far as you can for someone? For what you want in life? If there is a limit, how can you detect it? And when do you know if you're approaching it or if you crossed it a long time ago? What's Charlotte's limit? What's mine?

Instead of continuing on my journey home, I decide to lengthen my walk, and I eventually find myself at Target. I pick up a congratulatory card for Alice, choosing one with a big smiling sun on the front and lots of colorful flowers on a green hill. It says, "You Shine, Girl!" I tamp down my cynical, or perhaps just realistic, side as I shop for my niece. This is exactly the time you tell a young girl that if she wants to make chocolates or be a world-renowned dancer, if she wants to be a kindergarten teacher, a baker, a lawyer, or even the president of the United States, she can. She can set her sights on what makes her happy and go after those dreams. She doesn't have to know just yet that life is rough, that even when you do everything you think is right and you work hard, that even when you find your Prince Charming and you begin the novel of your grand life, at some point you will discover that there are limits. You will meet your limitations, and you will have to ask yourself, how do I overcome them? And you will learn if you have what it takes to do just that.

Right now, however, it is time to shine, so I add to Alice's inspiring card several bags of her favorite candy, Skittles; the latest Disney Blu-ray (and I keep the receipt because most likely Charlotte's already taken care of this purchase); and a couple of the chapter books she's been sinking her teeth into lately. Then, for the fun of it, I swing down the party supplies aisle. I grab bags of balloons, kazoos, and blowers to add to her gift bag. Sometimes you just need to be silly. As I check out, I plunk a greedy handful of large Peppermint Patties onto the conveyor belt. Comfort food.

Upon walking through the front door I'm met with both Marian's giggling from inside her bedroom and a pair of men's dress shoes parked beside a pair of her heels in the entry. Immediately I can't help but miss Adam. Then I quickly decide I will do myself no good standing in the entryway, getting lost in my thoughts of Adam, as Marian's "Sounds of Romance" playlist rings in the background.

I settle into bed early, with my earbuds in, latest Muse album on, and Peppermint Patties at the ready, and I find my romantic fix in the novel I've got queued up on my Kindle. I don't let myself get hung up on missing Adam or wondering when—even if—Adam and I will get to play our own lovemaking soundtrack.

Before lights out, I fish Alice's cheerful card from my canvas shopping bag and write a heartfelt note about how proud I am of her. I sign the standard *Love, Auntie Halley + Uncle Adam* at the bottom, and as soon as I finish the cursive *m* in Adam's name, I notice the habit. Had I given it some thought beforehand, I'd probably still have signed Adam's name to the card. No need to cause unnecessary drama and have Alice asking a thousand and one prying questions. It will already be awkward if Adam doesn't show up to her science fair, which I need to address tomorrow morning. No doubt Mom, Dad, and the whole group would then learn why Auntie Halley was solo for Alice's big day.

I'd also probably have signed Adam's name because there still is an Auntie Halley and Uncle Adam. There is no split. Only a little break. To accentuate the point that there isn't anything a ten-year-old needs to have any knowledge of, I add an *XoXo* underneath our names. Then I draw a big heart around the word *Love*.

When I look at my finished project, I realize I've just drawn attention to our problem. Overcompensation can scream horribly loudly. Not that Alice will notice. In fact, she'll probably think the big pink heart is creative and pretty. Charlotte will take one look at it and give me a sympathetic glance. Just the same, I slip the card into its yellow envelope, write a large cursive *Alice* on its front, and set it on my nightstand, to serve as a reminder to contact Adam tomorrow and find out if he plans on going to the fair.

I try to settle into sleep as I'm filled with anticipation of Adam's possible attendance. If he comes, then I can see him, and I do miss him. But if he comes, then that means I'll see him, and as much as I miss him, I'm upset with him. This may be *our* problem, but *he's* the reason we're here, the reason I'm second-guessing my greeting card signatures. The reason Charlotte and I are talking limits. I'm so incensed at the ridiculousness of it, I decide that as much as I miss Adam's smile and the sound of his voice when he says my name, I don't want him at Alice's event.

And so it begins, I acknowledge, that even in the absence of a divorce, sides are being chosen. This is *my* sister's daughter's day, and I'm going. Since we're separated, that means Adam shouldn't join. It's all so stupid, especially as soon as I consider my relationship with Nina. She's Adam's sister, for chrissake, but I'll be damned if she and I can't still share a friendship. We were friends long before Adam and I became a thing. The absurdity of the thoughts whirring about my head is a loud reminder that I'm falling into the trap of playing the role of vindictive, angry wife. I love Adam. This is our rough patch. Perhaps even our limit. I have to find a way to heal and not further dig myself into the dip in our road. If Adam wants to come to Alice's fair, I'll be pleasant. If he doesn't, I'll understand. We're figuring things out, that's what this is.

The bright-yellow envelope with *Alice* written across it, set on my night-stand, does its job the following morning. I'm reminded as soon as I awake both of my separation from Adam and that I need to reach out and ask if he plans on attending Alice's science fair.

I'm nearly out the front door when Marian, who emerges from her bedroom, rubbing her wrists together, then touching them to the back of her neck, asks, "Hey, want to catch a ride to work with me?" She clicks her way across the hardwood floor in her nosebleed-high navy suede heels, grabbing her Louis Vuitton purse and office bag, slinging both over one shoulder.

"Thanks, but I'm going to walk." Then I add, waving my cell phone, "Going to call Adam."

"Honey," Marian says as I pull open the front door, "please don't tell me my date last night got you missing Adam and now you're desperate dialing."

I'm proud when I tell her, "No, actually." Yes, her spicy evening got me thinking about Adam, but my longing for intimacy with my husband is not going to be some magical push to solve this separation business.

We begin our descent of the stairs as I tell Marian about the text I need to send Adam about next Saturday's shindig.

"You're torn between wanting him to come or not?" Marian astutely says.

"Yup." I put on my sunglasses. "So I'm leaving the decision entirely up to him. It's easier that way."

"Sounds like a plan. And speaking of plans, are you going to bring up that little timeline thing? Set a date?"

"Ugh." Like a child, I tilt my head back and say in a whining tone, "One painful brush with reality at a time."

"All right. A free pass there, darling." She withdraws her car keys from her purse and asks again if I want a ride.

"My walks do me good," I say. "They help with the tension, frustration."

"Sex is also good for that," she says with a laugh.

"Yeah, yeah. Who was the lucky guy last night, by the way?"

Marian flicks a lazy wave in my direction. "Just some guy from Research," she says. "We'd been playing cat and mouse for long enough. It was time."

"And?"

She gives me another lazy wave. "Ehh. Lousy tipper, turns out. Lousier kisser."

Without giving my words much thought, I say, "Then why'd you sleep with him?"

Marian raises both brows.

"Sorry," I say, waving away my insensitive comment. "That came out bluntly."

She shrugs it off and says, "A girl's got to get some action now and then, Hals. And you and I both know that men with the *it* factor are few and far between."

At the mention of the *it* factor I can't help but think of Adam. He has *it*. Loads of *it*. It's not often a woman meets a man who has *it*, and when she does, she'd best not let go. I'm suddenly overcome with sadness—sadness at the thought of potentially losing Adam, a man with all the *it* I've ever needed.

I straighten my posture and look to Marian, trying to brush away the depressing possibility.

"True. They can't all be Mr. Right," I say.

With a glossy look of longing in her eyes, Marian gives a breathy exhalation and says, "Nope, they can't."

"Well, there's a wide ocean of men out there, right?" I say, optimistic, and Marian just smiles and waves goodbye as she walks toward the underground garage.

I've made it to the first crosswalk on Cordova Street when I decide to send Adam that text. It's not that I don't want to talk to him. I just think a question as simple as *Are you still planning on coming to Alice's science fair next Saturday?* can be easily answered via text. Given our situation and general awkwardness, why further complicate things? If it comes down to a call, then I have no qualms with keeping talk light. Adam is my husband, after all.

Within two minutes I receive a reply.

I assume you're going? it reads.

I type back, **Yes. Are you?**

He responds with, **Depends. Do you want me to come?**

And this is what I didn't want to have happen but what I think was inevitable. Adam, of course, would take the noncommittal approach. Alice is *my* sister's daughter and therefore, since we've apparently begun this silly taking-sides game, it is up to *me* to decide whether Adam should attend *my* family events.

Growing upset at the childishness of what should be a simple ordeal, I decide to call Adam. As much as I know it'll pain me to hear his crisp, deep voice, it'll be more painful to text back and forth for the duration of my walk to work.

"Halley," Adam answers, surprise in his tone.

"Hey."

"How are you?"

I bite my bottom lip for a second before responding. "Fine. You?"

"Fine."

"So, about Alice's science fair?" To the point.

"Yeah." He clears his throat. "Do you want me to go?"

"I want you to go if you want to go," I say, the most immature of responses.

"Of course I want to go. I know this is important to Alice. We have it on the calendar to go."

"So you're going?" My tone is not quite acerbic, but I'm short.

Adam reads me loud and clear. "If it doesn't bother you, Halley, then yes, I'll go." Every single word is soft yet direct.

"Perfect. I got her a gift." I press the next block's crosswalk button. "And a card. From both of us."

"Have you . . . told anyone in your family?"

I press the button again, partly because of agitation with the red light but more because of how awkward this call to my husband is making me feel. "Only Charlotte."

"Are we keeping it a . . . secret?"

"I don't know, Adam. I haven't thought much about it. I . . . guess."

"Okay." He pauses for a beat. "Just wanted to know, in case I brought it up at the fair and no one knew."

I don't know what bothers me so much about this line—the idea that *he'd* be the one to bring up the separation, thereby somehow eliciting pity or making himself a victim, or the idea that this is something so important it just *has* to be brought up at a family function. For whatever reason, what he says bothers me, and I fight the urge to roll my eyes.

I once read that eye rolls between spouses can be a very damaging, albeit silent, weapon. What begins as a relatively harmless *You've got to be joking* or *This is so stupid* eye roll can later morph into *I don't respect you.* So, as much as I want to give Adam the old eye roll right now, I don't. Even though he wouldn't be able to see it if I did, I feel that once I commit that first eye roll, the second will only be easier, and the third, and the fourth, and before I know it, I'll be eye-rolling left and right. Anything vexing that Adam does will habitually result in an eye roll. Not exactly medicine for an ailing marriage.

So instead I close my eyes and say, "How about we don't bring it up?" To minimize its importance, I add, "I mean, it's just a separation, right?"

"Right."

Part of me wishes he would finish the sentence that is in my head: *Right. It's not like we're divorcing.*

But he doesn't. There's nothing but silence on the other end.

"Well then, I guess that's settled," I say. I tilt my head up some, not letting myself be overcome or distracted by emotions. That's not what this call's supposed to be about. "The fair starts at ten, next Saturday. And then Charlotte's having a lunch at her place."

"Sounds nice."

"Yeah."

The light finally turns. I briskly cross the street, and I'm about to tell Adam goodbye when he says, "I miss you, Halley."

My speedy walk slows, causing a man in a suit to bump into me from behind. He shoots me a rude look over his shoulder as he goes on his way. I can't give an apologetic wave or mouth, "Sorry," as I usually would. All I can do is stand with a slightly open mouth, taken aback by my husband's missing me.

Before I get mowed over or struck in the back again, I finally pull to the side of the walk and press a finger to the ear not pressed to my cell phone.

"It'll be nice to see each other next weekend," Adam says before I can respond.

A small smile tugs at the corner of my mouth, and I find myself nodding. "Yeah. It will be."

Before I can tell Adam that I miss him, too, he clears his throat again and says, "Hey, uh, I've got to run."

I spit out a, "Yeah, me, too," and our call is over.

I'm not sure how to take his *I miss you*. Does he miss me as I miss him? Is he wishing we could forget this stupid separation and go back to the way things were before he got this ludicrous baby notion? Does he feel different about that notion? Are we closer to ending this separation than I think?

I decide it's best not to read too much into an *I miss you*. As much as I love Marian and am enjoying much of our just-like-the-college-days reunion, I married Adam because I love him, because I want to spend my life with him. Not being with him hurts. Of course I miss him. I miss us.

Seven

As soon as I pull into a parking space at Springs Elementary School, I notice Adam's car a few spaces over. The USC decal on the bottom of the rear window of the midnight-blue 5 Series is unmistakable. Adam's head of thick dark hair and that confident slouch as he leans against the side of his car are even more unmistakable. My heart flutters at the mere sight of him. Before I can even shift my car into park, my palms feel sweaty.

I smooth out the back of my dress—the simple white cotton short-sleeved dress that hits right at my knees, one of the dresses I wore when Adam and I went to Seattle last summer. One of his favorites. My intentions behind choosing to wear this dress today are embarrassingly obvious. The white is a subtle reminder of our marriage, the very dress itself a not-so-subtle reminder of vacation memories, to make Adam's heart beat the way mine does when I look at him. It's a small way to say the *I miss you* that I didn't have the chance to say during our phone call.

Once Adam detects the sound of my heels clicking against the asphalt, he draws his gaze from his cell phone to me, and he smiles that crooked smile I so miss. I can't help but feel, however, that behind that smile he is, just as I am, a mixture of happy *and* sad that we're seeing each other again. Just the same, I smile and wave.

"Hey, Adam."

"Hey, Halley." His eyes travel up and down my body in a fluid way. "You look beautiful. I've always loved that dress on you."

"Thanks. You clean up well yourself," I say, taking note of one of his more casual pairs of tan dress slacks, paired with a navy blue long-sleeved dress shirt, the sleeves rolled up to the elbows. If I slipped into this white cotton dress to tell him I miss him, then I can surely believe those rolled sleeves, a look that Adam knows always makes me weak in the knees, are his way of saying that he meant every word about missing me.

"You taking a work call or something?" I point at his cell phone, wondering why he's waiting out here and not yet inside the school. The fair is probably under way; I'm right on time.

"I figured I'd wait for you." Adam pushes off from his car and is about to take my hand in his—his arm outstretched toward me, palm open and waiting. Old habits. Instantly he slips his hand into his front pocket. A sheepish expression covers his face. I'm not sure what to make of the gaffe.

"Right," I say with a rapid shake of my head, realizing why he's chosen to wait for me.

"It might turn some heads if we walked in at different times," Adam clarifies.

"Yeah. No. Totally." I can't help but look down at his hand stuffed in his pocket, his thumb resting at the opening, against one of his most worn brown leather belts. For a second I consider brushing my fingers against his hand, inviting him to finish the hand-holding gesture he started, but then he opens the door to the school and ushers me through. He doesn't do so as he usually does when he holds doors open for me, with that light press of his fingers to the small of my back.

I glance at Adam, waiting for him to follow closely behind, and as soon as our eyes lock I get all twitchy in the stomach. I give a loose smile, trying to rememorize the dark-mocha color of his eyes, the soft square cut of his jaw, the way his thin lips pull into a straight, sideways line as he smiles. I could never forget Adam's face, but having spent two weeks away from him, and not knowing how much longer our separation will be, I take the embarrassing moment to just stare at him, take him in.

Adam raises his eyebrows, and when I think he's about to say something, he nods, gesturing to something behind me. I turn around. It's Charlotte's husband, Marco, hurriedly walking toward us, as if he's forgotten something.

"Marco!" I cheerfully call out as he nears.

Marco's thick, broad chest is clad in a bright-yellow polo shirt. You could see him a mile away. He charges over in cargo shorts paired with Toms, the relaxed ensemble he often displays.

"Hey, guys," Marco says, swallowing me into a fast hug, then giving Adam the brotherly handshake and half-hug, back-clap greeting.

"Forgot something?" I ask.

"Always something with three kids," Marco calls over his shoulder as he passes by.

Before I turn back around, I notice a small smile tug at Adam's lips. I decide to ignore it, even though I know it has more to do with Marco's having three kids than with Marco's comical huffing and puffing in the battle of forgetfulness. How long has this baby fever really been going on? Or how long have I neglected to recognize it?

By the time Adam and I find the gym where several rows of tables are adorned with projects, experiments, and colorful trifold poster boards, all of Alice's esteemed guests have arrived. The entire Miller clan—Marco's parents; his brother, Bryan; Bryan's wife, Cat; and their baby—is here, as well as my parents and Ray, my mother's husband of two years.

No one particularly likes Ray. He's as tolerable as our mother, I suppose. He and Mom started dating a few years ago—one of my mother's very few serious relationships post-Dad—and of all the less-than-stellar men she'd introduced to us over the years, Ray was the least scummy. His hair was still as greasy as we feared his flirtatious moves on our mother had been. He has "oodles of money" (the exact words Mom used the very first time she mentioned Ray) thanks to a successful franchise of juice bars across Southern California. We all worried Mom would never see past the glitz and realize he might not be the best choice of life partner, but here you have it. Nearly three years later, they're still going strong, and I guess that's a good thing. If it works for them. He's a nice-enough guy, Ray, and he seems to temper the rougher edges of my mother, at least now and again. He makes her happy and she makes him happy, so what more can one ask for, right?

"Auntie Halley!" Alice squeals as soon as she sees me. She runs over and wraps her arms around my waist. "You came!"

"Of course I did, goofy girl. And look!" I hold out her gift. "Something for the science genius. Congratulations."

"I didn't win, Auntie Halley."

"Not *yet*," Adam says, appearing beside me.

"Uncle Adam!" Alice is about to give her uncle a hug when Adam scoops her up into his arms.

"Boy, you're getting big, Alice!"

"I'm a whole inch taller on the door now," Alice says with pride.

"A whole *inch*?" Adam is extraflabbergasted by Alice's height.

Marco and Charlotte have kept a constant tally of their children's heights on the inside of their entry coat closet door. At Alice's mention of her growth spurt, I'm reminded of a moment, which at the time I thought nothing of, when Adam saw the pencil tick marks with names and dates and said he really liked the nostalgic idea. As if he would ever need to bookmark it for his own future. Little did I know . . .

"Halley," Mom says in her idiosyncratic tone—a mix of chipper and judgmental. She appraises me, as she always does, deciding if she likes my outfit, my hair, my expression, *me*, before giving me a gentle hug. A very gentle hug, so as not to wrinkle her clothes or smudge her makeup. "I was wondering if you were going to make it."

"Hey, Mom." I kiss the air as we hug, letting her comment roll off my back.

"Have you tried the punch they're serving?" She hops straight to the most pivotal of topics.

"Hey, Ray," I say, giving Ray a hug as he steps forward. He's about to plant one of his signature kisses on my cheek, but I pull away in time. Among Ray's faults—the grease; the literal wad of hundreds he keeps in his pocket, bound with a rubber band; his mystifying affection for my mother—is his greeting routine. He can keep his wet kisses for my mother, thank you.

"The punch, Halley. Have you tried it?" Mom says in a nettled voice.

"Not yet, Mom."

"It's far too sweet," she complains. She looks at her Styrofoam cup in distaste. "Do they not realize these are children here? The juvenile diabetes cases must be through the roof!" Nevertheless, she knocks back a slug of the stuff.

"Not everyone can serve a Ray's Days smoothie," I say in a half-mocking way.

"Now there's a market to tap into," Ray says, ever the salesman. "The school system." His furry eyebrows knit together as he strokes his chin.

"Oh, Ray, you're a genius," Mom gushes.

Suppressing the urge to comment that I'm sure the LA County school system could certainly find in its strapped budget room for six-buck smoothies, I open my arms wide at my approaching father.

"Hey, Dad!" I say, grateful, in more ways than one, for his arrival. He embraces me in one of his signature bear hugs. These are the hugs I could live forever in.

"Auntie Halley," a jubilant Alice says, rushing to my side to hand me a space-themed name tag. "Can you wear this? You don't *need* a name tag, but they were fun to make."

"Oooh," Dad says as Alice hands me a safety pin. "That's a nice tag you've got there, Halley."

"Grandpa said I should have made you a comet," Alice says with a roll of her eyes. Dad chuckles. "But I wanted *only* planets and moons."

"I like planets and moons," I say, pinning on the computer printout that's been cut into shape, an *Auntie Halley* written on it in thick marker. "So I get to be Neptune?" I'm taking a wild guess.

"Neptune's *blue*," Alice says, like it's the most obvious thing in the world.

"Sorry," I say, looking to my father. He's just smiling at me with those crystal blues of his, slightly shaking his head.

"Your name tag is Titan," Alice informs me.

"One of Saturn's moons," Adam says, sauntering over. He gives me a wink, and I playfully smack my forehead at my faux pas.

"Not just *one* of Saturn's moons." Alice looks fondly at my affixed tag. "Saturn's *biggest* moon."

My father is beaming from ear to ear, and when I look over at Adam, he, too, is grinning.

"You're a smart cookie," Adam says to Alice.

"I see you didn't get Neptune, either?" I say to Adam.

"Ganymede." Adam glances down at his affixed tag. "Jupiter's largest moon."

"I see." There is no hidden agenda or intention behind Alice's name tag decisions. However, I can't help but think how fitting it is that Ganymede's world is not Titan's. That these two moons do not orbit the same planet. It's the kind of classic overanalysis I've been prone to since I can remember, a habit that was only fine-tuned when I was an English major.

Alice's fair is a success, with more impressive projects on display than I thought possible in the fourth and fifth grades. Alice's project, about finding the specific gravity of minerals, nabs the first-place ribbon.

While Dad helps Alice and Marco move the winning project to Alice's classroom, where it will remain on exhibit throughout the school year, Charlotte leans into my side, Leah still attached to her hip. "You guys come together?" she whispers.

I look over at Adam. He's with Bryan and Cat.

"No," I whisper back, my eyes locked on my husband.

"No one's the wiser."

I give Charlotte a knowing smile, then offer her help loading her car. She carries enough luggage for a weekend getaway whenever she leaves the house.

Charlotte shifts Leah to her other hip and leans in for another whisper. "How you doing? You two? Together here?" She raises her voice a notch as she says, "By the way, thank you for coming. It means the world to Alice. And me."

"Of course." I look at Adam, who's now gently running his hand over Bryan and Cat's baby's head. He's smiling, looking back and forth from Bryan to Cat to their son. "It's not as hard as I thought it'd be."

Adam then takes the baby into his arms, and I can't help but notice how natural he looks. He has about as much experience with babies as I do, yet he looks as if he does it all the time.

"Mommy." George's voice comes from nowhere. He's immediately tugging at the hem of Charlotte's plain grey tee. "Mommy, I'm hungry."

"We're going home right now," she tells George. Charlotte's got an entire catered lunch scheduled to arrive at her house, although judging from the strength of George's tugs, I don't think he'll be able to wait. "Okay, okay," Charlotte says with a light groan in response to her son's growing impatience.

Charlotte gives me one of her classic *I'll be back, sorry!* looks before taking George by the hand.

"Halley," Adam calls out, waving me over. He's still pulling baby duty with Bryan and Cat's son.

"Remember the last time we saw Davies?" Adam asks me. He's wearing the world's largest grin.

I look at the cute bald baby in Adam's arms. I have no clue when we last saw Davies . . . and I could have sworn it was Davis. "Christmas?" I say.

It couldn't have been Christmas, because Adam and I spent last Christmas in Aspen, a ski-filled adventure away from traditional family holiday dinners. Nothing against family and requisite holiday visits, but one of the privileges of being a married couple without children is that we can have Christmases in Aspen, Easters in the Bahamas, Fourth of Julys in Miami.

"Almost a year," Adam says in astonishment.

I'm not surprised. Bryan and Cat are Charlotte's in-laws, and aside from the rare holiday, birthday, or science fair, we don't cross paths.

Cat nods, looking to her son. "Time flies," she says. "Especially when you're a parent. Hard to believe Davies will be one soon."

Doing the math, I realize it was soon after Davies's birth that we last saw Bryan and Cat, and Davies, for that matter. I now remember that Davies was indeed much more baby then than now.

"How old is Davies?" I ask the polite question that every mother must get rather tired of answering.

"Ten months," Cat says, looking anything but exhausted.

"Like a little person already," Adam says. I suppress a laugh at Adam's comment, then realize laughter is the wrong response, given his following comment. "He probably already lets you sleep through the night now?" Adam asks Cat. "He's a lot easier of a baby now than when he was first born?"

Adam's questions are so obvious, I'm immediately peeved. He's asking these stupid questions with me here, having called me over, only to make the point that babies aren't that complicated. That I will be able to have sleep-filled nights. That all newborn troubles are short-lived and totally worth it when you have a cute bundle of smiling baby like Davies.

I bite back the resentment that's boiling up.

"Davies is a cutie," I say to Bryan and Cat.

Adam decides to take my compliment as an invitation, and says, "Here, Halley, hold the little guy."

I bore my eyes into Adam's, but he carries on. He cheerfully situates Davies in my arms. I'm no stranger to holding babies and ordinarily wouldn't mind doing it. But I know why Adam's putting on this little performance, and I surprise myself with how much I want to lash out at him. Right here, right now, in front of everyone. For something that's both so innocent and so manipulative.

With Davies snugly, although uninvitedly, in my arms, I give a few light bounces, and with gritted teeth stare at my husband.

"You're a natural," Adam says, beaming.

I want to kill him.

"Are you two planning on having one of your own anytime soon?" Cat asks with inquiring eyes. In any other situation, her question would be as innocent as my holding her son.

My eyes are still boring into Adam, but he responds before I can. "Maybe," he says with a grin.

"Probably not," I correct.

I lessen the blow of the truth (which is *Absolutely not!*) so as not to impress upon Cat and Bryan that I look down on their decision to have a child. In my years of experience at answering these kinds of questions, questions that people always seem to feel the need to ask a childless married couple in their midthirties, I've found it's best to tread carefully with the no that rests on my lips.

"You'd make a great mom, Halley," Adam says, adding insult to injury.

I look at Davies in my arms. He's putting a small finger through one of the eyelets in my dress. "Oh, I don't think I'm cut out for this," I say, then politely hand Davies over to Cat.

"What doesn't come natural can be learned, right?" Adam says.

I cut my gaze back to Adam, and it's all I can do not to drag him out to the parking lot and give him a piece of my mind.

With that, I turn to Bryan and Cat and say, "Adam and I decided long ago, before we got married, that we weren't going to have children."

Bryan and Cat, obviously uncomfortable, shake their heads, and Bryan says, "Yeah, parenthood isn't for everyone."

"Exactly." I meet Adam's eyes and give him that silent look that means he's crossed the line, then turn to Cat and Bryan and say, "It certainly seems to suit you two, though."

I notice Charlotte trying to balance Leah and her insurmountable amount of luggage, and I excuse myself from the conversation. I distract myself by taking off Charlotte's hands as much stuff as possible. The busying helps bring my elevated blood pressure down a notch.

"Whoa," Dad says when I accidentally bump into him as I spin around with an armful of stuff to take to Charlotte's minivan. He, too, has his hands full.

"Sorry, Daddy," I say, flustered. Determined to get as far away from Adam as possible before I erupt, I charge out of the gym, a diaper bag oh-so-ironically slung across my back.

It's on my way to gather the small load Charlotte's left at the entrance of the school that I bump into Adam.

"Halley," he says in a low and calming voice.

Anything but calm myself, I give a curt shake of my head. I have nothing to say to him. Certainly nothing that would be appropriate in front of a bunch of fifth graders.

Not getting the hint, Adam pursues me, even offering to take some of Charlotte's things off my hands.

"Stop," I growl under my breath. "I can't talk to you right now."

"Well, we're all going to Charlotte and Marco's for lunch," he swiftly points out. "Are we not talking there?"

I give him a biting look, a look that says, *Not here, not now.* He doesn't comprehend, or he doesn't care, because he presses.

I finish gathering all Charlotte's things, including a dropped sippy cup Adam grabs from the ground. I snatch it from him, indignant. I charge over to the minivan.

"Halley, I didn't mean to make you angry."

"Well, you certainly weren't winning yourself any points," I snap, voice low enough that only Adam, hot on my heels, can hear.

"It was a baby, Halley. Not a grenade," he scoffs.

"Exactly! It was a *baby*."

Adam and I both cast about, making sure no unsuspecting family member can overhear or spot us as we quietly air our filthy laundry.

"Halley, I didn't want to upset you. I just saw the opportunity. In hindsight, yeah, I guess it was stupid. I thought I'd point out that you *are* a natural with children, that's all. That we could do this."

I hold up a halting hand and momentarily close my eyes.

"Adam, I don't care if I'm a natural or if I have two left feet. I. Don't. Want. A. Baby."

I cast about again, and that's when I notice my father near his car. He's much farther down the row but is easily close enough to read our obvious body language.

"Look," I say in a hushed tone. I shove the last of the things into the minivan. "Let's not do this here. This is Alice's day."

I'm about to walk to my car, noticing that my father is still watching, when I turn back around to face Adam.

"Never do anything like that again," I say. "I mean, how are we supposed to put together the pieces when you keep breaking them and making more?"

My comment, ice-cold, leaves Adam speechless. With nothing more to say during what started as a perfectly fine and civil afternoon, we depart for our respective cars.

"What's going on?" my mother's voice peals from behind. Ray is several steps ahead of her, already getting into their silver Mercedes, when she stops right behind my car.

"What?" I breathe, unlocking my car doors.

With a quizzical expression, Mom looks from my car to Adam's, then again to mine. Her auburn hair, coiffed into her usual stately bob, sways slightly with a confused shake of her head. She points in Adam's direction, making shaky circles with her pointed finger. "What's with the two cars? Did you two not come together?"

Surprised my self-absorbed mother noticed, I find myself unable to come up with a plausible—or any—answer.

I glance at Adam. He's looking on, one arm lazily resting on the hood of his car, about to get behind the wheel.

"Halley?" Mom's hands are sternly on her hips. She tilts her chin down so as to make direct eye contact with me from behind her sunglasses. "Why did you and Adam not come together?"

Before she can say another word, Charlotte, folding up her umbrella stroller and stuffing it into the back of her minivan, shouts, "Come on, Mother! The caterers will wait for no one. Let's move!"

Flustered, Mom just shakes her head some more and makes her way to Ray, who's already reversed from his parking spot and ready to go.

I mouth a "Thank you" to Charlotte. She smiles and nods. We're only halfway through the afternoon, and the family drama is already taxing.

Everyone arrives at Charlotte and Marco's with only minutes to spare before the caterers arrive with a bounty of delicious food. Marco's making drinks to order; the garage refrigerator is packed with a variety of wine coolers, sodas, and beers; and a small picnic table for the kids, as well as a Slip'N Slide, is set up in the backyard. All the trappings of what should be a perfectly enjoyable family get-together.

Adam and I don't exchange words during the appetizers and drinks. In fact, he joins Marco on the back patio, where a makeshift bar is set up, while I sip my drink in the living room with Mom, Ray, Dad, and every now and then Alice, who's in fashion show mode. She wants to show all of us each of the three new pairs of jelly sandals her mom recently bought her. It's on the second pair, pretty aqua-blue ones with glitter, that Dad leans over the arm of the sofa and says to me, "You okay, kiddo? You don't seem to be . . . yourself."

While sometimes I feel I've made a career out of lying to my mother, always in an effort to keep the peace, I do not lie to my father. Ever. Not even when Danny Newman stole a kiss from me during our junior high dance. When my father asked if I'd kissed any boys that night—and looking back I think he asked in jest, not expecting my answer of yes—I told it to him straight. My father and I have always felt comfortable confiding in each other, keeping it real, honest, heartfelt.

"Guessing you saw the whole parking lot thing?" I say grimly.

"Are you and Adam doing all right?" Dad says, almost as if he knows the answer.

I cringe at the words before they even come out of my mouth. "No, we're not."

Dad's hand, the knuckles knobby and hardened with age, thick veins mapping the top, folds its way around mine.

"Oh, Halley." His tone is soothing yet commanding, something I will always adore about my father. Perhaps it's an effect of playing both maternal and paternal roles. He's understanding yet authoritative, kind yet stern. His hand squeezes mine some.

"We're having some problems," I say, voice hushed. "We're . . . separated."

My father looks surprised, but no judgment crosses his face. Only a twinge of sadness pulls at the wrinkled corners of his eyes, and his clasp on my hand strengthens. "Halley, I'm so sorry."

"I don't know how we'll pull through it, but that's why we're separated. To figure things out."

"You will."

I raise my eyebrows.

"You'll figure things out," he assures me. "You always do, Halley." He gives my hand a few comforting pats.

"I don't think I've ever gone through something so hard before, Daddy."

Yes, losing my pet rabbit was difficult. Taking the SAT five times in an effort to get a semidecent score was another sort of difficult. Breaking up with my first love in high school and being dumped in college by the man I was most serious about before Adam were other types of difficult. This is unprecedented.

Voice still lowered, I say, "He wants a baby." I look into my father's eyes. "Adam wants one after all."

"I see," he says with a pensive nod. "And you—"

"Don't." My father's known where I stand on children since Adam and I got married. In fact, it was clear to everyone in the family that the Brennans were not going to become parents, ever.

"Aha." Dad continues to nod.

"We just have to . . . figure things out."

He gives my hand one more squeeze and says, "I'm always here for you, Halley. I've always got your back."

"Thanks, Daddy."

"You'll do what's right."

I'd like to think that's true. It sounds good. But my heart and mind are at constant odds. One minute I think I will do anything to have Adam back. Another I'm so outraged that I want to call it like it is. We want different things, so how are we supposed to work it out?

"Thanks," I say again. "I hope so." I stand to go see if Charlotte needs any help in the kitchen, then say, "Oh, the separation isn't exactly common knowledge, Daddy."

My father briefly looks across the room to my mother, and says, with a small smile, "Dad's the word."

Sniffing a laugh at my father's silly humor, I make my way to the kitchen.

"Need a hand?" I ask my sister.

"How about two?" Charlotte hands me a knife and a spatula. "Cut away." She gestures to the lasagna.

"So Dad's officially in the loop about the separation," I say.

"I take it he was his usual levelheaded self when you told him?"

I chuckle. "Yeah. Thank you, by the way, for that parking lot save with Mom."

"Ugh. Mom. Seriously." Charlotte dries her hands on a kitchen towel and tosses it onto the counter. She rolls her eyes. "Never the time, never the place, always indiscreet."

"You think she suspects?" Not that it matters. I've long since done away with the aim of pleasing my mother. If I don't want her to know of my separation, it's merely because I want to avoid the inevitable drama that would come from her jumping to conclusions about divorce. The less instability added to an already unstable predicament the better.

As sisters often think alike, Charlotte replies with, "Does it matter?" In the grand scheme of things, no, it doesn't. "We all have bigger fish to fry," she says. "More important things to worry about. You've got your separation. She's got Ray's new pinkie ring. Did you see that thing?"

I laugh. I had noticed, because how can you *not* notice *two* pinkie rings on a sixtysomething-year-old man?

"This one has a diamond," I say.

"Guess we really do pick our battles, huh?" she says with a sigh.

I follow Charlotte's gaze out the kitchen window, where Adam and Marco are still on the patio. No longer concocting drinks, they're sitting on the steps of the small built-in Jacuzzi, talking, drinking beer.

Charlotte has a far-off look in her eyes as she watches her husband. Ordinarily, especially given the emotional roller coaster of the day, I would join her, fondly looking at Adam. However, it's almost as if my sister isn't here in the kitchen, standing right beside me. It's as if she's in a dream, caught up in thoughts of the object of her look. Her silence and distant gaze throw me off. I get a brief bout of goose bumps, even.

"Charlotte?" I say softly.

"I'm worried about my marriage," she whispers. Her eyes stay focused on Marco. "It's hard, Halley, marriage. I get why you and Adam are having your thing."

"Charlotte."

I'm not sure what to say. Her revelation, though I know she and Marco struggle with making all the pieces fit in a family of five, is like a punch to the stomach. *Worried about her marriage?*

Gaze still unbroken, Charlotte continues. "I didn't want to burden you, Halley. You and Adam have your own stuff going on." We're more alike than either of us realizes. "I know Marco and I married young. But I never thought it would come to this. No one ever thinks their marriage will be the one in two that ends in divorce." I can't believe my ears. "We were always so sure of each other. We even said, 'We may not know much of anything with certainty, but we know each other.'"

"Charlotte," I gasp, touching her shoulder.

She closes her eyes, opening them only a second later, still fixated on Marco.

"I don't want to jump to conclusions about what could happen to Marco and me. And the kids! Oh god, the kids." She exhales, long and loud. A panicked exhalation. "But couples rarely bounce back from this."

Is she saying what I think she's saying?

"Char—" I don't have the words. She does.

"How do you come back from infidelity?" At last her gaze on Marco breaks, and she looks at me with watery eyes. "How?"

"Oh, Charlotte." I wrap her in my arms.

She stands against me, limp. "I know this is *not* what you need to deal with right now, Halley."

"Shut up." I hold her tightly. "This is *exactly* what I'm here for."

Charlotte, as if from years of practice putting on the brave mom face, deftly suppresses any tears and sniffles. She looks anything but strong; however, she doesn't look as if she will break. It's almost robotic, her posture, the way she's talking, the way her eyes return to Marco.

"You know how I told you that you shouldn't have a baby for Adam if you don't really want one?" she says.

"Yes."

"I didn't even suggest that you should consider it."

"Yeah. I thought, what with you being Super Mom and all, that you'd say at least a consideration was owed to Adam. To myself." I look out the window at my husband.

"I didn't suggest it because I knew you didn't want to hear it," she says. "Because you *don't* want to be a mother, Halley." She turns to look at me. "I told you what I wished someone would have told me five years ago," she says. "That having kids for the wrong reason is one of the biggest mistakes you can make."

The pitch of her voice rises. "Don't get me wrong, I love my children to pieces. But having a baby to save your marriage, or because you think you *have* to, or because your husband wants one and you're not sure . . . don't do it, Halley." She looks me square in the face. *"Don't."* She looks back to Marco. "Making choices for the wrong reasons can lead you to make some very wrong choices later on. I'm not making excuses, but . . ."

"Oh, Charlotte. I'm sorry. I'm so sorry."

At first I am overwhelmed, then sad, and then I'm upset. I look out the window at Marco, who's laughing at something as Adam talks. And now I'm enraged. How dare Marco. To hell with it, how dare those two men out there! Breaking the rules. Changing the plans. Risking their marriages.

"Look, Marco and I haven't exactly talked about it yet," Charlotte says. "And the kids don't think anything's wrong. And I don't want a divorce. Really, I don't. I don't want this to ruin our marriage." She turns away from the window and leans against the sink. She crosses her arms over her chest. "I just don't see a way around this . . . this mess."

"How long?"

"May. Five months."

"Five months?" I say, surprised she's managed to keep such a secret for so long. I waited a good month or so before I told Charlotte about my problems with Adam, but *five* months? Why wouldn't she come to me with something as big as this? What she must be going through, all alone!

Now is not the time to chastise, and I remind myself that Charlotte and I really are two peas in a pod. Here we are, in the throes of the most difficult stages in our marriages, and we try to carry on without each other's support. When we need each other more than ever.

"I'm here for you, Charlotte," I say, touching her arm. "I know we're both going through some shit right now, but whatever I can do, just say the magic word."

She smiles weakly. "Thanks, Hals. I think right now I need to stay strong for the kids. They can't be made victims in this mess. I love Marco. I love my family. I don't want this to break what we have."

"I know."

"I just have to figure out what's best for everyone."

"And don't forget yourself in that equation, Charlotte," I remind my sister, who is always apt to put herself last.

"Eh," she says with a lackluster shrug. Then she groans and tosses her head back. "God. I never thought we'd have *this* conversation, did you?"

I look out at Adam, then to Marco, and bite my tongue. How dare he do this to my sister. After all she's sacrificed to give him a family, to make them a home. I want to hit Charlotte with a barrage of questions. *How did you find out? Are you sure? Is it just one woman or many? Is this the first time? How can you not want to leave him after this?* Again, now is not the time.

"No," I say with a sigh. "Never in a million years did I think we'd be here."

Charlotte hooks an arm around my waist and rests her head on my shoulder. "Never in a zillion years," she whispers.

The rest of the afternoon moves along with relatively little added drama—a feat given the conversation in the kitchen. George smashes his fingers in the patio door, and Charlotte shouts at Marco for not being more vigilant. Ray says something that gets under my mother's skin, but that is old news as soon as baby Davies pulls himself up with the assistance of the coffee table. I'm guessing this is one of many firsts for Baby. Adam and I split a piece of cake, which is an endearing gesture, though one that is made more for show than as an endearing couple's thing. Adam and I share a few words, mostly about work. At least we aren't snipping at each other as we did earlier. Mom brings up the topic of some longtime friends at her and Ray's country club and how after forty-three years of marriage they are divorcing. "Isn't that despicable and tragic?" Mom says, beside herself.

We all are thinking of the irony behind her words, Dad in particular as he inadvertently blows some bubbles into his cup of coffee. When she adds that it is even more tragic that all three children of this unhappily married couple are also divorced, I am alert. Charlotte is alert. Mom can steer a conversation anywhere she damn well pleases. Luckily, Ray finds something fascinating on his cell phone and interrupts the potential convo crash.

I am almost out of the woods, and for that matter, so is Charlotte, we daughters who unfortunately are potentially facing the same fate as the country club couple's. But when Adam gets up to leave, saying he enjoyed the afternoon and is very proud of Alice and her win, Mom asks, "Where are you going without your wife?"

Adam looks to me, blindsided.

"Uhh," I splutter.

"You're both here in separate cars. What's that all about?"

"It's nothing, Mom," I brush off.

"I've got some work to do at the office," Adam says. "And Halley—"

"I'm going shopping with Marian," I finish the lie. "At the Grove. It's easier if we drive separately."

"Oh." Mom shrugs, as if she never really cared to know the answer to her prying question in the first place.

"See you . . . at home," Adam says to me. The way he says this breaks my heart. It's so uncertain, a blatant lie, and sounds utterly contrived.

"See you," I say, but instead of Adam, Charlotte catches my eye. She's got her knees pulled to her chest, sitting on the love seat, her hands wrapped around the mug that reads "#1 Mom." She's looking at Adam with the most depressing of expressions. I know my sister well enough to know that she won't cry, not out in the open, in front of everyone like this. But I swear a single tear rolls down her cheek as she watches Adam walk out the door.

Yes, we're more alike than we realize.

Eight

The ballet is just what Nina and I need tonight. Since last Saturday afternoon at Charlotte's, I've been looking forward to a relaxed evening out with a friend who's a steady, calming presence—the person to remind you to enjoy the things you have that make you happy. When you want to remember that everything really is all right . . . or at least it's going to be.

The ride to the Los Angeles Ballet from LA's Westside, where I met up with Nina at her place, is like any drive with my good friend. There's the requisite stop at the Starbucks drive-through and a golden eighties Madonna song on the radio we can't help but turn up and sing along to. And there's Nina's classic fight with the GPS that offers continuous suggestions for alternate routes to beat the traffic. Nina insists there isn't a way to turn the setting off, and I think Griffin would figure it out if his wife weren't so inoffensive and cute in her battles with it. "Darn machine!" "Dang thing." "No, I don't want to take that route, dummy!" "Make it stop, make it stop!" There is never any worry that baby Rylan will pick up a swear word because his mother is behind the wheel.

I give Nina the scoop about last weekend, including how things still have yet to change with my nosy, judgy mother—this gives Nina a laugh—and how Alice won first place at her science fair. Then Adam comes up.

"We were not our best selves that afternoon, Nina," I confess as she switches lanes. "We had all the telltale signs of a separated couple. Downright embarrassing, actually."

"I know Adam's taking it a bit rough," she admits. "He doesn't like the way you two are interacting any more than you do."

Apparently, as Nina explains, Adam has taken to mountain biking. She compares Adam's newfound activity to my walks to and from my office.

"I'm glad you two are finding your own time to reflect and work things out," she says. "Many couples wouldn't make the effort. I think most would just call it quits without trying."

Nina's probably right. Even though the separation sucks, and the entire way Adam and I got here is so stupid, we're trying to save our marriage, our love. We're not giving up. There's comfort in knowing that neither of us really wants to be doing it. We're trying to find our ways, on our own, to responsibly and peaceably deal. Although, Adam wasn't earning any points with that whole "hold baby Davies" shtick. I don't mention this interaction to Nina, as much as it is a sign that Adam is throwing wrenches in what was a perfectly functioning relationship. I don't want to pit her against her brother. Instead I casually mention that Adam was very interested in baby Davies and I was not. We're not making much progress on the baby front.

"To be honest, I wasn't sure what to make of this whole separating idea at first," Nina says near the end of our drive. "It seemed so drastic. But I really don't think it's a bad idea, you two getting clarity, working things out *separately*, so you're not . . . tense together."

Tense is the perfect word for how Adam and I were around each other Saturday. *Hostile* would be too severe a word; *tense* is just right. And *that* is all wrong. Yes, there is an upside in all of this. The distance is what we need to try to make things right again, to step back and not live in constant tension around each other, so we can come to some solution. But if we couldn't spend what should have been a completely relaxed and fun afternoon without a baby-themed argument or unnecessary tension simply from being around each other, what does that say about us? How are we supposed to reverse that?

At the ballet, Nina and I settle into our seats. They're on the terrace level overhanging the orchestra—better seats than I could have imagined. That's a perk of being a corporate lawyer. I tell Nina to thank Griffin again for the tickets.

When Nina drops her hands to her bump, I'm reminded of the 4-D ultrasound she mentioned wanting.

"Do you have your 4-D appointment yet?" I ask, and her expression is not what I anticipated. Instead of giving an enthusiastic grin or clap of the hands, maybe even a bounce in her seat, Nina only nods. Her face is almost blank. "Are you still going to do it?" I query, confused by her reaction.

She smiles, lips pressed together. "Yeah, we are."

"Ah. Well, that'll be exciting, huh?"

She only nods some more, then tucks a lock of hair behind an ear decorated with a rock of a diamond stud.

"I wonder what it'll be like," I say. "Aren't they supposed to be pretty real looking? I mean, obviously they're *real*, but . . . you know." I faintly recall Charlotte's 4-D images of Leah. The clarity and definition put the classic ultrasound black-and-whites to shame.

"It'll be great," Nina says mistily. She presses a pinkie to the corner of her eye.

"Oh, Nina. I didn't mean to make you cry, honey."

"Emotions." She brushes it off with a sniffle. "It's fine. Thanks for asking me to come to this, Halley."

"My pleasure."

She rubs a hand on her stomach, her face glowing. "It's nice to have some me time. I know they say to enjoy all your free time and not to get too eager to meet Baby ASAP. Because once Rylan's here, goodbye free time."

"I bet."

"But it's so hard. I can't *wait* to meet him, Halley. He's going to be strong and beautiful."

"He will be."

"And healthy." Nina nods some more, as if to reassure herself. Then, from nowhere, she says in a timid way, "You know there's a chance?"

"A chance?"

"Of Down syndrome." Nina looks straight at me, now wearing a poker face. "I mean, there's always a chance, but since I'm over thirty-five, the risks are . . . higher."

"Aren't there tests for that?"

"Yes. There are lots of tests. *Invasive* tests, too. Tests that could even cause miscarriage."

I press my lips firmly together, not wanting to discuss the taboo topic of miscarriage. Nina's been down that road before, and it nearly took everything out of her.

Nina instinctively rests both hands on her stomach. "We did the noninvasive tests," she says. "First and second trimester. Then Griffin and I had a prenatal appointment the other day, and my usual doctor wasn't in. This doctor pestered us about why we didn't choose to do amnio or CVS, and then she rambled on about the risks and how if we did those tests we could be much more certain whether or not Rylan was a risk and—" She groans under her breath. "It bothered me."

"I'm sorry, Nina."

"There's a one-in-less-than-three-hundred chance of a woman my age having a baby with Down syndrome. And tests aren't always accurate, so swearing by them will only do you so much good. I mean, think of the women who are told they're negative, and they're that one in three hundred. Or the women who are told they're positive, and it's a false reading. There's one out there, somewhere." She sighs heavily. "As if I *wanted* to be thirty-six, nearly thirty-seven, by the time I had my first child! And even if I did, so what? Down syndrome is a challenge, yes, but not one you can't overcome."

I'm about to offer my support when she quickly says, "Griffin and I love Rylan no matter what, you know? We're ready for him *however* he comes. I want to *enjoy* my pregnancy. Not worry about tests."

"Completely understandable. What did your regular doctor say?"

The first set of bar bells rings, alerting the audience that the performance is about to begin.

Nina's body language and tone soften. "She's wonderful. Totally supportive. She knows how difficult it's been for us to conceive. Of course we'd steer clear of *anything* that could cause miscarriage, no matter how slight the chance."

"Then you're in good hands, Nina. Don't let this other doctor get you upset." I wave a dismissive hand.

"Yeah." Nina smiles weakly. "Just being made to feel like some over-the-hill, clueless mother . . . And all this test talk . . ."

"Gets your feathers ruffled. I get it. And, Nina, you're far from over the hill. Seriously. And you're going to be—no, you *are*—a perfect mom to Rylan."

"Thanks, Halley."

"And hey," I say with a chuckle, "I can totally sympathize with your 'supposed' over-the-hillness. Not a year goes by my OB doesn't say"—I affect a high-pitched, whiny tone—"'Your window is only open for so long.' *God!*"

"Oh, you poor thing," Nina says with a laugh.

The final alert of the ballet's commencement is made. Stragglers shuffle through the doors and into their seats.

"Honestly," I say. "Thirty-five. The magical year. I swear, I'm still a good half a year away from it, and it's haunted me more than thirty ever did."

"Why can't it just be accepted that some women wait to have children?" Nina says. "Or *have* to wait? I understand making us aware of potential complications, risks, et cetera. But does anyone ever stop and think, *Maybe they* can't *have a baby when they want?*"

I sniff and say, "Yeah."

"Or think, *Maybe they don't* want *a baby?*"

"And as if it somehow makes you less of a woman because you don't," I add. "Less of the person you're meant to be."

The lights dim and the orchestra strikes up, and two best friends, who couldn't be on more opposite ends of the baby spectrum, decide they're right where they want to be right now.

I'm looking through the refrigerator, trying to decide between having a bowl of cereal and actually making something for dinner. I cannot order takeout for the third night in a row. Marian and I haven't gone grocery shopping in a while, and I'm fairly sure the half-eaten Whole Foods sandwich that's been sitting on the top shelf for several days is no longer good. I opt for cereal as Marian emerges from her bedroom, ready for her date. She's a knockout, wearing skinny black jeans, narrowly pointed cherry-red Valentinos, and one of her many band T-shirts. This one says "AC/DC" in silver sequins.

"I didn't know Brian Johnson was in town," I kid. "Or is it Axl Rose?"

"Brian's back." With her handheld compact in one hand, Marian touches up her bright-red lipstick. "Impressed you're on top of the rock world, Hals."

"God knows I had to endure your selection of music back in college." Nina and I have much more common ground in the music department than Marian and I, although I'd be remiss if I didn't admit that Marian and I can rock "Stairway to Heaven" on Guitar Hero better than anyone we know.

"So a concert date?" I guess, pouring myself a bowl of cereal. "Who's the lucky guy?"

"I wish it was an AC/DC concert. Only dinner and drinks. Same-o."

"And the guy? Is he from work?" That seems to be the trend. Is there anyone else left for Marian to date from her office?

"Not this one. He's a doctor." She waggles her eyebrows.

"Snap."

"I know. He's like fiftysomething, so . . ." She shrugs.

Marian casts wide in the pool of dating, but rarely, if ever, does she bring home arm candy old enough to call Dad.

"But he's really sweet. And single," Marian says, nonchalant.

"That's important." I immediately think of Marco.

"And he asked." She leans over the breakfast bar countertop. "He so doesn't look his age, Hals. He's a marathoner."

"Endurance is key."

Marian cackles, then grabs her clutch. "Hey, a girl's got to keep her social life alive. Speaking of social, got any plans of your own tonight?"

I pour soy milk over my cereal. "I have a date with a book." I was going to work on my *Copper* article, but I forgot my laptop at the office.

"A book? A date that does not make."

"You suggesting I go on a date? I'm still married, Marian."

Marian and I have been over this before. Adam and I need a plan. Given the tension between us whenever we're within three feet of each other, I don't know where to begin. Agreeing on a timeline is scary. What happens when we reach the set time? Do we get back together? Do we . . . divorce? Does one of us concede his or her life's wishes and we figure it out from there? As painful as it is to be away from Adam, to have so much negativity fill the space between, I much prefer the vague, unknown space of our future to a solid decision.

"I'm not suggesting that."

"We were a disaster at Alice's fair," I tell Marian in defense of my not yet having figured out how this separation is to be productive. "Clearly we should keep our distance."

"I guess it's all about baby steps, huh?"

A spoon gripped in one hand, I drop my fists onto the counter and give Marian a crooked glance. "*Any* word but that, please."

She gives a throaty laugh as she makes her way to the front door, her long, silky blonde ponytail swishing with each step.

"At least have some wine with that book." She points toward the kitchen. "I picked up a Pinot Grigio on the way home. It's chilling in the fridge, and it has your name on it."

"I love you, Marian."

She blows me a kiss before stepping out the door, on her way to her hot-older-doctor date. It's a scene I've gotten quite used to since I moved in. I'm home, deciding between a book and work, cereal and takeout, calling Adam and hoping he calls me, Marian dressed to impress and living her wild social life. You'd think it'd get old, or at least that I'd get so fed up I'd switch things up a bit. But there's a warm and fuzzy comfort to wearing my pajamas before night falls, to opening a bottle of wine and settling onto the sofa with a good read, and to having absolutely no responsibility to make dinner for anyone other than myself. To wait for Adam to come home. To see what Adam wants to do over the weekend. To coordinate, to plan, to be a partner.

Except I can't help but notice there's an emptiness in my life, a hole. It's been there awhile, and I've chalked it up to Adam's being gone. Although, as I consider Marian's date tonight, and Nina's upcoming ultrasound, and Charlotte's busy calendar, I can't help but feel that that hole is there because of something more than Adam's absence. I know I don't need a baby to fill the space or make me feel as if I have purpose. I don't know what it is, or if this even does go beyond my missing Adam. I can't help but wonder, though, even if Adam and I do reunite, if we do make our way back to where we were, will I find myself sitting on the sofa, a book in one hand, a glass of wine in the other, the house peacefully all to myself before Adam comes home from work, and asking, "Is this it? Is this the life I want? Is this my purpose?"

Enough introspection for one night. I pour myself a second glass of wine and decide Adam filling that gap is what I need to deal with first and foremost. We need a plan. It's time to set a date. Our separation cannot go on forever.

I reach for my phone to send Adam a text. Even though tension erupts when we're together, and I've repeatedly convinced myself that space is what we need, Marian's right about seeing each other now and then. About staying in contact, checking in from time to time and trying to work things out on our own *and* together. Plus, we really need a plan.

How about we get lunch sometime next week? I punch out on my phone. My fingers are shaking at the thought of seeing Adam again, of having a date—of having to directly discuss our new marital status.

Adam responds almost immediately.

Lunch sounds great, he texts. Been to the new place on Fair Oaks? Pacific Café?

I haven't even heard of it. So he says I should look at the menu and see if there's anything that appeals to me, and if there is, he'll reserve us a table.

I decide to look on Marian's laptop. It's easier than using my phone, which can get wonky opening apps, and she doesn't mind my using it, though I rarely do, and not usually for anything more than placing takeout orders.

The screen comes to life, revealing a personal Facebook page. But it's not just anyone's page. It's Cole Whittaker's page. Like a moth drawn to flame, I can't help myself. I begin scrolling through the page. I mean, it's *Cole Whittaker's* page! Why is Marian looking at *this*?

I click through some photos. Cole's profile photo is of him with what I'm assuming is his dog. Although it could very well be the station dog, as it's a Dalmatian, and evidently, as the second photo confirms, Cole Whittaker is a fireman. A very fine-looking Glendale Fire Department fireman. I can't help but notice he's much more . . . *man* than when I last saw him some ten-plus years ago. Clearly he's older. He's more muscular. His jaw, speckled with light hair, is less soft, his chin more pronounced. His eyes look kind of tired, or as if they've seen a lot, been through a lot. His smile is still charming, dimples and all. His sandy-blond hair, which once hung shaggy past his ears in college, always disheveled like some surfer boy's, is now in a clean crew cut. He looks good. I could definitely see him in the annual fireman calendar.

I've clicked through what's probably fifty photos now—Cole with the firehouse dog; Cole with another dog (his?); Cole with a bunch of very beefy firemen; Cole at a restaurant table covered with drinks, toasting with some friends; Cole at the beach; Cole with friends at the beach—when I remember I should be looking at a lunch menu. But as moths are apt to do when a shiny flame's flickering, I can't turn away.

I quickly check Cole's bio details. His city of residency and career? Check, check. What about his relationship status? I scan three times and do not find *Married* or *Single* anywhere. No *Interested in* or *Looking for*. Nothing. And after a quick scan of a handful of photos, I don't spy a one that suggests he's involved with anyone. Sure, there are some women in a couple of the photos, but nothing that shouts, *Lover!*

I bite at the corner of my bottom lip, stumped. What is Marian doing looking up Cole Whittaker?

Cole and Marian have a history, and it's a labyrinthine one. I never imagined, after all these years, Marian would have Cole's Facebook page pulled up on her computer screen. I never imagined she'd ever bother to look him up, given their past. I don't want to be nosy, but it's not as if I'm reading an e-mail between the two. His Facebook page is as public on her screen as it would be on mine, I note when I see that Marian is not Facebook friends with him. Still, given their history, I feel as if I'm eavesdropping. *Why*, after all this time, after what happened, would Marian be interested in looking at what Cole Whittaker's up to?

Marian and Cole met freshman year in the hall of our coed dormitory. They were both looking at the bulletin board, interested in the twenty bucks you could make if you participated in a personality experiment in the Psychology Department. In the most perfect of meet cutes, they both reached for the same tearable paper slip hanging from the flier. Small talk ensued, and that night, at dinner in the cafeteria, Marian introduced Cole to our small circle of friends. He seamlessly joined our group.

Marian is outgoing, social, and always up for meeting new people and making new friends. Cole was the stark opposite. The sweetest guy, and super quiet, he had been homeschooled all throughout high school and arrived on campus not knowing a single person, unlike some of us, who made the transition from high school to college with familiar faces among us. He was a lone wolf, to say nothing of the social skills he'd missed out on honing by not attending a traditional high school. Cole wasn't a student athlete like Marian and me, who had easy opportunities to meet people and make new friends before classes even started. And Cole wasn't the type who felt comfortable showing up, party of one, at a free lunch put on by one of the departments or an informational meeting about intramural sports. Introverted Cole needed a friend, and Marian was just the girl.

If you asked any of our mutual friends back then who Marian's best friend was, it wouldn't have been a surprise if Cole and I tied, or if Cole even took the title. As Marian told me once, Cole was like that boy neighbor you grew up with your whole life, whom you built a tree house with, ate Pop Rocks with in your bathing suits on the lawn as the sprinklers sprayed, and maybe even went to the school dance with. It didn't matter that you had boy-girl sleepovers or even went to the school dance together, because you were *just friends*. The best of friends.

Come junior year, Cole had come more into his own. He had his own group of friends and was more comfortable in social settings. Marian's extroversion had had that effect. However, Cole hadn't quite mastered the girlfriend thing. Marian, on the other hand, dated around the clock (some things never seem to change with Marian). She couldn't manage to pin one guy down for longer than a couple of months, but in the middle of junior year she came out of a breakup with a cheating Sigma Pi. The relationship hadn't been serious, although it had lasted for almost three months, which was nearly an eternity for Marian, but it crushed her.

It was during this breakup period that Marian learned that Cole was still a virgin. It wasn't a big surprise, seeing as how he'd never had a girlfriend. Marian was the only woman he truly felt comfortable around. She was down about her breakup, and Cole confessed his embarrassment at being twenty-one, his college graduation around the corner, and still a virgin. The next thing either of them knew, they were having sex. Marian told me right after it happened. She referred to it as *mutual sympathy sex*. She said they'd agreed to do it as friends. He could put away his anxiety about his first time, and she, ever the loyal one, willing to literally bend over backward for her friends, stepped up to the plate.

I still don't understand how the arrangement worked, how both agreed it was a good idea. Though my first time wasn't exactly special in the way that sex would later be with someone I loved, it was still a big deal, with my first serious boyfriend in college. I wanted to share that experience with him. Doing that with a friend? And for the first time? I don't know how you can do that and then come away with still only a friendship. Maybe that's just because I've never had such a friendship with a man, the way Marian did with Cole.

In any event, they had their moment, and it was strange how it changed Cole, practically overnight. It could've been all in my head, since I was the only one, aside from Nina, who knew about the onetime friends-with-benefits move, but Cole gained significant confidence, particularly with women. He had a positivity about him we couldn't explain. (Well, I could.) A week later Cole asked a rather emo drama major out, and before any of us knew it, he had a girlfriend. Marian, by that point, had already landed herself a new frat boy to call her main squeeze, and in the bizarro way the universe seems to work, Marian and Cole carried on with their friendship as if no romp in the sheets had ever happened. One hell of a friendship, you could say.

It was at the start of senior year that that meet cute at the bulletin board actually became the classic romantic prelude. Cole and Marian became more than just friends, and not friends with benefits, onetime or otherwise. Cole had broken up with his girlfriend over the summer, because he'd realized his deeper feelings for Marian. He wanted to be with *her*, *she* was the One, and that was that. At first Marian thought it was weird. Naturally. I mean, all this time as friends and now they were supposed to . . . date?

Marian was hesitant. Countless nights we sat on our kitchen counter, sharing a bottle of cheap wine, talking about the pros and cons of her shifting from a friendship to a relationship with Cole. Before we ran low on bottles and had to break into our even cheaper backup box—an emergency party replenishment—Marian decided she owed it to Cole and herself to give a relationship a try. She loved her time with him, and she'd missed him over the summer. He'd done an internship in San Diego, so unlike during the previous summers, they hadn't gotten to spend much time together. Her summer had been filled with fast and loose dates, which she'd enjoyed, but the quality time she spent with Cole was missing. Maybe dating your best friend was the ideal answer. The best of both worlds.

Within weeks of dating, Cole had told Marian he loved her. That he had always loved her. Marian was officially swept off her feet. She'd never been told *I love you*, and she'd never said those words herself, until then. And just like that, Marian and Cole were a serious item. Marian's final spring break was not spent on some beach, drunk, getting tattooed and collecting phone numbers. She spent it with Cole, they went to the beach, and right there, as the sun was setting over the Santa Monica Pier, Cole proposed, Marian said yes, and the wedding planning commenced.

Like any bride-to-be, Marian experienced a wide gamut of emotions, from elation to surprise, from nervousness to anxiety. Then downright fear. Terror, even. When fear arrived on the scene, Marian knew she was no longer like most blushing brides. Yes, plenty of women ask themselves before their wedding, some even as they're walking down the aisle, if this is what they should be doing. How many are overcome by the urge to run in the opposite direction? That thought, that notion to bail, gave Marian serious pause. Because even when you're feeling a surge of complex, mixed emotions on your wedding day, terrifying, gripping, overwhelming fear should not be among them. It certainly shouldn't be the most prominent.

Marian had confessed to me, drunk and loose lipped, during her bachelorette party, that she wasn't 100 percent sure about marrying Cole. It was the first time she'd ever voiced her doubt. Was marrying the man you'd spent more time with as best friends such a good idea? Were they more friends than lovers? Better suited to being BFFs than married partners?

I was shocked at her uncertainty and could only offer the advice that I'd want were I in her position: make sure you're absolutely, 100 percent certain before you commit. Like the way I was with Adam. I knew without any shred of doubt that I wanted to spend the rest of my life with him, as his wife. How can a person be so sure? That, I couldn't tell Marian. She'd have to look deep into her heart, and search her soul, and answer for herself.

Well, she did. On the day of her wedding, Marian Kroeber was a real-life runaway bride. It may have been cute when Julia Roberts did it, but the Marian-and-Cole version was a disaster. Before the church doors opened, revealing a bride at one end of the aisle and an groom waiting at the other, Marian tore out of there like a bat out of hell. She fled toward her awaiting limousine as I chased after her. When I finally caught up, she reached out for me, wild eyed, and the grip she had on my forearm was intense.

"Hals, *please*," Marian cried, barefoot, heels in hand, her veil askew. "*Please* tell Cole I'm so incredibly sorry, but I just—just—I just can't go through with it!"

As you can imagine, it was the most awkward social situation Cole, I, or any of us had found ourselves in.

The entire audience turned to watch me charge down the aisle, my head low as if that were going to make the moment somehow surreptitious or less embarrassing. I whispered to a confused and eagerly awaiting Cole what felt like half a dozen times under my breath what had happened. At long last, with a glazed and dubious expression, Cole managed to utter, "She what?" And then we just stared at each other, in all the awkward glory of the moment.

Then, as he staggered down the aisle, a hundred-plus heads following his every move, I stepped in front of the mic. In the most gracious and upbeat tone I could affect, I announced, "Change of plans." I giggled half-heartedly and paused for laughter that never came. "The wedding's been postponed," I announced before turning to the officiant and shrugging (I still don't know why I did that), and, like Marian, like Cole, I bailed.

Marian was nowhere to be found until the following morning, when she showed up on my doorstep, fresh from Cole's, hungover and in tears. She'd spent the night in her honeymoon hotel suite emptying the minibar and watching television. Once dawn broke, she went to Cole's, to the apartment they had shared since graduation and were set to call home as Mr. and Mrs. Whittaker. She apologized to him profusely and explained that she realized, however stupidly late, that marriage meant one man forever. And that one man was more friend to her than lover or partner. Cole was her best friend, and that wasn't enough. I've never been sure if Marian just threw the line at Cole—"I only see you as a friend"—to ensure a breakup; I've never been sure that she wasn't attracted to him in the way a wife should be to her husband.

No matter. Cole and Marian said their goodbyes the day after their deserted wedding, and as far as I know, they have never spoken since. If Marian could have discovered her true feelings earlier, perhaps the two could have salvaged their friendship. At the very least she might not have torn out the poor guy's heart. And at the altar of all places.

As unfortunate as Marian's discovery might have been, however, I have never begrudged her decision. Many brides have finished their walk down the aisle not only questioning their choice, but with a voice screaming in their head not to finish that walk. Marian might have been the talk of the town and she might have broken Cole's heart, even broken her own, but she was true to herself, and she was honest with Cole. It would have been selfish to marry Cole for the wrong reasons, to commit to a marriage that she viewed differently from him, to give only a part of herself when her entirety was needed.

As my father always says, the universe is filled with possibility, perhaps even infinite possibility. When a star dies, it explodes, creating a supernova that may burn only briefly but whose light is vibrant and travels far. When you think it's over, it isn't. Stars shoot out elements and debris, and from these form new stars, planets, moons. Possibilities are spread across the universe, new opportunities dotted left, right, and all across. It's when you think that everything's coming to a halt, that the world's about to end, and when you feel incredibly conflicted, when an overwhelming ache of sadness fills you, that a world of opportunity is before you, brighter than ever. I may not be proficient in the sciences, but this analogy is an encouragement from my father that I have never forgotten and that I always call to mind when I'm in a hopeless kind of situation. It's easier said than done, though, to pick up the pieces and stay optimistic when you've been through the wringer.

I'm brought out of my run down memory lane as I open a new tab on Marian's computer, remembering I need to search for the Pacific Café. The menu looks delicious, so I send Adam a text that he should go ahead and reserve us a table for lunch on Tuesday.

After closing the tab of the restaurant's website, I look at Cole's profile photo again. Seeing it fills me, oddly enough, with a sense of hope. Given my lunch plans with Adam, I can't help but wonder, as I look at Cole's photo, if Marian and I are in the midst of what happens once stars explode. If worlds of opportunities are awaiting us—a reconciled marriage with Adam, perhaps a reconciliation with Cole, whatever that may mean. A found-again friendship, another stab at something more? Life's a funny thing, and as life changing as an exploding star is, so too is the chase down one path, after one opportunity, one possibility.

Nine

Pacific Café is only three blocks from my office. I arrive on time, so as not to appear too eager with an early arrival or too insouciant by being late. I hardly believe Adam would read into my being early or late, but it's something I would most likely read into with him. Adam is already there, standing by the restaurant's double wooden doors. *Just early? Or eager?*

"It's a beautiful day, isn't it?" Adam says when he sees me.

He gives me a quick kiss on my cheek. I kiss the air in return, lightly vexed at his immediate turn to the weather for a greeting. It's the kind of comment one makes to a coworker or to a person one is meeting for the first time. Not one's spouse.

Gaining my footing on optimistic ground, I point to Adam's head. "It looks good," I say, referring to his hair. I can tell it's been cut within the past several days. The sides are thinner and shorter than usual, making the sometimes unwieldy thick growth on the top more pronounced. I like it. It's got a youthful, hipster sort of vibe to it. "You look good."

"You look beautiful, Halley," he says. "As usual." He points to my hair. "I always love when your hair is curled."

It isn't often I curl my hair. Usually I'll straighten it, or if I'm feeling lazy I'll pull it back into a neat ponytail or a high-set bun.

"Thanks."

We're seated at a small table for two near a back corner, where the wooden-framed windows to one side are opened wide, letting in the fresh October air. The restaurant is filled to capacity, with an even blend of tables for two and larger tables that are occupied for company lunches, judging by the business attire. The pink gerbera daisy in the vase in the center of our small table lends the right amount of romantic-meets-casual. Though the restaurant is filled, our corner table feels private. Adam's picked a perfect place.

Well after we've placed our orders, I gather my nerves and get straight to the point of today's lunch. "I've been thinking," I say. "About a timeline, a plan."

Adam's eyebrows rise.

"I think we need one." I take a nervous sip of my water. "A date we set that can serve as a guidance in this separation."

"A plan," Adam says with a crooked smile.

"Yeah. A plan." I take another nervous drink, realizing that the most prep I've done for this conversation is deciding we need a plan. What that plan should be, I have no idea. "This weekend marks one month since we separated, Adam. Do we take another month? Two more?" I put out feelers, hoping he'll bite.

He fingers the edge of his napkin, eyes cast down, and says, "Yeah, I've been wondering about that, too. I think"—he clears his throat—"I think that's a good idea."

"Good." *And?*

"How about . . . after Thanksgiving?"

Our meals arrive—always impeccable timing, these kinds of things—and I don't know what to say. We're only halfway through October; Thanksgiving feels like a lifetime away. Do we need to stay separated for so long? Then again, is a couple of months even long enough? I've heard somewhere that you should give yourself an entire year—a full round of seasons—to come to terms with the loss of a loved one. Could it stand to reason that at least a full season in separation is a fair amount of time to figure out a marriage, a lifetime together?

"What about . . . our trip? Our Thanksgiving plans?" I ask gingerly.

"Halley, be honest. Do you see yourself vacationing with me right now?"

To be honest, as much as I hope to have our troubles figured out before we've got our boarding passes in hand, I can't picture myself spending Thanksgiving all alone with Adam on some remote island. I don't give myself a second more to consider this thought, because I know I'll beat myself up over it. *Your marriage is doomed, see! You two are a train wreck! You don't even want to spend time with your husband in paradise!*

"Right now, no."

The fact of the matter is, I can't picture spending a holiday in paradise with Adam because wounds haven't been healed, questions haven't been answered. We're not ready. Will we be ready in one month? I don't know. I suppose that's why "after Thanksgiving" will be the plan.

Adam picks up his fork and knife and looks at me as he says, "I think we should spend a holiday apart, Hals. I don't know how long this will take, but I'd rather give it more time than less and do it right. And maybe a holiday away will give us some introspection?" His expression says he wants to stick to this plan, that he believes it will bring the closest thing to a solution we can find.

I pick up my utensils and say, "Okay."

Maybe that's it. Not a season apart but a holiday. Or both. At the rate at which things are being planned now, it looks like we'll have both.

"I'll take care of the cancelations," he says.

"Okay." My voice is small, my disappointment apparent as I push a walnut about my plate. "Thanks," I mumble.

"It'll all work out, Halley." He gives me a faint smile that doesn't help to quell my heavy heart.

"Yeah," I say, both in agreement and to instill confidence in our decision to cancel our holiday plans, to spend months, and Thanksgiving,
separated. "You're right."

"Unless you have a better idea?"

"It's not like I've ever done this before." I take a bite of my salad.

"I know. There isn't exactly a book on how to do this," he says.
"Actually, I'm sure there are plenty of books on saving marriages . . ."

The thought of Adam perusing Vroman's shelves, looking for books
on saving marriages, separation, and, god forbid, divorce, throws me off
balance. I can't shake from my mind the stack of books I can see piled
on his nightstand. Would his collection grow so large he'd start setting
some on my nightstand? Is he going to search for a podcast to listen to
on his drives to and from the office? Some dry and obnoxious self-help
nonsense about how you learn to move on, how you'll find love again,
how some marriages are beyond saving?

"Halley?" Adam tries to meet my eyes, bending his head low.
"Halley?"

My eyes meet his, and, blinking several times, I say, "Sorry. What?"

"How does Christmas sound?"

"Christmas what? Where?"

He does a breathy, brief laugh thing. "We spend Thanksgiving apart
but plan for Christmas together. How about that?"

"How about that." I sniff. "And at Christmas we . . . what?"

Adam looks at his plate. "I'm hoping we resolve this before then.
Either stay separated and keep working on it, or . . . I don't know . . ."

I don't know? I don't know? This is code for divorce, the ultimate
failure!

I clear my throat. "It sounds like we have a plan," I say. I'm about
to take a bite, even though I've lost my appetite, when I abruptly say,
"What if we . . . I don't know." I'm grasping at straws. "What if we
decide sooner?"

"Decide to get back together before Thanksgiving?"

"Yes." I'm hopeful.

"Then perfect. Assuming things can change before then." Adam takes a drink of his iced tea.

I turn my head to look out the window. Sunshine is falling in slivers across the grass of the adjacent park, where birds hop about and the occasional person saunters along.

"Will anything change?" I say, my voice low and soft. I keep my focus out the window, but in the periphery I can see Adam shift uncomfortably in his seat. "Have things changed yet?"

Adam and I look at each other. His face is covered with the same sadness that suddenly swells in my stomach. I have my answer. He has his.

I can't help but wonder if things will ever change if they haven't already. And if they do, just *what* will those changes be?

"I still don't want a baby, Adam."

"And I still do."

The sadness is swiftly replaced by tension. There it is again. When Adam and I are together, sans baby talk, things are okay. Not easy or smooth, but given the fact that we're separated, it isn't all that bad, if I'm honest. As soon as babies are brought up, it's as if we emerge from our corners of the ring, ready to duck, swing, and jab. Is this not telling enough? Is this not enough of a sign that a child is not what we need? That the tension exists because we are trying to force what was meant to be a family of two into becoming one of three?

"Let's enjoy our meal, Adam." I take a bite. "No baby talk."

"Deal."

"Until after Thanksgiving."

"Exactly."

"And if we want to see each other before then for a lunch like this, that's still okay?" I say, hoping he'll agree.

Adam smiles in a sympathetic way, the tension being exchanged for sadness. "Yeah, Halley. Me seeing you is always okay. I love you."

"I love you."

A weight lifts from my shoulders. I feel like sighing in relief and saying, *I love you and miss you so much, Adam.*

Before I even manage to exhale, Adam says, "I wish we wanted the same things, Halley. It'd sure make things a whole lot easier."

Deflated, unsure of what to say, I can only nod. Because yes, if Adam had stuck to our plan, the original plan we *both* wanted, and hadn't proposed some new arbitrary one that involved staying separated or getting back together, then *yes*, it'd sure make this a whole lot easier. But he didn't. And now we're here. And after Thanksgiving, what then? I'm beginning to wonder what the point of having a timeline is. Are we only delaying the inevitable breakup? Are we trying to get used to not having each other around so a breakup will somehow be easier? Is each of us honestly waiting for the other to change his or her mind?

It's the same questions, over and over again, and the same nonanswers. Frankly, I'm sick and tired of it. So I decide here and now that I will not wait on a hope and a prayer for some earlier resolution. I will not expect Adam to come knocking on my door, saying he was wrong and we should head to Maui for the holiday after all. I will not expect him to change his mind or forget any of this ever happened, until we have to return to baby talk sometime after Thanksgiving.

I will not be pessimistic, but I will not cling desperately to hope and wonder day in and day out if what we have can survive this. If what we want out of life together is still possible. It may seem like limbo, but neither of us is prepared to make a decision right now, nor am I prepared to battle every waking moment, reeling over the possibilities that come after that star explodes. Now's the time to, I suppose, float about. See what happens, take each day as it comes, surf along in the debris of an explosion until my next path presents itself.

It's something I'm both proud and disheartened to admit: I've gotten used to doing things for one. It takes twice as long to fill up the hamper for a load of laundry and half the time to make the bed. I pull one pillowcase out of the dryer a week, not two. When Marian's not home for dinner, it's setting out one place mat and one wineglass. It's making four cups of coffee instead of eight.

When I tell Marian this, she, ever the optimist, says, "Sleep with two pillows and hog the bed. Place mats? Who uses those, other than grandmas and event planners? As for the wineglass, ditch it and grab the bottle. Four cups of coffee? Time for a caffeine cutback?"

"Then you'd see a girl with real problems," I say.

"Then switch to tea. Or take your coffee at Starbucks. Or get one of those French press thingies and make coffee for one. Change it up if it ain't good for you, Hals."

It isn't every day a woman, after eleven years of marriage, realizes how capable she is of doing things on her own, for one, even despite the hurt.

It isn't every day you find yourself having to.

It's on Saturday morning, with a bright-blue sky, nary a cloud in sight, a temperature of that perfect autumn-crisp-warm seventy-five degrees, that I find myself on my way to Burbank to visit Charlotte. I called her yesterday, filling her in on my lunch with Adam. I mentioned that even though it was still a ways off, I'd be happy to help her plan Thanksgiving dinner, assuming she'd be hosting as she does each year. (She would be.)

When I asked how she was holding up, she insisted I come over this morning. Marco has a tee time with some buddies from work, Alice is at a friend's for a sleepover, and George has a playdate. Charlotte and I will have the house to ourselves, with only little Leah to tend to. I detected the pleading and urgency in my sister's voice when she said, "I could use some adult time."

"Amazing, isn't it?" Charlotte says as she leads me through the living room to her backyard. All the toys are in their buckets, the carpet free of even the tiniest toy car or block. "As soon as everyone was out of the house, I went into cleaning mode." She proudly surveys the space.

"I'm impressed. Your first second of respite and you clean?" I say.

"Sad, huh?" She snickers. "It won't stay like this for long, but you have no idea the sense of accomplishment one feels when they have a living room that doesn't look like a twister tore through it."

Despite the twisters that my nieces and nephew can be, Charlotte manages to keep quite an impeccable home. One would swear she had a housekeeper—the floors are vacuumed daily, kitchen spotless, bathrooms fresh. Spend five minutes with Charlotte and a full house and you'll notice it's all her doing. One minute she's handing out snacks, the next she's vacuuming up the crumbs left behind. Juice duty, mop duty; toys out of the box, toys in the box. I don't know how she does it.

Charlotte turns up the volume on the baby monitor and sets it on the patio table, ready to announce when Leah's awake from her nap.

"How's it going?" I ask my sister, who's got one knee tucked into her chest. Despite the warm temperatures, she's wearing a pair of purple leg warmers over her leggings. In addition to her cleaning, she's spent part of her morning with the house practically to herself by getting in an in-home aerobic routine.

Charlotte looks at me with wide, unblinking eyes.

I get right to it, knowing that I'm here because she wants to talk, and that in the Miller house you take advantage of any silent moment. "Have you and Marco talked about . . . it . . . yet?"

Biting her bottom lip, Charlotte casts her gaze across the yard.

"Oh, Charlotte," I say. "Omigod, you did, didn't you? That's why you wanted me over. You told him you know he cheated and—"

Charlotte's shaking her head harshly.

"Oh. You didn't tell him you know?"

"Halley—" Her face suddenly goes blank, the blood draining away. "Halley, it's *me*. I'm the one who cheated."

I can feel the blood drain from my face, all color lost to shock.

"You didn't know?" Charlotte breathes. She brings a hand to her opened mouth.

"I just a-assumed," I stammer. "I assumed it was Marco."

"Because the man is usually the cheater." She rolls her eyes. "Yeah, well, not in this case." She tightly hugs both legs to her chest. "*I'm* the cheater. *I'm* the one who hurt my family. *I'm* the one who's ruined everything."

"Charlotte."

"I know." She looks across the yard again, this time her gaze glossy and empty.

"I assumed Marco because . . ." I try to think back on Charlotte's infidelity revelation. To the best of my knowledge, either Charlotte or Marco could have been the perpetrator. But I never thought it'd be Charlotte. Never. I never thought her capable of something like this.

"I'm sorry I didn't come right out and say it. It was hard enough to talk about. I didn't even think that it could come off any other way. I've been carrying this guilt, this ugly secret for so long—for *five* months now. *Five!* I feel like it could only be me. It *is* me."

I place a hand on her knee. "How? When?" A barrage of questions is probably not what Charlotte needs from her big sister right now, though, so I backtrack. "You don't have to explain, Charlotte. Just tell me how I can help. What do you need from me?"

She forces a weak smile. "I think it'd do me some good getting it out."

"Then get it out, hon."

"A kind of prep for"—her bottom lip quivers—"for telling Marco. Oh, Halley." She shakes her head. "What have I done?"

I wait patiently, supportively, and then, after a few silent beats, Charlotte's posture goes rigid and she gets a far-off look in her eyes.

"It started in May," she says in calm, even tones, "when I met . . . Damon."

The mere sound of his name, as trivial as it is, makes the entire affair so real.

"That's when the affair actually started. I slept with him only once. Several weeks after we met." She swallows. "I'm not making excuses, and once is as bad as any amount of times." She pauses. Only the sound of the pinwheel in the yard can be heard as the gentle breeze spins its wings.

"The affair started as soon as I began seeking companionship with him, from day one. Coffees together . . . then lunches . . . and then . . . his place. The feelings he gave me and the way I sought them out are unforgivable. I had a physical *and* an emotional affair." She closes her eyes and sighs. "Damon noticed me, Halley. He talked to me. He made me feel . . . alive. I have fifteen more pounds on me that I didn't have before I had Leah. And ten more on top of that after having had Alice and George. I know I won't have my pre-baby body back. And that's okay. It is. I'll be able to lose ten, fifteen pounds, if I stick to my work-outs and healthy eating. I know that." She looks to me, despondent. "In any event, I haven't felt very pretty or desirable for a long time. I know it sounds banal and vain. There's more to a beautiful woman than her weight."

"Absolutely."

"But it's how I feel. I don't feel like myself. And on top of that, I wear yoga pants and track suits so often it's considered dressing up when I put on jeans and a T-shirt. I have to use so much darn concealer under my eyes or I look like a drug addict."

"Charlotte, you're ridiculous. Your eyes are fine."

"That's the concealer. I'm tired, Halley. Utterly exhausted. And I've lost myself. For years I've looked in the mirror and haven't seen anything. I don't say that to be overly dramatic. I mean that I literally look in the mirror and I don't really take the time to notice that the reflection belongs to *me*. That I should actually care for it. Instead, I see the circles, the extra weight, the hair in desperate need of new highlights, the stains on every piece of clothing I own. I don't see me, my identity. I'm Charlotte the mom. And Charlotte the wife. It's almost like . . . like I've forgotten how to be me."

Static briefly crackles over the baby monitor. No sounds of an awoken Leah can be heard, so Charlotte carries on.

"My priorities are my children, and I am by no means making an excuse for my behavior. But it's so difficult to focus on anything *but* those priorities. I don't take the time to take care of myself, even though I know I should. I don't know what it's like to not be tired every single day. And I'm always cleaning. *Always* cleaning—"

"Charlotte," I interrupt. "I know a clean home is a happy home." It's her mantra. "But putting down the vacuum one of the five times a day you're running it, and maybe, I don't know, reading or opening a magazine, or pulling up something mind-numbing on YouTube instead, will help. Tiny you moments."

"I know. I obviously found *some* me time. I had a damned affair, Halley. I'm just in a terrible rut. You know I can't stop cleaning—the kids are always making messes. And Marco works all the time. I can't ask him to help when he gets home from work."

"Why not?"

She gives me a deadpan look, as if I can't possibly understand what it's like to run a household that's more than just *moi* and my husband. I can't argue with her.

"You know I believe a clean home is a happy home because it's something I can control," she admits. "When there are crumbs on the sofa, I can vacuum them away. When there's spilled milk, I can mop that. When you let everything go to hell in a handbasket, then there's strain and chaos in the family. Look at our mother! She couldn't give one iota for how our home—or we—looked. Daughters with ratty hair? Whatever, she had appointments to go to. Messy kitchen? Not her problem, she had dates. I need a clean home, because I need a happy home, and I need a family that stays together."

Charlotte runs her hands through her long, wavy hair and sighs. She affects a false laugh and says, "And look. I'm so obsessed with striving to keep that perfect home, not wanting to have my children grow up in a broken one, that I've really done a number and have caused the ultimate damage. Ironic, isn't it?"

"How long have you felt like this, Charlotte? Felt . . . lost?"

She sniffs. "Since I had Alice."

I grip her knee once more at the painful admission that my sister's felt such pain for so long. I knew she was worn out and juggled a circus, but to feel so lost for so long? And to keep it bottled up to the point that she reacts by having an affair?

"It wasn't as severe then, of course," she says. "It's increased over time. With each child. With each year. I think I just . . . finally broke. Finally. Had. Enough."

"And Damon made some of that frustration, that brokenness, go away?"

She stares across the yard again, her voice calm, words chilling. "It all started with my routine coffee stops on the way back from dropping the kids off at school. Wednesdays and Fridays. The days I drop Leah off at day care for some of the few three-hour breaks a week I allow myself not to feel guilty over—some of the only me time I really get in the week."

"Sure."

"The man in front of me had paid for my coffee."

"Damon?" I ask, and she nods.

"He said he was in the middle of writing a movie script, and the leading guy picked up the leading lady by buying her coffee while waiting in line at a café. Said he thought he'd see if it worked in real life."

Smooth mover, this Damon.

"It did," she says. "He turned out to be a nice guy. Really easy to talk to, interesting. He's only two years younger, works in advertising but decided to chase his dream of screenwriting."

A corner of Charlotte's lips turns up as she reminisces. "Damon took on this representation of freedom, of choice, of chasing passion. Of *being*. And I was taken in, Hals. You know, I've never gotten over the fact that I never made it to law school, that I just kind of . . . gave up my dreams." She glances at the silent baby monitor and says, "I had a lot of dreams. Having a family was one of them, but I had more dreams. I . . . I still do. It's silly, really."

"No, Charlotte. No, it's not."

She shrugs and says, "Well, I guess Damon just represented what I didn't—couldn't—have. I'd always gone to the same coffee shop every day Leah had day care, but I had a new reason to go. Of course I told Damon that I was married, that I had three children. It didn't matter. He didn't mind. Nothing really seemed to matter when I was with Damon. It was like I could be the Charlotte I wasn't. I could focus on *just* me.

"In the back of my mind I knew there were healthier and better ways to focus on myself. I could take that spin class I'd been meaning to. I could find the time. I could trade in my coffee dates for meetings with a nutritionist, or go to the salon and get my hair done, or any other cheap quick fix. Anything but an affair. But I simply liked the way Damon made me feel beautiful and young and like I was more than a wife and more than a mother. I liked being more, Halley. I liked being *just* Charlotte, the woman. Somehow I've lost her along the way."

She pauses, and I take the moment to ask, "Are you still seeing each other?"

"No," she says firmly. "Like I said, we slept together only once, and right after it happened I told him I couldn't see him anymore. And I didn't."

Good. This is good.

"I was guilty. I screwed up big-time, and I knew I had to stop. But it was hard, Halley. When it was just coffee, I *constantly* thought about how wrong it was. How I shouldn't continue things. It was never innocent. But I was addicted to the feeling. To feeling beautiful and special. Validated. Like, despite the yoga pants and the stains, I was interesting and desirable to someone who didn't have any reason to give me a second glance. It's so terribly . . . cheap. Cheap and humiliating."

She shifts in her seat, turning to face me. "I'm broken, Halley. I won't play victim, I won't make excuses, but I am horribly broken, and I need help. I don't . . ." Her shoulders shake as she inhales against the oncoming tears. "I don't know how to be me anymore. I've lost Charlotte, and I want her back. I want my marriage and my children and my family and my life *back*. I want to be me again."

I pull my sister close, and as soon as her face presses to the side of my neck, she bawls. She pours out what sounds like years of pent-up pain and secrets and longing. Years of feeling as if she's had to fight, and fight alone.

"The guilt is eating me alive," she says. "I can't carry on with this secret, this lie. I can't do that to my marriage. I can't live a lie, Halley. I can't."

"And you shouldn't."

"Even if I slept with Damon only once. Once is enough." She grips her heart. "The emotional affair kills me the most. I . . . I'm sick about it. It's unforgivable." Her whole body heaves in uncontrollable sobs. "Never did I think it would come to this. Never."

"It'll all be okay, Charlotte," I soothe.

It's hard to believe my own words, but this too shall pass. We never think life will hit us with one hard blow and then another, but eventually we dust ourselves off, we move on. In the end we are all right. Whether Marco and Charlotte can move beyond this and repair the damage or they go separate ways, in the end I believe we are all all right. We have to be.

"I can't believe this," Charlotte says, aghast. She pulls back from the embrace and spits out, "I'm our mother! I never thought I'd see the day, but I am Monica. Oh god!" She covers her face with her hands and wails, loud and hard.

"Charlotte, look at me." I force her hands away from her tearstained face. "Look at me."

"I'm a home-wrecker. Like mother, like daughter. You know I hated Mom for what she did to Dad? To us?"

"I know. We all did. But you are *not* Mom. Okay? You are a wonderful mother. You're a strong woman. You love and care and do for others at the expense of yourself."

"Not with this. Not with Damon."

"Nobody is perfect, Charlotte. Nobody. Everyone has their demons, their challenges. This one is big, I'll grant you that."

"Massive. Catastrophic."

"But you are not our mother. You love unconditionally. You want to fight for your marriage, your family. You want to right this wrong."

"I do. Oh, Halley, I do. I messed up, but I want to fight."

"And you will." I hold her firmly by the shoulders. "You will. Mom didn't fight. Mom cheated, over and over again. She hurt all of us. She never really loved Dad. Hell, she never really loved us. Not the way a mother should. We were her accidents."

"Children aren't accidents, Halley. They're just early and/or additional blessings."

"To *you*. To Mom?" Jaw locked, I slowly shake my head. "There's the difference. One among many. You are *not* Mom, so get that out of your head right now. You understand?"

"Okay." She sniffles.

"You'll get through this, Charlotte. You'll find your way. This is your . . ." I furrow my brow. "At the risk of sounding trite, this is your cross to bear. You can do it. You can work to make it better."

"What if Marco leaves me?" She bites her quivering lip. "I couldn't blame him, but the children! Oh god, what have I done?"

I hate to be the bearer of bad news, but I haven't allowed myself to ride on the back of false hope with Adam. And I can't, in good conscience, let Charlotte with Marco.

"That is a possibility," I say. "That does not mean he will, though. Okay?"

"Okay."

"And if he does, you will be all right. Alice, George, and Leah will be all right. I know it's not the example you want, but you and Dad and I survived Mom's messes. Present dramas aside, we turned out all right."

This gets a laugh out of Charlotte.

"First things first," I say, rubbing her shoulders. "This affair is absolutely over?"

"Absolutely."

"No more coffees at this place?"

"I steer far and wide from that coffee shop."

"Good."

"Then I think you need to tell Marco."

"Oh god. This is going to be the hardest thing in the world." Charlotte tightly runs both hands over her head, smoothing back her auburn hair.

"It will be. I'm no professional, but—" I pause, alighting on an idea. "Maybe that's what you need straightaway. A professional. A therapist, some counseling? Work toward fixing this, Charlotte. In *any* way possible. Like how Adam and I are trying to fix things. In our own curious way, but we're trying. Tell Marco. Try."

"You're right." She blows her nose and wipes away her tears. "God, how do I begin?"

I note the irony of my advice when I say, "Baby steps, Charlotte."

When Marco comes home from his game of golf, Charlotte and I are outside, stretched out on towels in the sunniest part of the lawn, pants rolled up as high as possible, trying to tan ourselves, like when we were teenagers. Only back then we weren't discussing affairs and separations as a two-year-old scampered about the yard with a pail and shovel. Marco's arrival takes us by surprise, and we immediately end our conversation. There is hardly a chance he's overheard anything—Charlotte and I see him enter the yard well before he's within earshot. As he approaches, his bag of clubs over one brawny shoulder, I glance at Charlotte and can't help but notice that her face looks as guilty as mine feels. She watches her husband, on tenterhooks as he lumbers across the lawn.

"Hey, girls!" Marco calls out. He bubbles with cheer, clearly—and fortunately—clueless about the goings-on.

Charlotte quickly leans over and whispers to me, "How could I have done this to the person I love most in the world? Look at him. How stupid am I?"

As I drive home along the Ventura Freeway, I keep running Charlotte's question through my head. Traffic's heavy, as it often is on Saturday afternoons. How does one find herself hurting the person she loves most? Is the hurting some sign that you may not love that person as much as you think you do, or claim to? Do we all hurt the ones we love most *because* we love them so much? Do we hurt as badly as we do because of the strength of our love?

I laugh under my breath at the thought of having some kind of a self-help podcast streaming in my car right about now. I click on the radio. As I'm about to turn up the volume, my cell phone rings. The caller ID on my dash reads "Adam."

We said we'd have lunch again. It hasn't been long since our last one, and he's already calling to plan our next. Is he eager? Should I read into his eagerness?

"Hey, Adam," I say after I press the "Call Answer" button on my steering wheel.

He doesn't respond immediately, so I ask if he's there, if the line's cut out.

"Halley." His voice is clipped, as if saying my name takes an enormous amount of effort.

Immediately I jump to panic. "Adam, are you okay? Did you get into a wreck or something?"

Whenever there's a heady pause over the phone or I can detect someone's about to deliver bad news, I always assume a car accident. I don't know if it's because of my own car accident years ago or the state of anxiety that visits whenever I get behind the wheel.

"No, no," Adam says, promptly allaying my fears.

I am relieved. And, oddly, a twinge joyful. I've never doubted my love for Adam since we committed to the separation. You can't help, though, but wonder how committed you still are after a month apart. The thought of Adam merely scratched and bruised in a car wreck sends stinging needles all over my skin. Makes me want to take him into my arms, kiss him, hold him, and never leave his side.

"Is everything all right, Adam?"

Another lengthy pause gets my heart thumping, and then he says, "It's Nina. The baby. She went into early labor." There's a slight nervous shake to his voice.

"Omigod." I try to calculate the remaining length of Nina's pregnancy. She's only seven months along. "What happened?"

"Everything's okay now."

"Is she at the hospital? Where? I'm on the road right now. I'll go—"

"She's home now."

"She had Rylan?" I gasp. "What . . ."

"No, no, no. The doctors were able to stop the labor."

"Thank god," I breathe.

"She's fine now, back at home, and on bed rest."

"Oh my goodness." I ease my grip on the steering wheel. "And Rylan?"

"He's okay. Everything's better now."

"Omigod. What on earth happened? Are you with her now?"

Adam's answer doesn't come quickly enough, so I ask if he's still on the line.

"I'm at home," he says.

I know Adam like the back of my hand. His pauses, his dazed and shaky tone, his calling me to share the frightening news.

"Adam, would you like me to come over?"

"Could you, Halley? Could you come home?"

Ten

I never thought I could feel like a stranger in my own home. Everything looks the same. All the framed photographs are where they were when I left, the living room throw still on the sofa's right arm, the coasters still stacked on the coffee table shelf. It smells the way I've always known it to—like apple cinnamon potpourri. The remote controls are still scattered about the furniture, the magazine bin still filled with already-read magazines that have yet to find their way into the recycling bin. At a casual glance, this is my home. Yet when I sit on the sofa, the soft golden light of the evening spilling through the windows in its routine way, my husband an arm's length from mine, I feel like an intruder. Everything's familiar yet foreign. Everything's where it should be yet misplaced.

Adam looks up from his cell phone. "That's Griffin," he says. "Says again that everything's all right."

"Good."

I slowly shake my head, imagining the sheer terror that Nina and Griffin had to go through today. They were having their usual Saturday-morning brunch. They'd invited Adam along, as well as Nina and Adam's parents. What started as a pleasant family brunch turned into an emergency rush to the hospital when Nina experienced sharp pains in the abdomen. They'd turned out to be contractions. Serious contractions, Adam explained, and not the light ones many women experience a few weeks before their due date. Nina was going into labor a good nine weeks too early.

Luckily, the doctor was able to bring the contractions to a halt and stop the labor. However, Nina will have to be on bed rest for the remainder of her pregnancy. She is now considered high risk. The doctor assured her that if she stays on bed rest, keeps her blood pressure low, and doesn't endure stressful or high-pressure situations or physically exert herself, Rylan should arrive in the healthy late-thirties-to-forty-weeks zone.

I'm confident Nina, who does not usually succumb to stress, if she stays in bed as the doctor orders, will have nothing to worry about. Still, the thought of Nina's having to endure a high-risk pregnancy or any complications tears at my heart. Hasn't she been through enough trying to become a mother?

"Nina asked me to call you," Adam says. "Tell you what happened and that everything's okay."

"Thank you."

"I would have called anyhow."

I look at Adam, into his warm, comforting eyes. He's only two feet away, but I miss him.

"It doesn't seem fair, does it?" he says, reading my mind. "Nina doesn't deserve this."

"She doesn't."

"I knew Nina wanted to be a mother. Above and beyond anything." Adam's fingers toy with the throw's fringe. "But tonight, seeing the horror on her face when the doctor told her she was in early labor, and seeing how relieved and happy she was when she was told everything would be fine so long as she stayed in bed. Damn, Halley." He sighs. "She wants nothing if not this baby. To be a mother. It was . . . grounding. Being told you can't leave bed for so long, most people would probably grumble to no end. Think they got a raw deal. Not Nina. I swear, it was like she won the lottery with the doctor's news."

"After facing the potential of a premature birth or worse," I say, "I can imagine."

"Thank you for coming over."

"No problem." I tuck a piece of hair behind my ear. "It's nice to talk to someone after something traumatic like this. Your nerves sounded a bit shot."

He sighs in response.

"I'm . . . glad you want to talk to me," I say cautiously.

He shifts in his seat some. "At the risk of sounding selfish at such an inappropriate time," he says, sheepish, "I couldn't help but think of you, at the hospital. And how much I missed you, Halley. How you were the only person I wanted to talk to. The only person who could make me feel all right during such a shitty time."

"That's not selfish." I consider extending my hand toward his, letting my fingers touch his. But I hold back and say, "I'd want the same."

"It's been a weird couple of months, hasn't it?" He stops toying with the fringe. One hand now lies limp in his lap, the other resting on the sofa cushion, in the space between the two of us.

"I think that's a bit of an understatement." I inch my hand closer to his.

"In the hospital, when I wasn't thinking about Nina and praying that everything would be all right, I couldn't help but think about loss. About us. I don't want to lose you, Halley."

I let my fingers find Adam's, and despite the discomfiting sensation of being a stranger in my own home, as soon as my hand finds his, I know exactly where I am.

"I don't want to lose you, either, Adam." I let my hand tighten around his.

"I love you. Always have, always will." He pulls our hands toward his side, naturally making me inch closer to him. Our eyes lock.

"We're still not fixed, Adam," I whisper.

It isn't a romantic thing to say, in the way the connection sparked by the emotional roller coaster of the day and the low lighting are romantic. It's warranted, though. It's a caution.

"But we're not broken, Halley."

Adam looks from my eyes to my lips. He studies them the way he sometimes does before he kisses them, softly at first, and then hungrily. It's this gaze that makes me move that inch closer, that makes me whisper his name right before he presses his lips to mine. His kiss is exactly the way I remembered—soft, then hungry, then tender and every single perfect adjective a woman can write about being in the heat of the delicious moment.

As Adam moves his kiss to my neck, leaving a trail down my nape and along my shoulder, I give in to the space of unbroken yet not fixed. I'm filled with a cocktail of emotions—grief at the potential loss of Rylan and everything that Nina wants; joy that everything I want is right here, in my arms; worry that Charlotte will not find her way out from under the rubble; and sadness over just how much pain life can bring.

Both of Adam's hands now press firmly, eagerly against my hips. My head rests on the arm of the sofa as Adam hovers above me, his mouth only inches from mine, breathing heavily and looking deeply into my eyes. I am also filled with a reassuring and convincing hope—despite my best efforts to stay optimistic without playing into the hands of false hope—over just how much beauty life can bring.

Adam and I unexpectedly make love, and in a way we never have before, that quiet early Saturday evening, when the light is low, the words unsaid are many, and the rekindling of the connection between husband and wife is attempted. We give in and make love even though we will have to face the problems we set aside for this intimate moment when we unwrap our arms from each other, when we say goodbye and I go home. We make love as if it's the first time and the last, a unique compilation of desperation, defenselessness, and desire. He moves inside me the way he always has, and I hold him as if I never want to let go. He looks at me as if he doesn't want this moment to end, and I close my eyes and say his name in the same throaty and pleasing way I have since our first time. It's as if time stops or something. As if in this union our problems are put on pause and we can attempt to return to a happier time, a simpler, less messy time. There's no thinking about what comes after or how we got to this point. There's just the moment of now. The very complicated now when we ignore reality and cling to what we know, what we miss. And it is that complication, that image of clinging to hope and the past, that hurts.

I come shortly after Adam, and then we hold each other, breathing heavily, collapsed in exhaustion on the sofa, wrapped in each other's arms.

He runs his fingers through my sweat-dampened hair. "Some things never change, do they, Halley?"

I touch the speckling of coarse hair across his cheeks and chin. I kiss two fingers and press them to his lips.

It isn't what never changes.

But what has.

I don't leave until the next morning. When I glance at my cell phone I notice a text message from Marian: Guess you're at Charlotte's for the night. See you in the morning! XO

"How about breakfast?" Adam says with a grin.

Front door wide open, I'm about to step outside when he places a hand on my hip. "At your favorite place, Le Pain Quotidien?"

Adam's touch sets loose butterflies in my stomach, but not the kind I'm used to, not the kind I want to feel. Rather, I feel vulnerable, as if I should be anywhere but here. So I say, "That's all right. I should get home. Marian's probably worried sick about me." I hold up my cell phone. It's a lame excuse.

"Text her you're A-okay." His hand remains on my hip.

Exactly. Lame excuse.

"Adam," I whine playfully. I step out onto the front walk.

"Halley." I turn back. Adam has one arm crooked over his head, resting against the doorway. "I really enjoyed last night."

"I did, too."

I hug my purse tighter to my side. The pointy edges of the heavy silver eight-by-ten photograph frame dig into my armpit. It's one of my favorite photos of ours, taken on the Greek island of Mykonos. Adam and I had booked lodging at what turned out to be, unbeknownst to us, a gay resort. We had a fabulous time, though we were the oddballs on site. It was a vacation not at all short on laughter and good memories, and this photo represents that. A simpler, happier time. A time when all that mattered was that we were together.

I don't tell Adam I've taken it. Not because I want to see if he'll even notice it's missing but because taking it is such a nostalgic move. When we separated, I took mostly my clothes, bathroom products, stuff I need in my everyday life. I didn't pack up my collection of books and movies or select photos and knickknacks from around the house. My taking this one photo isn't necessarily indicative of the state of our marriage, but what if Adam sees it that way?

"Thanks for coming over," Adam says.

As great as last night was, I can't be here any longer. I can't watch a tempting Adam standing before me, barefoot, hair askew, T-shirt raised by his stance, exposing the sexy section of tanned torso where his abs end and his pelvis begins. And he's wearing that crooked grin of his, with a dark overnight shadow—it gets me every time. If we hadn't had sex last night, you could bet that we would right about now.

No, I can't be here any longer because it hurts too much. It hurts too much to feel as if I'm somewhere I shouldn't be.

"You know," he says, rubbing his jaw, "I didn't expect this to happen."

"I didn't, either," I assure him.

He leans forward and says in a husky voice, "But I'm really glad it did."

I scratch at my eyebrow and look up at him, face pulled tight in confusion. "Look"—I glance behind me, body language for *I really should be going*—"I should go. Call me if you hear anything from Nina. I mean, I'll talk to her, but in case she needs me, or you need me, or . . ."

"I will, Halley."

"Okay," I say in a high, nervous pitch. "Then . . . have a good day."

"You want to do lunch again?"

I'm already halfway down the walkway when he asks. I pause, drum my fingers against my purse strap.

"Adam, I love you, and I loved last night, but . . . it's confusing. Complicated. You know?"

"It's just lunch, Hals."

"Lunch." I nod to myself. It is just lunch he's offering, not an afternoon delight. Lunch. Something we agreed to do more often together anyway. Before last night.

"Yeah," I say, "*lunch* is good."

"Then I'll call you about another *lunch*." He smiles.

"Like, next week? Or the week after?" I need some space. Need to regain my footing. I feel as if I'm blushing bright red.

"Sure."

Before I get into my car, I look back at Adam. His arm is still raised over his head, T-shirt pulled up past his waist, biceps flexed. He gives a loose wave with one hand. I wave back and get behind the wheel.

"Shit," I say under my breath, starting the engine. "What now?"

"Oh. My. God!" Marian's sitting on the sofa when I break the news of last night to her. Her response is exactly what I expected. "This is *huge!*" She's still in her pajamas—a pair of boy-shorts underwear and a loose-fitting black tank—and her hair is in a loose bedhead bun. A blanket drapes over her legs, her computer is opened beside her, a glass of orange juice is in her hand.

I fill her in on all the details, including the unfortunate reason for my showing up on Adam's doorstep.

"Poor Nina," Marian says, clutching a hand to her chest. "I'd lose my frickin' mind if I had to stay on bed rest. How's she doing?"

"Doing well, so I hear. I'm going to go visit her next week. I'm sure she could use the company, what with bed rest here on out."

"Damn, well, at least she's okay."

"Definitely."

"And at least you got some!" Marian playfully smacks my thigh. "Hear, hear." She hands me her glass of orange juice. "This is toast-worthy."

I take a sip of what turns out to be a mimosa and hand the glass back to her. "I wouldn't say toast-worthy."

"You and Adam slept together. You had sex! This is awesome."

"*Awesome*'s one way to describe what happened last night. It's still . . . really good." This, despite the conflicting emotions, cannot be denied.

"Of course it is. It's like riding a bike." Marian takes a long drink of her mimosa. "You don't forget." She leaps from the sofa and busies herself with refreshing her drink and making me one.

"But it was . . . different," I say, tucking my bare feet into the ends of the blanket.

"How so?"

I groan, dropping my head against the sofa back. "I don't know if it's because of the high emotions with what happened with Nina, or because it's been so long, or because we're technically separated. It was like . . . conflicted. Like we were having sex to try to get over our problems. Pretend they weren't there."

"Screwing your way to a solution?" She cackles. "Honey, you guys are married. It's totally normal to have sex. God, don't read too much into it. And makeup sex is some of the best."

"Marian," I say, looking to her as she sails across the living room floor, two filled glasses in her hands. She slides the partially opened balcony door all the way open with her shoulder and says we should sit outside. "It wasn't makeup sex," I say. I lie on my side on one of the chaises and face Marian.

"Well, sex it was." She holds her glass to mine. "Cheers."

Our glasses clink. Then I shake my head.

"We were close, yet somehow far away," I say. "It was the same—the motions—but different."

"Same motions, different emotions," Marian says.

"Yes! And then afterward I felt like I'd crossed a line."

"A line?" she says, perplexed.

"Like, I can't help but feel that by being intimate with Adam I was trying, in some twisted way, to ignore or suppress how complicated things are." I pause. "Like I'm trying to ignore that things have changed. Because things have, Marian."

"Go on."

"Sex with Adam shouldn't feel like a desperate act to go back to the way things were, you know? It shouldn't feel like a safe place to escape answering questions. It shouldn't feel . . . *different!* And at the heart of it, this stupid *difference*, this change, hurts. It hurts so deeply I found myself wanting to be anywhere but there, with him."

"Oh, Hals."

"I don't know." I rub the side of my head. "There's a very good chance I'm reading too much into it."

"It sounds like it."

"But there's still a very good chance that I'm not, and that Adam and I are slipping away. That our problems really are bigger than us. Bigger than we can handle."

"Prob-*lem*. Singular, honey."

"Problem. Problems. It's still a mountain to climb." I take a sip, and Marian does the same. "Part of me wishes we hadn't had sex last night. Because then I wouldn't know that it could be different. I wouldn't have to think about *why* it was different."

"I get you. But Halley, if it really was different, then don't you think, even though it sucks to feel this way, that it's *good* you know *now*? So you can make a more informed decision?" She firmly presses her lips together and tilts her head in a knowing way. "Better to know sooner rather than later?" With a heavy sigh, she sets aside her drink, leans back, and tucks her hands behind her head. "In a manner of speaking, I've been here before, Halley."

"Cole," we say simultaneously, and my eyes widen.

"Marian, I saw Cole's Facebook page open on your computer."

Marian is nonchalant as she says, "I look him up from time to time."

"Omigod, Marian." I sit upright.

"It's pretty pathetic, actually. I've been doing it for years."

"What?" I can't believe my ears.

"The age of social media. Don't tell me you've never looked up an ex."

"Yeah, that's one thing. *For years* is another. And you and *Cole*? I—I—I thought you guys were done? Through! Absolutely finished?"

"I did, too."

"What?" Marian's got to give me more to work with here. "What happened?"

"That whole sooner-rather-than-later thing?" she says. "How I probably should have figured out I didn't want to marry Cole *before* I put on the big white dress?" She looks to me with two raised brows, and

I nod. "Well, son of a bitch, I should have realized sooner rather than later that I'd made a terrible mistake."

"But you didn't *really* know you didn't want to marry him until you wound up at that church," I remind her.

"No, Halley. The mistake was that I *ran*. Period. I should have married Cole."

My jaw is on the ground.

"I shouldn't have left him. We could have worked through what I was feeling. Not being together is . . . wrong."

"Marian, I'm sorry if I'm a bit slow, but bear with me. You've felt this way for *how* long?"

"Years," she says with a sigh.

What is with all the pent-up feelings my girls have been having, for years on end? For that matter, Adam, too, with his paternal instincts kicking in? How is it possible to be so sidelined by so much drama in so little time?

"Years?" I parrot, baffled.

"Yeah, but only once you and Adam separated did I start realizing the gravity of the decisions we make about love," Marian confesses. "It made me question my breakup with Cole, and it got me to start examining my life. For real. I've always missed my friendship with him, and I can't help but wonder if I made the right decision. You know?" She moans. "I know I have no right to feel this way. *I'm* the one who ran from *him*."

"You always have a right to your feelings, Marian."

She gives a limp smile. "I guess I wonder *what if*. So"—she gestures to the living room behind us—"sometimes I look him up on Facebook, Instagram. Imagine *what if*." She rolls her eyes.

I think of sex with Adam last night and say, "Doesn't that make it harder? Doesn't it make you miss him more? Confuse things somehow?"

"Sometimes. Usually." She takes another drink. "But it makes me feel a little connected still. Maybe hanging on to silly hope, huh?"

"I don't know, Marian."

"It sounds cheesy, and don't take it the wrong way, but . . ."

"Yes?"

"Seeing you and Adam go through all this shit . . . and now you two hooking up last night! I mean, love's a complicated thing, isn't it?"

"That's putting it lightly."

"It's made me realize what I want. What I've missed." She turns in her seat and looks at me head-on. "I know that it's too late for Cole and me. It wouldn't be fair to him to tell him I've rethought things all these years later. It just sucks to realize that you used to have what you want."

Trying to regain my footing in all of this, I say, "Marian, you've been in the place before where you weren't certain. When you decided that marrying Cole, the friend, was not enough. Can you say that you're the same amount of certain today as you were then, that deciding *not* to marry Cole was the wrong thing to do? That you're certain you want Cole, the friend *and* the lover?"

Marian's green eyes turn slightly glassy, and she swallows hard. "I've been as certain as a girl can be, for a long time, Halley. I've pined over Cole for years. I don't think I've ever stopped loving him." She titters to herself. "I guess you realize how much you want something when you can't have it. I've made a mistake, Halley. I know that now. God, more than ten years later. It's so dumb."

She rolls her eyes, then reaches a hand out to me. I clasp it.

"That's why I want you to know how important it is to get this right with Adam," she says earnestly, squeezing my hand. "Whatever that means. Whether you get back together or you guys d—"

"I know." She doesn't have to say the D word.

"Because when you let go and move on, that door closes, Halley. Another one opens, but it's the door that's locked shut that you want. Promise me you'll be as sure as you can be before you decide."

"As sure as I was when I married Adam," I say. "The surest I've ever been."

"Good. Because this feeling blows." She rapidly blinks away the tears.

"Marian?"

"Yeah?" she says, forcing a smile.

"When you told Cole that you couldn't marry him because you didn't see him as more than a friend, did you mean it?" I've always wondered.

"Yes and no."

"Ugh, Marian, nuanced answers are not helping."

"Yes, because our friendship was *so* strong. We'd been friends for *so* long, it scared me. Were we really able to be a married couple? Everything happened so fast. We dated, were engaged, and about to be married all within a year. That's crazy!"

"You'd known each other a lot longer before that, though. It's not as crazy as you're making it out to be," I note.

"That's part of the problem," she says. "I felt like our friendship was stronger than our romance." Again, rapid blinking grips Marian. "It was a very stressful decision to make, leaving Cole. Our relationship had moved so quickly. We were graduating. We were searching for jobs, trying to establish the start of our careers. There was so much change, Hals. Big change. And then the wedding, all the people . . ."

"It was a stressful time, I remember." I recall my own experiences during that period. "But are those reasons really enough to decide you and Cole shouldn't be married? You said yes and no. When you told him you didn't see him as more than a friend, why *didn't* you mean it?"

"It was the only way I knew he'd accept my leaving him. What I said hurt him. It hurt me. I didn't know how else to pull back, so I pulled away the hardest I could. I was afraid, Halley."

"Oh, Marian."

"A few days before the wedding," she says, and then pauses, adding, "I've never told a soul this before."

Immediately my mind is whirling with an abundance of dramatic possibilities. "What?" I ask, waiting anxiously.

"I was a week late," she confesses. "And that's not normal for me." Marian's period runs like a Swiss train—insufferably reliable and on time. A week late would definitely have her in full-on panic mode.

"Omigod, Marian."

"I was a complete wreck. Life was moving *way* too fast for me already. I was *not* ready to be a mother. I couldn't even take a test I was so angry. I got my period the next day. It must have been all the stress delaying it. But do you know what ran through my mind when I thought I was pregnant?"

I wait in suspense.

"I was terrified. I didn't want to have a baby. I didn't want all of this commitment."

"Alice came too early for Charlotte," I say in support. "It's normal to be scared, but it doesn't necessarily inform anything about your relationship with Cole." It may not be the greatest example, seeing as Charlotte's going through a crisis in part because of that early surprise. "You and Cole could have worked through it, figured it out."

"I stopped," she says, "looked in the mirror, and realized that if I was afraid of being pregnant with my husband-to-be's child, then what the hell was I doing marrying him? How could I *not* ask myself that?" She has a point.

"It just wasn't the right time to get married," I say.

"Definitely. The feeling of relief when I got my period made me the happiest I'd been all week. It was my *wedding* week, Halley! A girl shouldn't feel happiest that she isn't knocked up. She should be looking forward to the honeymoon, the promise to have and to hold, the happiest day of her life!" Another salient point.

"When I finally did think of all that happy wedding stuff," she says, "even after I realized I wasn't pregnant, I don't know, I just . . . I was overwhelmed. I wanted the world to stop. Slow down. Life was flying by, and I felt like I had no control over it. Was this what I really wanted? I couldn't honestly answer that question then."

Marian pauses, and neither of us says a word. She dabs at her tears with the palms and backs of her hands, then blows her nose into one of the tissues from the box I fetch from the bathroom.

"I know now that I ran from Cole for all the wrong reasons," she says. "I was scared and immature. I just wasn't ready to get married, that's all. Maybe, had we stepped back and waited, we'd eventually have gotten married. Or maybe we'd have learned that we really were only friends. But now we'll never know." She blows her nose.

"Losing Cole is my greatest mistake. I'll never forgive myself. I'm not genuinely happy, Halley. Yes, I have an amazing career, more money than I know what to do with." She waves a hand at the scenic view. "A killer town house, fancy little convertible Audi, a Carrie Bradshaw kind of wardrobe. I rampage-date, because that's the only way I know how to do 'relationships.' Because I don't want to fall in love with anyone who's not Cole. He has *it*. The *it* factor. You know what I mean?"

Of course I do. Adam has *it*. After one date, I knew.

"It's like," she says, "what you do end up with—the packed little black book and meaningless sex and nonexistent relationships, all the things you thought you wanted with the freedom and noncommitment you craved—are the very things that make you realize that you want what you lost after all. You'd think I have it all, but I'm missing my great love. I'm missing Cole."

"Marian?" I say, pensive.

"Hmm?" She folds her arms across her chest and lies back in her chaise.

"You know how we've both established how important it is for Adam and me to be absolutely certain about a decision before we commit to it?"

"Yes."

"And you remember how I told you when you and Cole broke up, how brave I thought you were to walk away? How admirable it was, despite how hard it was, that you were honest with yourself about what you wanted? Or, rather, what you thought you wanted then?"

"Yes."

"By that logic, then, don't you owe it to yourself, and maybe even to Cole, to at least see if there's something still there? Even after all this time?"

Marian bolts upright, a flustered look on her face—mouth open, eyes round, brows raised.

"Looking at Facebook and longing from afar isn't going to help you heal and move on," I say. "I know it's a lot to ask and consider, and I'm sure there's a valid argument we could make for how this is so unfair to Cole, but you're talking about examining life, the gravity of love, doors closing and locking, wondering *what if*. Well *what if* you saw Cole? *What if* you told him why you really ran away? *What if* you told him you made the greatest mistake? *What if* you told him how you really feel?"

"Telling him I ran because I was terrified at the prospect of having his baby is going to make everything better?"

"It's honest."

"He'll just question the depth of my love for him anyway. I mean, saying I ran because I thought everything was moving too quickly, that I was scared. That's convincing love!"

"It says you got it wrong. We all make mistakes; we don't always get it right the first time. It says you're human, you messed up in a major way, and, even after all this time, you want to try to make it right. Whether right means you get back together or you have a friendship or you just forgive and move on, don't you think you should give it a shot?"

She bites her cheek and looks off to the side. "I don't know, Halley. I don't know if anything could be had between us. After all these years. The damage I did. It's unforgivable."

165

"I think that's up to him to decide."

"I couldn't," she says, obstinate. "I couldn't do that to him. Or to me."

I take a chance and say, "Because you're afraid of the answer? You have a sliver of hope now. He's the great lost love, the one you let get away and can secretly pine for on Facebook, without his knowing? Without risk? So long as he's nothing more than a picture on the screen, there's hope and fantasy for reconciliation. But when a decision's made, hope's time is up. Like Adam and me, it's about timing. It's about delaying the painful and holding on to hope. It's fighting for the hope."

"Exactly."

"You think there's nothing scarier than the answer you don't want to hear, so you cling to what you've got left—hope, possibility, a chance."

"Yes."

"Until, Marian"—I lean toward her—"you realize that the scariest thing of all is not the answer but what can happen when you let life beat you. I'm not the best spokesperson for this right now, but I'm trying. Take control of your life, Marian. Chase your happy."

"And if I do tell him how I feel and he wants nothing to do with me? And I just hurt him all over again?"

"It's probably a cheap response, but you know he won't be the only one hurting. You hurt him, you hurt yourself."

"Ain't that the truth."

"Ask yourself if getting your truth is worth the pain and the heartache. The possibility of loss, forever. And then," I say with a shrug, "if it is, run *to* him, Marian."

Eleven

Halley, it's beautiful," Nina says, holding up the cream silk newborn onesie I bought at a baby boutique that Charlotte recommended. A small gesture of encouragement after what Nina went through. Nina sets it across her lap and places the matching cap above it. "Thank you. I love it."

"So is Griffin at your constant beck and call now that you're on bed rest?" I ask, sitting cross-legged at the end of Nina's king-size bed. "Treating you like a queen?"

Nina's seated upright, propped up by a mountain of pillows. She has two large bottles of Evian and various snacks on her nightstand, and scattered across the bed are books, pens and pencils, her laptop, her cell phone, her reading glasses, the television remote control, and stacks upon stacks of papers, one thick sheaf bound.

"Griffin spends half his business hours working from home now," Nina explains. "And then Desiree, his sister, comes by twice a week for a couple of hours to help me. She's a nurse, so this is easy-peasy for her." She scoots up. "And the rest is all me. I sleep, I snack, I work in bed, watch my soaps, listen to music. I can move around lightly for one or two hours a day, but other than that just basically to use the toilet, which feels like every hour with Rylan constantly pushing on my bladder. You're jealous, aren't you?"

"You are living in the lap of luxury," I say with a waggle of my eyebrows.

When I ask Nina how she's handling being away from work earlier than planned, she holds up the thick bound sheaf—a manuscript with red and blue pencil marks all over it.

"The bonus of the editing gig," she says. "You can do it in your pajamas in bed."

She sets aside the manuscript, reaches for the light-pink paperback among her papers, and hands it to me.

"Here," she says, "I finished reading this. It's one of our house's newest women's fiction releases. Not one of my acquisitions, unfortunately, but a complete gem."

Following Home, the cover reads. "A tearjerker?" I speculate.

"Only a little. It's inspiring, actually. In typical women's fiction fashion, it's about a woman who sets out to find herself. She's fresh out of college and embarks on an open-ended trip around the world. No budget or timeline."

"A trust-fund baby?"

"No. She actually does it all on the cheap—hitchhikes, sleeps in hostels, does odd jobs, and works under the table to earn her keep. It's about finding yourself and not coming home until you do. It's really quite sweet. Give it a read. I think you'll enjoy it."

"Thanks."

Nina's fingers glide over the onesie. There's a tender and heartwarming quality to the way she stares at it, to the way she lightly smiles as she brings it up to her face. She touches the soft fabric to her cheek, then brings it to her nose and inhales.

"You know," she says, "it sounds silly, but I can't wait to smell Rylan. That baby smell, you know?"

"I do," I say, recalling from Charlotte's children that gentle, clean scent that only a baby has.

Nina smooths the onesie and cap back out across her lap. "I was absolutely terrified on Saturday."

"I can't imagine, Nina."

"When it was happening, I wasn't thinking about myself at all. I wasn't thinking about what was happening to my body or what the pain meant for me. All I could think about was Rylan and how I wanted him safe. How I couldn't lose him. How all that matters is that Rylan joins our family."

"You're already a mom, and he isn't even here yet, hon. You'll be spectacular."

Nina's hands move from the onesie to her growing belly. She sighs, a smile peeling across her lips.

"It may not exactly be easy right now, but it's entirely worth it." She looks up at me. "I've never wanted anything so much in all my life, Halley."

On my way home from Nina's, I decide to take a small detour and swing by Griffith Observatory and see my father. It's been a draining few days. Hell, the whole summer and now autumn are taking their toll. I can't take away Nina's worry or do more than give her company and bring her lunch and baby clothes as she sits and waits out this precarious time. I resent this sense of helplessness. But Nina is confident and hopeful. She's determined that she will deliver a healthy baby Rylan. And I don't doubt she will.

As for Marian, I don't know what more to tell her about Cole. I'm just beside myself at how long she's hidden these feelings, how long she's swum in conflicted love.

And Charlotte! God, how long she's battled losing herself, and how she's had to deal with the burden and guilt of infidelity.

And then what the hell did Adam and I do the other night? Were we ready to finally come to a conclusion? What did it say that our night together was different? Or was it all in my head? Or, even worse, some kind of self-fulfilled prophecy?

I park my car in the nearly empty lot of Griffith Observatory after the long, scenic, winding drive along the slope of Mount Hollywood. The sky is a gorgeous painting of orange, purple, and pink, the expansive view of Downtown and the Los Angeles Basin truly breathtaking. The tall trees bend against the slight breeze that gently whips up high in the mountains, as if to wave farewell to the last of the observatory visitors and welcome the evening skies.

"Hi," I say to the janitor—Neal, his nametag reads—sweeping the entry, around the Foucault pendulum, which persists in its meticulous and gentle swaying.

"We're closing in a few, darling."

"I know," I say. "I'm here to see Dr. Robert West. He hasn't already headed home for the night, has he?" Then I quickly add, "I'm his daughter."

"Does Dr. Robert West *ever* go home?" the janitor replies. "He's around here somewhere. You want me to call for him?"

"No, thanks. I'll find him."

I stop by the exhibits on the ground level and come up empty. I make my way to the lower level and journey down the Cosmic Connection Corridor. As I near the end, I hear my father's voice call from behind.

"Halley! What are you doing here?" Dad saunters down the lengthy hall, dressed in my favorite blazer he's had since forever, a charming tweed. "Neal said a daughter of mine was here looking for me." He gives me a hug.

"Oh, I'm on my way home from Nina's. Thought I'd see how you were doing."

"I'm doing just fine, Halley. Just fine." He leads me down the hall, back to the mezzanine level, his briefcase in hand, an old-school puce leather case with well-worn brass locks. "We had three elementary class visits come in today!" He beams. "I had the honor of presenting at the planetarium for all three of them. How are you doing, sweetheart?"

I tuck a piece of hair behind my ear. "Been better, but I'm hanging in there."

"Everything still . . . the same with Adam? You guys are . . ." His grey mustache twitches as he moves his pursed lips from side to side.

"Still the same, Daddy." Random night of passion aside, but a girl's not going to spill those beans to her father. "Still separated. Still figuring things out."

"Progress takes time," he says with confidence. "How's Nina?"

We make our way toward the entry.

"She's on bed rest, poor thing," I report. "But she and Baby are A-okay."

"Oh goodness."

"Hey, don't know if you've heard yet. I'll be joining you guys for Thanksgiving at Charlotte's."

"Wonderful." I can tell, as he looks at me with a tight-lipped smile, that he's wondering if I'll be coming along with Adam.

"Adam'll spend it with Nina and his parents," I clarify.

"Okay." He closes his eyes and nods, Dad's affable way of dealing with news that could have gone in a better direction.

I ask if he's ready to close shop for the night, and when he says he is, I suggest we go out to dinner.

"What do you say, Dad? Did you have dinner plans?"

He checks to see if he's got his usual pen in his front shirt pocket, then motions to the exit. "Does a frozen TV dinner count?"

"Omigod, Daddy. Come on. You need a real meal, and I need emotional counseling."

We find ourselves at Debut Steakhouse. Since Dad insisted on paying, and since they serve some of the best steaks in Los Angeles, we claim two of the few available seats. At the bar we place identical medium-rare fillet orders and await our drinks.

"It'll be nice to have you at Thanksgiving dinner, Halley," Dad says. "It's . . . been a while." He smiles.

It's been at least three, maybe four, years since Adam and I have done "the family thing" for Thanksgiving. Last year it was Vancouver, the year before that the Caribbean. Always taking advantage of holidays from work, living the DINK dream.

"Yeah. It has." I look to my father and smile, refusing to let Adam and broken plans resurface. "I'm looking forward to it."

Our drinks arrive—Dad's his usual gin martini with two olives and mine a Scotch neat. It's an order that surprised me as much as my father, as I'm ordinarily one to order a chardonnay or pinot. I ordered Scotch for the simplicity and because I just want something really strong. Something that'll burn as it goes down, that'll give the proper nod to the crappy swell of emotions going on inside me.

"I know how much you and Adam like your romantic getaways and adventures."

I nearly roll my eyes at the mention of Adam and our travels. Instead I knock my glass to Dad's and say in an acerbic tone, "Well, I don't think we'll have to worry about us taking any of those this year."

"There's always Christmas. Or New Year's."

My father, ever the optimist.

I shrug, then take a sip and wince slightly at its strength.

"Halley, I don't mean to talk poorly about your mother."

His words take me by surprise. First, I didn't expect my mother to hijack the evening even in her absence. Second, though it'd be entirely warranted, my father doesn't speak ill of his ex-wife. Though no one would ever hold it against him, it isn't in his nature to ridicule, lay blame, or complain.

"It's something I think is important for you to hear from me, Halley. I'm sure you already know it, but I want to be clear."

"What, Daddy?"

His forehead wrinkles. "You're not your mother."

His words chill me, but not for the reasons one might think. They're the words I said to Charlotte when she disclosed her infidelity.

"You and I both know your mother never shone in the maternal department," he says delicately.

"That's a diplomatic way of putting it."

He pats the bar top twice, palm down, and says in a humble tone, "I know you don't want children, Halley. I want you to know, though, that if you were to have a child, you'd be anything *but* your mother."

"Daddy, it feels good to hear this. Especially from you." I value my father's advice more than almost anyone's. "But Mom's lackluster efforts are not why I don't want to be a mother." I pause to consider my words, biting down on the bottom corner of my lip.

My father patiently waits, his warm eyes encouraging, comforting, accepting.

"I suppose, *yes* . . ." My words come out slowly. "To some degree I've been influenced by not having had the best example of a mother. But . . . it goes deeper than that, Daddy. There are a lot of reasons one can give to *want* a child, and the same goes for *not* wanting one. And I have my reasons. They may not be 'good enough' or acceptable to some. They may not be shared or understood, but they're mine. And they're real."

"I figured as much, Halley." He smiles. "I felt it important that you heard it from me, just the same. You are your own woman."

"Thanks." I cup a hand over his.

"There's a lot you could blame your mother for," he says with a light chuckle, "but I played a role in the divorce, too."

"Don't defend her."

"It takes two to tango, Halley."

"Oh, Daddy, come on."

"Halley, listen. Looking back all these years, I've learned a thing or two. I know I could have been more emotionally available for your mother. Now, I don't know if that would have saved our marriage, and I can't speak for it doing anything for her . . . maternal instincts. God knows it probably would have only delayed the inevitable divorce a short while. But I could have done more. I could have fought harder." He takes a sip of his martini. "Halley, I know you came to your old man tonight because life's beating you up lately."

"*Oh* yeah." I raise my eyebrows for dramatic emphasis.

"And I'm out here sipping an overpriced seventeen-buck martini to tell you that life's hard."

I laugh louder than I would have expected and say, "You don't need to spend seventeen bucks on a drink to tell me that."

"Well, that's what we're doing. And I'm telling you that life'll beat you up, and you'll have to stand again. When it puts up a fight, you fight back. And harder. But don't beat yourself up when things don't go the way you plan."

"Things definitely aren't going according to plan, Daddy."

"See?"

"But I'm not naïve enough to believe everything *does*. And will."

"That's not naïve, that's hopeful. I mean, what's the point of making a plan if you don't expect it to . . . go according to *plan*?"

"That I'll toast to," I say, raising my nearly empty glass.

"I loved your mother, and I think a small part of me still does."

It's not often I hear my father mention my mother and the word *love* in the same sentence. And I certainly never imagined he *still* loves her.

"A part of me will always love her, because she's the mother of my children. I have two beautiful daughters out of my marriage with her and three amazing grandchildren. I'm, despite the hell that woman put us through, the luckiest man in the world." He takes a drink, sets his glass on the cocktail napkin, and looks me in the eyes.

"Expect that a part of you will always love Adam." He swallows hard before he continues, almost pained by his own words. "If you and Adam don't come out together at the end of this, know that it's perfectly normal to pine for him, Halley. To find yourself still loving him. Sometimes marriages last; sometimes they end. It's not black and white. Whatever way it turns out, I'm saying not to beat yourself up. Not to mistake your love and longing for a reason to do something untrue to who you are."

"Don't stay for the wrong reasons," I say.

"Don't live a lie."

"I don't want my marriage to fail, Daddy."

"I know you don't, sweetheart. No one wants to see their marriage end." He squeezes my hand. "And, if it came to that, I wouldn't look at your marriage ending as a failure."

"Daddy. Come on."

"No," he says, steadfast. His shoulders broaden some; he sits up taller. "It takes a lot of guts to call it quits on something that is no longer working. Fight? Yes. Take the high road and try to figure out a real and honest solution? Hell yes. Suffer? Live a half-fulfilled life? Live untrue? No, no, no, Halley. Life's too short for that. I could have stayed with your mother. I was the one who finally called for the divorce, and she ranted and raved, fought tooth and nail to keep the marriage."

"Really?" I'm taken aback. I'd always figured it was mutual. Mom was, after all, the one who ran to the overtanned, bleached-teeth divorce attorney with the giant billboard over Wilshire Boulevard that advertised cheap and quick divorces. Perhaps that was out of spite, or defensiveness, or a wish to surrender.

"Really," Dad says. "Life'll hand you more than you think you can handle. Don't look at a plan gone wrong as a failure, but as a different plan. Your course has shifted."

"Easier said than done."

He laughs some, then says, "Halley, you know what I've always said?" He finishes his martini just as our steaks arrive. My father, in all his wisdom and knowledge, is an overflowing wealth of sage advice. It is one particular tip, though, that he's made his life's motto.

"If it isn't hard," I recite, "it isn't worth doing."

He smiles and adds, "The rewards are in what's hard, never in what's easy."

I can't help but say, with a grin, "What happens when *every* path is super-duper hard? Which do you choose?"

My father doesn't answer, and he doesn't have to. Because I believe there is no clear, straight, single answer. Love is not simple. It is universal, but it is not uniform. It is not a clear-cut equation or an easily explained scientific formula. Love and life's paths and choices are not things you can quantify, put under a microscope, toss around some hypotheses about, and after extensive evaluation come out with a foolproof answer to. Love, like life, simply is varied. And I can live with that. The problem is just deciding what difficult answer—what hard path—will be the one I do choose to follow.

It's after nine by the time I get home, and Marian, instead of being hunkered over her laptop, putting in the sixty, seventy, or however many workaholic hours she clocks each week, is hunkered over a bowl of instant oatmeal. The signature scent of the peaches and cream I grew up on fills my nostrils as soon as I walk through the door.

Marian's standing at the kitchen counter, one elbow plunked down on it, the side of her head pressed into her hand, spoon in mouth. She looks as if she's suffering from a hangover.

"Drink too much, Marian?"

"That's tomorrow's plan."

I toss my purse aside. "What's going on?"

Marian pulls the spoon from her mouth, making a suction sound. "I went to the firehouse."

I shake my head, confused.

"The firehouse. In Glendale." She widens her eyes at my doltishness.

"The *fire*house?" My eyes match hers now, my mouth hanging open in disbelief. "In *Glendale*?"

Licking more oatmeal from her spoon, she says, "That's right. *The* firehouse. In Glendale. Frickin' firehouse number Twenty-Two."

"Did you . . . talk to him?"

She sets her jaw in a determined way. "No, I didn't talk to him. I drove there, like a pathetic, lovesick puppy, and I just watched him. He looks freaking gorgeous."

"This is the first time you've been?"

"Yup. I'm amazed I lasted this long. For years I've known where he's stationed. Good ol' Twenty-Two."

I feel responsible for Marian's little trip to see Glendale's bravest.

"Marian," I say cautiously. She raises her brows, spoon in mouth. "When I said run *to* Cole, I didn't necessarily mean, like, ASAP and all stalkery. No judgment!"

"Judge away, Hals. It was pathetic. I'm pathetic. And don't blame yourself for my behavior. This was a long time coming." She makes a disgusted face at her bowl of oatmeal. "This is my third instant packet. I think I'm going to be sick."

I take the spoon and bowl from her.

"Come on," I say, walking into the living room. She follows.

"I'm so stupid, aren't I?" she says. "I don't deserve any pity. I'm completely to blame for all of this. Stupid, silly girl in love."

"Marian, when you drove to see him, did you plan on going to see him? Actually *see* him?"

She sits next to me on the sofa. "Yeah. Kind of. I don't know. I just drove straight after work. I didn't think it through, to be honest with you."

"Sounds like it."

"I didn't get out of the car, because I think part of me wanted to just see him. To find out if seeing him made me feel differently. Stupid, huh?"

"No. I can't say it'd be all that helpful, but . . . did it make you feel differently?"

"Ha! All it did, girl, was make me realize what a big fat mistake I made. And then I got so nervous, I couldn't get out of the car. What would I say to him? What would *he* say? Ugh! You know he trains therapy labs? He raises cute puppies, trains them, and gives them away? As if his career isn't already Mr. Hero, he's perfect and selfless in his hobbies." She sighs.

I take a bite of the delicious oatmeal. "So where do you stand now?"

She throws herself down, dramatically sighing and turning so that she can rest her long, tan legs against the sofa back, her bare feet crossing at the ankles. "Six feet under." She laughs to herself.

Spoon in my mouth, I lean toward the coffee table to snag the remote control. "Honestly, Marian."

"Honestly? I will go to that firehouse again. Firehouse Twenty-Two, where there's one Mr. Cole Whittaker, the one who got away and still has my heart."

"You're going back?"

"*Oh* yeah. I don't know when, exactly. God knows when I'll gather the nerve. But next time, I'm getting out of my car. And I'm going to talk to him."

"That's what I'm talking about!"

"But before I do, I'll have a plan. I'm going to think things through and not just drive over there in a flurry, on a high from selling an assload of Diazepam. I don't know exactly *when* I'll dust off my balls and go over there, but I will!"

"You and the dusting of the balls," I say with a laugh.

"I sure as hell can't carry on like this, Hals. All lovesick and stupid. Wondering *what if.*"

I turn on Netflix, and Marian asks what I'm up to for the night.

"What we've always done best," I reply. I find *Friends.* "Binge-watch our favorite TV show, bemoan men and wacky love, and pretend that *Friends* equipped us with all the right and realistic life lessons a girl needs."

"Hey, out-of-work actors and coffee waitresses can totally afford big Manhattan apartments," Marian says, situating herself next to me.

"Or," I say with a grin, "best friends can wind up married and happily ever after."

Four back-to-back episodes of *Friends* don't quite do the trick I'm hoping for. It is some nice escapism, and it helps lull Marian into sleep. She beats herself up pretty hard after the second episode, when we pause our binge-streaming to take off our makeup and get into our pajamas—our roommate reunion is an eerie reflection of our first time living together. Marian gets really upset, calling herself names and saying she deserves to feel this way, that she deserves for Cole to potentially break her heart, the way she broke his. Then she gets really downcast and considers forgetting about seeing him again, talking to him. It is time for some roommate cheering up. I tell her to put the entire idea of Cole to bed for the night, sleep on things, and let *Friends* take care of the rest.

Our TV night doesn't bring the calm I'm looking for after an emotionally difficult day, however. So with Marian sound asleep on the sofa, lights out, I tiptoe into the living room and retrieve my laptop from my workbag.

It's been years since I got out of bed, either straight out of a dream or because I couldn't fall asleep, and picked up a notebook or sat at my computer to write. In college, because I had the spare time and lofty career ambitions that hadn't yet had the chance to be diminished by the real world—gotta get that job that offers benefits!—I'd do it all the time. I actually wrote a couple of novellas and even a novel back in college. When an idea would strike and I thought I'd found gold, I'd rush to my notebook or sit in front of the screen and go to work. The inspired moments didn't amount to much, as all that writing just sits dusty on disks today, and I left many stories untold, breaking off somewhere halfway through when I grew tired of the characters or couldn't figure out where the plot was going. It was a hobby I enjoyed, nevertheless.

Tonight, though, I can't resist the urge to sit up in bed, laptop open and a blank screen on the page. The cursor awaits my first sentence, and as in that magical moment in *Jerry Maguire*, words pour out so fluidly, so perfectly, so honestly, I don't stop until I say all that my heart feels and all that my fingers can type. I don't stop until I complete the piece that matters more to me than anything I've ever written, or would ever write, for *Copper*. It's more important and more personal than the strong-female-in-fiction series, which I'm proud of, which is already on its second feature. That ambitious passion project is indeed important, something I really wanted to do, but it hasn't filled that creative void as I hoped it would. This, though. This is bigger. So much bigger. For the first time in a while I feel a sense of purpose.

When I'm finished, I scroll to the top of the page. I notice the time—2:14—in the upper right-hand corner of the screen, but it isn't the lateness of the hour that fills me with urgency. It's the first line I've typed. And it fills me with an urgency to pat myself on the back, to realize I'm standing up and fighting life back, throwing the best punch I've got in me.

"A Letter to My Twentysomething Self," reads the first line.

I read through my letter once, then twice, making a few minor adjustments. After my third reading, I consider it finished enough for the night. There will be no maniacal *Jerry Maguire*–like moment where I run down to the print shop and churn out stacks of shiny copies to pass around the entire *Copper* office. No, tomorrow I will read through it again, edit it, polish it. Then I'll submit it for publication consideration. It will be its own feature in *Copper*, if I'm lucky. I don't know if Chantelle will approve it, but I don't care.

What if, right? And why the hell not?

Twelve

A Letter to My Twentysomething
Self, by Halley Brennan

To My Twentysomething Self,

Listen, girl. Plans are good to have, as are backup plans.
But I'm going to let you in on a little secret: make a
plan. In fact, make lots and lots of them. And then brace
yourself. Life has a mind of its own. It's going to knock
you on your ass, sock you in the arm, throw you for
one loop after another. There are few guarantees in life.
Think you'll be immune? Even the girl with the glittery
life—the important job, the dreamy husband, the stamp-
filled passport—even she will find her ever-prepared self
scratching her head, going, "I didn't see that coming."

Don't worry. It happens to the best of us. And the
worst. It happens to us all, and I'm here to tell you not
to be surprised when it happens to *you*.

There will come a day when you realize that stressing over a term paper at two a.m. in the college library was far from your low point. When you will realize that your best friends and your own sister, women with whom you practically share a brain, can harbor secrets and pain that you never saw coming . . . and won't be able to fix. When you will realize that the spark you felt when you first met your husband has faded. It will change. If you're lucky, it won't blow up in your face but just morph into a new kind of spark. One of those familiar, warm, fuzzy sparks—the kind you feel when you share a blanket and a bowl of popcorn, watching reruns of your favorite sitcoms, which, you will also realize, did not prepare you for real life as much as you may have thought. When you will realize that you're not as mature in arguments as you thought you'd be by thirty; that you're not processing problems and facing challenges as gracefully as you thought you could by thirty; that you're not quite that well prepared for the unexpected, because no contingency plan is *ever* enough for what life will dish out to you. When you will realize that if you haven't yet tackled *War and Peace* or learned how to play backgammon or mastered your grandmother's cookie recipe, you're probably still going to be waiting to tick off those boxes come your forties. When you will realize that there are also some things perhaps that are probably meant to be bucket list items forever. When you will realize that no magical cream will ever remove stretch marks, and that, yes, stretch marks will present themselves, even if you don't become a mother.

And since we're on the topic of motherhood, let me tell you that you may think you want a family, and you may think you have a life plan all figured out. You'll conceive your first child at twenty-eight, which gives you and the hubs plenty of time to build your careers, acquire a mortgage, put up a fence in the yard, lease a minivan. Baby two will come two to three years later, when you've got potty training with your firstborn down, and then once one is off to kindergarten perhaps it'll be time for the family dog, or at the very least a goldfish. Life, however, has other plans. Baby one comes earlier than expected, sending your entire plan—your life—into a tailspin. Or baby one doesn't come. You try and you try, and you find yourself waiting and wishing for something you slowly begin to believe may never happen.

Or you'll have met the perfect guy, if you're fortunate enough. (And trust me, you very well may not have at this point, so if you do, consider yourself a leg up on life. And if you haven't, do not despair. Life *will* throw something else your way.) So you and Mr. Perfect meet, and you mutually agree that it's you and he against the world, sans children. And then, out of nowhere, someone will change his or her mind. Someone will suddenly want a baby. It can happen. (Don't say I didn't warn you.) And if and when it does, you need to pull out this letter and remember that life does not care what you have planned for it. You're responsible for only so much of what happens in it. You can make decisions and hope for the best, but don't be so shocked if you find the wind knocked out of you. If you find yourself asking, "What do I want out of life? What is my purpose?" If you find yourself wanting to rail against the world, even against the one you love most in it, because you feel the pressure to conform, to save your marriage. To do something that is not who you are or what you want, not even for the person to whom you've promised your heart and life.

The best thing I can tell you is to find a way to stay standing. Find a way to get up and fight back for what you value. Build another plan and prepare to have the rug pulled out from under you, again and again. But be true to you, whatever the hell that means.

Don't get all pessimistic, though. Contrary to how this letter may read, pessimism is not the answer. I believe the best dress for life is one woven out of . . . let's call it healthy realism, with a smattering of optimism and a can-do attitude! Trust me when I, a women's magazine contributor, say that full-on pessimism is not the new black. It's so last season and doesn't look good on any body type.

Realize, sweet Twentysomething, that men are predictable in that they will never fail to surprise you. Realize that love is a rainbow of colors, from the conditional to the unconditional. Realize that true friends are invaluable and kindness and humility never go out of style. Realize that life is filled with bridges, and you've just got to find your way from one side of them to the other. And lather, rinse, repeat.

Realize, darling, that you're strong and powerful and beautiful, and if you put your mind to it, you'll figure out most things. Keep on planning, and keep on preparing, because expectations and hope keep us going. And from time to time, well-laid plans do pay off, because the hand of Murphy's Law—which states that anything that can go wrong will go wrong—can only stretch so far, so often. When it does, though, remember that thirty will be just as fabulous as you expect. *And*, to your great dismay, it will also be *un*fabulous in ways you could never expect.

But through it all, know that you will be all right. If you find you. If you be you. If you do you. It'll all be all right. In the words of Ms. Charlotte Brontë, "I try to avoid looking forward or backward, and try to keep looking upward."

Keep looking upward . . .

XO love,

Your Thirtysomething Self

P.S.: Even though the damn cream does little to thwart the stretch marks, don't discontinue its use. Perhaps liberal use in your twenties slows the progress of the inevitable dastardly little lines. It's worth the hassle and expense.

Thirteen

Like kismet, or maybe because I gave life a little of the old one-two, Chantelle and the entire editorial staff love my letter. They said, and I quote, "We love how raw it is." It'll make it into *Copper*'s next issue, gracing newsstands Thanksgiving week. I'm ecstatic—so ecstatic that I nearly do what I've always done with good news from work. I almost e-mail Adam a copy of the letter, with a note sharing the thrilling publication news. I then decide that his seeing my piece as an actual feature, in print, will have a stronger impact. On a page in a glossy mag, it'll say, "Halley's done it! Halley's written something that matters, something she's passionate about, something real." Adam'll be proud, and he'll tell me he knew all along I could do it if I put my mind to it.

The upcoming issue date reminds me that Thanksgiving is nearing, and that means so, too, is my next big step in solving the mystery that is my marriage.

When Charlotte called over the weekend about Thanksgiving, I asked how she was doing overall. She's clearly got heavier things on her mind than dinner, and a lot to say, but it's all so overwhelming at the moment. She told me she'd decided to wait to tell Marco about the affair until after Thanksgiving. So the family can enjoy the holiday and, as she said, "Hopefully get to repair some of the damage before Saint Nick comes round."

I know it's eating her alive. She isn't her usual chatty and chipper self. Even in the face of exhaustion, she dons the Super Mom cape and tries to wear the mask of doting wife. She'd argue she hasn't been herself in a long while. And I could make that argument, too. She's more subdued these days, even more so than when she was directly under the cloud of remorse, when she bared her dark secret to me.

Charlotte told me that she keeps her chin up, and she tries not to set Marco off, have him wondering if something's wrong. She drives Alice and George to and from school. Leah is in tow when she's running errands. She tidies the house and prepares the dinner. She does it all without complaint, all by rote. She makes sure Marco's dress shirts are back from the cleaner's well before he needs them, and when he asks if she's okay with him going golfing on Saturday, she says of course and breaks out the Play-Doh and the goldfish snacks, and even manages to call me for a few minutes, from the temporary silence of her closet. It's business as usual so as to keep the familial peace.

I know the holiday will be a big breath of fresh air for Charlotte, and not just because she'll have a full and joyful home, with plenty of distractions from the routines of everyday life. Also because that'll mean she's on the cusp of a solution. Or, at the very least, a day away from a confession that's eating her from within and pleading to be released. Hopefully, in her moment of truth, in her naked honesty, she'll find that solution. She'll be able to let the weight lift from her tired shoulders, though only to be replaced by another sort of weight, I'm sure. This won't be easy on her marriage, and I hope to god that she and Marco have the strength to endure and overcome. Because if there's something I've learned from my separation from Adam, it's that love requires a hell of a lot of strength. Falling in love is the easy part; staying in it is so much harder.

Every now and then, usually right before I fall asleep, I find myself asking if staying in love *should* be so hard. If it's true and requited and real, should it really be so difficult to keep? Then again, maybe true love, maybe requited love, maybe real love is the kind of love that should be so hard. After all, if it isn't hard, it isn't worth doing, right? Or does that not apply to something so unquantifiable as love?

A crisp, shiny new copy of the latest issue of *Copper* rests carefully in my canvas tote. "A Letter to my Twentysomething Self" by Halley Brennan is on page thirty-one. Adam's name is on the cover, by way of a Barbie-pink Post-it.

Tomorrow is Thanksgiving, and that gives the city of Pasadena the chance to shut down by midafternoon on Wednesday. Everyone rushes to exit the office so the turkey can be stuffed. Men swing by the grocery store for the forgotten potatoes; women make a mad dash for the last of the frozen piecrusts. The festive four-day weekend is upon us, and I'm kicking off the holiday by clocking out at two with the rest of my comrades. I'm in my car, making my way not to Whole Foods but to Adam's. The wine and chips have been bought, as well as the organic pumpkin pie Marian asked me to pick up for her—her contribution to the Kroeber family Thanksgiving dinner she'll be headed to tomorrow afternoon. Today I give myself permission to share with Adam something I've been itching to share for weeks.

I contemplated giving a copy of the magazine to him during our lunch on Monday, endless stacks of the new issue of *Copper* piled about in the office, one all ready and waiting for me to share with my husband. I chose to wait, though, until I can slip it surreptitiously into his—our—mailbox. Right before Thanksgiving, when I know he'll have time over the long weekend to get around to it when he wants. I don't want to hand it to him in person, over lunch, where I'd run the risk he'd pry it open right there and read it in front of me. Naturally I want to share with him something I'm proud of, and I know with all my being that he, too, will be proud. But what will he think of the actual letter? It is personal, direct, and yes, raw. It's filled with things I've never actually shared with him, or anyone. Things I, as the title clearly states, wish I'd known a long time ago. And it is nothing if not honest.

Adam's and my occasional lunches have gone smoothly, even the first lunch after we slept together. It took nearly two weeks for either of us to initiate that postcoital lunch, but it was like every other meeting we've had since we've been separated when there wasn't any baby talk. When we kept talk simple and didn't touch on the serious. I don't want to spoil the good run we have going, especially before the holidays. Before we'll see each other, on that vague date of "after Thanksgiving," to discuss where our marriage is headed.

Right now seems the best time to share my magazine news, so with an "Adam, Have a great holiday. XO Halley" scrawled on the Post-it stuck to the magazine's cover, I lift the metal flap of our mailbox. I briefly considered hand delivering it—knocking on the door and waiting no more than twenty seconds for Adam to answer. I'd give a casual happy-holiday greeting, tell him to say hi to Nina and the family, and let him know that there was something on page thirty-one he might want to check out. And off I'd go.

Adam's car isn't in the driveway, though. He's most likely one of the busy guys at the office who won't be calling it a holiday until tomorrow morning.

When I watch the last corner of the magazine slip from view and drop to the bottom of the mailbox, I'm hit by a curious package of emotions. Some odd mixture of pride, anxiety, excitement, and wonder. It is now, in the shaded corridor of the condo complex I haven't officially called home in more than two months, that I realize this is the first time since I can remember in our separation that I've stood here, in our residence, and felt a sense of contentment. It's strange, given that my cocktail of emotions includes some anxiety. I chalk it up to gathering the courage to write something that I probably should have written a long time ago—something that gives me a sense of accomplishment, despite its being only one small feature. It's something Adam will be happy to see that I've done. Maybe, even, it's something that will bring Adam and me together. Something that will bring us to a resolution. To a better place.

One can hope.

A couple of hours after I get home, Marian arrives, and we decide to slip into our running shoes and pound some pavement. Preparation for the caloric overload we'll suffer tomorrow.

Our pace is mild—more ten-minute mile than my usual seven or eight, which allows for steady conversation, even a few laughs. Marian and I cross the railroad tracks and make our way toward a stretch of road less congested by traffic and pedestrians. The winds that started off as a gentle breeze in the morning and have become gustier hour after hour are notably stronger now, in the late afternoon, proving a challenge, as our course is now head-on into what is shaping up to be a Santa Ana.

"So I didn't get a chance to tell you what happened yesterday," Marian says loudly.

"Your Christmas bonus came early," I guess, thinking of the plethora of carrier bags I saw on the dining room table this morning.

"It did, actually."

"I saw you did some damage with it already."

"Don't you know it."

Marian points to the left, suggesting we make a turn on Marengo. Eager to no longer run into the wind, I take the lead and turn.

"That's not what I'm talking about, though," she says. "I went to the firehouse again. Finally."

"Omigod. And?"

Marian's bleach-blonde ponytail swishes wildly in the wind, in step with the slowly increasing pace of her run. I kick up my pace to stay alongside her. I can see that the mention of Cole is getting her blood pumping harder; perhaps even an adrenaline rush has begun to course through her body.

"I promise, it's the last time I'll go as a chicken," she says.

"You didn't talk to him?" I ask, bewildered.

Brow wrinkled in embarrassment and what I assume is regret, she whines out a no.

"Marian," I scold. "This stalker business is no good."

"Says the girl who drops off mail in her own mailbox instead of actually seeing her husband."

"That's not the same." Similar, yes. But not the same.

"I *do* want to talk to him," she says.

"Sitting in your car and staring at him will definitely accomplish that."

"I've only 'stalked'"—she actually uses air quotes—"him twice, Hals. I really do want to talk to him. So badly. I'm insanely nervous."

"I get that."

"Look, third time's a charm. I'm taking a page out of the Halley-and-Adam playbook and doing this whole 'after Thanksgiving' thing." Marian pauses to catch her breath. Our pace abruptly settles back to that of a more comfortable ten-minute mile. "I just don't know how to say what I need to."

Thanksgiving dinner is delicious and plentiful. Charlotte pulls out all the stops, and Marco spends much of the early afternoon tending to the final smoking hours of the twenty-four-pound turkey that takes a spot beside Charlotte's honey-glazed ham. Thanksgiving at a beach resort never looked this delicious.

I slip through the closing gap between a dashing George and a hot-on-his-heels Alice, engaged in a spirited game of chase, and join Charlotte in the kitchen.

"I'm faster than you!" George screams, vanishing down the hallway.

"Kids, chase is an outdoors game," Charlotte calls out, not the least bit threatening with her high-pitched voice. She looks to me, a whisk in hand, and gives a defeatist sigh. "Right about now, you're wishing you and Adam were on some tropical island," she says with a laugh, returning to her mixing.

"Oh, Charlotte," I say dismissively, plucking a carrot from the relish tray.

"Mom knows, by the way," she quickly adds at her surface mention of the separation.

"I figured as much," I say at the confirmation that the separation is common knowledge now. Adam isn't here with me today—obvious cause for Mom's alarm bells. Since no one questioned my apparent singleness when I walked through the door, not even my outspoken mother, I figured the cat was out of the bag.

"Mom knows what?" My mother's voice startles both Charlotte and me, coming from nowhere.

I give my sister a stiff glance, then turn to face my mother and say, "About Adam and me."

A nearly finished martini in one hand, one brow raised high in inquisitiveness, lacquered lips pursed, my mother says in even tones, "Yes. I heard about that." She gives a pointed look to Charlotte. "Not, of course, without having to play detective. Honestly, Halley, why you keep something so momentous from your own mother I'll never—"

Charlotte cuts in with, "And detective you played very well, Mom. She asked me point-blank, Hals."

"It's okay. It isn't exactly a secret." I shrug. There's no need for Charlotte to feel she owes me an explanation for why she directly answered a direct question. I'd do the same.

My mother drains the remains of her drink. "Well, I'm very disappointed."

"Everything's fine, Mom," I brush off.

"Halley, I'm not going to make this day all about you," she says, and I look back at Charlotte in curiosity. My sister just shakes her head, whipping her mixture even harder. "Because today is a family holiday, and while I know you haven't exactly *had* one of these in a while, always bolting out of town with Ad—"

"Mom," I cut her off. "You're already making this more about me than I think you intended."

"I just wanted to say that I think you and Adam are making a terrible mistake."

The way she says *terrible* makes me cringe, makes me want to knock back a martini of my own.

"Thanks for your input, Mom," I say.

"I consider my divorce my greatest failure, Halley."

"Not your daughters?" Charlotte says under her breath. I have to suppress a laugh.

Mom tilts her head to the side and looks over my shoulder to Charlotte. "What, Charlotte?"

"Nothing."

Mom blinks rapidly in annoyance and carries on. "I'm not sorry about much in life. There's no point in running around being apologetic, now is there?"

Charlotte and I share a pointed glance.

"But I am sorry I had to go through that terrible divorce," Mom says. "Divorces are so . . . disruptive." She wrinkles her nose. "I'm only telling you that divorce is failure, and I don't want the same for you, Halley."

"I appreciate you not wanting me to fail," I say, oddly appreciative of and surprised by my mother's words. "But," I say, thinking on my father's, "I don't think divorce is necessarily a failure."

"So you *are* getting a divorce?"

"No," I groan. "I'm not saying anything definitive right now."

"Well, are you two back together?"

I did not want to undergo an inquisition at Thanksgiving, and certainly not with my mother, and in front of Charlotte, whose own marriage is precarious.

"Mom," I say through a tired sigh, "Adam and I have to do what's right for us. If that means a . . . divorce"—I swallow the bad taste in my mouth—"we'll have to work that out together. But don't see it as a failure."

"It is! It's a *complete* failure. You can bounce back, of course. I love Ray. He's the best thing that ever happened to me."

"Not your daughters," Charlotte quips nearly silently.

"Okay," I say, wanting to concede defeat and move on.

Charlotte senses the torpor in my voice and says, "Mom, how about we stop *actually* making the day about Halley and just have some fun. It's Thanksgiving, so let's stop the Stasi-like interrogation."

I can't help but laugh, and Mom only looks from Charlotte to me and back to Charlotte, mouth tight in disapproval. "I'm only trying to give a mother's advice," she says, stoic.

"I appreciate the effort," I say, knowing full well the bite behind the way I word this sentence. The effort is there. The rest leaves much to be desired.

"A failure," Mom can't help but whisper to me, eyes boring into mine, before she turns on her tall heels and returns to Ray's side on the love seat.

"She's wrong," Charlotte says to me.

I smile at my sister. "I know she is."

There is a small bit of truth to what our mother said, however. I already feel a sense of failure at the separation. No doubt I'd feel a greater sense of it with a divorce, if things came to that.

But Charlotte says exactly what I'm thinking, and it helps me digest my mother's harsh words and make sense of them. "You've never striven to please our mother before, Halley. Don't start now."

"Divorce hurts," I tell Charlotte, for her sake as much as, if not more than, mine. "And I'm sure it feels like failing, but it isn't the end. It doesn't have to define you or break you."

Tears fill the rims of Charlotte's eyes as she nods. "I know."

Fourteen

It's Saturday afternoon, and though I know Adam was busy at his family's on Thursday, and there's still the rest of the holiday weekend, I'm rather thunderstruck he hasn't contacted me. Surely he opened the mailbox when he got home on Wednesday, saw the magazine and the Post-it, and was planning on calling. Or at the very least texting. I suppose the wait is what I deserve for not hand delivering the mail, saying to his face, "Happy Thanksgiving. Oh, and read this."

Or maybe Adam has read my letter and he hates it. And now he's furious with me. The letter isn't exactly roses and rainbows about love and marriage, about the unexpected that life brings a woman. Just the same, it is something I want him to read. A bold move and career success I want to share with the man I love. And, yes, some intimate insight into where I am and how I'm feeling.

I'm starting the next chapter of the paperback Nina lent me, *Following Home*, when Charlotte calls. It's the other of the two calls I've been anticipating this weekend. I cross my fingers before answering. I hope all is as well as can be on the Miller front.

"Hey, Charlotte."

As feared, Charlotte blubbers out a hello.

"Oh, Charlotte."

"I told him," she wails. "Oh god!"

"You want me to come over?"

"No," she says with a heavy sniffle. "No, no."

"I'm sorry, Charlotte."

"Oh, it's just awful, Hals. Obviously! How could I imagine it'd be any other way?"

"Is he . . . there?" I ask tentatively. "Where are you?"

"I'm in my car."

"Where'd you go?"

"Nowhere. I'm in the driveway."

"And Marco?"

"In the house. With the kids," she replies before falling into another fit of crying.

"Where are you going, Charlotte?"

"Nowhere. I had to get out of the house, away from Marco. After I told him, he went for a drive. He was gone for hours."

"Oh dear."

"He came home a little while ago. Totally silent and cold. Stiff. I've never seen him like this. Oh, Halley, he hates me."

"Charlotte." I try to calm her down. "Charlotte, we knew this wasn't going to be easy, that you couldn't predict how he'd react to something . . . like this."

"He hasn't said a word since he came home. I told him I was going to be in the car. He just glared at me, like he could see straight through me. I don't know if he's in there now planning my murder or his escape."

"Do you want me to come over? Meet you somewhere?"

"No. No, I'll be okay. I have to figure this out." The sound of her blowing her nose rings through the receiver.

"I needed to talk, to let it out," she says. "To get out of there. I don't blame him, but I don't know what to do, Halley. When I told him, he was in denial at first. Wouldn't believe me. God, what torture it was, telling him over and again that it *was* true. When I said Damon's name, that's when Marco flipped. I kept telling him how sorry I am, that it's over with Damon, that it was the biggest mistake—a *true* failure in life, biggest ever—and that I want to fix us. I told Marco I love him still. Always have. There was all this shouting—we were in the backyard, away from the kids—and our neighbors officially know as much as Marco. Oh god, Halley. What a total mess!"

"I'm so sorry, Charlotte."

"I'm so embarrassed, so sickened by myself. It was awful." She blows her nose again. "I was *begging* him, Halley. Begging. And then he said he had to leave before he did something he regretted. *Regretted*, Halley! Like my murder!"

"Oh, Charlotte. Marco is not going to murder you."

"Hit me!"

"He would never hit you." Then I quickly add, "Would he? Has he?"

"Oh no," she says firmly. "Never. But god, isn't anything possible? I'm a cheating whore who deserves eternal damnation."

"Stop it, Charlotte."

"It's true!"

"No. What you did was wrong. This is a mess. A terrible mess, yes. But calling yourself a whore isn't going to do anyone any good. Come on," I encourage her. "When you're ready, maybe it's best to go back inside. Focus on the kids. But . . . let *Marco* be the first to talk. Let him process this." This is far graver than what Adam and I are going through, but I pause to consider my own horror at Adam's springing his baby wishes on me. I needed time to process that before I could attempt to react somewhat sanely.

She exhales a drawn-out sigh. "You're right."

"Be strong, sis. Fight for what you want. And call if you need *any*thing."

We hang up, and I cross my fingers once more and look up to the sky. I ask whoever may be out there listening that Charlotte and Marco find their way. This day has been coming, and it was never going to be an easy one.

"Halley!" Marian screams, startling me as I rub the towel over my wet head. "Halley!" Her voice has taken on a shrill trill. "Halley, Halley, Halley!"

"What?" I yank open my bathroom door. A giant pillow of steam bellows out, meeting a flustered, wide-eyed Marian head-on. She's wearing her loose-tank-and-boy-short-underwear pajamas, and her nose is covered in a dark-green exfoliating mask.

"Omigod, Hals!"

"What is going on?"

She jabs a finger behind her.

"Words, Marian. Words."

She swallows, eyes still wide with bewilderment, and gasps out, "Adam." She swallows again. "Adam. At the door."

I look down at my half-naked self, clad in a simple grey T-shirt bra and cotton panties. Much like Marian's attire, this is a girl's Sunday best.

"At the door?" I say. "Seriously?"

I take a quick look at my reflection in the foggy mirror. My hair is wet, hanging in dark, heavy strands. My face, already quite oval, just looks more drawn down when my hair's in this state. I've had better moments.

"Did you let him in?" I ask.

Marian, still looking as if her panties are on fire, shoots upright in her stance. "Shit. I didn't." She turns around, about to dart to the door, when I grab her wrist.

"No, wait!" I blurt. "It's better if he waits outside." I pick up my pajamas from the floor. "Let me at least look presentable." I pull on my pajamas, considering them suitable-enough attire for going to the front door and seeing why Adam's here. After all, Marian answered the door half-naked and looking as if she were halfway through a spa treatment.

"Omigod, Halley." Marian's now wearing a wide grin. "I bet this is some big romantic gesture." She claps her hands together in delight and presses them, clasped, to her chest. "Omigod!"

I laugh. "Calm down there." I wrap a towel around my hair, turban-style, and slip past my overly jubilant roommate. "Don't jump to conclusions." A thought strikes me. "Hey! It could be Nina. In labor! Still a bit early, but . . .'"

"Okay, okay." Marian pushes me down the hall. "Jumping to conclusions here. Find out what your man's doing on our doorstep!"

"Adam." My voice is high and pleasantly inquisitive.

Adam's standing at the front door, both hands in his front jeans pockets. His thumbs are exposed, and his left one makes aimless, maybe nervous, circles. His dark-blue button-up pulls at all the right places, revealing that cut chest of his I can feel pressed against my cheek if I let myself get lost in reminiscence.

I don't have a chance to, though, because Marian's darted into the living room. She's hidden from Adam's view but is in my clear line of sight, distracting me as she stares on, an acrylic French nail in between her teeth, eyes still wide as ever. She's impossible.

"Halley," Adam says. I'm surprised by how taken aback I am by the sound of his voice. It's so warm and familiar—the perfect voice to say my name.

"What's up?" I try to stay casual. Try not to look as gobsmacked as I am that he's here.

Adam leans slightly forward, but his entire body, head included, is still outside the town house. He turns his head to the left and the right and asks in a low voice, "Now a good time?" He's clearly wondering if Marian's anywhere within earshot.

I shrug one shoulder, self-consciously crossing my arms over my stomach. I don't know why I feel vulnerable and exposed. This is my husband, and it's not as if I'm naked. I'm in my pajamas. And even if I were naked, this is *my husband*.

Nevertheless I say, "Sure. What's up? Nina okay?"

"Yeah, Nina's great. Says hi. Missed you. For Thanksgiving."

"Yeah . . ."

Adam clears his throat and casts his gaze to the floor before pulling from his back pocket a rolled-up magazine.

"Is this how you really feel?" He looks into my eyes, the issue of *Copper* held up for me to view. The Post-it is still on it, and I'm hit with a wave of nostalgia for the way things were. When Post-its were given. And they were given a lot, but never like this.

"Yes." I hug my arms tighter to my stomach.

Looking at me, he gives a small, crooked smile, and says, "Want to go for a walk?"

"I'm not exactly dressed for a walk."

"I'll wait downstairs." He rolls the magazine back up and claps it against an open palm.

"Yeah," I say in a flurry of confusion. "Okay. Just a sec."

He turns on his heel and, just before descending the stairs, calls out, "Hi, Marian."

Marian giggles like a schoolgirl and immediately rushes down the hall, following me into my bedroom.

"Omigod," she squeals as I quickly change into a black V-neck tee and my loose-fitting light-wash jeans with the holes in the knees. "This *is* his grand romantic gesture, huh? Sweeping you off your feet? Saying he was all wrong, that he doesn't want a stupid baby. That all he wants is you. You, his wife, his soul mate!" Those clasped hands go back to her heart, and she bats her lashes.

"You're insufferable, Marian," I say with a laugh. "I love you, but insufferable. Really." I tie my mess of wet hair up into a high bun and slip into one of my many pairs of Old Navy flip-flops.

"This is it, isn't it?"

"This is what?" I tuck my keys into my back pocket and head down the hall.

"Your 'after Thanksgiving' meeting? Your time to decide?"

I stop and give the assumption some thought. "Yeah," I say with a small smile. My smile then begins to grow, warming my cheeks as they tighten in what is now a full-on grin. "Yeah, I think it might be."

"And? Are you ready?"

Bottom lip bitten, hands in my back pockets, I nod aggressively. "I think I've been ready for a long time, Marian."

"You haven't changed your mind, huh?"

"No," I say without any hesitancy. "I've always wanted one thing and only one thing."

Marian looks toward the front door, left open wide by Adam's arrival. She sighs and looks back to me. "And that one thing's waiting for you."

"The question now isn't if I've changed my mind," I say, my smile instantly fading as my mind spins with possibilities, "but has he?"

I meet Adam at the foot of the stairs. He's still got the magazine, rolled up, in his hand. There isn't any hesitation when, as soon as I plant both feet on the concrete path at the base of the stairs, Adam extends his free hand and his fingers graze my palm.

Holding my hand, he smiles and says, "Let's walk."

I initiate the conversation, unable to stand the buildup, wait in the wake of his unexpected visit. "It's that 'after Thanksgiving' talk, isn't it?" I say.

His hand tightens around mine. "It is." He holds up the rolled magazine and says, "Your letter."

"My letter." I give a quirky, childish nod—two shoulders shrugged, lips pressed tightly together, a somewhat sheepish expression on my face.

"I'm really proud of you, Halley. You're a very talented writer. Always have been. It's clearly your passion."

"Thanks. It is."

"You know, you don't give yourself enough credit."

"What do you mean?"

"You should do more of this." He holds up the magazine. "Go after what you really want, write from the heart, follow your passion. This"—he gestures to the magazine—"this is good. It's . . . real."

"Thank you, Adam. That really means a lot." It's my turn to give his hand a squeeze.

"So, Thanksgiving, by the way, was not the same," he says, abruptly changing topics.

"Oh yeah?"

"Oh yeah. Not just because I drank beer and watched football instead of cave diving with exotic fish."

I laugh. "Tell me about it."

He pushes his aviators atop his head. "It wasn't the same," he says, looking at me, "because it was without you."

"Yeah."

Adam stops walking, and his grip on my hand tightens again. He faces me straight on, those strong shoulders of his broad and in perfect posture, the wrinkles around the corners of his eyes deepening as he speaks, as he smiles. "I love you, Halley. I miss the hell out of you."

"Oh, Adam, I love you, too." I can't help but squeeze his hand tighter in confirmation. "I miss the hell out of you, too."

"I want you back." He draws close. He tucks the magazine into his back pocket and swiftly yet gently moves his now-free hand to my lower back. His intimate touch sends a riveting sensation up my spine. I can feel goose bumps cover my upper arms, travel to my lower arms. "At any cost. I want you, Halley."

Both his hands are now firmly and longingly touching my lower back. I'm pressed up against his chest, my neck craned as I look into those deep chocolate-colored eyes of his.

It takes all the strength I can muster to whisper, "At *any* cost?" I bring my hands around his waist and tap the magazine in his pocket. "You read the *whole* letter, didn't you?" He nods. "The part about not wanting to be a parent? About wanting to rail against the world? Even against the one you love the most in the world, because you feel the unfair pressure to conform? To do something you wouldn't do for anyone, not even for the person you've given your heart to?"

As I say aloud the painfully honest words I've written and released for all of Los Angeles to read, I realize for the first time how truly frank they really are. And how painful they might have been for Adam to hear. The brutal honesty in them only adds to the already painful words, and now I have no idea what to say.

"I did, Halley. I read it all. And I'm standing here, telling you that I love you. That I don't want to lose you. I don't want to lose *us*."

I'm trying to wrap my mind around just what this means for *us*, for our marriage, for the reason we even wound up in this mess in the first place. Finding the courage to ask the question I hope to hear the honest answer to, I say, "So you changed your mind? About a baby?"

Adam doesn't answer, so I word it differently—directly—no room for nuance or misunderstanding.

"Do you still want a baby, Adam?"

It takes too long for him to answer. A swelling begins in my gut, and I can feel acid tingle on my taste buds.

"Adam?"

"I want you, Halley."

"I know that. And I want *you*. I want *only* you." I wrap my arms tighter around his waist. "That's enough for me. That's all I've ever wanted."

"And I want *you*."

"Adam, no." I stay determined. "Do you *still* want a baby? That's the question."

There's a long silence before he finally comes right out and says what I know, deep down, has been the answer since he first told me that the plans had changed. His answer is the same as on that night, on the drive home from Nina and Griffin's.

"I do," he says.

Tears spring forth without warning. Those two words that once meant eternal devotion and commitment are now wrought with pain and torture. They represent the pieces that are broken and cannot be put back together.

"But Halley, listen," Adam implores. He grips me firmly—encouragingly—around my forearms. "Listen, Halley. I want a baby still, yes. I can't help feeling that, just like you can't help thinking you still don't want one."

"Not think, *know*."

He rocks back on his heels and groans. "But I want what I have right now, Halley. I want *you*."

"So nothing's changed."

Gripping my arms even tighter, he says, "Yes! Things have."

"How?" I say loudly. "You can't have both. You can't have me *and* a baby, Adam. I have not changed my mind, and I never will. I'm sorry. I can't. I just can't."

"Never say never," he says with a light roll of the eyes.

"Adam, no."

"Halley, hear me out."

"I haven't changed my mind, and clearly neither have you, so we're back at square one. What the hell was the point of being separated?"

"We both know two pots about to boil over under one roof wasn't going to solve this."

"And evidently being apart didn't do much good, either," I say bitterly. "What are we doing, Adam? Seriously?" I wave a hand between us. "What the hell are we doing here?"

Adam steps toward me, the gap between us now closed. He moves one hand to my hip. "Things have changed," he says softly.

"*How?*"

"I'm willing to look past my wanting a child. Remember how I said I wanted you to consider having one? Well, I'm choosing now to consider not having one."

"Adam," I say, brow furrowed. "This is confusing and—"

"Halley, look. I want what I have now, with you." He cranes his head lower to meet my averted eyes, his grip on my arm now pleading. What was only seconds ago an encouraging hold is now desperate.

"I can move past wanting a baby," he says. "If you end up wanting one, then great, we'll have one!"

"Adam—"

"If you don't, then . . . we don't. But we'll have each other. That's what matters, isn't it?"

"Can you honestly stand here right now and tell me that you want to have a baby? Never mind how I feel. Can you tell me that you want to become a father someday?"

He nods before saying, "Yes."

"But that you'll put that aside in order to be with me?"

"Selfless love, Hals."

I step back from his hold and grip my head in confusion. "Adam, this is . . . a love that's conditional. It shouldn't be like this."

"No, Halley. The only *condition* is that I have to learn to settle with the very real possibility—*likelihood*—that I won't be a father. But I love you. I want you." He gently pulls me close. Bringing his lips nearer mine, he whispers, "I've had a lot of time to think this through, Halley. If you'll have me, I want to go back to the way things were."

It's all I've ever wanted, to have what we once had. To go back to the way we were.

So why, as Adam holds me against his chest, as his lips come to meet mine and taste me, dance with me, shower me with the love we share for one another, do I feel as if we can't go back? As if there is no having what we once had because nothing has truly changed? Or because everything has?

Adam still wants a child, only he is now willing to suppress his paternal urge—*settle!*—out of some selfless love for his wife.

And his wife? She's the woman who gets what she wants at the expense of her husband's wishes. Of his fulfilled life, his joy, his happiness. So it is Adam's choice to choose the two of us over a family of three, but why doesn't it feel right? Why doesn't it feel like enough?

"Adam," I say, pulling back from the kiss.

"No, Halley." His tone, his eyes, his embrace are pleading. "You win."

"I . . . *win?*"

"Yes. We don't have to have a baby. You don't want one."

"And you still do!" I can't help but point this out, again and again.

"You and me, Halley." His voice is unwavering. "*That's* what I want. Let's not lose us."

"Yeah," I say, looking down at the concrete under our feet. "That's what I want, too."

Adam lifts my chin. Our eyes lock. "I love you, Halley."

"I love you, Adam."

"Come home." His thumb runs along my lower lip. "Move back in. Before Christmas."

"Yeah?" I'm trying to digest all of this. Everything seems to be happening so fast, even though we've been separated for so long. It feels like an eternity. I should be leaping at his suggestion to move back home. I mean, this is what I want! I wanted Adam back. I wanted to be just us again. I wanted him to concede having a baby.

Concede. The word is foul, like *I do.* Like *separated* and *baby* and *settle* and . . . *divorce.* Like *You win.*

I shouldn't win anything. Marriage is full of compromises, yes, but winning? Conceding? This is a marriage, a true love. There aren't sides to take or victories to be had or games to concede.

Despite the storm swirling inside my stomach and the heavy cloud that still seems to be hanging above our heads, even on this arbitrary date sandwiched between holidays when we've evidently reached our happy solution, I look into my husband's eyes and I acknowledge that the man I want to spend the rest of my life with is right here, before me, declaring his love for me, wanting what I want. So he wants a little more, and something I won't give; he wants *me.* And I want *him.* Isn't that enough? Isn't that all that really matters when it comes to a real and lasting love?

"Before Christmas," I agree, although rather absentmindedly. I expected to feel a greater sense of satisfaction at this conclusion. I suppose it's the sudden nature of its arrival and the discomfiting idea of winning and conceding that throw me off. I let a small smile form on my lips. Adam is grinning from ear to ear.

"Say . . . tomorrow?" Adam suggests.

"Tomorrow?" I ask in surprise.

"I want you back home yesterday. But you take whatever time you need to pack up and come home." He kisses my forehead. "I'll be there, waiting." His hand finds mine and we begin our walk back to the town house.

After a few steps, I say, "How's next Saturday sound?"

His face lights up. "Next Saturday sounds perfect."

And just like that, the date is set.

"Girl, this is *great* news!" Marian says. "He wants to make it work. You guys are getting back together. Oh, I'm so happy for you!"

I immediately curb her enthusiasm by telling her how Adam still wants a baby but that he'll let it go and we'll make it work.

"You *can* make it work, Hals," Marian insists. In an effort to assuage any worries, she pitches her classic worst-case-scenario speech. "Okay, Hals, what's the worst that could happen?" she says.

"The worst?"

"Yeah, the total worst."

Before I can answer, she does for me. "Worst-case scenario is you and Adam get back together and years later, or whatever, he decides, after all, he can't suppress his fatherly feelings anymore. He just *has* to have a baby." She presses a palm to her heart, for dramatics. "You guys agree to disagree and move along your own ways. You decide on an amicable split, and that's it. You did the best you could, and you move on."

"Yeah, that'd be the worst," I soberly agree.

"*Or*, you get back together now, work things through, rekindle that spark, and this baby thing never comes up again. He realizes his silly paternal desire wasn't as great as he thought. Happily. Ever. After." She smacks my thigh.

"You're right." I let my wet bun come undone and shake my hair about.

"Attagirl!"

"Adam's come to his senses," I say. "I mean, he could have said he doesn't want a baby after all, but—"

"Tiny, surmountable details," Marian brushes off.

"You should have seen him," I say dreamily, thinking of Adam's face close to mine only minutes ago—his inviting smile, telling eyes, soft lips. "I don't doubt he loves the hell out of me."

"I don't, either, Hals. Never have."

"And I love him more than anything."

"It's written all over this pretty little face." She draws a finger in the air about my face.

"This is right," I say in a convincing tone. "This is."

"You bet it is."

"We're getting back together." My voice rises in pitch toward the end of my sentence, delight at our resolution beginning to bubble forth.

"Hell yes, you are!" Marian rubs her hands together and gets a devilish grin on her face.

"What?"

"So, when do we get your stuff packed and back home?"

"Are you kicking me out?" I say with a laugh. "I actually thought I'd stay here for the week and move in over the weekend?"

Marian seems surprised. "Stay as long as you like," she says. "If you want my opinion, though," she adds with a sly look, "I'd run into that man's arms."

"The goal's before Christmas," I assure her. "Saturday's the plan."

She squeals, then says, "I'm a bit bolstered by your happily ever after."

"Oh?"

She nods, lips pursed. "I need to try to get one for myself. I think someone's paying a certain firehouse a little visit soon."

"Seriously?"

In theory, it seems like something Marian would do—finally confront Cole after all this time. But I can't picture it, because I cannot, for the life of me, imagine how it will all go down. What will she say? What will he say? Will there be tears? Oh, there will have to be tears. *And* shouting. But can they forgive? Can they move on?

"I'm doing it, Halley," Marian says with pride and insistence. "I've waited long enough. We all need our happily ever after somehow, someday."

Fifteen

It's been days since I've heard from Charlotte. Sometimes no news is good news, although in situations like these, and when one's got a creative mind that won't quit, it's not entirely out of the realm of possibility that no news means very bad news. I could never imagine Marco taking his anger out on Charlotte in a violent way, but this crazy year's taught me that Murphy's Law is a thing, and anything is possible.

So I decide our silence has gone on long enough, and I've given Charlotte enough space. I send her a quick text. Everything okay, sis?

Her response comes only a couple of minutes later. Surprisingly yes. Call you tonight?

Absolutely, I type back.

I don't let the phone ring more than once when I see Charlotte's name pop up hours later. I cheerfully answer the call. "Hey! How are you doing?"

"I'm alive."

"That's important. And Marco?"

"Also alive."

"Also important."

I'm relieved at the lack of the crying that I had expected to hear, as during our last call.

"So, how do things look?" I get right to it.

"We went a solid forty-eight-plus hours not talking," she says, her tone regretful.

"Oh, Charlotte."

"He's been sleeping in the guest room, using the guest bath. We have dinner together. For the kids. Basically there's been as little contact with each other as possible. But the moratorium lifted after two days."

"Oh?"

"Before I crawled into bed, by myself, Marco was in the room. And no, he didn't have a knife or a golf club."

"Okay," I say with a laugh.

"He didn't say much. He was reserved—still a bit icy but not frigid. He said he didn't want to lose me."

"Omigod, Charlotte. That's good!" I breathe in grand relief.

"But that he's really angry with me. Unbelievably angry."

"Understandable."

"He says he wants to go to therapy. To try counseling. To work through this." At long last she begins to cry, but her gentle sobs and lack of moaning, and the turn of events itself, tell me they're tears of joy, relief, hope. "He said he wants to work to save our marriage."

"I'm so happy for you, Charlotte. That's wonderful news."

"It is. We've still got so much to work through. This is a start, though. This is just what I want. What we *need.*"

"Exactly."

"I love Marco so much. So incredibly much. I've just . . . lost my way." She inhales deeply, a high note of exhausted relief pealing over the line. "We need counseling. We need help. We're finally going to get it, and I think we can work through this."

"Of course you guys can."

"Well, I need to get going," she says at the sound of her kids in the background. "I wanted to let you know things are working out, slowly, one step at a time."

"I'm so glad."

"Yeah," she says in a small voice. "We're still not talking much, and we're still in separate beds, but we're under one roof."

"Isn't that half the battle?"

As the idiom goes, when it rains it pours, and my oh my does it pour on Thursday night. What is supposed to be the night I settle in with a bath and the final chapters of Nina's book turns out to be a scene from *Sweeney Todd*. That's an exaggeration, but blood may as well be flowing.

"I can't believe it! I can't believe it!" Marian screams. She's got her hands fiercely clapped to the sides of her head, her acrylics boring into her scalp. She messes her hair while screaming, "I'm an idiot! Idiot, idiot, *idiot*!"

"Marian." I try to soothe her, but it's no use. She's run amok, charging up and down the hall . . . into my bedroom, into hers . . . through the living room . . . briefly stepping onto the balcony, then back into the living room, all the while shouting obscenities and insults at her own expense.

"Marian," I try again. My low voice drowns in the reverberations of her tirade.

"I can't believe what I've done. I've ruined everything! I'm such a fool." Her hair a complete bleached rat's nest, her cheeks tear soaked and stained black with running mascara, Marian plunks her shaking body onto the hardwood floor. "Everything bad has just become a million times worse!"

It takes what feels like forever to get her to stop shouting, to quit pulling her hair and pounding her fists on the floor, to suppress the tears for at least the length of one breath.

"Marian," I say in a cautious tone. I'm sitting with her on the cold floor, pushing her long matted hair away from her face.

It doesn't take a genius to realize that Marian's wild outburst has Cole written all over it. I knew she'd been planning to finally step out of her car and actually approach Cole. I wasn't sure when, but when she stormed through the door a couple of minutes ago, like a bloodthirsty maniac ready to attack, I had my answer. I'd had a horrible suspicion this approaching-Cole thing wouldn't go down so well. However, I hadn't quite imagined the deafening rampage. I'd hoped it'd be more like Charlotte and Marco's recent episode, even mine and Adam's. More forgiveness and fewer mascara-stained cheeks.

At long last, with Marian at the most vulnerable I've ever seen her, curled up in a fetal position in my arms on the floor, she explains what happened.

"After work," she says, "I drove to the firehouse and waited a couple of minutes in my car to see if Cole was there. There were a few guys out in the drive and in the garage, but none was Cole." She swallows. "The longer I waited there, the longer I started to doubt my intentions. I probably should have taken that as a sign to get the hell out of there." She sighs with obvious regret.

"I was just about ready to go back home, deciding I don't have what it takes to tell Cole how I really feel, when, as if on cue, he appeared."

"Yeah?" I say, curiosity thick in my voice.

"My heart raced." Her eyes grow wide. "And I was filled with crazy optimism. Like . . . like I *knew*." She presses her palm to her chest. "I *knew* in my heart of hearts that I was *supposed* to see him. I can't explain it. It was a heart or a soul thing."

Her words bring to mind Adam's similar words when he first explained to me that he wanted a child. There are some things you can't explain—matters of the heart. Deep and true matters that stir your soul and drive you to do things that are equally unexplainable.

"It was the strangest thing, but all my fear just flew out that car door as soon as I opened it," Marian explains. "As soon as I saw him. As I walked straight up to him." Goose bumps start to prickle my arms. "I tell you, Halley, as soon as our eyes met, I couldn't feel any part of my body." She exhales slowly, as if living the scene all over again and trying to gather the strength to do what she went there to do.

"It sounds corny, but as soon as I looked into Cole's eyes, I—I—I knew what I was doing was right. I knew it was dangerous and in some ways cruel. But it felt right." She pounds a fist on her chest. "It hurt, but it felt like *finally* I was being real. Being honest." She pushes her hair behind her ears and sits up out of her fetal position. "He was so beautiful, Hals. And he didn't run off or shut me down. He heard me out."

"That's good," I say in a peppy tone.

She tilts her head to one side and raises a brow. "Just wait." She shakes her head as she continues. "God, I've never forgiven myself for hurting him, Hals. I really owed him an apology and an explanation, so I just kept telling myself that over and over. I had to follow through. And then he said my name, when he saw me, and I nearly lost it. The way he said it was kind of empty. Like he was shocked, yes. Angry, yes. Confused, definitely. A little glad, maybe? Anyway, I told him everything, right there, just spilling it all. I knew if I stopped I'd lose the stamina, the courage. Probably break down in tears."

At the mention of the word *tears* her eyes start to get watery. I embrace her, which gives her the push she needs to keep calm.

"I told him it was all my fault," she says, pulling back. "The running away, the being afraid, the lie about *only* feeling like friends. I told him I've realized after all this time that I was my truest happy when I was with him. No one's ever made me feel the way he has. He was my most real relationship." She looks down at her hands in her lap. "And I told him it wasn't just that way because I hadn't had many, if any, relationships that lasted longer than a few months. Like, he's the longest relationship so it must be the right one. *No.* I *love* Cole. I always have. If there is a one for me, Halley, it's him. It's only ever been him."

"I know, Marian." I tighten my hold around her. "He's got *it*."

"Exactly! Anyway," she says helplessly, beginning to pick at her nails. I lightly swat her hand. She'll only be upset with herself for damaging a fresh manicure fill. "I say all of this to him. And I say that I know this is entirely unfair to do to him, that he can hate me if he wants—which, obviously, I don't expect him to. God, right?" I nod.

"And I tell him the reason I'm there is because I want to tell him how I really feel, tell him the truth, after all this time. That I miss him and love him. And I made a *huge* mistake. That if there's any chance in hell he feels the same for me, don't we owe it to each other, and to ourselves, to give it a try? Like you said! We only get one shot at life, so . . . might as well see. Right?"

"Good. And?"

"And"—she bobs her head from side to side—"I asked him to forgive me. That above all, I was sorry. Even if he wanted nothing to do with me after all this, I had to tell him how sorry I was to run off, to hurt him like I did. Even though I'd apologized the day after I ran out on our wedding, it was just so rushed, and everything was so fresh, you know? I was in an awful place. I told him I was selfish with what I'd done then, and that maybe even now I was selfish springing this on him. I told him, though, that if he felt about me, today, the way I do, I'd hope he'd come and tell me."

"That's good, Marian. Good! And then what'd he say?"

"Well . . . since I was being honest . . . I told him about the pregnancy scare."

I suck in a breath. "And?"

"That was a shocker. Probably only added to his hating me."

"He doesn't hate you."

"Oh no, he does." She firmly presses her lips together, as if to quell the onslaught of tears. "He hates me."

"Marian—"

"After all this, after asking him if he doesn't want to see if there's something that can be had between us after all this time—even a friendship, you know?—then if anything I beg for his forgiveness. I hurt him, and I was hurting him some more, and I've never forgiven myself for it, because . . . he didn't have the chance to forgive me first."

"So . . . what happened? What'd he say then?" I almost don't want to ask.

She blinks away some tears and says, looking up at the ceiling, "Not much. But enough."

There's a long pause as Marian tries to compose herself. When she still doesn't say anything after a lengthy silence, she begins to grip the sides of her head again. She scratches her fingers in her hair.

"I'm *so* stupid! So, so, so *stupid*! I deserve this pain." She squeezes her eyes shut and violently shakes her head. "I deserve this rejection. This misery!"

"You're not stupid, Marian. And you don't deserve this."

"I've brought this upon myself. I deserve it, Hals. Deserve it all."

I rub her back in slow, soothing motions.

In a small and broken voice, she says, "It hurts so much I almost wish I could trade this in for the hurt of not knowing."

"You don't mean that."

"Halley, he told me he's single."

"Okay," I say in a drawn-out way, thinking this a peculiar thing to make note of.

"He said he dates, sure, but that he's never gotten married. He was engaged at one point and broke it off. Never married. You know why?" I shake my head. "He said after what happened with us, he's not sure he believes in marriage." She breaks down into a fit of tears. "Can you believe it?" Her words come out wet and mumbled against her palms. "He told me I hurt him more than he ever thought possible. And he said—"

"Yes?"

"He said he wished I wouldn't have come to see him. That all I was doing was hurting him all over again. Which I knew! I knew there was that chance. Oh, Halley, it hurts so much."

Rubbing her back and rocking her in my arms, I say, "We'll work this out. The pain will eventually go away."

"No, it won't," she says. "It may lessen, but it'll never go away entirely. I lost my forever, Halley. I'm glad I was honest with him and that I gave our what-if a chance, but that chance is lost and gone forever. I waited too long, and now it's all ruined."

"Marian?" I say after some time sitting and rocking in silence.

"Hmm?" She sounds sleepy. I look down at her face. Her eyes are closed, clumps of mascara and runny eyeliner all over them.

"You have your answer now. What you did was really brave," I say. "He may not have said what you were hoping to hear, but he listened, and he responded. That's something."

"It's something, but it's not enough."

"Maybe he needs some time?" I'm reaching here. "Like Adam and I've needed time."

"Oh god, I know this is so selfish, but you can't leave me now!" Marian cries at the realization that she'll be roommate-less soon.

"I'm not running anywhere just yet," I assure her.

"It's super selfish of me, but please, Halley, just . . . stay here a little bit longer."

"I'm here, Marian. Don't you worry about that." I smooth back her hair. "Maybe Cole needs a little time to process all this," I say, upbeat. "You've had a lot of time to think about approaching him. He didn't see this coming. For him, you were there, at the firehouse, telling him all this, out of the blue. Honestly, it sounds like he handled it a lot better than most guys would."

"Of course he did. Cole's perfect."

"How about we turn on some *Friends* and let this one pass for the night?"

"Always sleeping on our troubles," she says with a resigned sigh.

"Better than sleeping with them, right?"

That gets her to laugh, and since she's Marian Kroeber and, god, I love her for it, she says, "Maybe sleeping with bad-boy trouble ain't such a bad idea right about now."

I laugh. "You sure you're prepared to settle down with Cole, one man, for the rest of your life?" She gives me a stern sideways look and I say, "Sorry, too soon."

"Not having Cole is why I don't want commitment, Hals. For me it's Cole—"

"Or no one," I finish, and she smiles and nods.

"I get that, Marian. I *completely* get that."

Time can be a magical healer of wounds. Though in the thick of it, when the wound is fresh and gaping and you're exposed and vulnerable, the last thing you want to hear is this silly feel-better adage, and you can't possibly imagine how you'll ever heal. In that moment the pain is too much to bear. The idea of healing is so inconceivable all you want to do is crawl into bed, draw the blinds, and wallow in pain, pity, and despair. Yet sure enough, days pass, and time begins to heal. Slowly.

Marian has been anyone but herself lately, although she's much closer today than she was a couple of nights ago, curled up in that vulnerable fetal position. I called Adam right away after the Marian-and-Cole blowup, letting him know that Marian really needed me now. I still planned on returning home before Christmas, but I didn't see the use in running out on my best friend when she needed me most. Not when Adam and I had already been apart for so long. What was a few more days?

The way he said "I love you" at the end of our call in only one way—the way it's meant to be said and heard between a husband and wife—reminded me that this is the right decision. Adam is my perfect other half. He's my partner, my love, the man I want to spend my life with. That's why when I return home next weekend I will accept the fact that in our separation we have decided on a compromise. And if that compromise is enough for Adam, the one who's making the sacrifice, it should sure as hell be enough for me.

With only a few weeks before Rylan's due date, I check in with Nina. She's in the homestretch and grateful to be on bed rest. I offer to drop by after work, but she insists she's in no condition to see anybody or do anything.

"I feel like I'm carrying two giant watermelons," Nina says over the phone. "I'm always too hot or too cold, and I've got to pee every five minutes. I don't even bother with makeup at this point. I just sweat it all off."

Despite her ticking off one miserable point after another, I find Nina's tone and exasperated sighs comical.

"I'm not kidding around," Nina says, laughing along with me. "Every pregnancy book I've read says the last few weeks are like this, and boy, are they right."

"Well, you're a trouper hanging in there."

"I can't even watch reruns of *The Office* anymore, because I almost pee myself from laughing so hard."

"Oh, Nina," I say, laughing so hard myself I'm nearly in tears.

"And I've seen every episode, like, a hundred times, so you'd think they'd get old. Nope. I just laugh. And then I pee."

"Nina, you're too much."

"It's just as well. I shouldn't be watching so much TV anyway. Probably rotting Rylan's mind before he's even here. I've been reading a ton."

"Hey! That reminds me. I finished the book you lent me," I say.

"And?"

"I really enjoyed it. Thanks for that." The novel came at an ideal time in life—a story of a woman trying to figure out her place in the world, her role in life, her purpose.

"And the ending?" Nina says.

In the end the protagonist returns home to rural Virginia to discover that it is not home. And neither are any of the countries and exotic lands she'd visited. Home is a global concept to her, and so she sets out for another vagabond-like adventure as soon as she arrives stateside.

"Didn't quite expect it, but I like how it wrapped up in a way of not wrapping up," I say.

I glance at my watch and note that I should be heading over to Charlotte's. She called earlier, lamenting that her babysitter had bailed at the last minute and her backup wasn't available. Before she could get a chance to ask, I said I'd be over to watch the kids. Today is Charlotte and Marco's first counseling session. On top of being nervous about their first session, Charlotte had to deal with finding a sitter with only hours to spare.

"Well, Nina, I'm on my way to Charlotte's now," I say. "Babysitting duty. You hang in there, okay? Only a little while more."

"You got it," she says cheerfully. "And hopefully I'll see you at the hospital soon."

"I'm sure Rylan will come early," I say in an effort to lift some of that weight off her. "Not too early," I add, "but when he's good and ready."

"Thanks, Halley. I'm glad you called. And I'm really glad you and Adam have worked things out."

"Me, too."

I arrive at Charlotte's within minutes of her and Marco needing to leave to make their appointment on time. As I make my hurried way to their front door I notice Marco behind the wheel of his idle car. His unexpected presence in the driveway causes me to do a double take. He gives me a brief glance, his face pinched. Unnerved, I give a weak wave and tight-lipped smile. He doesn't return the wave. Rather, his expression moves from tense to vacant before he turns his head and looks straight ahead at the closed garage, one hand coming up to grip the steering wheel.

As soon as I walk into the house, Charlotte gives me a quick rundown on who needs what to eat and when, and opens up the kitchen pantry door to point out the list of emergency phone numbers taped to its inside. I tell her I've got it handled and wish her good luck. (She's going to need all she can get, judging by Marco's expression.) Then she flies out the door, leaving me with Alice, George, and Leah, all of whom are pleasantly silent and entertained in their own ways. Alice, with her book, is seated solo in a beanbag in a corner of the living room. George, with his plastic cup of Cheerios, is methodically placing one piece of cereal on top of each of his Hot Wheels cars. Leah, with a sippy cup in her mouth and plush pink blanket draped over her tiny body, is slowly fading into sleep on the baby mattress Charlotte keeps in the living room for sporadic naps (or time-outs). At first glance the gig's not bad. But give me a few rowdy hours and I could very well be pulling my hair out.

As I cast about at my well-behaved and self-entertaining nieces and nephew, I realize I have the best job in the world when it comes to kids. The role of the aunt, even though it has included some diaper changing and has required me to administer discipline on rare occasion, is perfect. As an aunt you have such great love for the tiniest members of your family, and you get to spoil them with gifts, adventures, and giant auntie hugs, while skipping the tiresome day-in and day-out parental duties. You get the kids without the raising, without the round-the-clock responsibilities, without the motherhood. While this afternoon confirms for Charlotte and Marco that they are going to work on their marriage and save what they have, it confirms for me that I was always meant to be an aunt and never a mother. And there is nothing wrong with that. I am no less a woman, no less a person with a purpose.

"Auntie Halley?" Alice asks as she closes her book, carefully placing her colorful bookmark between the pages.

"Yes, Alice?" I temporarily stop gathering the Cheerios George has littered across the floor and sofa.

"Do you have a Christmas tree yet?"

Charlotte, who usually breaks out the Christmas decorations and makes sure the family room is sporting a Monterey pine at least twelve feet tall during Thanksgiving weekend, has only retrieved the boxes of decorations from the garage. Seven large plastic storage containers are stacked in the corner of the dining room, an immediate reminder that she has greater things on her mind than tinsel and stockings.

"No," I answer Alice with a smile. "Not yet."

"We don't have one, either." Alice's face goes long.

"I bet you will soon."

She shrugs and says, "I don't know. Mommy and Daddy seem kind of weird."

"Weird?" I'm immediately hyperaware of my words and tone. I know Charlotte and Marco have kept their children in the dark about their marital troubles. Up until now I assumed the kids, including oldest and wise-beyond-her-years Alice, were safe and sound in that dark space. I shouldn't be surprised by Alice's comment, though. I was always vigilant about my parents and their constant tension and fighting. I'm sure Charlotte and Marco have kept their arguments to a minimum and away from the children, but it'd only be a matter of time before the kids would begin to suspect something was off.

"What do you mean by weird?" I ask.

She shrugs again and says, "Mommy seems sad, and Daddy's really quiet."

"Hmmm," is the best I can come up with. This area definitely falls under motherly duties and not an aunt's.

"And we don't even have our Christmas tree yet," Alice sadly points out yet again. "It's weird."

"That is weird," I say, a bit aha-like with my tone. "I think if Mommy's sad and Daddy's quiet, it's probably because they haven't had time to pick out a Christmas tree yet."

"Or put up the decorations?" Alice's expression reads somewhat hopeful. I'm on the right track.

"Definitely. I bet once they find time in their busy schedules to get that tree and decorate for Santa, they'll be happy. They won't be quiet."

"Yeah." Alice nods repeatedly, smiling. "I think you're right, Auntie Halley."

"Hey," I say, alighting on an idea. "How about we look at your mommy and daddy's wedding album?"

If there's proof of a couple that is happy, proof that can easily win over a ten-year-old girl, it's her parents' wedding album. Alice enjoys looking through old photo albums with my father, and she's always jumping at the chance to show off her new school and soccer photos every year.

Seconds later Alice snuggles onto the sofa next to me, her long-eared stuffed bunny tucked under one arm. She helps me open the pearl-colored cover of Charlotte and Marco's wedding album. The first photo is a large black-and-white engagement shot of them, a profile kissing shot in a park. As soon as Alice sees it she coos and says, "Mommy and Daddy are kissing." Then she wrinkles her nose and begins to giggle.

"Like your Barbie and Ken," I say.

"Yeahhh."

We turn the pages, commenting on how beautiful Charlotte's gown is, how funny Marco looks with cake on his face, how happy her parents look dancing together. Alice is completely enthralled, and little George even runs over when we're halfway through to see what all the commotion is about. When Charlotte and Marco are embracing and kissing in one enlarged reception photo, George covers his eyes and begins laughing. He shouts, "Ew, kissing! Ew, kissing!" As he spins wildly about the living room, Alice telling him that it's good—"Mommy and Daddy love each other, George"—a waking Leah stirs.

As Leah's small moans turn into groans and then whimpers, I take a second to soak in the loving embrace and locked-eyed pose of Charlotte and Marco in one of their wedding photos. Both of them look unbelievably happy, smiling, holding each other close, Charlotte's newly ringed hand gripping the back of Marco's head, his forehead pressed to hers. It is, without any doubt, the happiest day of their lives. They're right where they belong.

Leah is now crying, and I tear my eyes from the photo and move to scoop her up in my arms. I bounce her on my hip to soothe her and watch Alice carry on with the photo album without me. She's as awed by her parents' beautiful wedding album—that romantic and happy photo—as I am. Her grin doesn't leave her face as she pages through the entire album. The activity has the distracting and uplifting effect I'd hoped.

I can't help but notice, though, that I haven't seen Charlotte and Marco look at each other like that in a long time. Not even half that happy, half that consumed by each other. As Leah's tears dry and she becomes fascinated by my necklace, I catch myself hoping that Charlotte and Marco will find their happily ever after again. And that I can find mine with Adam, too. As Marian said, don't we all deserve one? Someday, somehow?

When Charlotte and Marco return home, all three kids go crazy. George clings to Marco's legs, Alice vies for her mother's attention, and Leah jumps up and down on her haunches, waiting for someone to pick her up.

Marco, whose face is fortunately no longer pinched or glazed over, asks me in low, even tones, "Were they well behaved?"

"A-pluses all around," I say cheerily.

Marco's eyes meet mine for the first time since he and Charlotte returned. "Good," he says. For only half a second does the corner of his mouth twitch upward, as if about to make the smallest of gracious smiles. "I'm glad to hear. Thank you, Halley."

"Absolutely."

Marco's eyes move to Charlotte when I ask, "So did you have a good time on your date?" *Date* being the code word for today's parental outing.

"It was really good," Charlotte says. She meets Marco's neutral gaze. He gives a nod and reply of, "Really good."

"That's great," I say, relieved. Relieved to hear the session went well, relieved to hear so from *both* of them, relieved to see that tension has been replaced by what I think the murmurings of reconciliation look like.

"Look, if you need me in a bind again—" I offer.

"Thanks, Hals," Charlotte says. "If we're in an absolute bind, yes, we'd love the help. But our sitter expects the same day, same time every week, so hopefully we won't have to bug you much."

"It doesn't bug me," I say, rubbing Alice's head. She looks up at me with a grin. "Every week?" I glance from Charlotte to Marco. I don't want to be nosy, but does that mean this is a good sign? That they've both decided to work through this?

"Once a week," Marco says.

"You and Mommy are going on dates every *week*?" Alice says dramatically.

Marco ruffles Alice's hair. "That's right," he says, his voice turning up in a friendly tone, as it often does when he's talking to his children.

"But what about us?" George whines.

Marco takes Leah from Charlotte's arms and says, "Mommy and Daddy's dates are good for all of us."

Charlotte gives me a small, hopeful smile. "Baby steps," she says under her breath.

Marco looks to his wife. He may not be smiling, but he is present in a way he wasn't earlier. Whatever happened behind closed doors, and maybe even in their alone time during the drive there and back, must have really done wonders. I'd hardly say Charlotte and Marco are a happily married unit, but I think they're well on their way.

"Mommy! Daddy!" George cries, stealing Marco's gaze from Charlotte. "When are we going to get our Christmas tree?"

"Yeah!" Alice chimes in. "And the decorations! You said after Turkey Day and it's *after* Turkey Day!"

I grab my sweater and purse and move to the front door.

"Thanks again, Halley," Charlotte says, touching my arm and giving me an optimistic look before I step out the door.

"What are sisters for?"

"Daddy! Mommy!" Alice and George howl in unison.

Charlotte turns to her impatient little ones and says, "You want a Christmas tree, huh?"

"Yeah!" they shout.

Charlotte looks to Marco as Marco says, "Then I think we better go get a Christmas tree."

"I think that's a great idea," I hear Charlotte say as I make my exit.

Sixteen

I squint at the screen of my vibrating cell phone. Its persistent and heavy vibrations have woken me from a dead sleep. The alarm clock reads half past five in the morning. I can't imagine who'd be calling at this hour. I squint some more, trying to make out the name on my phone. Unable to read it with sleepy eyes, I blindly answer the call.

"Halley!" the caller shouts.

"Yes? Who is this?"

"Nina went into labor."

"Griffin?"

"She's five centimeters dilated," Griffin says, clearly electrified by the news.

I shoot up in bed. "Oh my—"

"Rylan's coming a bit earlier than expected—three weeks—but the doctor has given a healthy thumbs-up. Nina is great. If we're lucky, we'll be popping open that champagne sometime today!"

"Oh my goodness!"

Griffin says there's a bet going on the hour Rylan will arrive. I ask if he'll share with me some of the wagers. He's going with ten in the morning—"It's aggressive," he adds, "but I'm just so ready to meet him!" Nina refuses to bet, and I assume that has something to do with her bouts of moaning and heavy breathing in the background. Griffin's parents both bet noon, his sister and brother both two o'clock, and Adam four.

I switch my phone to my other ear. "Is Adam there?"

"No," Griffin says. "We're actually asking everyone to hold off on visiting until Rylan's born. Give us a few hours, maybe even a day, depending on when he comes," he explains, adding that they are excited to have everyone meet their son, but they want to soak up the very newness of their firstborn and early moments of parenthood as just the two of them.

"Absolutely," I say. I couldn't imagine, if I were to ever go through labor—and that is obviously a hypothetical—that I'd want the whole world pouring into my room, seeing me at my most vulnerable, most exhausted, most uncomfortable. Besides, I've always thought it rather unfair that when a newborn arrives everyone showers the baby with adoration and attention, while the poor mother, who did all the work, plays second fiddle. Yes, a newborn is thrilling, but I can't think of what would put me into postpartum depression faster than that kind of a reception.

"I'll come over whenever you and Nina like," I say.

"Great." Griffin sounds hurried, for obvious reasons. "Oh, you want to bet?"

"I'm in." I consider Adam's four o'clock bet and decide to follow closely behind. "Put me down for five."

"This evening?"

"I sure hope so, for Nina's sake." God, the possibility of being in labor for twenty-four-plus hours!

Griffin says he'll contact me when Rylan's born, and then let me know when to head over for a visit. The anticipation of one of my best friends welcoming into the world the thing she's wanted for so long, more than anything else in life, is almost too much to bear. I can't imagine what Griffin and Nina must feel like. In my anxious anticipation I almost forget to apply mascara to my left lashes, and at work I accidentally trash two important e-mails instead of moving them to a folder.

Shortly after two o'clock, Griffin sends a text message complete with a photo of a tiny, swaddled, blue-beanie-capped Rylan. Rylan James Burke is here! Griffin's text reads. 6 lbs, 2 oz, 18 in. Mother and baby beautiful and healthy.

My heart swells as I read the announcement and gaze at the photo of my nephew. This is indeed a perfect day for Nina, for Griffin, for everyone who gets to be a part of this special little boy's life.

Griffin sends another text message shortly thereafter, letting me know I'm welcome to visit sometime tomorrow. In my excitement I call Adam before I respond.

"Hals, have you heard?" Adam blurts over the phone as soon as I say hello.

I laugh and say, "Yes! Rylan's here!"

"Omigod, Halley. It's incredible. This is so exciting! And isn't he adorable? He's so small!"

I laugh again and say, in a joshing tone, "Well, he is a baby, Adam."

"Omigod," Adam says, as if he hasn't heard me. "It's just, I'm so happy for them. I'm so excited to go and see him. Omigod, Hals." For a moment one might mistake Adam's exuberance for that of an expectant father's. The idea sends a pang to my heart, but then baby Rylan's face flashes into my mind, and I feel nothing but pure joy at the news.

"Hey, uh," I cut in. "You want to drive over to see him together tomorrow, maybe?"

"Damn." Adam's voice is thick with disappointment. "I can't get out of the office until after seven."

"Okay."

"But I can manage a lunch-break visit."

Because I don't want my visit rushed so Adam can return to his office on time, we agree we'll drive separately and meet at noon tomorrow. Ready, at long last, to meet our nephew and godson.

"Hey, Adam," I say before we hang up. "Congratulations."

"Adam!"

As soon as I spot my handsome husband walking toward the entrance of the BirthPlace in Westwood, where I've been eagerly awaiting his arrival, I let my excitement burst forth. I wave my hands overhead.

"Adam. Oh, I'm so excited to meet him!" I squeal, letting myself fall into Adam's welcoming, tight embrace.

"Have you met him yet?" Adam asks with a broad grin.

"Are you kidding? Meet him without you?"

"Come on." Adam takes my hand in his and leads the way inside, his smile never leaving his face. Not as we walk up to reception, nor as we swing by the gift shop to pick up a bouquet of white roses and a giant balloon of a stork delivering a blue-blanket-swaddled baby, and not as we walk down the lengthy corridor to Nina's room. His already massive grin even miraculously grows when he lays his eyes on his nephew for the first time.

"Nina," I whisper. Nina's sitting upright in bed, her hair sleekly brushed straight and tucked behind her ears. She looks both the happiest and the most exhausted I've ever seen her. "Congratulations!"

Nina holds her arms out and I carefully hug her. She rubs a hand across my back, and when I pull out of the embrace, tears are instantly streaming down her cheeks.

"Oh, the emotions," she mutters, fanning her flushed face. "They're all out of whack." She points to the end of her bed, where Griffin is standing proud and tall, the tiniest bundle of baby in his arms. "And every time I look at him and hold him I just get even more emotional."

Adam sets aside the gifts and kisses his sister's cheek. "Hey, sis. How are you doing?"

"Never better." Nina pulls a tissue from the box by her bed. "Best I've ever been."

"Congratulations, you two." Adam turns to Griffin, who's completely enamored with his son.

"Guys," Griffin says, gingerly adjusting a tightly swaddled Rylan in his arms. "Meet Rylan. Rylan, meet your uncle Adam and aunt Halley."

Adam moves toward Griffin, and I stride up to Adam's side. I loop my arm around his waist. Adam doesn't peel his eyes away from Rylan for a second.

"May I?" Adam asks.

"Absolutely." Griffin's about to place Rylan in Adam's arms when Nina clears her throat. "Oh, yeah." Griffin brings Rylan back toward his chest and motions with his head to Nina. "Disinfect time."

"Right," I say, remembering Charlotte's constant warnings to squirt some disinfectant on our hands before handling her newborns.

When Adam and I are prepared, Griffin carefully places Rylan into Adam's arms with the slow, extracautious motions of a brand-new father. Rylan doesn't stir. His eyes are shut tight, his lips so small—his mother's—his cheeks puffy, eyebrows dark. He is a beautiful and perfect mix of his parents. He's wearing the blue beanie he wore in the photo yesterday, and judging by his eyebrows, I bet he's already got a good amount of his father's gorgeous dark curly hair on his sweet head.

"He's beautiful," I say. I run the side of my index finger across his impossibly silken cheek. "Amazingly beautiful. Good work, guys."

Adam doesn't say anything. He just stares at his nephew, that broad grin of his ever present, pulling at his eyes in that wrinkled way it has. Adam seems almost mindful of his breath, as if he is concerned that his usual exhalations might wake the sleeping baby. His arms are strong, supporting and protecting Rylan, though his touch is gentle, just like his voice.

He quietly says, "Hi, Rylan. I'm your uncle Adam. We're going to have a lot of fun together." I tighten my hold around Adam's waist. "I'm going to teach you everything you could want to know about sketching." Adam speaks softly. "And your dad and I are going to play ball with you. And you're going to love the ocean. You're going to have a lot of adventures, little buddy."

I lightly touch a hand to Rylan's bundled body. "You're very loved, Rylan," I say to him in a whisper.

"Very, *very* loved," Adam repeats in earnest.

I cast a glance at Nina, and she's looking on in wonder and joy, much like Adam, like Griffin . . .

I watch as Adam holds Rylan against his broad chest. He gingerly shifts his weight from his left to his right, rocking and swaying in his stance. Like a natural.

"Halley?" Griffin asks. "Would you like to hold Rylan?"

Before I can formulate an answer, I find myself struck by the sheer beauty and perfection of this moment. I'm struck by the naturalness with which Adam holds Rylan. The beauty of Adam's genuine grin as he holds his nephew in his arms. The perfection of my husband holding a baby. I'm struck not only by the joy that fills me at this special moment but also by the immediate, unexpected, and overwhelming sadness that I feel. As Nina sheds tears out of joy and an abundance of emotion, my eyes brim with tears out of sadness at the sight of my husband holding what he wants so very much in his life.

"Halley?" Griffin says.

I swallow the gripping knot in my throat and allow Adam to carefully settle Rylan into my arms.

Adam gazing down at Rylan snug in his arms was enough to bring on the storm of emotions in my heart, but the look that takes over my husband's face as I hold our nephew for the first time is enough to bring me to tears. A river of tears. I am enamored with my nephew, but the look in Adam's eyes is a lot like the look in Nina's, in Griffin's, in Charlotte's when she had each of her three children. It's not the same, of course. There's nothing quite like holding and looking at your own baby for the first time, I imagine. But there's also nothing quite like holding and looking at your heart's desire . . . and knowing you can't have it.

"Hi there, Rylan," I say, my voice quaking slightly. "I'm your aunt Halley." I swallow hard. "And I love you so much. You're so very, very special. Do you know that?"

I look up at Adam, and his eyes say everything. Everything I need to know. They confirm that what I am feeling is justified. They tell me exactly what he said all those months ago, when he told me that he wanted me to consider having a little Rylan of our own.

I exhale a long, shaky breath, trying to keep back the tears that now blur my vision. I kiss the air above Rylan's head and gently hand him back to Adam. As Rylan leaves my arms and once again rests safely in Adam's, I see things as clearly as I ever have since Adam and I separated. Far more clearly than when Adam and I agreed to move past this silly separation and reclaim our marriage and our love and move back in together. Right here, right now, I can see how much my husband wants a child of his own. I can see how much he wants to share this experience with me, but not as an uncle and an aunt. Adam's heart and soul want a baby. It's that feeling in your heart that words cannot explain.

I'm moved by the clarity with which I can finally see what our whole time apart was about. It wasn't about changing minds or reneging on plans. It wasn't about taking a breather or each of us hoping the other would come to his or her senses. It was about discovering what we want so deeply, about listening to our hearts and learning what matters most in the world to us. It was about this, right here. About digging down deep, uncovering the truth, struggling through the pain and denial, and learning that sometimes nothing and everything change.

In the blink of an eye, during an evening's drive, over the course of an eleven-year marriage.

There's no prescription for love, no indisputable explanation for how your heart feels or what you do because of love. It's that raw, unexplainable feeling you have when you hold a baby in your arms, when you gaze into your partner's eyes, when you accept that love comes in a variety of forms, happiness in a number of shapes, individual truths in all kinds of sizes.

Adam keeps his eyes on the gently awakening baby in his arms. He's in awe. As Rylan stirs some, Adam makes an instinctual cooing sound and soothes Rylan back into a slumber.

I press my lips firmly together, blink free a few tears, and turn to Nina. "How are you feeling, hon? You've got to be so tired," I say, moving to her side.

I welcome the distraction from my thoughts, making them now all about Nina, all about baby Rylan. Nina had a hard but healthy labor. Rylan was born three weeks early, but he arrived as expected—as a healthy baby boy, with a complication.

It's only when Griffin walks Adam out so Adam can head back to the office, Rylan sound asleep in his bassinet by Nina's side, that Nina tells me, "Rylan has special needs."

"What?" I gasp. I look to the helpless infant who looks perfectly healthy. That's impossible.

"He has Down syndrome." Nina's incredibly calm as she delivers the startling news. Her hands are folded, resting in her lap. Her face is gentle, with no expression of concern or despair.

"Wha—I thought you had the tests done to determine—"

"We did," she says with stately calm. "The noninvasive ones. And they reported a high risk. As positive a result as those types of tests can yield."

"Omigod." I clasp a hand to my mouth. "I thought you just had the tests. I didn't think they were . . . positive."

"That's a big reason we were urged to do the rest of the tests, to prove, with certainty, the results. There was still a slight chance of a false positive, but very small. We weren't counting on it. Hoping, yes, but not counting."

"Nina." I sink into the vacant chair next to her. "What . . ."

"It's okay, Halley." She pats my hand. "We've been preparing for this. It was hard to accept at first."

When she says this, I begin to recall moments throughout her pregnancy when she seemed low. Like at the ballet. What could have been the anticipated ups and downs of an emotional pregnant woman could have also been the emotions a mother experiences when she learns that the road ahead may not be quite what she expected.

"But I thought . . . ," I say as I reflect on the ballet. When Nina and I had a heart-to-heart about such tests and Rylan's health. "I was under the impression, at the ballet, that your test results weren't cause for any alarm. Did you . . . You knew? You've known for so long?"

"Yes." She smiles. "As sure as we could be. I had blood work done the same time we found out we were having a boy, to confirm the previous results. It was really difficult to hear, but learning Rylan was a boy!" She presses a hand to her heart. "I look at it this way. I had a one-in-four-thousand chance of getting pregnant. *That* was my focus. Having Rylan, here with me, is all that matters."

"You're absolutely right, Nina," I say, smiling. "He's all that matters."

"You know, I was sad at first, scared. And then I remembered that I was pregnant, Halley. I was going to have a baby! *That* was the miracle. The rest Griffin and I could learn, could figure out. And you know what? Having all this time to prepare and to expect, we realize we've been beyond blessed. Having a special needs child will be a challenge, yes. But it also means we get to spend so much more time with him than we probably ordinarily would have. He's our entire world now, Halley. And not just because he's our son but because he needs us more than ever."

She looks to Rylan. "I planned on returning to work after a few months. But now?" She closes her eyes and shrugs. "I don't even think about work. Sure, eventually I may go back part-time, but Rylan needs me full-time. It's a blessing. I get to not only be a mother but a full-time mother." She sighs gleefully, and I grip her hand.

"I've been a part of an online moms' group for children with Down syndrome," she says, "and they're so supportive and encouraging. Every day Griffin and I learn something new; we're growing together. And now we get to do that with Rylan. They say that in the difficult things there is a lot of beauty and joy to be found. They're absolutely right. Gee, Halley, we already love Rylan *so* much, and he isn't more than a day old!" She laughs.

"Wow," I breathe, looking to my sleeping nephew.

"It's a feeling I can't explain," Nina says, making a fist over her chest. "It's the most amazing feeling in the world. My son needs me, and I want to be there for him. Griffin is so committed, so in love with him. We have everything we could ever want. It won't be easy—"

"But is anything easy worth doing?" I can't help but say.

Nina's glowing. "Exactly."

"Why didn't you tell anyone?" I ask. "If you and Griffin knew all along and . . . You didn't want to share with anyone?"

"We weren't embarrassed," she says. "We weren't ashamed. It was just something we didn't want to receive pity over. I wanted my pregnancy to be about the hope and the love and the joy—the healthy baby boy—that it was about. Not condolences or apologies." She looks at Rylan. "He's a miracle baby, and I'm going to spend the rest of my life loving him." She looks to me. "He's my purpose, Halley. He's my truth."

I know what I have to do. I've never been confident in making decisions, least of all the difficult and big ones. This one, though, I have to make. It's one of those heart-and-soul matters, and I can make it. The clarity I experienced at the hospital is still with me. Even clearer, hours later. The stabbing pain of its reality causes some doubt, but then I just have to think about Rylan and the way Adam looked as he held him, and how Rylan is Nina's everything, and all my doubt recedes. The pain is still there, but so is the clarity.

Nina didn't plan for Rylan's having Down syndrome. She didn't plan to spend a decade trying to conceive. Her love for her son is stronger than any challenge—he's her truth. When she follows her heart, she's led to Rylan. And Adam's truth is out in the open, clear as day, and he needs to follow it. My truth is staring me in the face, too, waiting for me to finally act. To do what I'm so afraid of doing. To do what I never planned for. But I suppose that's the way these things can go. You can plan, prepare, practice, and in the end, love's a strange and wild beast. You can try to fight it, or you can fight *for* it, in all its different colors, shapes, and sizes.

With the bathwater running, I slip out of my clothes and light the large rose-scented candle at the foot of the tub. The sound of a gently played piano fills the space when I turn on the "Relaxed Evening" playlist on my cell phone. I drop my cold hands to my stomach, flinching at the chill. I forcefully distend my stomach and look at my profile in the mirror that's already lightly fogged by the heat of the running water. I've never done this before, imagined what it'd look like for me to be in the early stages of pregnancy. Then again, this year there's been a lot of "never done this before."

I rub my hands across the slightly distended shape, as I'd seen Nina do so many times.

"Christ," I say, shaking my head.

I shut off the water and slip into the steaming bath, sinking down until the water's surface meets my ears. I close my eyes, drowning out the loud silence of clarity.

Seventeen

It's hard to breathe. My pace through Old Pasadena down Colorado Boulevard is strong and steady. I pick up speed as I approach the crosswalk each time the green pedestrian light moves to red, making the light right in time. I charge across every street, no matter what the countdown is signaling—ten seconds, seven, two. When I'm stopped, I anxiously tap a beat with my foot. When the light doesn't turn quickly enough, I start a drum solo with my hands on my upper thighs. I'm a woman on a mission—a quasi–Brooklyn Bridge kind of mission.

I duck into the Starbucks along my route, because that's how this was supposed to go. Well, not entirely, but coffee was a part of the original idea, and when all else fails, there's always coffee, right? I order two grande lattes—one with soy milk, one dry—then continue my mission to the quiet office park where I've asked Adam to meet me tonight. It's the closest I can come to the Brooklyn Bridge/Long Beach Freeway bridge scene Marian and I came up with. The park I've asked Adam to meet me at is located near my favorite part of the city, in Old Pasadena. It's usually quiet, there are benches, and it's pretty at dusk this time of year, the trees decorated with Christmas lights. It's neither my office park nor Adam's, and it isn't a place that holds any sentimental value for either of us. It's the neutral ground I'm looking for.

As soon as my eyes fall to Adam, standing from his seat on a bench, brushing his hair back with one hand, I feel helpless. As if I can't do what I came here to do, can't say what's weighing on my heart, can't say what's needed to be said all along.

"Coffee?" Adam says as I stride up to him.

With my arms open at my sides, coffees raised in both hands, Adam steps close, bringing his supple lips to mine. I close my eyes as he kisses me.

When he draws back, I see him trying to read the Sharpie scribble on the cups.

"Soy's mine," I say. "Dry one is yours."

"Thanks, Hals. Felt like coffee?"

"Uh . . . yeah." I hike my purse higher up my shoulder. *Since public drinking is frowned upon,* I want to add, but I refrain. A beer would help, but coffee will have to do. I've mustered the courage to come out here tonight, and I've done a lot of thinking about what I will say. I barely slept a wink the last two nights, ruminating over what couldn't wait another day more to be shared with Adam. I knew that the more nights I slept on it and the longer I waited to say what I felt in my heart, the higher the likelihood I'd lose my nerve, the words would go unspoken, and Adam and I would be, at some point down the road, back in the very rough spot we find ourselves in now. I am just as confident today as I was at the hospital about my decision, about Adam, about us. I have mulled over all the possibilities, the pros, the cons. I've dug deep and I've searched my soul. And I know.

"So, you all packed?" Adam says to me cheerily. We sit on the bench.

"I've packed some."

"Been packing all week, I take it?" The corners of his eyes crease with a knowing smile.

I take a cautious sip of my hot coffee. Adam does the same.

"Adam." I turn some in my seat to face him. My knees begin to turn to jelly. I breathe slowly and steadily, fearful I'm about to hyperventilate.

I set my coffee underneath the bench, then press a palm to my warm cheek. "Adam, you want a baby."

Before he can utter a response or rebuttal, I add, "And I've decided I can't take that away from you. I'm not going to take away something you want so badly."

"So . . ." His mouth freezes in a tight *O*, suspended in incertitude.

"I saw the way you looked at Rylan. The way you held him. The way you lit up when he was in your arms."

"Okay? And?"

"You want a baby of your own."

He casts his gaze to the sprawling lawn. "He's my nephew, Halley. My godson. Of *course* I was . . . lit up." He says "lit up" in an exaggerated way.

"I don't blame you for wanting a baby, Adam."

"What are you saying, Halley?" Before I can respond, he clears his throat loudly and says in a stilted voice, "Halley, I already told you. I'm willing to put aside my wanting a child if it means being with you."

"I know." I grab his free hand and hold it tightly in support.

"I'm willing to fight for *you*. I want you. I want us." He squeezes my hand. "Whether or not you want to have a baby."

"Don't you see, Adam? You can't do that to yourself. And I can't do that to you. I can't take away what you want. What your heart wants."

"My heart wants *you*, Halley," he says earnestly. "We're meant to be together."

"Are we?" The words steal my breath, and from the look on Adam's face—color drained away, mouth frozen open, eyes wide—the words have not fallen on deaf ears. "Adam, listen." I put both my hands around his now-limp one. "I love you *so* much."

"Don't." He looks up at the sky, jaw locked.

"Adam. Adam."

He slowly looks to me.

"Adam . . . you love me so much you're willing to forego having a child. And I love you so much . . . I've decided I am not going to take that away from you."

"That's bullshit."

"No, Adam. Bullshit is living a half-fulfilled life. It's us being that couple who comes to fight and yell, passive-aggressively tear each other down over the years, because they have this giant unspoken cloud of angst, of lies, of lost hopes and dreams and incomplete lives." I pause to steady my nervous breathing. "It's you, whether you know it or not, coming to resent me for never having a child. And it's me, whether I know it or not, coming to resent you for feeling incomplete in our marriage for not having one. We're not going down that path."

He hisses an unintelligible response, yanking his hand from my grasp. He sets his coffee on the ground.

"How can you do this? Huh? Giving up on us? It's like . . . it's *easy* for you!"

"Nothing about this is easy, Adam," I say, my voice rattling. *"Nothing."*

"So you're saying . . . what?" His eyes bore into mine.

"I'm saying that I think we've reached a point in our relationship where we can't go any further. You want something I can't give, and I want something you can't give."

"But I *can*. I *can* choose not to have a child."

"Adam."

"Dammit, Halley."

A lone tear trickles down my cheek. "Adam, this is the hardest decision I have *ever* had to make. And I need you to stand with me on this. Do you want to live a half-lived life? Do you want to live a lie?"

He doesn't answer.

"I talked to Nina," I begin, and Adam's head shoots up.

I'm about to assure him that no one is complicit in my decision when he spits out, "Omigod. Is this about . . . Rylan?"

"In a way."

"So that's it? A baby's hard enough. But a baby with a compli—"

"No!" I say sharply. "Is that your honest opinion of me? That I'm that shallow?"

He doesn't speak.

"It's about Rylan in the sense that Nina has her purpose," I explain. "She has her truth. Yes, life gets messy and things don't always go according to plan, but at the end of the day, Nina can look in the mirror—look at her life—and declare it *hers*. She can live it with honesty and pride. I want that, Adam. I want that for me, and I want that for you." I soften my tone, lower my voice. I reach out to take his hand, and he reluctantly accepts. "I want a complete and honest life for us, and the best way for us to achieve that is to move on . . . from one another." I exhale a deep, quivering breath.

Adam drops his head into his hands and groans. "This whole separation . . ." He looks to me. "The point of it . . ."

I swallow the lump in my throat. "It was necessary. It gave us time to gain some clarity."

"God, Halley." He leans back in his seat, eyes wide in disbelief. "Then why did you agree to move back in?"

"I didn't know I felt this way until two days ago."

"With Rylan."

I nod. "I think the answer was always there, that you weren't going to want a baby any less, and I wasn't going to want one any more. We just had to figure out what that meant for us." I bite down on my lower lip. "That's why I think I'll be happy . . . if . . . if I . . . let you go." Hot tears run down both my cheeks. "That's why I think you'll be happy if you can find someone to have a child with. Someone who wants what you want." I grip his shoulder, forcing him to look at me. "Don't for a second think this is at all easy. Or even what I want." I blink away another run of tears. "I want us to go back to the way we were. Back when we agreed it was always going to be Adam and Halley, and that was all. When that was enough. But we can't go back there. It . . . isn't . . . enough."

"Shit, Halley. This . . . this is . . . *insane.*" He shakes his head in disbelief. "So . . ."

He makes a fist with one hand and claps the other over it, an old habit that says he's digesting something he knows he has to accept and can't change, try as he might.

"I think it's the solution that's been in front of us the whole time," I say.

He tightly presses his lips together. "So? I guess that means that we—what? Divorce?"

No other word sounds as ugly as this one. No other word tastes so rancid coming out and hurts so much once it's been said. Nevertheless, with calm, clarity, and confidence, I say, "Yes. A divorce."

"Shit." He runs a hand through his hair. He stands, picks up his coffee. "Forgive me," he says angrily, "but I thought my *wife* was moving back home tomorrow. Now she's asking for a divorce."

I blink through the tears that refuse to quit. "I'm sorry."

"So am I." With a powerful arm, he throws his coffee into the neighboring trash can. "So am I, Halley."

I decide now is the time to leave, to let Adam process, to let myself grieve. To run into Marian's arms and cry. To go home and not look back. Because at this point, in all its clichéd literary beauty, there is no looking back. We are finally, *finally* looking upward.

Marian's an angel sent from heaven. When I tell her what happened— the decision I fell asleep on last night and awoke to this morning, unchanged and ever determined, despite the pain it would cause—she wraps me in her arms and tells me everything will be all right. She says she's proud of me, of my bravery in doing what I felt was honest, no matter how difficult it was. Then she presents every bottle of wine, beer, and spirit she has on hand, before opening the freezer and revealing a stash I didn't know existed of a wide variety of Ben and Jerry's pints.

"Kind of suffering from my own breakup hangover," she says with a one-armed shrug. "Want to eat away our problems?"

"Sure," I say, listless.

And then I don't hear anything anymore. Marian's lips are moving, her eyebrows and shoulders are animated, presumably matching the peaks and dips of her tone. Then my ears begin to ring. The grating pealing fills the entire space of my mind. Of my body, now numb, that is standing here in this kitchen, staring at a sea of ice cream . . .

"Halley? Halley?" The repetitious tone and word—my name, I recognize—snap me to. The ringing subsides.

"Halley?" Marian says. "Are you all right?" She returns the two pints of ice cream to the freezer and quickly touches the back of her hand to my forehead. It's slightly chilled from having rooted about in the cold. It feels refreshing.

I close my eyes, take a deep breath. "It's over," I whisper. "My marriage is over."

Marian pulls her hand from my forehead, and I open my eyes.

"Adam and me. We're . . . It's . . . ." I press my own hand to my forehead. "Shit, Marian." I wince, looking to my best friend. "It's . . . *actually* over."

When it hits, it hurts. It hurts as nothing ever has. A burning in my chest and in my gut. A sinking feeling in my heart. A release in my back, yet a bearing down on my shoulders. This is what divorce, what heartbreak, feels like. This is what it looks like. This is . . . it.

"Come on," Marian gently coaxes.

We move from the kitchen to the living room, Marian's supporting arm around my waist, guiding my suddenly frail body—as if I've forgotten how to breathe, how to walk, how to *be*.

"I . . . ," I say once I'm seated. "I . . . never thought I'd say it's . . . over."

Marian doesn't say anything, and she doesn't have to. Her being here beside me, a box of Kleenex held at the ready, and that awaiting stash of ice cream say enough. Her knowing and understanding that sometimes it's just over, that sometimes life simply does not go according to plan, is her saying everything. It's her saying, *It'll all be all right.* And it will be. Eventually, everything will be all right.

When I can't imagine any more tears (or Kleenexes), I take Marian up on her ice cream therapy. With a pint of Sweet Cream and Cookies in my hand and a pint of Chocolate Fudge Brownie in Marian's, we sit on the sofa in silence. Only the occasional sniffle or licking of a spoon clean can be heard.

"Is it helping some?" Marian asks after a long while. Nearly half my pint is gone, and I have no plan of stopping anytime soon. "It's a temporary feel-good at best," she says. "Is it even that much?" She gives me a worried, sympathetic expression.

"It is, actually." I lick the sweetness from my lips. "Thank you."

"You know, if you need it, I can always get you some Percocet," she says, only half kidding. "Vicodin. Oh! There's a new drug out—"

"Thanks, Marian," I cut her off, chuckling. "I think I'll stick to this." I hold up my ice cream.

"Well, you're stronger than I could ever be."

"I'm on day one. Let's see how long I can pull it off." I glance at the nutritional information on the carton but don't actually read anything. "Or how long I can last with these and still fit into my clothes. It should get easier, though." My tone invites affirmation from Marian, and she, as a best friend does, answers the call.

"It *eventually* gets easier, Hals. But I'm not so sure the sadness ever goes away entirely."

"Cole."

She shrugs. "You learn to move on. You start to think about it less. You're not so wrapped up in it. But it still hurts some." She sighs. "And then when you go and muck it up and make a total fool out of yourself, you just invite the damn hurt back in, and it kills."

She takes a bite as I say, "I guess the big lesson is that life doesn't always turn out as planned. Even when you plan."

"Amen, sister."

"And that a breakup or a divorce isn't necessarily a failure."

"Absolutely not."

"Yes, it hurts, and of course I'd rather have made my marriage work. You'd rather things had worked out with Cole."

"Another amen," Marian says drily.

"It's sad and bleak and depressing as hell and all that cry-into-your-ice-cream crap."

"Mmmhmm."

"But . . . I'm kind of desperate for hope right now," I say. "Kind of counting on it, trying to keep my chin up as best I can."

"I get that." She pauses. "But . . . even though Adam was willing to put his wanting a child aside for you? To save your marriage?"

I stick my spoon in the slowly melting remains of my ice cream. "It hurts to come to this. It really does. But . . . it wouldn't be fair to him, Marian. That isn't the kind of marriage or life I want. The kind of love I want."

After a few beats of silence, Marian says, "I get where you're coming from, Halley. I really do. And I respect the hell out of it."

"Thanks."

"But damn, I'd do *anything* and everything for the man I love. I'd have a baby for him."

"That's because you want a child some day."

"I suppose."

"You've been there, Marian. Going after what you want, being true to you. Even when you weren't sure if things would go as you hoped."

"I'm a great example of living true to yourself." She rolls her eyes.

"You are."

"Halley, you fail to see that my running away from Cole put me in this nasty, miserable spot."

"But would jumping into marriage with Cole when you had all those doubts and fears really have been right? Would it have maybe damaged your relationship? Your marriage? Eventually?"

"It's just . . . it's a fine line, living true to yourself and making a horrible mistake that you'll only realize is a mistake much later on. Maybe even when it's too late."

"Maybe. That's life for you, I guess," I say. "But I've done the separation. I've done the thinking, and this is the decision I've made, Marian. At the risk of sounding corny, I know in my heart that this is the right thing to do because my heart is terribly heavy." I press a fist to my chest. "But I also feel like a burden's been lifted, you know? There's a lightness, like I've finally found the solution, finally come to acceptance, and now I can try to move forward. No half-lived life, right?"

"Yeah . . ." She takes a small bite of ice cream, eyes fixed on the coffee table. "I respect your decision, Halley. Really, I do. I'd just do anything to have Cole want me the way Adam wants you. It's so unfair. I wish we could trade places."

I let my eyes follow hers, fall into my own stare. I don't know what to say.

"I guess that's just my pathetic way of saying I love Cole," Marian says.

"Yeah. And Adam saying he'll forego having a child to be with me—that's his way of saying he loves me. My way is letting him go."

"Shit, Hals. This requires ice cream *and* booze."

"I should unpack," I say resignedly, standing. "I've got a partially filled suitcase in my room, and the sight is too depressing."

Marian grabs my forearm and pulls me back into my seat. "Later," she says. "You're home now. It can wait."

She's right. In fact, unpacking my suitcase will probably only make me more depressed than its being there half-packed.

With my ice cream in hand, I nestle close to Marian. She reaches for the remote control and selects an episode of *Friends*.

"Moments like these call for some *Friends* and then a night out," she says with pep. "What do you say? There's this new bar I've been wanting to try. I think we deserve to treat each other to a drink."

"Maybe."

"And hey, since you're going for the optimistic road and all, look at one of the grand life lessons *Friends* offers us."

"What's that?"

"Yes, divorce bites, but at least you're not Ross," she says with a smile.

"Right," I say with a laugh. "Three divorces by thirty."

Three days later, my half-packed pile of clothes is still sitting inside my opened suitcase. Three neat stacks that greet me every morning and disappear into the darkness every evening before bed, reminding me that I am not returning home. Adam is no longer my home. Part of me wants to close the piece of luggage and shove it and all its contents into my closet—out of sight, out of mind. Denial of the impending divorce. And another part of me wants to keep it in sight, in mind. Encouragement that the impending divorce is that necessary step in this love story, painful as it is.

I don't expect to hear from Adam soon, so I'm surprised when my cell phone rings in the early afternoon and I half expect it to be him. It's Charlotte. She and Marco had their second counseling session on Friday—probably around the same time I was meeting with Adam, I can't help but think.

Their session went well, which excites me to no end, and they'll be starting twice-weekly sessions after the New Year. Marco hasn't yet forgiven Charlotte, and Charlotte is far from forgiving herself. However, they're talking, they're fighting for their marriage, they're chasing their truths. When Charlotte asks about Nina and Rylan, I catch her up on the birth and Rylan's condition, and then I realize I desperately want to visit Nina and my godson. Right now, Rylan is both my nephew and my godson, but with the divorce, our familial ties will be legally cut. Will my future with Adam change more than *our* relationship? Will Nina and Griffin think it best to choose another godmother for their son, given the circumstance?

Nina invites me over the following day after I call to see how she's doing. She and Griffin have gotten into the swing of being home with their newborn, though neither has gotten more than two simultaneous hours of sleep since. Yet despite their exhausted states, they're all smiles and positively jubilant when I drive over after work.

"You're wearing fatherhood well," I compliment Griffin. He's comfortably barefoot, dressed in a pair of linen pants and a short-sleeved tee. He's let his facial hair grow out some, but it's maintained in a neat beard. Though he hasn't gotten much sleep, his eyes are bright, his mood cheerful.

"Not as well as Nina wears motherhood," Griffin replies. He looks on adoringly at his wife, who's gingerly making her way down the winding carpeted staircase. Rylan, bundled like a baby burrito, is nestled silently in her arms.

"That's for sure," I say, giving Nina a kiss on the cheek. She's still wearing her pregnancy glow, leading me to believe that she's seamlessly transitioned from glowing expectant mother to glowing-with-pride mother-at-last. With Rylan, Nina will always have her glow.

"You ladies enjoy some girl time," Griffin says. He and Nina make the baby handoff as if they've been doing it for years.

Nina and I settle into the cozy front sitting room. Their home, in spite of having welcomed a newborn, is immaculate and therapeutically silent. There's even some jazz lightly streaming from their living room that, thanks to the unbelievable peace, can be heard all the way in here. I'm sure that if Adam were here he'd point out that having a baby clearly doesn't have to disrupt one's life entirely, flip it on its head. I love my sister, but I can picture Adam comparing the two drastically different examples of child-filled homes, saying that we could write our own version of parenthood. That I had nothing to worry about.

It doesn't take more than a few seconds for her to give me a sideways smile and say, "I heard."

"Yeah. It wasn't easy. It *isn't* easy."

"Divorce never is." Nina smooths her dark hair back with both hands. "Halley, I want to let you know that nothing's changed. You will always be my sister. Sister-in-law or not, you are my sister."

"Nina, thank you. That means a lot."

I hesitate before saying, "I understand if you want a married couple for Rylan, but I love being his godmother. I want to be, if you'll still have me. It's an honor I don't take lightly."

"Oh, honey." Nina waves a dismissive hand. "That is not changing. You're tied to that sweet boy forever. Regardless of what's happening with Adam."

Relief washes over me. I'm sure it'll be strange when Adam and I, divorced, will attend Rylan's baptism together, standing side by side in front of everyone important in Rylan's life, promising to be his guides. It'll be weird when we cross paths, such as when I see Nina, as a friend, a forever-sister, and Adam is around. It'll be hard to see Adam, knowing he's no longer mine, and I'm sure it'll be just as hard for him, but our love for Rylan is greater than any awkward moment or stiff hello.

Griffin then brings a lightly fussing Rylan into the room. "I think he's hungry," he says, returning Rylan to Nina's awaiting arms.

Nina discreetly begins to breastfeed her son.

"Everything's going well with you and Rylan?" I ask. "A-okay healthy?"

"Everything's perfect, Halley. Absolute perfection."

"Good. That makes me happy to hear. Oh! Before I forget," I say, reaching for my bag. "I really enjoyed it. Thank you." I set the paperback copy of *Following Home* on the ottoman.

"My pleasure. The house is enjoying the sales," she says with a wink. "It's a hit."

"I can see that."

"I wish I would have been the lucky editor to have found it. Wasn't it just inspiring? Her travels? Adventures?" She looks down at her peaceful bundle and draws her thumb across Rylan's forehead.

"It was. We should all go on a life-changing journey like that."

Nina looks up at me and, with a confident and kind smile, says, "Aren't we, Halley?"

I pause to consider the simple truth.

"Yeah," I say with a small smile. "I suppose we are."

Eighteen

It's been nearly a week since I've heard from Adam. Since that fateful evening in the park. My luggage is still half-packed, and I've decided it'll stay that way until Adam and I talk again. And I've decided the ball is completely in his court. Not to pass the buck but to give him the time that I was able to take to recognize the clarity. I don't know if he'll come to it before our divorce proceedings begin, and I don't even know if he'll agree to a divorce, though it need not be a mutual decision. I do hope it'll be amicable and easy—a quick, clean, and friendly divorce. Well, as friendly as one can be.

I have the name and number of an affordable and efficient divorce attorney scrawled on a Post-it in my jacket pocket. Mika, a junior editor at *Copper*, went through her own divorce last year—an amicable and clean one, hence the recommendation. During my walk home, the Post-it starts to burn a hole in my pocket. I blame the Christmas tree lot on my right. The inescapable scent of pine wafts over and fills my nostrils. The cheery red sign of the chain-link-barricaded lot to the left with "Ho-Ho-Ho" written on it *and* the one to the right advertising, in the same cheery red, "Christmas Trees" officially do me in. It's everything I can do to keep from falling into nostalgia's trap and missing Adam unbearably. Will I always feel sad when I pass a Christmas tree lot, thinking back on when Adam proposed? And how we broke our vows? Will I ever be able to look at a Christmas tree lot—or a Christmas tree, for that matter—the same way again?

My fingers alight on the Post-it deep in my pocket. I make a fist around it in defiance of the pain that swells within at the mere sight of a stupid Christmas tree lot.

That's the way we show our love for each other. I think back on the conversation Marian and I had postpark. I try to pull myself up by the bootstraps, give myself a kick in the pants to keep on walking. Don't let myself get all misty eyed, become dreary about the holidays this year. God knows it's not going to be an easy Christmas to get through.

My mind turns to what Marian said about love, about her love for Cole. How she'd do just about anything to have Cole want her the way Adam wants me. The way I still want Adam, but can't.

I don't know if it's coming off the heels of finding the courage to confront Adam and admit that a divorce is our tragic answer, or if the damn Christmas tree lot is doing a number on my olfactory sense, or maybe it's the Post-it with the divorce attorney information on it that's fanning the flame, but I stop right here on bustling Green Street and pull out my cell phone and request a ride. There's not a minute to spare to run home and get my car, for a chance to think twice. A gold VW sedan pulls up minutes later, asks if I'm Halley, and then whisks me away to Glendale. To firehouse station number Twenty-Two.

I'm impressed that I remember the house where Cole Whittaker's stationed. Marian mentioned it on only one occasion. The drama with which she did, though, probably helped ingrain it in my brain. I'm apprehensive when I emerge from my ride, wondering if I really do have the number right. Wondering if this was such a hot idea after all.

It's too late at this point, my driver disappearing down the road, two intrigued firemen staring at the displaced girl standing in their driveway.

"Are you lost?" the taller of the two asks.

Both men begin their approach, and I mentally scold myself for not thinking this through better. I had plenty of time to formulate a plan on the ride over. I'm the Queen of Plans, and all I could think of was Marian's face if this all went well. Then I tried to picture it if it didn't. I thought hard about that one. So that is why I've resolved to keep my little romantic stunt to myself. There will be no point in telling Marian I've gone to Cole's firehouse to tell him she's lovesick for him, because if he doesn't reciprocate, or at least tell me (and Marian) to bugger off once and for all, then what'd be the point in telling her about my adventure? It'd add even more insult to injury. Now, if Cole does hear me out and reach his own clarity, as I optimistically think he will, then Marian surely won't be angry with me for going behind her back and doing a tad of prodding. She'll be ecstatic! After all, wouldn't she do anything for Cole?

It's this entire line of thought and wondering that consumed my time on the drive over. So now I'm here, standing in front of two beefy firemen, the sun beginning to bake the little brains I'm beginning to think are all I have upstairs, no more sure of what to say to these two strangers than of what to say to Cole himself.

"Can we help you?" the shorter of the two asks.

Before either jumps to breaking out the gurney or offering first aid at my idiotic stand-in-silence-and-stare routine, I stammer out, "I-I'm looking for Cole. Cole Whittaker."

The two exchange a look I can't quite read. It isn't what I'd expect from complete strangers. As if Cole routinely gets strange girls walking up the driveway, asking to—

Oh. Right.

The taller one says, "You change your hair?"

"Right," I say with an understanding nod.

"It's not her," the shorter one says. He looks to me and hitches a thumb behind him to the house. "Cole's here. But, uh . . . who may I ask is looking for him?"

"I'm . . ." I stand up straighter and say with as much confidence as I can muster, "Look, guys. I know Marian—"

"Marian. That's it," the taller one says, snapping his fingers.

I refrain from rolling my eyes and say, "I'm Marian's best friend. But I'm also old friends with Cole. We all went to college together. I won't keep him long, I promise. I'd just really appreciate it if I could talk to him. Please." I press my hands together in supplication. "I'm not here because Marian sent me. I'm here . . . because I have nothing left to lose."

Now they're both stumped.

"Look," I begin again, but the shorter one stops me. He waves me on to follow.

"Come on, darling," he says. "I'm not a fan of daytime dramas and I'm not about to step into a real-life one I have nothing to do with."

"You'll let Cole know I'm here?" I ask excitedly.

"We'll do you one better," the taller one says. He points toward the opened garage. "He's right there. You can let him know yourself."

It takes me a second to identify Cole, as there are three guys in the garage. Two in those sexy fireman pants, suspenders hanging at their sides, tight T-shirts revealing cut biceps, are working on a fire truck. The other, not in the sexy pants but still showing off ridiculously muscular arms in his tight tee, is fiddling with tools on a shelf. If the two guys who played bodyguard to Cole were in a real-life soap opera, then I am living a girl's fireman calendar dream.

The man working with the tools turns to look in my direction. He has changed since I last saw him—he's stronger, ruddier.

"Cole," I say as I approach the opened garage with hesitation.

Cole looks at his partners, then looks back to me. "Halley?" he says in a confounded tone. He's wearing as bewildered a face as one would expect. It's been twelve years since we've seen each other. Marian may have been the last person he'd ever expect to see grace his station's driveway, but I'm sure the faithful friend and trusted bridesmaid comes in a close second. "Halley West?"

"Halley Brennan, actually." Then I immediately correct myself. "West, yeah," I say in an uncertain tone. The correction marks the first in a long line of firsts as I embark on my divorce.

Cole's jaw locks. "Did Marian ask you to come here?"

"No." I don't like the way he says her name or that her asking me to come here sounds like his worst nightmare. "Cole, look. This is something that's entirely out of character for me."

He doesn't say anything. He just stands here, towering over me as he's always done at a good inch or two over six feet. His arms are akimbo, his face pulled tight in confusion.

"I know Marian came here. I know she spilled her guts. I know she really hurt you a long time ago." He winces. "*And* when she came here. But that's not what I want to talk about." I wave my hands. "I don't know what it's worth, but since I've got nothing left to lose, and since I, well, actually *did* kind of lose everything . . ." I shake my head, realizing I'm spinning into a tangent that Cole most likely couldn't care less about, much less follow.

"The point i-is," I stutter, "Marian loves you. She's screwed up and she knows it, and she's taken a long-ass time to figure things out, but she's never stopped loving you. And I applaud her for owning how she feels. For stepping up and putting it all out on the line. She's in love with you, Cole. With her whole heart and soul. And I know this not just because she's told me. And not because I can see it in her face when she talks about you or when your name is mentioned. Or even how she gets this glazy-dazy look when she sets off the fire alarm because she's really not that great of a cook."

Cole sniffs a small laugh, and it's the encouragement I need to power on through my speech.

"I know it because I've had to take a step back and relearn what love is. What honest and unconditional love is. Sometimes love is taking a step back; sometimes it's moving forward. Sometimes it's letting go; sometimes it's holding on. Sometimes it's taking it back . . . chasing it. But it isn't anywhere in between. It isn't in some stupid, drawn-out separation. It isn't in a decade of waiting and pining and wondering. It's in the action. In the decision you make *now*." I shrug, then slip my hands in my rear pockets.

"I couldn't save my love, but you and Marian can save yours," I say. Cole looks entirely confused, no doubt wondering what my losing love has to do with anything. "I'm here to tell you Marian loves you so much she'll do anything to have you back. But she does understand if it can't be that way. I swear, I'm here of my own accord. I'm just here to beg you to . . . to . . . to . . ." I sigh heavily. "To find it in your heart to give her another chance. Give the two of you a chance. I know I'm out of line here and all, but, hell, I guess I still have faith in happily ever afters. And part of me has kind of hoped that you haven't decided yet—whether to let her go or to take her back." I give a nervous laugh.

"You're single, she's single. Maybe I'm that little push you need to decide," I say, making a small driving-fist movement.

There. That's it. I've said what I came to say.

Now I wait awkwardly. Cole doesn't say anything. Even his blank expression doesn't change.

When I'm hoping that the bodyguards or the two working on the truck or even the firehouse dog who's got to be around somewhere would come and break the silence, Cole says, "What makes you think I haven't made a decision already?"

Crap. He's right. Perhaps he has made his decision, and it doesn't involve running after Marian.

Feeling like an idiot, I say, "Well then, if you have, you have. If you've moved on, if you don't love her, then . . . okay. Point taken. It was worth a shot." I adjust my purse over my shoulder. "Then I'll just bow out now, wish you merry Christmas, and leave, terribly embarrassed." I can feel a hard blush crimson my cheeks.

"Halley?"

"Yeah?"

"It isn't just about love. It's about a whole hell of a lot more than my loving her."

My ears prick up. "You still love her?"

Cole doesn't answer, and I don't think he has to. He's said enough. There's still room for hope, and maybe it's even more hope than Marian thought she had. Maybe it's just enough.

I quickly write down my and Marian's home address on a sheet of paper from the small notebook I always keep in my purse.

"Here," I say, stuffing the note into Cole's hand. "It's where she's at, if you decide your love's the kind you chase."

"And if it isn't?" he says.

"Then it's the kind you let go." An intense aching grips my heart.

He looks down at the crumpled note in his hand.

"If my opinion's worth anything," I say. He raises one brow. "I know a letting-go kind of love. And yours and Marian's isn't one of them."

Men. Seriously. It's been a week since I pulled that crazy stunt at firehouse number Twenty-Two. Still no word from Cole. No one's riding in on a white horse, and, on Marian's end, there is no inordinate Ben and Jerry's consumption. At least not more than the usual inordinate amount. And it'll be two weeks tomorrow since I've heard from Adam. Not that Marian and I are exactly Miss America with our grace, patience, and understanding—a real party to hang out with, chase after. I can't blame Adam for wanting to slam shut and double-bolt the door on the divorce topic. Neither of us really saw it coming, and he'd hoped—planned—for reconciliation.

While Cole may not ride on in, relief at last does, in the form of a phone call right before I get ready for bed. It's Adam.

"I think you should come over," he says.

I'm puzzled. *Come over* as in move back in? Or *come over* as in we need to talk?

It's neither.

"I'll help you pack," he says, morose. "I picked up some boxes."

I can't help but stand at the foot of my bed, cell phone loosely in hand, in surprise. Adam's done more than come to accept the decision to divorce, he's gone to Home Depot, loaded up with boxes, packing tape, bubble wrap, and god knows what else? A dolly, for good measure? I know I have no right to stand here, incensed, when I'm the one waving the divorce papers in front of him. My eyes land on the half-packed suitcase on the floor of my closet, and I let the moving boxes fade from my mind, the anger slowly roll off my back. If a backward version of the Brooklyn Bridge–esque moment of cutting the ties and a half-packed bag are what I needed to begin the painful journey of moving on, perhaps Adam needs some moving boxes and packing tape.

"Sounds good," I say, my tone neutral. "When works for you?"

"Tomorrow night?"

Tomorrow night?

I swallow hard, and that darn suitcase comes into sight again. It has been two weeks. Adam has had time to mull things over. And it isn't in Adam's nurturing and kind character to vindictively shove me out of the house. It simply is what it is. We are getting a divorce. I am moving out.

"Tomorrow night is fine."

"I'll pick us up some tacos." Then he quickly adds, "If you like."

That's my Adam. A smile pulls at my lips, and I can almost smell pine, Christmas trees. Nostalgia envelops me and I give a confirming "Mmmhmm" to tacos, to the meal that brings on a sudden sadness and a lone tear trickling down my cheek. Only this time it isn't because we've inadvertently made Taco Tuesdays a thing of the past but because tomorrow we'll have put all tacos—and all Tuesdays—in our past.

Dragging my feet and listlessly checking off menial tasks is pretty much how the day goes at work. I'm uninspired to write my next strong-females-in-literature feature, and I'm even more uninspired to tackle the secrets of a tasty Tuscan bruschetta. I'd be remiss if I said it doesn't have a thing to do with the way I plan to spend my evening tonight.

I know this isn't going to be the last I see of Adam, and it most likely won't even be the last time I'm in my old home. The evening, complete with one more round of tacos, however, very heavily marks an ending. And a beginning, Marian perkily insisted this morning when I told her my plans for the night.

I've never been too fond of the notion of new beginnings. There are no do-overs or restarts, are there? Not in this life. You're born and you die, and everything that happens in between is life and moves along with time. You can't pause it or rewind or fast-forward, no matter how hard you try. My father's logical and scientific approach to the world we live in influences me as I consider the notion on my drive over to Adam.

We are all along for the ride of life, and a lot is out of our control. As much of a fan as I am of planning and being prepared, there is repose in knowing some things are up to fate and chance. Decisions have to be made at certain points, and sometimes they're really tough ones. And rather than declaring an ending here and a new start there, you have to keep moving on, constantly. There is no stasis. I want to remember the past and its memories, and let the past inform my future and be a part of my now; I also want to look forward to possibility, to chance, to whatever may lie ahead. I suppose my divorce is not an ending nor is what follows a new beginning, as in a book, but rather the next chapter in my life. The next part of the story.

Oddly inspired in my daydreaming drive to Adam, wondering where this kind of inspiration was when I was at work and all dried up, I park my car on the street in front of our condo. Adam's car is in the driveway, with plenty of room for me to park alongside him. I park here instead. Perhaps this is just another one of those firsts. I am the visitor here, not the resident.

As Adam said, he's picked up moving boxes. And bubble wrap and shipping tape. And tacos. The familiar fragrance of Tito's Tacos hits me as soon as Adam swings open the front door.

"I got our usual," he says, pointing to the white bags on the dining table, grease already seeping through the paper. "Hope that was okay."

I become rigid at the use of the impertinent words *our usual.* "Great," I tell him. "Thank you. You didn't have to."

"I wanted to."

Adam looks better than I thought he would, and that makes me happy. His hair is freshly washed, wet and slicked back, and he smells wonderfully of newly applied cologne. He probably went for a run after work, then showered and picked up dinner. I can't help but think about how whenever we had our last jog together it was, in fact, our last jog together. And then I wander down the dangerous road of thinking about our last shower together, our last night in bed together, our last kiss, our last spur-of-the-moment drive to the beach, our last vacation, our last this, our last that. Our last everything! I thought Adam would be the last man I would ever sleep with. Now that is no more a guarantee than anything else in life.

I can feel myself being moved to tears—chest tightens, stomach churns, eyes sting—and I restrain myself with every ounce of will I can find. As much as I wanted Adam to be in accord with our divorce, and as much as I believe it will come to be a mutually accepted decision, it is *I* who have brought on this pain. *I* have decided to make every last our last.

As Adam pours the tortilla chips into the sunflower-yellow bowl, I note it was a wedding gift from Charlotte, and then, when I'm in the middle of thinking who will get it in the divorce, and how we'll divvy up everything else under this roof, I inhale deeply and tell myself that if I am to blame for calling for a divorce, then Adam is to blame for getting us to this point. And if—

"I got extra green," Adam says, holding up a large cup of salsa verde. "Since you drink this stuff."

And then I stop. There is no blaming. There is no finger pointing. Just as there are no endings or new beginnings. We are here, now, and though it is bittersweet, it is honest.

Adam and I make small talk with ease, and when there's only one taco remaining and nothing but crumbs at the bottom of the chip bowl, we move on to the purpose of my visit.

We begin in the bedroom, my side of the closet the largest challenge. When we've filled half a dozen boxes of clothes, Adam says that he didn't intend for us to completely move me out tonight. I tell him that I figured as much, and that it was a good idea to just start. Start somewhere.

I drop into the bottom of an empty box my navy blue down jacket, an item I rarely wear but one I wanted so badly for Christmas a few years ago. Adam surprised me with it, and snug inside one of the pockets were two ski passes. I know now that if I were to slip my hands into the pockets and fish around for paper, I'd come up empty handed, obviously. The fact that I'd pull out balls of lint, at best, hurts, silly as the thought may be.

The thought of paper in pockets brings to mind the attorney I discovered.

"I was talking to someone at work," I say in my best casual voice. There is no easy way to segue into the discussion of divorce attorneys with your husband.

"Oh yeah? You have a new feature idea?" Adam says.

I smile at the fact that Adam's first thought is of my writing.

"No, uh, a coworker of mine got divorced recently. Said it was amicable and really clean. Affordable, too. She gave me the number of her attorney."

"Oh." Adam finishes taping closed a box. "You have an attorney already?"

"Not officially. Do you?"

"No."

"Good, because I was thinking, if you wanted, we could use the same one?"

His eyebrows raise.

"That's what Mika did—the girl from work," I explain. "She said she and her ex-husband wanted it fast, efficient, and cheap, and no drama, and their attorney was really great. Maybe we want to meet with her? I have her information. You can contact her on your own, if you like. See if you're inter—"

"If she's good enough for you, she's good enough for me, Halley." He begins assembling another box.

"Okay."

"I think that's a good idea, actually," he says, tone a bit upbeat. "Sharing a lawyer. I didn't even consider it." He pauses, then says, "To be honest, I haven't really considered an attorney or anything to do with divorce proceedings. Actually, why not ask Griffin?"

"Griffin? He's a corporate attorney."

"Not Griffin himself. His firm or someone he knows."

"Adam, do you really think it's such a great idea to involve family in our *divorce?*"

He gives a self-deprecating laugh. "You're probably right. So, we've got an attorney?"

"Potentially."

"Potentially. Good." He looks into my eyes. "I wish we could have found a better solution, Halley. A solution where we stay together."

"Me, too."

"I've thought about us and this whole mess nonstop. It isn't easy."

"No, it isn't," I say solemnly.

"The fact that it's not easy and we're still doing it, though, is kind of that flashing light."

"Flashing light?" I scrunch my brow. "What do you mean?"

"That flashing light that says, this is the right thing. A wake-up. Our obstacle is . . . insurmountable."

I wanted with my whole being for Adam to agree that our relationship should take a different course. That the problems before us could be met with a solution that neither of us wanted to admit was the best one. For both of us. Now that he does, it all becomes so real, so palpable, so final.

"I've visited Rylan twice since the hospital visit," he says. He's seated on the edge of our bed, his hands limp in his lap, a tiny smile playing on his lips. "I can't get enough of him, and babies grow so fast." He looks over at me. "I can see now that you're right, Halley. It hurts, and I don't want to let you go, but I can't let go of wanting to become a father someday. I should have been able to see it all sooner—how I felt, how you felt. I mean, your letter in *Copper!*"

I nod, my lips pressed together, my hands firmly clasped in front of me.

"You've always made it clear that you don't want to become a parent, and I think I lost respect for that along the way," he says. "I got so caught up in what I wanted that I thought time could persuade you otherwise. Or I just wanted to live in denial, simply say, 'It'll all work out' without really giving genuine thought to if and *how* it would work out. Like you said, water and oil don't mix, Hals. Okay, maybe for a brief moment when you shake them together everything seems to be cohesive, but let time pass and they're no more suitable to one another than a man wanting a child and a woman not." Adam looks at me with glassy eyes. "If we're both honest with each other, I think the most honest thing we can do is part ways. I'm sorry it ended up like this, Halley."

"I am, too." I crawl across our bed and move beside Adam, slipping my arms around him. "I am, too, Adam."

Everything he's said, as difficult as it is to hear and as painful as it is to digest, is right. It's how I feel. It's heartbreaking and relieving.

I pull back, brushing my hair from my face. Adam stands, clears his throat. He moves away, picking up a stack of folded clothes at the head of the bed, and begins to pack them.

"You think this will ever feel . . . normal?" he asks, pensive.

"Not being together anymore?"

"Yeah."

I shrug. "At some point," I say, hopeful. "I think so. I think it will when . . . when you find someone to have a child with." My heart aches at the idea, at my admission. At my letting go of Adam. "When you . . . become a father."

"And what about you?" He raises his brows.

"Well, we covered that. No babies for me." I force out a half laugh.

"That's not what I mean." He stops packing. "Halley, if we're going to pull the honest card and divorce because of it, then I want you to go out there and live your life with every bit of purpose you can find."

"I can't think about remarrying, Adam."

"That's not what I'm talking about." He moves across the room and stands right in front of me. "I'm talking about you living your purpose. You saw how Nina has hers with Rylan, and you tell me to go become a father and fulfill that role."

"Yes."

"What about you?" He places a hand on my upper arm. "Halley, you're an amazing writer."

"Let's not compare having a child to writing articles for a women's magazine," I say with an eye roll.

"Halley, you're not happy at work."

"What?" Where is this coming from?

"All right, yes, you've had some wins lately," he says.

"Damn straight."

"But writing's your calling. Can you honestly tell me you're writing what you're passionate about?"

"It's a job. I need the money. And it's a *writing* job," I say, starting to become irritated at the strange turn in conversation.

"I'm only saying you deserve to be happy. And you're not happy at work."

"Granted, I could be happier, yes." I give him this.

Adam's eyes lock on mine. Both his face and his grip on my arm are imploring, encouraging.

"Halley, whatever it is for you, be true to yourself. Go after it. You've got your whole life ahead of you and so much potential. Live honestly." He drops his hand from my arm and takes a step back. "Maybe it isn't for me to say, but I will. Write that novel you've always wanted to write. Go *be* that author you've always dreamed of being."

I crinkle my nose at his carpe diem monologue. "O-kay," I draw out.

"I'm serious. I think you should do it. Like you did with your letter, put it all out there—without fear, with honesty, *passion* . . ." He crosses his arms over his chest. "Share what you've got inside that very talented head of yours." He smiles, his eyes creasing in that forever-memorable way of his. "You've got it in you. I believe in you, Halley."

"That . . . that means a lot, Adam."

"I think it's time you go do what you've always wanted to do. Write the next great American novel!"

"Ha! Well, if I were going to write a book, I wouldn't attempt the next great American novel."

"Whatever it is, just do it," he pleads. "Okay? No more excuses. Be true to who you are. Promise me?"

"Promise you that I'll write a novel?" I say through a laugh.

"Yes." He's absolutely serious. His shoulders pull up toward his ears, his arms still crossed. "I know you've got one in you. Hell, probably a dozen. What have you got to lose?"

I jut my bottom lip out in response.

Truth is, I have let fear and lack of confidence get the better of me. I've used the excuses of "no time," "*Copper* is my job—my paying job—not writing novels," and "I'm probably not good enough to make it," and allowed them to foolishly dictate my chasing my dream. I have always wanted to write and publish a novel—even, as Adam suggested, a dozen—but what if the words didn't come out right? What if no one believed the story or felt for the characters? What if I wasn't any good? *What if . . . what if . . . what if . . .*

"Look," Adam says, snapping me back to the conversation. "I'm just saying, if we're going to do this whole live-honestly thing, Halley, then for god's sake, *go* for it! *Do* it!"

I nod. "Yeah. Yeah, I know, Adam."

It's so much easier to say than to do, I want to tell him, but instead, I continue nodding and say, "I've got it. Don't talk but also walk."

"Exactly."

I keep nodding, as if convincing myself as much as Adam that I will consider filling that void—that hole—in my life. Conquering fear, self-doubt, apprehension. Pursuing my purpose, living true.

Adam leans over the bed to grab another stack of clothes.

"Who knows," he says, "maybe sitting down and focusing on a book will help you through the . . . divorce. I know I plan on mastering this mountain biking thing." He catches my gaze and smiles.

"I heard about that," I say in a flirty kind of way. "Mr. Tame the Mountain, are we?"

I watch as Adam neatly places my folded clothes into boxes, as he clearly labels, tapes, and sets one box after another aside in an orderly stack. There's a mechanical yet also thoughtful and emotional approach to his system of packing away his wife's belongings. A peculiar analogy to the passage of time and life pops into my head once again. I start to think about how we compartmentalize things in life—this goes into that box, this in that one. How we discover coping mechanisms, seek answers, and ultimately solve one problem after another, often battling what the heart wants and what the head says. How sometimes we choose to hold on to something—this blouse, this relationship, *yes*— and let go of others—this pair of jeans, this marriage, *no*. How we create systems to try to make sense of things. How we fill gaps, pass time, and eventually learn to heal and move on after our hearts break. Or, at the very least, try to. It may seem trite and perhaps even a little defeatist. Although I suppose, for the eternal optimist, there is also a great deal of hope in it. It's peculiar how hope and love are uniquely, inextricably paired, yet also at odds with each other.

One thing this is—to use yet another literary cliché—is bittersweet. I know most wouldn't drop their divorce into the bittersweet category. Bitter, yes. I'd like to think, though, that in my and Adam's divorce there is not a change just in the love and relationship between a husband and a wife, but also in the hope and possibility of a child, a parental love that deserves to be awarded and explored and lived. And, yeah, maybe even that next great American novel, too. We'll see. Whatever lies ahead, I have to believe that with the turn from one chapter to another there is a future that Adam and I will come to look back on and admire, knowing we lived as fully and as honestly as we could. Even if it wasn't together forever.

I tell myself that Adam and I will look back on all of this not with heavy hearts but knowing we made the best call we could in a shitty situation. I tell myself this because I want it to be true. And because I need it to be true. Bittersweet it may be, but divorce is never easy. Not on the one who calls for it in the first place and not when it's mutual. And certainly not when you still love each other, when you have to learn how to let your love change. It's a transition—a chapter—and learning something new always takes time. It always hurts before it heals. It's always bitter before it's sweet.

"Halley?" Adam's got a load of my paperbacks in his arms, having moved on from clothes to another subcategory of my personal items.

"Hmm?"

His eyes lock with mine in the way only his eyes can. "I love you."

I look at the paperbacks in his arms. My eyes instantly gravitate to the bright-orange spine that reads *The Baby Name Wizard*. My throat constricts and my stomach tightens. And like that, tears begin to well, but not before I look back into my husband's eyes, swallow down the pain, and whisper, "I love you."

I was wrong. *This* is the heaviest *I love you* I have ever—and will ever—say. It is the hardest. It is our last.

Nineteen

The appointment with the divorce attorney has been made. I wonder if this is how Charlotte felt when she made that first marriage counseling appointment. That first official, bring-in-the-third-party step of attempting to repair a damaged relationship. Things suddenly become so much more real. As if everything that preceded the appointment—the separation, the anguish, all that waiting—weren't enough. While Charlotte and Marco are on their way to marital reconciliation, Adam and I are on our way to what Marian's lovingly coined *individual identity reconciliation*. I get what she implies—Adam and I don't hate or resent each other; we're not angrily pulling the plug on our marriage, vengefully calling it quits, fighting over assets and finding ways to apply pressure, get in the last word and final dig to the side. We're reconciling with each other on an individual level. He's to find himself, and I'm to find myself.

Adding the appointment with the divorce attorney—my last entry for the year—to the calendar on my cell phone and scrawling it in red marker on the calendar on the kitchen wall emphasize the realness and permanence of it all. To tell me and all who pass by that calendar that what is happening is not a nightmare, nor a theory, nor a thought.

Needless to say, it puts a very odd spin on Christmas this year. Never mind that I can't pass by a Christmas tree lot without tearing up, but Christmas is a time of cheer and festivity. A time to be around loved ones. A time of hope and wishful thinking and gratitude. Marian and I are each other's rock, more so now in the aftermath of our tragic love stories. Had either one of us known what a hellish year this one would be in the love department, we'd probably have purchased stock in Ben and Jerry's. Heavy doses of calories and broken hearts bring best friends together like nothing else.

But the vibe in our home is anything but merry. It's downright depressing. Alice's complaint about the lack of holiday decor in her home is warranted here. Marian and I don't have as little as a silver strand of tinsel out, much less a tree or two single-girl stockings hanging above the fireplace. It's just wrong.

I'm about to tell Marian that I think we could both use some cheering up by finally getting into the spirit of the season when she beats me to it.

"Merry Christmas! Happy Hanukkah! Happy Kwanzaa! And all the merry-merries my best girl deserves!" Marian trills, waltzing from her bedroom with a large brown carrier bag in hand, "Gucci" inscribed in gold across the center.

"Christmas isn't for another two days," I say in protest, but not because I'm a stickler for opening gifts only on Christmas morning. I haven't given a single thought to any Christmas gifts this year. It's terrible. I have nothing for Marian. Or anyone, for that matter. This is entirely unlike me, and I find myself using my divorce as a cheap cop-out. I wonder how often and for how long I will be able to use divorce as an excuse for brain-dead moments?

"I know," Marian says, "but it isn't the eighties anymore, and you still blast eighties tunes like they're today's hits."

"That I won't argue," I say with a laugh.

She presents the carrier bag to me by holding its handles with two fingers, the nails freshly painted a Christmas red.

"You got a mani," I note.

Marian's been out of sorts because of the whole Cole thing. She even let her dark roots start to show, which she never used to allow, since she still didn't buy into the whole bleach-blonde-hair-with-black-roots look. *Super skanky*, I think she called it. I was as relieved to see her touch them up a few days ago as I am to see that her nails are back to their maintained selves.

"I may be heartbroken and unable to move on, but I'm not about to go super skanky on myself," she says, making me smile. "Come on," she urges, dangling the bag in front of me. "Open it!"

"Damn, Marian." I take the bag into my hands. "I feel horrible. I haven't done my Christmas shopping yet."

"Who cares? Open it." She claps her hands in excitement.

As the bag indicates, Marian's outdone herself and bought me a Gucci handbag. It's a classically designed tote, and I am immediately obsessed with it.

"Marian, this is way too expensive," I say as soon as it sinks in that this bag costs more than any single item in my closet. More expensive than any bag I already own or that coveted pair of hot pink SJP heels Adam got me for my last birthday.

"I got a great bonus, and I have a well-paying job, Hals," she says breezily. "And it's not about the cost. It was my pleasure."

"Well, thank you." I run my fingers across the leather straps.

"And I love to shop," she says with a cackle. "Besides, I can't watch you go off to work schlepping that boring nameless bag you carry."

"It does the job," I say, defending my trusty large black bag.

"Well, Gucci does the job, too, in style."

"That's for sure."

"Open it!"

"Open it?" I look down at my bag, noticing there is something inside.

It is a medium-size black box. As I pull it out and discover what it is, I immediately smile and look to Marian.

"Thank you, Marian. My gosh . . ."

Marian returns the smile. "Now you can easily make—"

"Coffee for one," I finish.

"I was going to say, 'healthier amounts of coffee,' but you get the idea."

"Thank you." I set my new French press on the sofa and wrap my best friend in a hug. "Thank you, Marian. For *everything*."

"I figured you could use the gifts early," she says. "Things have been so damn depressing lately, you know? And what Ben and Jerry's or *Friends* can't fix, Gucci can." She runs her fingers along the bag.

I quickly fetch the purse I've been using, a very worn camel-colored leather bag, and transfer the essential contents to my brand-new designer bag.

"You going somewhere?" Marian asks. "Giving your bag a test run?"

I toss her her keys lying on the coffee table. "*We* are going to get a Christmas tree."

"Do you think there's anything left? We're two days away. Hals, there are probably only Charlie Browns left."

I slip on my lightweight zip hoodie and proudly rest my new handbag's straps on my shoulder. The ensemble as a whole leaves much to be desired, but with this bag I could walk out the door naked and feel dressed to the nines.

"Well then," I say nonchalantly, "we'll get a Charlie Brown. We'll save it from the wood chipper so it can fulfill its Christmas destiny." I give Marian a wink. "Besides, a Charlie Brown tree is probably fitting for this year's Christmas, wouldn't you say?"

"All right," she gives in. "But we're only buying one. You're not going to pull a Phoebe on me and get me to buy up all the sad Charlie Browns."

Fortunately, Marian and I find a lot with plenty of beautiful and full Christmas trees ripe for the picking. I, as Phoebe on *Friends*, always find it a bit sad, really, when we're this close to Christmas and there are still so many trees that haven't found rightful homes yet. This late in the game, most unwanted trees will either see the wood chipper or, if they're lucky, fall into the hands of two thirtysomething women down on their love luck and in desperate need of some Christmas cheer.

"Are you sure we didn't go too big?" I ask Marian, unsure about the size of our tree and the height of our living room ceiling.

"Are you kidding?" she spits, tugging at the rope that's wound about the tree and my car roof. Her high-set bun is coming loose, now a lopsided mess. "I snagged this particular town house because of its tall-ass ceilings."

I maintain my doubts, even though Marian's ceilings are indeed quite high. This tree is taller than I'm used to. It'd never fit in my old place, and I really doubt it'll fit here.

"The guy at the lot said it's a fourteen-footer, and my ceilings are, like, fifteen. Or something." Marian pulls free the rope and I assist her with carefully rolling the tree off the roof and somehow into our arms. The tree is unbelievably heavy, so it doesn't stay in our arms for long.

"Damn," Marian breathes. "This sucker's heavy."

"Because it's fourteen frickin' feet," I say with a laugh. "Marian, I'm not so sure."

"Hals." She gives me a stern look, one hand on her jutted hip. "We need to stay positive here. We have greater challenges than finding out if this beast fits or not."

"We need to figure out how we're going to lug it up the stairs," I say succinctly.

Marian instructs me to take the top portion while she handles the trunk. "I've been doing fifty push-ups a day," she says, which is supposed to suggest she's the stronger of us and can therefore handle the heavy bottom.

"Fifty?" I say, impressed.

"One, two, three, *lift*," she says, and up goes the tree, back into our arms.

"Fifty," she breathes out. "You know, between the Ben and Jerry's and the realization I've lost my greatest love, a girl's gotta do what a girl's gotta do."

I lead the way to the stairs, moving with slow, stunted steps so as not to put any more of a burden on Marian. My end is surprisingly light. I move farther down the tree, almost to the midsection. It'll lessen the load on Marian as we ascend the stairs and take the corners.

We're halfway up the miserable flight of stairs when a male voice shouts out, "What are you doing?"

"What the hell does it look like we're doing?" Marian bellows from under a blanket of pine.

Assuming we're holding up the stairwell, I blindly shout, "We're almost out of the way. Sorry!"

"Are you two insane?" comes the voice, still as stern and rather condescending.

Like that, the weight of our overgrown Christmas tree is lifted from my shoulders. I crawl out from underneath the mesh-contained green and step up to the landing, my eyes growing wide at the sight before me.

"Halley?" Marian calls from under the tree.

"I've got it. I've got it, Marian," Cole says.

Marian emerges, eyes also wide, from under the tree. She's on the midway landing just below me. Cole, our colossal tree on his back, is in between us in the middle of the stairs.

"Coming up," Cole says, taking the steps two at a time.

I dart out of his way, my mouth now hanging open.

"House two-eleven, you said, right?" he calls out.

I glance down at Marian.

"You said?" she mouths to me, incredulous.

"Yes!" I call to Cole, still looking straight at Marian. "Two-eleven."

"Halley . . ." Marian's jaw is tight.

"I may or may not have gone to see him," I say bashfully.

She blinks a few times, then rushes up the stairs.

No one says a word as I unlock the front door. No one says a word as we enter the town house, Cole with the tree still slung on his back.

Finally Cole breaks the silence. "Where should I put this?"

Dumbfounded, Marian and I look at each other and don't respond.

"Living room?" Cole suggests.

Marian looks to be in a complete state of shock, her arms listlessly by her sides, eyes and mouth opened wide.

"I think this tree might be a little too big for these ceilings," Cole says with a light laugh.

I smack Marian on the shoulder to wake her from her trance. I gesture with my head to Cole and the oversize tree. "Say something," I whisper.

She doesn't. Total shock.

"That's what I feared," I say, walking over to Cole. "We got too big a tree."

"Well, where should I put it?" He casts about. "Corner? Window?"

Marian speaks at last. "By the fireplace." She points, like a woman pointing to an apparition, to the awaiting tree stand next to the fireplace.

"The fireplace?" Cole says, perplexed.

"Mmmhmm."

"Seriously?" Cole shakes his head, and I can see the corners of his lips turn up ever so slightly.

"Yeah, uhh," I jump in, since Marian's still playing the ghost-sighting girl. "Probably not the best idea, huh? Fires and all?" Discomfited, I dig my hands into my pockets.

"Something like that," he says.

I move the tree stand to a corner of the living room, one as far from the fireplace as possible. Cole sets the tree into position.

"What are you guys doing just now getting a tree?" he asks casually. "I'm surprised you found such a nice one so late." He hitches a thumb to the tree. "Looks like a big one."

"It is." I'm trying to keep the air from becoming stale. Marian still won't snap out of it. "Not a Charlie Brown, like we feared we'd end up with."

"What are you doing here, Cole?" Marian says, voice calm yet stony.

Cole looks from me to Marian, and as soon as he does, his expression morphs into one filled with pain and hope and a hundred questions and answers. I take this as my cue to leave.

I'm halfway across the living room when I whisper, "I'll leave you two alone."

"No," Marian says, grabbing my arm. "Stay, Halley."

I comply, taking my awkward position next to her, hands folded in front of me like an obedient child.

"Cole," Marian says.

"Marian."

"What are you doing here?"

"Marian," I whisper beseechingly, "let me leave you two alone."

"No, he won't be here long. Stay," she insists.

Now I'm confused. I didn't expect Marian to put on her best upset face if Cole were to finally mount that white horse and ride on over. Then again, he may have ridden over, but maybe not on that white horse. Maybe he's here not to declare his undying love, but . . .

Oh hell, what do I know about love?

"Marian," I try to protest once more, but this time Cole cuts in.

"You can stay, Halley," he says. "In fact, you should stay."

"I should?"

"Yeah. You're why I'm here today."

From the corner of my eye I see Marian look at me with a bewildered expression.

"Well," Cole says, "I'm here *for* Marian, but . . . you know."

"What the hell is going on?" Marian bursts out.

I decide my place in all of this is on the sofa, knees against my chest in a protective kind of way, completely neutral about whatever's going to go down. Passive, observant at most.

"Marian," Cole says. He takes two steps toward her and stops when she takes one step back. "When Halley came to talk to me, she said a lot that made sense." He takes another step closer. This time Marian doesn't retreat. "I don't like how we ended things all those years ago. Or when you visited me."

"I didn't like it, either." Marian's voice is quaking. "But you said I hurt you more than you thought possible. And I did. I *did*, Cole. You said you wished I wouldn't have come to see you, and I get that."

"Marian."

"You said all I was doing was hurting you again, and I get that, too." Her voice rises.

"Marian."

"And that you don't believe in marriage." This line causes Marian's voice to squeak.

"Marian."

"No!" She holds up a hand, stopping him from advancing any farther.

Cole slips both hands in his front pockets and rocks back on his heels.

"I heard you loud and clear, Cole. And yes, I've spent all my wishes on you, hoping you'd come back. But . . . why? Why are you here?" She squeezes her eyes shut, fighting back the tears. "Why, Cole?" she begs. "Because everything I said to you . . . Nothing's changed. I still love you. I still want you back."

"Marian." He smiles. "Can I answer why I'm here?"

She groans and rolls her eyes, caught up in emotion.

"I didn't say everything I should have when you came by the station," he says. His voice is low and collected. "I told you I'm not sure

I believe in marriage anymore, but that was only half of it. I was afraid of admitting to you why I don't believe in it. Yes, you hurt me. Badly." He inhales deeply, steadying himself. "I was engaged once, and I broke it off."

Marian's wearing a face that reads, *Why are you telling me this again?* I'm pretty sure I am, too.

"You know why?" he rhetorically asks. "I'd rather be single than incompletely in love."

"What?"

"I may have been angry with you, but I've always loved you, Marian. I've never come to feel for anyone what I felt for you. What I . . . still feel for you. Granted, I've been hurt and angry, but my love for you has been constant. It's you, Marian. It's always been you." He reaches a cautious hand forward, and when Marian doesn't react, doesn't move away, doesn't flinch, he gently places it on the side of her shoulder. "I really don't know where we go from here. But if what you said to me is true, and if what Halley—who, seriously, is one hell of a best friend—said is all true, then . . . like you said, I think we owe it to each other to see if there's still something there. Something we can still have."

Cole hesitates in bringing his second hand up to Marian's other shoulder, but then Marian brings her hands to her face and gasps.

"Marian?" Cole looks at her expectantly, both hands now on her shoulders. "This is me chasing our love. I should have run after you the first time. I don't want to let you get away again. I'm not sure how we start or where to go from here, but we still love each other, and I think with that we can go pretty far."

"Cole," she cries.

"Look, I know how much you love grand romantic gestures. I'm twelve years late, but . . . we should give us a try again."

Marian squeezes her eyes shut, her face filling with a blush. "Cole, I don't—I don't know what to say."

"How about to start, a yes to my asking you on a date?" he says with a growing smile.

Marian presses her hands to her face again, lightly pulling down taut the skin on her forehead—the quintessential image of disbelief and joy.

"Yes!" she shrieks. "Omigod."

Cole wraps her in his arms, and like something straight out of a fairy tale, he kisses her. And then they kiss as if they're making up for lost time, which I suppose is exactly what they're doing.

"We have a lot to catch up on," Cole says, his head pressed to hers.

"A lot to talk about," Marian says. "A lot of forgiving and explaining."

"We've got time." He runs his thumb along her cheek, and I decide to slip silently from the sofa and make my way to my room. The credits are rolling. It's time to leave the theater.

Before I can complete my escape, I hear Cole say to Marian, "I'm going out of town for Christmas. How's a New Year's Eve date sound?"

"Perfect," Marian says, and then she says my name, halting me in my tracks. "But I can't leave my main girl, Halley, alone. It's New Year's Eve."

"Hi." I wave sheepishly. "That's me, the lonely divorcée."

Cole looks surprised, and he's about to say something when I add, "Marian, don't worry about me. You have yourself a fabulous New Year's Eve. It's time. Really."

She turns to Cole. "It's a deal."

There's no use in my hiding in my bedroom at this point, because Cole is out the door seconds later, reminding us once more not to place our Christmas tree by the fireplace and, preferably, not to use the fireplace while we have the tree up.

"Oh. My. God!" Marian screams, jumping up and down as soon as Cole leaves. "Omigod, Halley! Can you—Did you—What—"

I jump up and down with her, her hands in mine.

"I know," I say. I tell her about my firehouse visit and Marian's beside herself, absolutely gleeful.

"Halley, consider your Christmas gift for me finished. *That* was more than I could have ever wished for!"

An hour later, our tree still wrapped, our eyes still wide with disbelief, Marian and I are sipping champagne on the balcony.

"Did that really happen?" Marian asks.

I laugh. "Oh yeah."

"Wow." She exhales loudly. "Wow, wow, *wow*." She looks over at me. "God, can you imagine if neither of us had said anything? If I didn't go down there—if *you* didn't go down there? I can't help but think of all the time Cole and I've lost. Twelve years! So much time lost. But now we have our future. I mean, I don't want to get ahead of ourselves, but . . . this is huge, Halley. Huge!"

"I'm so happy for you, Marian."

"Omigod." She presses a palm to her forehead.

"You know," I say, glancing back at our tree that, affirmative, is a good half foot too tall. The point is bent at a complete ninety.

"Hmm?"

"All that time away from each other, while it sucks, was just your guys' journey to get to here. Life never takes you where you think it will, you know?"

"I like that notion, Halley."

"I do, too," I say, looking out at the palm tree–lined street below, inspired by the thought of winding roads and the unexpected places they can take you.

The winding road on which I find myself on Christmas Eve is the one leading to Charlotte and Marco's home. It's an annual tradition in the Miller home to host on either Christmas Eve or Christmas Day. On the rare occasion that Adam and I were in attendance, usually Mom and Ray would make an appearance, as would Marco's parents and his brother and his family, and always my father. This year, Charlotte and Marco have decided to open their home for both Christmas Eve and Christmas Day. Invitations were extended to come to either or both. It was, as Charlotte told me, her and Marco's way of strengthening their family unit, reveling in what brings loved ones together.

Tomorrow everyone will come together under the Miller roof to celebrate. Tonight it'll be a cozy few—just Dad and me. Mom and Ray were supposed to join but are apparently winning big at the slots and tables, so they have extended their festive Vegas retreat another night— no one's exactly made a fuss over their change in plans. I'm really looking forward to the quiet, intimate evening. I'm also looking forward to tomorrow's larger gathering. It's been a long time since I've spent Christmas with family, and I think it'll be a while before I'll be able to stand strongly on two feet during this time of year. The holiday season may have marked the proposal of my marriage as well as its conclusion, but in time I think it will come to be a reminder to hold close what is dear, to stay hopeful, to remember that we don't get a second shot at life, so make the most of the one you've got.

"Finally," Marco says with two thumbs up. He saunters in from the hall.

"The kids in bed?" Charlotte asks, hopeful.

"Better. They're asleep."

"All of them?" Charlotte's beside herself.

Marco proudly nods and says, "Reading *The Night Before Christmas* will do that."

"As does the threat of Santa Claus not stopping by homes where children aren't sleeping," Dad says with a chuckle.

"Shall we?" Charlotte asks, smiling and looking to Marco. She pulls the throw from her lap and stands.

Marco rubs his hands together. "Let's get 'em," he says of Santa's delivery, ready to be made now that visions of sugarplums are dancing in their children's heads.

To the unaware observer, Charlotte and Marco are a happily married couple, clashing over nothing heavier than whether to let *A Christmas Story* or sports play on TV. Underneath they are healing, working hard to repair the frayed places. They're actually doing quite well, all things considered, as Charlotte informed me earlier in the evening. But they've still got a very long road ahead, she also said.

"I thank my lucky stars for it being Christmas," Charlotte told me in the kitchen when we had a rare moment alone, uninterrupted by enthusiastic pajama-clad children running around. "We're so focused on the kids and making everything festive and fun and happy this time of year. It helps."

While Charlotte and Marco heave seemingly endless gifts from closets and secret hiding places to put under the tree and on the hearth, my father waves me into the garage.

"Wait till you see what I got Alice," he says, beaming. He flips the garage lights on, bathing the space in fluorescents. We make our way past Charlotte's minivan and over to a busy corner. Dad moves aside Marco's set of golf clubs, followed by a few lightweight boxes I help move out of the way.

"You're not here to show me some nest of mice babies, are you?" I say, suspicious. My father, for whatever reason, thought it cool to show young Charlotte and me a nest of mice that had claimed space in our garage. We both had nightmares about mice in the walls, in the ceiling, in our beds, for weeks.

Dad laughs to himself. "Just a valuable lesson in the ceaseless wonders of biology." He grunts, lifting the surprise upward. "Here we are." With a wide grin, he sets between us a black telescope. It has silver knobs and appears heavy, really solid. It isn't a state-of-the-art professional scope, but it's a far cry from the inexpensive ones you find at Toys "R" Us.

"Daddy," I gasp, lightly running my fingers over the telescope. Immediately I think back on the telescope Charlotte and I had growing up. It was found one Christmas morning on the hearth, and it looked much like . . . "Is this?" I say, looking to my father.

He's still wearing a wide grin. "It is. Your and Charlotte's first telescope."

He, too, runs his fingers nostalgically across the dull black body. It's clearly used and aged but is still in impeccable shape.

"I figured Alice would really enjoy it, the science buff she is," he says.

"Oh, definitely."

"And maybe George will have some fun with it, too. Leah, when she's a bit older."

"Charlotte and I loved this," I say, thinking fondly of the evenings my sister and I would share with our father in our backyard, stargazing, moon watching, planet searching. "I can't believe you still have it. I thought Mom got rid of this long ago."

"Oh no. I've had this ever since the divorce." I can sense Dad flinch at his last word. He knows that Adam and I are about to begin divorce proceedings, and while he's already conveyed his support and understanding of "whatever you decide and need, Halley," it clearly hurts a father when his daughter follows, in a sense, the footsteps he'd rather not have made.

Not letting the joy of the present become lost, I quickly say, "I'm so glad you didn't get rid of it, Daddy. This is a fantastic gift for the kids. Alice will love it. She'll go nuts, in fact. You know she's been begging Charlotte and Marco to get her one of these?"

"I know." Dad lightly pats the telescope. "And dreams shall come true." He lifts the telescope and gestures for us to make our way out of the garage. "Now that the kiddies are sound asleep," he says, "how about we give this baby a test run?"

The air is crisp, a chillier December evening than most we've had recently. The sky is dark, few stars twinkling against the orange glow of the city's lights. However, it is so clear tonight that those few stars are quite visible.

Dad fiddles with some knobs with his trademark scientific precision and care. I pull the cuffs of my wool sweater over my fingers and hug my arms to my chest, tilting my head back to survey the gorgeous Christmas Eve sky.

"There . . . we . . . go . . ." Dad squints through the telescope, then turns one more knob. He holds a hand out, inviting me to take a look for myself. "As good as new."

I bend down and look through the telescope. A slice of the right side of the moon meets my eye. Its dark craters are just as awe-inspiring and magical as they have always been, no matter how many times my father and I have stood under the LA skies during nights much like this, observing the wonders of the universe.

"It's still there," I say of the moon in a childlike voice, something I rather preciously told my father every time we turned the telescope to the sky.

Dad laughs and says, "It's waxing . . . Do you remember?"

"Oh, Daddy." I stand upright. "It's been so long."

Ever a tad dispirited by the science aversion of his offspring, he says with a forgiving smile, "It's waxing crescent."

"Right. Of course. How could I forget?"

"Tomorrow night the moon'll be first quarter, and if we have clear skies like tonight it'll look—"

"Magical?" I say, recalling another childhood memory.

"Magical."

"Gosh, Daddy," I say as my father looks through the telescope. He huddles over it interestedly, moving the scope with care.

"What's that, Halley?" His voice is low, almost a whisper, as he focuses on a view that he's seen countless times but one that he's never tired of.

"I'm sorry I didn't really appreciate this growing up."

He stands tall, looks at me, and points to the telescope. "What are you talking about? You and your sister loved this thing."

"It was fascinating," I assure him. "But it was spending time with you, on nights like this, in the backyard, that we loved most. We could have been looking at nothing more than a pitch-black sky with you, and we still would have been thrilled to no end."

Dad smiles, his eyes wrinkling and his nose scrunching. "I know that, too, Halley."

"What I mean is, I'm sorry I didn't appreciate it as much as I could have," I say. "Like become some smart and accomplished scientist."

"Oh, Halley."

"Now you've got Alice."

"Alice is a kid wonder. Halley, you not being a scientist has never disappointed me."

I shrug. "I guess, but . . . it probably sure would have been nice to have been able to really share with your child what you love."

"You know, Halley." Dad leads me to the bench at the far corner of the yard. "We shared time together, and that's what I loved. That's what *you* loved." I nod. "That's all any father can ask for of being a parent. The chance to spend time with and love his children. To know that they're happy."

I sit next to my father, close enough that his warmth can radiate onto me against the cold breeze in the air.

"You didn't have to become a scientist to make me proud, Halley."

I laugh and tell him that of course I know that. "I've been a bit of a hot mess lately, though," I add with a self-deprecating laugh.

"I want you to do what brings you joy, Halley. If that's writing for your women's magazine, splitting atoms, or running a metal detector along the Pacific Coast in search of buried treasure, you do Halley."

"Be honest with me, Daddy," I say, looking straight ahead.

"Always."

"Do you think I'm making a mistake, choosing not to become a parent? Choosing to let Adam go because I won't change my mind?"

My father sits silently for a moment. At last he says, "I want you to arrive at your decisions on your own, Halley. You know what's best for you."

"And you've always said to surround myself with loved ones and people who support and challenge and are good for me. That we're not in this alone."

He smiles and pats my knee. "Well then, my humble, honest opinion?"

"Yes."

His brow knits and one side of his lips turns up in contemplative thought. He rubs at his chin and, without saying anything, looks up at the sky.

"Halley," he breathes into the night, "I know this is hard for you. You and Adam divorcing is something you never saw coming. Something you never planned for. I know you'd never make such a decision lightly. And I don't doubt for a second that what you're feeling right now is a lot of pain, a lot of uncertainty, a lot of new questions needing all-new answers."

He looks to me for a second, eyes warm and gentle, before looking back up toward the sky.

"Your mother's and my divorce was very different, Halley. But an unexpected change—a love you have to let go of and move on from— nevertheless is not an easy hurdle. You know you were unplanned, your mom becoming pregnant with you?"

"How can I forget?"

"I wanted you before you were ever born—were ever even a blip on our radar. And that's why we named you Halley."

"Halley's Comet. Edmond Halley." I knew the story. My astronomer father loved his unexpected gift of a child, just as he loved the possibilities of the universe. My name was his nod to his beloved community and life's endeavors.

"That's right. Edmond Halley was a brilliant and inquisitive mind. Extremely accomplished. You're in great company, scientist or not," he says with a smirk. "Halley's Comet comes around every seventy-six years. It, like many comets, used to mystify the ancients. It used to be thought of as a forewarning of disease, famine, war, great storms. Today, we know it to be a comet. When I think of Halley's Comet, and when I look up into the sky or through a telescope, I think of the endless possibilities out there, the unknown worlds, the universes we can't even begin to identify and explore. So much possibility. So much beauty."

Dad looks to me and says, "Halley, all I've ever wanted for you—all that any father wants for his child—is for her to live a full, happy, and meaningful life. We don't know what kind of hand life will deal us. We all start with a clean slate."

"A fresh page," I say, running with the literary imagery.

"A fresh page, exactly. Then words appear on the page. You write your story. And then your muse visits." I smile. "And words you didn't plan for—you didn't expect—appear, and they take the story in a different direction. And on and on and on you go, writing your story. We make hard decisions, and that's the way of life. Adam is one of your hard decisions."

"He is. I love him so much, Daddy."

"I know you do."

"I love him so much that"—I take in a big drink of air—"so much that I have to let him go."

"I know you do."

"And I really hate that this kind of love is one I have to let go of."

"Do you know how I see this?"

"How?" I snuggle closer to my father, and he wraps an arm around my shoulders.

He points upward. "Your love for Adam, and your next chapter"—he winks—"is kind of like Halley's Comet."

"Forewarning of a disaster to the ancients?" I kid.

He ignores my jesting and says, "Halley's Comet is on an amazing and lengthy journey. It, like everything in our solar system, is in free fall around the sun. It travels an enormous distance, falling to the edge of our solar system. Most don't know that, that a comet's falling."

"Oh god," I say in a tone of dread at the moribund sound of things.

Dad gives my shoulders a squeeze. "It's falling away, and you think it's just going to disappear. Go away, never to return. Like you and Adam right now, you're falling. And it hurts."

"Yes."

"And then," he says enthusiastically, "when the comet reaches the edge of our solar system it comes back around, free-falling its way *back* to the inner solar system. It starts its return. Let's call that return your healing. Your . . . moving on to the next chapter." The thought makes me smile.

"Halley's Comet never leaves," he says. "It's in an orbit, free-falling back and returning to our skies, like clockwork, every seventy-six years. We can predict where in the sky it will return and on what path. It's always there, Halley. Always has been, always will be."

"Like my love for Adam. It'll always be there, just in a different form, maybe?" I say.

Dad gives a closed-eyed nod of satisfaction. "Like your love for Adam," he parrots. "And also like your movement from one chapter to another in life. Halley's Comet returns, with a glowing halo and tail, letting you know it's still there, burning bright as it shines across our skies. It never stops its journey. Love and life are like that, Halley. And you don't want to miss out on a second of it."

"Oh, Daddy." I rest my head on his shoulder and let his arm envelop me, pull me into his side.

"Burn bright, Halley," he whispers against my head before kissing it. "Burn bright and strong and with courage, no matter what you're doing."

"You know what, Daddy?"

"Hmm?"

"I think I'm going to get through this."

"Of course you are."

I sit up and look at him. "But not just get through it. Adam's right. You're right. We've got a whole life—a whole sky—out there. It's our job to make the most out of it."

My father smiles. "That's all we can do."

As we lean back on the bench, heads tilted, eyes skyward, I decide on two things.

"Are you going to be in town for New Year's?" Dad asks.

"I will be," I say happily of the first of my two decisions. I'm actually looking forward to, as with Christmas, not jetting off for a holiday vacation but spending it with family.

"There's a full moon at the start of the year, so it's not the best of telescope conditions. But if we're lucky we'll be able to see the Quadrantids. They should be spectacular!"

"Meteor shower?" I guess.

"You bet. It's best to go out to the mountains or the desert for that. The city light can make visibility difficult. If you want to join—"

"I'd love to."

"All right then." I can't think of a better way to ring in the New Year than with my father as we watch a beautiful, glittery light show in the sky.

It's also under the soft glow of the moon and the evening sky where Santa's making his rounds, making wishes come true, that I make the second of my two decisions. Now is the time to find myself. Whatever that means. Although I have a pretty good idea. I'm fairly sure it has something to do with courage. With that fresh, empty page. With that new chapter, waiting to be written by a Halley Brennan . . . No, Halley West, working writer, aspiring author. Like a comet, I've got to rocket to the edge of the solar system and back, fearless, shining in the sky and burning bright on the journey that is this messy and complicated, and nuanced, big beautiful life.

Epilogue

Two Years Later

It's that time of year again. That time when the winds get gustier, the nights get dark earlier, the street lamps are bedecked with red-ribboned wreaths. It's that time of year when you show your gratitude for those important in your life, when you look back on the year and recall its fond memories, when you say to yourself, *Boy, time flies* as you rip open the new calendar and prepare to hang it on the wall—a fresh set of days, weeks, and months, brimming with possibility and opportunity.

I drop my cell phone into my Gucci tote, a gift that represents one of the most significant and also most trying Christmases of my life better than it represents wealth, class, and sophistication. I check twice to make sure my keys are also inside my tote. I don't have a roommate I can count on to open the door when she gets off work in the event that I forget them. (Although Marian does have a key to my place—my home is always hers, hers mine.) Marian and I live across town from each other now. I have my own place—my first own place—and I love it. This quaint first-floor studio apartment in a quiet Pasadena neighborhood, exactly zero minutes from my office, is home.

Marian and I lived together for a year after the divorce, which turned out to be a very speedy, clean, and drama-free ordeal, as Mika had promised. Fifty-fifty, everything down the middle. Marian and I had a lot of great times together as roomies, and she really helped see me through my divorce. But it was time to get a place of my own, turn toward that next chapter. I'd saved up some money and gotten some in the divorce settlement, and I came into some additional funds that helped me get on my own two feet.

It was also time for me to move out to make room for Cole. He and Marian did, indeed, go out on that New Year's Eve date two years ago. And they did, indeed, make up for a lot of lost time. Marian actually offered for me to stay on as her roomie once Cole moved in. "It's not like he needs his own room," she'd said. The thought and offer were sweet, but it was time for Marian to fully live her happily ever after.

And now, during what I'm sure will be another historic, romantic Christmas season, I have a feeling someone's going to be getting engaged soon. It's hard to believe that Marian and Cole have been going out for two years, and have so much history on top of that, and they've yet to take that plunge. But they both insisted they weren't going to have a repeat *Runaway Bride* moment. They'd take as long as they needed until the time was right, and no matter how long it took, it didn't really matter, so long as they had each other.

They won't be taking that much longer, though. Last week, when I was doing some Christmas shopping on Colorado Boulevard, I bumped into Cole in front of Tiffany's, and he had the unmistakable Tiffany-blue bag in his hand. My mouth dropped open, his eyes grew wide, and he said, "Shh. Don't tell," a finger to his lips. It has taken everything I have not to call Marian and shout the exciting news.

What can I say? Some happily ever afters do turn out like fairy tales. Not all, but some.

I'm on my way to dinner with Marian and Cole right now, and I'm curious if she'll be sporting something sparkly.

I pick up Marian's Christmas gift, and I'm about to tuck it into my tote when I notice that the gold bow has popped off. Its sticky backing is weak, unusable, so I pull a spool of gold ribbon from my desk drawer and sit down to properly fix the wrapping.

With my Christmas playlist still streaming on my computer, I look at the holiday cards I've amassed over the month, pinned to my corkboard. At the very top of the display, in the center, is a large white-and-gold-accented photo card. "Merry Christmas from the Millers" runs along the top border, above a beautiful family photo. Charlotte, Marco, Alice, George, and Leah are posing in their backyard, with their one-year-old golden retriever puppy. They're each wearing some sort of a tacky Christmas sweater—this year's holiday card theme, Charlotte told me.

George is wearing his "cheese" smile. As soon as he sees a camera or hears the word *cheese*, he gets a tightly pulled, all-teeth-bared grin. The fact that he's missing a few teeth only adds to the charm. Alice is hugging her sister, Leah, both of them smiling their identical head-tilted-to-the-side closed-mouth smiles. It's their mother's standard photograph grin, although Charlotte isn't wearing hers. Instead, with one arm around Marco's waist and Marco holding Charlotte by hers, she's smiling a familiar and heartwarming smile. It's the kind of smile you can find when you page through her wedding photo album. And Marco's wearing that same look that he shared with his wife on their wedding day. When I see it, I can't help but brim with joy and think again about happily ever afters. Some are not like fairy tales. Some are messy and ugly. Some are just plain real life. It's that resumed-happily-ever-after smile and that promise at the altar of we did and still do that matter.

Charlotte and Marco are still going to marital counseling, but only once a month. Charlotte says it helps remind them that they have to always work for their marriage, even when things are—as they are now—going better than they have in a long time. Also, she says, it's a great excuse to make a date night of the appointments and get some time away from the kids.

Marco's started to do more around the house and with the children, showing Charlotte that he's committed to making her and their family a priority. Work e-mails are checked only once on the weekends, cleaning dishes after dinner is now a joint effort, Marco takes the kids for golf lessons at the club once a week, and Family Friday Nights are mandatory fun nights when each week one child suggests the family activity. They are both equal disciplinarians and shoulders to cry on for their children—a real team effort.

Charlotte refuses to ever wear tracksuits in public unless she's working out, and she will never again set foot in a coffee shop wearing one. More seriously, she consciously makes a point of showing her love for Marco, whether it's with a thoughtful text message in the middle of the day, sex on a weekday, a batch of his favorite chocolate-chip-and-walnut cookies, or a Post-it love note stuck to his travel coffee mug (my suggestion). She tanks up his car when she notices it's running low, and he unexpectedly brings her her favorite flowers. It's the little things, Charlotte says. It's the effort.

Among the parenting books stacked atop both their nightstands are self-help and relationship advice books. Charlotte's taking care of herself. She's lost a little weight and, more important, she looks refreshed and happy, fulfilled. She started law school this fall, and she's loving it, even making some friends and reviving the social life she'd lost. She says Alice will probably graduate from college before she will get her juris doctor, but it doesn't matter. She's going after her truth, and for that I commend her. Charlotte will always bear the scars of her mistake, but they do not define her. She is not broken.

When I asked Charlotte what Marco thought of her idea of applying to law school, she said he'd asked her if she really wanted to take that challenge on right now. If that wouldn't bring on more undue stress.

Three kids are demanding, no matter the level of help from a spouse. Charlotte told him that, yes, it would be stressful and hard. It'd be hard as hell. She was driven, though. And besides, nothing worth doing is ever easy. When she told Marco her plans, he showed up from work one evening with the paperwork she'd need to apply. Something as bright as that Tiffany-blue bag tells me that Charlotte will be wearing that cap and gown sooner than she thinks.

I move my focus from the Miller family Christmas photo card to the gold ribbon between my fingers. I pull free a length, then snip and wrap it around the rectangular gift. I knot the ribbon at the front, then curl the free ends with a pair of scissors in a fast motion. Perfection.

I fluff the curls into a decorative, wispy ball, then tuck the gift into my tote. I reach for another gift, identical to Marian's but with its gold bow still intact. A padded, addressed postage-paid envelope rests underneath it. I run my fingers over the address I've scribbled onto it. I consider how some numbers are as ingrained in your memory as your birth date. No amount of time or number of following addresses can wipe clean from your memory such pertinent digits.

As I look back up at my collection of holiday cards, my eyes fall to Nina and Griffin's greeting. The Burkes didn't opt for the classic family portrait like the Millers. Their card, however, is even more personal and touching than the sweet family-of-three photo that they sent last Christmas. This year Nina's scanned onto simple white card stock a finger painting that Rylan made—his interpretation of a Christmas tree. It's a green-and-pink triangle with blue and yellow ribbons and dots of red, and lots of tiny fingerprints that I interpret to be presents dotted about the bottom in a muddy orange-brown hue.

Nina and Griffin are the proudest and happiest parents I've ever seen. At two, Rylan is just the rambunctious, joyous toddler you'd imagine. As his godmother, I've done my fair share of spoiling. We make sure to see each other as often as possible, and lots of phone calls are made, videos and photos shared. I may not be his aunt in the eyes of the law, as

I am no longer Nina's sister-in-law, but Rylan will always have a special place in my heart; Nina will always be my sister.

Despite Rylan's condition, he's a healthy, happy, and apple-of-his-parents'-eye baby boy. Rylan wants for nothing. Nina tells me there are very challenging days when she stops and asks herself how, as a new mom, she's supposed to handle what she doesn't know, what she doesn't understand. Then she says all she has to do is take one look at Rylan, and she realizes that this world is new to both mother and baby. They're in it together. All that matters is that they finally have their happily ever after.

I hold the wrapped gift in my hands, admiring the perfect crosses and folds of the small bow in the center. I've never been prouder of a gift selection or more confident about giving it. Or more confident about whom I was giving it to.

As I look back to the holiday cards, my eyes move, without hesitation or mistake, knowing precisely where to look, to one particular holiday greeting in forest green—a family portrait.

I glance down at the envelope and the address written across it— my old address. Mine and Adam's.

A year ago Nina told me that Adam was getting married. An elopement. With a woman he'd met at our old breakfast spot, Le Pain Quotidien. She, like him, was eating by herself, and I guess one thing led to another. I didn't ask Nina for the details, and she didn't offer them. All I knew was that Adam had met someone—someone who was in her early thirties and wanting children—and had fallen in love. He was happy, and on some white sand beach he promised to have and to hold her, for better or for worse.

It hurt, I won't lie, but I am happy for him. It was time. It'd been a year since the divorce, and though Adam's second marriage seemed to happen quick as lightning, who am I to judge? Love can be like that. And besides, Adam's forty, and he wants a family. And if his wife's desire to have children was half of what Nina's was, who could find fault with a quick elopement? This was to be expected. This is what both Adam and I wanted. It's time to pick up the pieces and carry on.

The last time I saw Adam was about four months ago. I was at a restaurant with Marian, one of our routine girls' nights out that we'd never missed since I'd moved out. Adam was with his wife. His new, young, beautiful, and very pregnant wife, Bianca.

The sight of him, and then her, was stinging at first. I just stared in shock across the restaurant. Adam saw me, also wearing a surprised expression. Then the shock kind of melted away. We smiled at each other and waved, and that was enough. Adam's wife turned in my direction to see if she, too, knew the person on the other end of Adam's wave. Still waving, still smiling, and with Marian now looking on, Adam leaned toward his wife and whispered something into her ear, and then she, too, smiled and waved. It was a weak and hesitant wave, as was her smile. Awkward. But I just looked to Adam, still smiling, hand in the air in a dying wave, and he gave a small nod. He looked happy. And that made me happy.

It was then that I realized that the happiness I feel for him now that he's moving on with his life is finally greater than the pain I feel from no longer having him. That's the healing power of time, I suppose. And Ben and Jerry's. And *Friends*. And friends and family. And focusing on, as my father said, burning bright and fearless.

My eyes move from the envelope back to my corkboard, to the holiday greeting in forest green—the holiday greeting sent from the new Brennan family, with a casually dressed and smiling Adam and Bianca on the beach, with their infant daughter in Adam's arms. The holiday greeting that reminds me we made the right choice.

Nina had asked if it was all right if she gave my address to Adam, that he wanted to send me a Christmas card. I had a sneaking suspicion I'd be getting a Brennan family portrait greeting, like the one I surely did get. I've always been a stickler for sending out holiday greeting cards, and, even though my Christmas two years ago was a mess, I still got out my cards—a month late, but they were still sent out. One of those cards had Adam's name on it, and I did the same the year after and this year, graduating from "Adam Brennan" on the "To" line to "The Brennans." Adam's sending me a card was his way of saying he'd gotten mine, he'd appreciated them, and, yes, perhaps it was his way of saying, *Thank you. It was a hard choice but the right one. I've found my purpose.*

When the Brennans' holiday card arrived in my mailbox, it didn't sting as I'd thought it would. It was that feeling of greater happiness than pain that saw me through, and the fact that I, too, had found my own purpose at long last.

I decided on watching the Quadrantids meteor shower with my father after the New Year, the Christmas of my divorce. As Dad had promised, the desert night sky was positively forgiving. Not even the full moon could detract from the brilliant light show of the meteor showers.

I also decided to overcome my self-doubt and chase my passion. I finally wrote that novel. It's not the next great American novel, but it's real, it's heartfelt, it's mine. And it's great enough to have landed me a two-book deal (and a very generous advance—those helpful additional funds). Writing a novel was something I'd always wanted to do, and so one night I sat down, dug deep, and I started to write. I made the time, I ignored the insecurities, and I wrote with abandon. I wrote and I wrote and I wrote until, nearly a year later, I had completed my first novel, *The Gravity of Love.* A novel about a woman trying to find her place after a failed marriage. Seeking answers to questions she never thought she'd have to face. Trying to fly when she's in free fall.

When I finished, I told Nina what I'd done and told her the synopsis, wondering if she maybe wanted to give it a read, tell me what she thought. She was no longer in the publishing business, Rylan her full-time focus, but her experience and sharp eye as an editor could give me some insight on improvements. She read it, and when she told me she'd found an acquisitions editor at her house to buy it I thought she was joking. That was impossible. Yes, I believed in my work, my characters, my story, but a publishable novel? Nina said "nepotism" may have gotten my foot in the door, but it was the honest and resonating story that got me the publishing contract.

As soon as my advance came in and I'd worked through my budget, I gave my notice at *Copper*. I'd been given the chance to follow my dreams, and it was about time I started chasing them, started making them a reality.

The wrapped gift on my desk, just like the one for Marian snug in my tote, is a brand-new, soon-to-be-released paperback copy of my first novel. There's a hot pink Post-it on the inside of this copy. "As promised, Halley," it reads. I slip the book into the envelope addressed to Adam Brennan, grab my tote and jacket, and make my way to the front door.

On my drive to meet Marian and Cole at an upscale sushi restaurant that's just opened, which Marian says "has like a two-month waiting list!" I swing by the nearest mailbox.

"Here goes," I say.

I kiss the envelope before dropping it into the big blue abyss. I have a flashback to the last time I slipped something I had published in the mail for Adam, and I can't help but squint out a smile at how peculiar life is. How full circle yet how utterly chaotic it is.

Nina once asked me, after reading my novel, how I was handling the divorce. She asked if my novel writing was my way of trying to heal, trying to start fresh, that new beginning. The novel's storyline is clearly inspired by what Adam and I went through for love. For our brand of love. I told her that my divorce, just like my marriage, was a chapter in my life. Adam and I, I had come to learn and accept, were always supposed to be each other's chapters—a very significant and special relationship in each other's lives. We were not each other's entire story, not each other's life, not each other's happily ever after. And that was perfectly all right.

No, our chapter was about learning to find oneself. Learning how to live and love honestly, and that life is anything but fair. Learning that to love sometimes means loving a different way than you planned. That it sometimes means for only a while. That sometimes love means forgiving and letting go. That sometimes love really hurts. Some loves are not eternal, and some change. There are all kinds of happily ever afters, any writer knows. Not every love is the "to have and to hold" kind, not every plan one to be followed through on, not every purpose clear. Happiness means something different for everyone. It's having that baby, at any cost, however long the wait, no matter the challenges. It's fighting for your marriage and doing what's hard, even when the line that's been crossed seems fatal. It's putting yourself out there and risking heartache, if only for a second chance. It's that comet shooting across the sky, reminding you to burn bright.

Not every story is a fairy tale, and not every story has a happily ever after. But some do. And many have their own versions of happily ever after, their own brands of love, their own truths. And I know, as I scan the crowded sushi restaurant, my first novel tucked proudly in my tote, my giddier-than-usual best friend waving to me wildly, that I have found mine.

Acknowledgments

Where do I start? I suppose with the woman who made *Everything the Heart Wants* happen sooner rather than later, Kelli Martin—editor extraordinaire, warm heart, kind soul, and my drink of no-freak-out-water. Kelli, I'm still pinching myself that you found that bright cherry-red cover out of nowhere, read and fell in love with Gracie and Juliette's story, and decided little ol' me needed to join the Lake Union family. You have opened wide the doors and did the impossible: you made writing even *more* fun. Thank you for believing in me and, of course, for keeping in check my freakouts.

Many thanks to my wonderful developmental editor, Lindsay. We were peas in a pod on this novel. I had so much fun shaping this story with you. Let's do it again!

Thank you to Sadie, Stacy, and the entire editing team. It's tough work sifting through one word after another, but your efforts have helped make this a novel one of which I am so very proud. (Look, no annoying preposition ending!)

Heartfelt thanks to everyone who worked on this novel with me, from Women, who inspired and informed the story, to the teams of designers, editors, and everyone who has welcomed me and my life's passions into the Lake Union family and helped get my books into readers' hands.

Much gratitude to my dear friends and family for being in my life and adding sparkle to it. For supporting and loving me. For celebrating my wins and encouraging me during the not-quite-wins. You mean the universe to me.

Last, and never least, *HUUUGE* thanks to my husband, Christian. I may be a writer, but words still cannot express how much I love you and how thankful and happy I am to be your partner. To the edge of our solar system and back, *ich liebe dich*.

About the Author

Savannah Page is the author of *Everything the Heart Wants*, *A Sister's Place*, and the When Girlfriends series. Sprinkled with drama and humor, her women's fiction celebrates friendship, love, and life. A native Southern Californian, Savannah lives in Berlin, Germany, with her husband, their goldendoodle, and her collection of books. Readers can visit her at www.SavannahPage.com.